PENGUI

The Ch

Victoria Prince spent over twenty years writing and editing for women's magazines and newspapers including *Cosmopolitan*, *Glamour*, *Fabulous*, *The Sunday Times Style* and *OK!*

Growing up in Hertfordshire, Victoria studied Spanish and Latin American Studies at university in Granada, Spain, and Xalapa, Mexico, before travelling the world and returning to the town in which she was born. She lives there with her husband, two sons and cat Margot and is a fan of Latin beats, giant polka dots and pub quizzes (Victoria went on *The Weakest Link* and won it).

The Chalet Girl

VICTORIA PRINCE

PENGUIN BOOKS

PENGUIN BOOKS

UK | USA | Canada | Ireland | Australia
India | New Zealand | South Africa

Penguin Books is part of the Penguin Random House group of companies
whose addresses can be found at global.penguinrandomhouse.com

Penguin Random House UK
One Embassy Gardens, 8 Viaduct Gardens, London sw11 7bw

penguin.co.uk

Penguin
Random House
UK

First published 2025

001

Set in 12.4/15pt Garamond MT
Typeset by Falcon Oast Graphic Art Ltd
Printed and bound in Great Britain by Clays Ltd, Elcograf S.p.A.

The authorized representative in the EEA is Penguin Random House Ireland,
Morrison Chambers, 32 Nassau Street, Dublin d02 yh68

A CIP catalogue record for this book is available from the British Library

ISBN: 978–1–405–98254–2

Penguin Random House is committed to a sustainable future
for our business, our readers and our planet. This book is made from
Forest Stewardship Council® certified paper

MIX
Paper | Supporting
responsible forestry
FSC® C018179
www.fsc.org

For Jackie

Chapter One

As Emmeline Eversley thanked the crew and exited the budget aircraft, she paused at the top of a rickety staircase overlooking the tarmac and inhaled. The air felt crisp, clean and fresh, despite all the jet fuel in the vicinity. The snow-capped mountains in the distance called to her. Zurich was spelled out in huge, pristine letters above the terminal building. She truly opened her eyes for what felt like the first time in a long time. And felt invigorated.

Inside the terminal, passengers gathered at a set of double doors while they waited for a shuttle to take them to the arrivals hall, immigration, and their baggage. As Emme idly waited, she became aware of a presence, amongst all the people gathering around her, waiting for that same shuttle train; a powerful one. She knew just from the way the man, tall and strapping and smelling of bergamot and sage, looked at his Patek Phillipe watch on his tanned wrist that he had come from the private jet that had parked up next to her plane. Emme deliberately didn't look at him, despite his immense allure. This kind of man was infuriatingly used to people looking at him, and she didn't want to give him the satisfaction, so she kept her gaze firmly fixed on the countdown clock. The terminal train would be arriving in two minutes.

As Emme waited, she rewound her mental clock to one week ago. A Halloween wedding. A monstrosity of a dress. *Always the bridesmaid*, she thought. Her peach satin gown (verging on orange) was a shade that very few people could pull off, and it had done nothing for Emmeline with her warm apricot cheeks and gilded chestnut shoulder-length bob. And it drowned all 5ft 2in of her. Had Chrissy done it on purpose? As Emme looked at the other bridesmaids in shades of sorbet, buff and blush, in shapes that suited their figures, she considered her own: off-the-shoulder, puffball and drop-waist. It might be Halloween but did she have to look like a pumpkin?

It was obvious the bride didn't like her. If Emme was honest, the feeling was mutual. Not dislike, more like polite disdain. She knew Chrissy only asked her to be in her bridal party because she felt obliged to. And the truth that was worse than the dress: Chrissy was marrying the love of Emme's life, and Emme was the one who had set them up.

Three years ago Emme and Tom had been drinking after work in one of their favourite City haunts, as they often did, even on a school night, when a goddess with black hair tied back like a show pony put a coin on the pool table and gave Tom a wink. Emme took umbrage with this. Not because she and Tom were a couple, they weren't. Even though they'd been for tapas and rioja before hitting the bar, like couples do. Even though they'd been to the cinema the weekend before and watched a film so gory, Emme had curled into Tom's arm. Like girlfriends do. Everyone always said they *looked* like a couple. Emme hankered for them to be a couple, conflicted by the fact that Tom was her best friend. He had been her best friend since they were paired up on a trip to London Zoo in primary school and they held hands in hi-vis bibs. The woman, who introduced herself as Chrissy, was dazzling. So dazzling, in jeans, a blazer and YSL heels, that Emme foolishly encouraged Tom to get her number as their dismal game went on. Tom's happiness meant more to Emme than her own. And when he didn't dare, Emme handed Chrissy her cue and said to her, 'Winner stays on.' Leaving them to play pool, while she headed home to her flat in Balham. Boy did Chrissy stay on.

One week ago, a murder ballad played as Emme walked down an aisle illuminated by squash and pumpkin lanterns behind the bride sheathed in Vivienne Westwood. As they reached the altar, Emme saw Tom glance away from his wife-to-be for just a second, to wink at Emme. A wink of friendship, a wink of love, a wink of pity given her regretful outburst – before he looked back at his bride and welled up.

As Emme waited now for the train, still aware of the man with aviator shades and a Prada holdall, she rolled back to the excruciating night *before* the wedding, when Tom knocked on her hotel room door after the rehearsal dinner and asked why she was thinking of leaving her job.

'My sister told me,' he said, blindsided. 'Why would you give up your brilliant job, your flat, your life in London – your friends . . .' Tom stopped himself from saying the word *us*. 'Why would you give up all this to be a nanny? Anywhere in the world? At a moment's notice?'

Emme had been the trusty executive assistant to Dominique Henry, chief financial officer and leader of the board at ConCore Consulting for six years. Tom had sent her the job alert from the HR department when it came up two months after he'd started on the graduate training programme to become an auditor. They thought it would be fun working together. It had been fun working together.

Tom looked at her pleadingly. Emme had tried to bite her tongue but that wicked cocktail of champagne and heartache finally made her blurt it out it.

'Because of you, Tom,' Emme had replied with a desperate sigh. A tension hung between them; they both knew she was teetering on a precipice. 'I'm in love with you.'

As Tom looked aghast, Emme whizzed through all the almost-moments in the zoetrope of her mind: the times she and Tom snuggled on the sofa lost in a movie and she wanted to caress his face; or dancing in a nightclub, high on beats per minute and she wished he didn't look at her like a sister; or the time she saw him cry when his mother died and she felt such immense love for him. If only she had declared it then.

Tom was so shocked he needed the doorframe to hold him up. He shook his head.

'I don't think you are Em. You know me too well to be in love with me. It's all got blurred in the lead-up to the wedding, emotions are heightened – Christ, do you think I haven't had my doubts?' He looked up and down the corridor.

Emme was taken aback. Did he mean doubts about Chrissy, or what-ifs about her?

'Have you?' she asked, trying not to sound hopeful.

They were interrupted by Tom's father-in-law, thundering down the corridor sloshing a large glass of red in his hand.

'Come here Larner! Important men's talk to be had . . .' he said, as he commandeered him away. Tom looked back, but Emme had already closed the door and slunk down the other side of it, knowing that either way, it was too late.

Shaking off her regret Emme snapped back to Zurich as a slick futuristic train pulled in exactly on time and the thick double glass doors opened in a whoosh. Passengers spilled on, keen to collect their baggage and start their adventures or return to their beautiful homes. The man, who was so well-dressed he looked like Switzerland might be his home, held back to let Emme on first and she found a corner to stand in, an internal thrill quashing the simmering nerves. Love and regret could be left in London. Nannying in Switzerland was not going to be forever, but here, on this train, surrounded by hot strangers and wholesome-looking families as she careered to a new future, Emme realised she could be anyone. Tom might have been right, she might have been mad to give up her brilliant job, at the brilliant company she worked at with him, to be a nanny, but possibilities outweighed fear right now.

As the train glided through a tunnel, the carriage lights dimmed and the tunnel walls became illuminated with a kaleidoscope of Swiss scenes. Cows pasturing on lush meadows with spring flowers. Medieval turrets and crystal lakes. Snowy peaks and picturesque mountain villages.

'Hi, I'm Heidi . . .' said a voiceover. 'Welcome to Switzerland!' Children and adults alike looked around at the screens illuminating the tunnel, enchanted. Strangers smiled at each other. The man from the private jet looked at his phone, sunglasses still firmly on despite it being dark, and Emme wondered if she would ever be as blasé about being in such a hilariously brilliant place as he was.

Chapter Two

At Bloch railway station a guard with an elaborate moustache straightened his cap and blew his whistle so loud, it made Emme jump from inside the train. She looked out of the window and watched as a woman with a snowboard tied to her backpack rushed towards the door.

As the doors beeped to a close, she managed to squeeze in, just in time, the doors almost catching the board.

'*Hijo de puta*,' the woman muttered to herself, before turning sideways and hitting an unsuspecting man on the arm with it.

'Ah, sorry,' she said, in accented English. He gave a forgiving nod. The woman looked up and down the packed carriage for a seat, and saw one opposite Emme, next to a mother with a son on her lap.

'This seat, is it taken?' she asked the mother.

'*Nein, nein.*'

The woman was more careful with her snowboard now as she eased herself in past the child, nodding gratefully at the mother. She gave a relieved and theatrical, 'Oomph!', as she placed her backpack and snowboard clumsily on the floor between her snow boots.

Emme had made it from the airport to the mountain train at Bloch with fifteen minutes to spare. The recruitment agent who had fixed Emme up with the job assured her that it would be enough time.

'It's Switzerland, trains run like clockwork,' she said, when she talked Emme through the route from SW12 to the remote mountain village of Kristalldorf, nestled high in the Swiss Alps.

Emme looked at the screen at the end of the carriage and panicked to see the destination saying Alpentor and not Kristalldorf. As the train pulled out of the station, she realised it was too late. She stared at the screen, hoping that she hadn't got on the wrong efficient train. She absolutely didn't want to be late – or worse, end up on the other side of the country and be late. Emme started to panic and wondered whether she should message the mother of the family.

Shit.

The Harringtons were meant to be meeting Emme off the mountain train at Kristalldorf and Emmeline Eversley was never late for anything. In all the years she had been Dominique's PA she had never missed or mis-scheduled an appointment. She did not want to give the wrong impression when she was so nervous and keen to make a great first one.

Dammit.

There was low chatter in the carriage. Polite conversation in French, German, Italian, Spanish and English.

Shit shit shit.

She imagined the children's faces, remembering them from their hastily arranged Zoom call earlier in the week. A boy of nine with auburn hair and big brown eyes; his younger sister, seven years old, whose hair was redder, her freckles brighter. Their mother and father had flanked them on the screen, smiling hopefully, backs as straight as rods, as if they were both willing Emme to be the right fit. Emme had smiled warmly and taken diligent notes while the mother told her the expectations of the job: getting the kids their breakfast, doing the school run, taking them to ski lessons, clubs and playdates, overseeing their piano practice and the bedtime routine. She said most of the work would be during the week while the father worked in Zurich, although she would be expected to cover some evening babysitting. It all seemed so manageable, Emme had tried not to look as desperate as the family to make it work.

Emme cleared her throat.

'Excuse me please,' she asked the woman with the snowboard. Her wayward hair and well-worn baggage told tales of someone who knew the mountains. 'Is this train going to Kristalldorf? It's just it says Alpentor on the screen . . .' Emme nodded and swallowed hard.

'I hope so!' the woman said. 'I'm working there tonight!' She let out a loud and husky laugh and looked over her shoulder at the monitor at the end of the carriage.

'There are about five stops until Alpentor and then another three to Kristalldorf. The screen must have got stuck. The mountain train always goes to Kristalldorf, unless it's snowed in. It's the end of the line.'

The end of the line.

Suddenly Emme was hit with a sense of doom. What had she done? Her dad, mum and sister had all looked at her with sorrow when she announced over lunch last Sunday that she was moving to the Swiss Alps for a season. They had known about her hairbrained scheme to maybe one day take a sabbatical and sublet her flat, but they didn't think she was suddenly going to become a nanny in Switzerland.

9

'Why would you do that, love?' her mum Marian had asked.

Her sister Lucille was holding one of her five-year-old twins to her chest, while her brother-in-law Ryan had taken the other one into the garden to run around before pudding. It seemed like the right moment to drop the bombshell.

Because I'm too fucking embarrassed to take my lunch break with the love of my life when he's married to someone else?

She couldn't tell them that.

'A change of scene and some fresh air!' Emme had said with a forced smile.

'But what will Ms Henry do without you?' her dad lamented. Geoff Eversley always puffed with pride when he saw Dominique Henry on *Newsnight* or *Business Daily*.

'She said I could take a sabbatical. For the season.'

'But you've never skied!'

'I did once actually,' she said guardedly. 'In Colorado. With Tom.'

Lucille furnished her sister with a worried glance.

'You know I've been thinking about a change of scene. Tayla will look after the flat. The agency I've registered with called me yesterday morning, about a very short-notice placement with a family in the Swiss Alps. I'll head out later in the week.'

'You're going to be an au pair?' Marian looked mystified. 'You're twenty-eight!'

Emme looked at her sister for solidarity, but she was comforting her niece Zara.

'A nanny. Not an au pair. And it's just for a season.'

*

Emme wasn't lying, a change of scene was just what she needed. And although it seemed sudden to her family, she had trained to be a nanny in her teens and spent the summer after her A levels with a family in the United States while Tom was teaching a football camp out there. She hadn't loved nannying, but she'd been pondering this idea since she received her Save The Date last spring. It seemed her only way out.

So Emme spent months scrolling websites for international jobs, and kept landing on Nomad Nannies, an agency that paired young British women with British families around the world. Emme had interviews with the agency, and candid chats with Dominique, who was the only person Emme confided the real reason for wanting to get out of the country. Dominique said she'd support Emme and would give her a reference, keep her job open, but for six months max.

Emme understood.

'Six months is all I need Dominique. Promise.'

The snowboarder noticed the ambivalence on Emme's face.

'Don't look so worried about it! There isn't anywhere more beautiful to get snowed in.' She winked.

Emme smiled unconvincingly.

'And I should know because I am from the *second* most beautiful place on earth.'

'Where's that?' Emme asked, looking down the carriage to check her suitcase was still teetering on the luggage rack. Of course it was, she was in Switzerland. Surely no one would steal luggage.

She looked back at the woman with the gypsy curls; glad to shift the focus.

'Patagonia, southern Argentina. The scenery is not so different to this,' she said, nodding out the window.

That's not what Emme had expected, at all.

'Really?'

'Yes. I live on the edge of a glacier: beautiful blues and whites everywhere. Kristalldorf is much more accessible – even if it doesn't seem it to you.'

Emme gazed out of the window as the train started snaking up the mountain.

'I'm Catalina, Cat,' she said, thrusting a hand forward.

Emme was taken aback, but took off her mitten and returned her hand. 'Emmeline, but people call me Emme.'

'Emme. *Mucho gusto*,' Cat said, shaking her hand effusively. 'First time in Kristalldorf I guess?'

'Yes, I'm starting a new job.'

Cat's eyes widened, as if to say *tell me more*.

'I'm nannying. For an English family who live there.'

It was Cat's turn to look surprised.

'Interesting, I know everyone in Kristalldorf. Who?'

Emme lowered her voice.

'The Harringtons.'

Cat widened her eyes, ringed with kohl and mischief, and said, 'Ooooh, right . . .'

Emme looked nervous at this response.

'What?'

Cat waved her hand.

'Nothing . . .' Her smile didn't wane.

Shit.

'They come to parties at my family's home, where I chef. I didn't know Jenny that well.' Cat had wide, gossipy eyes as if there was some salacious tea to be spilled.

'Jenny?'

'Their *niñera* – their nanny – but I've been in Argentina for a few weeks so I don't know what the story is with that . . .'

'Story?' Emme pushed.

'Oh doesn't matter, you'll be great.' The smile was still there, but it definitely faltered for a second.

Emme looked up and down the carriage as the train rolled to its first stop. On one side of the track stood a pretty pale-yellow building with lilac shutters and a pitched roof. The word *Gesundheitzentrum* was painted in an ornate font on the façade. On the other side was a basketball court, with children in down coats playing in the last of the day's sunshine. Some of the buildings around the station had onion-shaped domes on their spires – beautifully preserved medieval architecture spaced out on flat rectangles of grass at the base of the mountain.

'What's the family like?' Emme asked cautiously.

Cat's voice was loud, which made Emme immediately regret asking.

'Mama's uptight. Very British. Sorry.'

Emme shrugged as if to say *that's OK, I am too.*

'The kids seem OK, bit whingy. Jenny was close to them, I think. Very dedicated.'

Emme already felt inadequate.

'As for Beeel . . .'

Cat looked up and down the carriage as if she had some very interesting intel on him, but stopped herself. 'Actually he works in Zurich in the week, he might be on the train.' She flirtatiously put a finger to her mouth.

'I'll tell you later,' she said with a wink.

*

13

As the train continued to ascend, the lush lake-level meadows dotted with grazing cows gave way to pine trees and the green hues faded to a colder palette of greys and white. The clickety clack of the track was peppered with the occasional sound of a cow bell in the distance, as the train stopped at each station, and fresh Alpine scents permeated the carriage.

'So you said you're a chef?' Emme asked, glad to be shifting the focus from the nerves she felt about meeting her host family.

'*Sí*. For a family.' Cat said the word *family* as if it were loaded. They probably were if they lived in the most expensive ski resort in Europe and had a private chef among their staff. 'The Kivvis,' she said, as if that explained everything. Emme looked blank.

'You haven't heard of them?'

She shook her head.

'Viktor Kivvi, richest man in Europe? Born penniless, made his money in escalators and elevators.'

'Wow. He really went up in the world!' Emme couldn't help but release a giggle at her own joke.

'The Kivvis own the prime real estate in Kristalldorf. He built Seven Summits, where I live with the family,' Cat said proudly.

Seeing Emme's blank face, she went on to explain: 'Seven "chalets". Swiss engineering, very cleverly built into the mountain.'

Emme nodded.

'The Kivvis own *four* of them. They rent three out – you know Abishek Joshi?' Cat asked excitedly.

'Sorry,' Emme replied, feeling terribly unworldly.

'Bollywood royalty!' Cat exclaimed. 'He and his wife Priya are my neighbours.'

She didn't get round to telling Emme that a British Formula 1 driver and his Iranian model girlfriend lived in another, and a Danish songwriter and his husband in the other. There was plenty of time for that.

'Who owns the other three out of the seven?' Emme asked.

'Well it's a funny story – Viktor's nemesis, Walter Steinherr, who owns most of the town, bought the other three, just to spite Viktor I think.'

'Sounds a bit mean.'

'That's rich white men for you!' Cat joked.

'Isn't it your boss's choice who he sells to if he built them?'

'Well, he co-built them with a Russian billionaire . . . but that's another story for another time,' Cat added and quietened down. Gossip on the mountain train was ill advised because there was often a Kivvi, Steinherr, Sommar or worse, a Stognev, on the train. Or one of their staff, and the staff always knew *way* too much. 'We need to go out. When you're settled in, every night is party night. Give me your number.' Cat thrust her mobile into Emme's hand for Emme to type her number into. Emme happily obliged.

'Don't you have to work evenings?'

'Well, maybe not every night. But when I've cleaned up dinner and prepped breakfast; when my friends have wiped down their restaurants, we meet up. The nannies not so much, you often have to babysit while Mr and Mrs go out, although I don't see *Los Harrington* out much . . . Even Tiago gets one night off a week . . .'

'Tiago?'

'My guy Tiago – poor dude, he works the supermarket by day and is the night manager in the Steinherrhof six nights a week.'

Cat made a pitiful face that showed she had it good, then did a sudden double take as she looked up. Emme turned to see what had caught her attention. She saw the back of a silver-haired man carrying an attaché case in one hand and a wool coat slung over his arm, walking hastily up the carriage.

'That's your boss!' Cat mouthed. 'Best I . . .' she drew a zip across her mouth, and Emme didn't know if it was for her benefit or Cat's.

After almost an hour of further chatter, about Cat's life in Argentina – her grandmother's funeral she had just been home for – and happily not much about Emme, the train pulled into Kristalldorf station, where a beautiful gold and cream clock lit the darkened platform like a bejewelled moon.

All the remaining passengers – commuters, families, holidaymakers and thrill seekers – gathered their coats, scarves, ski paraphernalia and suitcases; as this was the last stop, Emme took her time. Cat looked at her colourful Swatch watch with the energy of someone who was always in a hurry and Emme didn't know whether she felt invigorated or exhausted by her. She'd left her flat for Gatwick at 6am and now the sun had just set.

'Gotta fly, catch up soon yeah?' Cat said. She fist-bumped Emme on the shoulder, hauled her backpack and her board over her shoulders, and weaved off the train.

Emme wondered if Catalina would ever bother – why would she? She was the chef for a super-rich family and always had friends to party with. But she already knew Kristalldorf wasn't big enough to avoid anyone. Not that she wanted to. Cat had a warmth and a sparkle about her that had helped calm Emme's nerves.

Chapter Three

'Happy birthday, Daddy!' gushed doe-eyed Vivian Steinherr, youngest daughter of Kristalldorf's most powerful hotelier, as she raised her champagne glass and looked adoringly at her father, sitting at the head of the table next to her. His two sons were out of town but Walter was celebrating turning seventy with his beloved daughters, Vivian and Anastasia, Anastasia's husband Dimitri, and their three children, Orfeas, Ophelia and Olympia, named after their father's Greek ancestors, who were home from boarding school for the occasion. On Walter's other side was his wife, Kiki, who trailed a pointed fingernail in figures of eight on her husband's arm.

'Thank you, Vivi,' Walter said, raising his Baccarat glassware and chinking it against Vivian's. He wasn't in a celebratory mood, but he put a good face on it. He had been particularly grumpy since repeat mystery infections had led to his recent cancer diagnosis, which he was keeping from everyone except his physician, Dr Blitzer, who he spoke to about the cancer almost in code.

Walter wasn't particularly frightened of his cancer – he was not a young man – he was more inconvenienced by the myeloma, because it was causing increasing pain in his bones, and by the increasing amount of appointments he didn't really have time for. He didn't want aggressive treatment either; at his age it felt rather pointless. For now, Dr Blitzer recommended a 'watch and wait' strategy, and Walter decided not to tell a soul. Not his wife. Not his children.

Vivian was thirty-one, as charming as she was composed, and had the most luminous complexion in Kristalldorf. Walter was an imposing man with pale-blue eyes like his daughter, white hair and a bushy moustache. He wore a shirt and a cardigan with thick gold buttons.

Despite his devoted daughters insisting he have a party for his birthday, *he* insisted not. There were always parties in Kristalldorf: hotel launches, restaurants celebrating their Michelin stars, the Kivvis' annual Christingle, The Kristall Ball, the spring music festival, the list felt endless. So the last thing Walter Steinherr wanted to do was attend another damn party.

He might have had his pick of venues, seeing as he owned most of the town, from the restaurant at the Steinherrhof to the terrace at the Alpenrose. Sometimes, when Walter was feeling mischievous, he hosted private dinners in one of the three vacant and enormous chalets he owned at Seven Summits. Each of the seven chalets had at least five bedrooms (all with ensuites with rain showers and mountain-view balconies), private ski rooms, wellness areas, a hammam and elevators. Finnish tycoon Viktor Kivvi had worked closely with Russian developer Alexey Stognev, and world-renowned architect Ludwig Smythson, to the highest spec, with his own Kivvi elevators installed into each premises, of course.

No one else in Kristalldorf had the money or the inclination to do what Walter did: cut a private deal with Stognev behind Kivvi's back to buy three of the villas just to spite him – and then leave them mostly unoccupied.

The small consolation for Viktor was that he and his family lived in the largest of the chalets, which was the only one of the properties to have its own cinema, card room and bar.

The wasted income on Seven Summits was something that irked Walter's children, especially his eldest daughter Anastasia, who was sitting at the opposite end of the long table to her father. Anastasia had ideas, if only she could have a closer look inside the empty properties. Walter was very guarded about them. He was becoming more guarded, more private in general lately.

Tonight Walter wanted an early dinner – he had always liked to eat early – in his mansion at the foot of the mountain; a mansion that looked more like a Snow Queen's palace, its turrets and gables giving it a Disney-like charm. Inside was a sturdy sweeping staircase, elaborate tiled floors adorned in ornate rugs, crystal chandeliers and crackling fireplaces.

Anastasia had tied scores of gold balloons to her father's chair, which made him look a little ridiculous – as if this serious stalwart of a man might just take off and float out of the mansion towards the mountains.

Walter didn't like to be made to look ridiculous. He had expensive but demure tastes, which is why it was such a shock to everyone when he married Kiki five years ago. American Kiki had white-blonde hair, a baby-smooth forehead, pneumatic tits and lip fillers that made her look *older* than her thirty-five years. Vivian did a better job of disguising her disdain for Kiki than Anastasia did; Vivian was good at making polite chat, asking Kiki how her day had been, even though the answer would predictably involve shopping or a spa. Vivian was partly relieved that her father had a companion. Anastasia, however, loathed their stepmother, who was two years younger than her and a money grabber as far as Anastasia could see. But then Anastasia had loathed all her former stepmothers. In her eyes no woman would ever live up to the saintly and distant memory of their dead mother. No woman would be good enough for their father. No woman would not be a perceived threat to her inheritance.

Next to Kiki sat Anastasia's two daughters, Olympia and Ophelia, who were ten and eight and had hooded eyes like their father, Dimitri, a lawyer for his father-in-law's businesses. Anastasia, with her dark locks and perfectly symmetrical face, was at the other end of the table next to their twelve-year-old son Orfeas, who had impeccable manners and wore a blazer as sharp as his bowl cut.

Walter's butler entered the ornate dining room and silently furnished glasses with wine while two maids brought plates of smoked salmon, chateaubriand, escargots and river trout garnished with dill. The adults raised their wine glasses; the children drank *apfelsaft*.

'Yes, happy birthday, Papa,' oozed Anastasia, not to be outdone by her sister. 'To the strongest seventy-year-old man on the planet! We *adore* you.'

Walter smiled wanly. He felt a pang of guilt, but he raised his glass and drank to that. He squeezed Vivian's hand as his eyes filled a little.

He was a tough man with a ridiculous work ethic, but when it came to his family, he was mush.

Walter's grandfather, Ernst, had been a sheep farmer in Kristalldorf at the turn of the twentieth century, when he saw an opportunity with the mountain train opening up from the settlement of Bloch down the valley. Ernst had the foresight to turn arable land into tourism and he opened a guesthouse at the foot of the mighty Silberschnee, the majestic mountain that overlooked the village, then three more as tourism started to grow. Ernst's son, Walter's father Gerhard, bought more land along the banks of the Glanzfluss river, and turned guesthouses into luxurious hotels when Kristalldorf started becoming as popular in the winter months as it was in summer. In the 1940s, the Steinherr family joined forces with the Sommars and the Kochs, two other founding families, to fund the first chair-lift from the village up to the mountains, which by now were being fashioned into ski runs.

Despite war raging in Europe, Kristalldorf was booming with Swiss visitors, or Paris's exiled elite, all looking for an escape. When Walter was born in the 1950s, he had his grandfather's foresight and his father's taste for grandeur, and over the decades he expanded his portfolio of hotels, with the Steinherrhof, the Alpenrose, the Kristall Palace, the Silberblick and, in the 1990s, Vitreum – the most luxurious, modern and exclusive hotel he'd built yet, perched high on a ledge overlooking the town. With his growing fortune, Walter alone funded a superfast train from the north bank of the Glanzfluss up to the slopes. The mountain train enabled skiers to get from the village to the slopes in three fast minutes, which brought a bigger boom and cemented Kristalldorf's reputation as the finest – and most exclusive – ski resort in the world.

For the past five years he'd focused on building the lofty glass box by the river, a beauty to rival Vitreum, which he'd carelessly lost in a bet at a casino in Monte Carlo. When it was finished, Walter gifted the Anna Maria hotel, a tribute to his late first wife, to their daughters for Christmas, to see if the sisters could come together in business. A test to help Walter identify an heir to take over the Steinherr empire.

Anna Maria Steinherr had died of ovarian cancer at home, opposite the site of the hotel that would one day be named after her. She was only thirty-four. Her daughters and two sons were all aged ten and under. Vivian was just a baby, she never knew her mother. She didn't remember wife number two, Mechthild, who took on the heartbroken billionaire and his four young children with matronly gusto, but Walter was too grief-stricken to let her in and the marriage was over within three years.

Wife number three was wicked stepmother Susan, an Englishwoman whose own husband had died in a car accident. Susan endured the teen and young adult years, a tricky time as eldest brother Lysander and Anastasia were particularly combative. Susan stayed in Kristalldorf long enough to receive a tidy divorce settlement for her fifteen years of service. Before them there was a nurse Walter alluded to if he was misty-eyed or tipsy, but he shut down the conversation when his children ever asked more. And there was Kiki. Wife number four who Walter met when he was playing blackjack in Monte Carlo five years ago. Half Walter's age with absolutely no shared interests apart from poker.

'*Proscht*,' Walter conceded. 'Anna Maria would have loved to watch you all grow up,' he said sentimentally. 'To see what beautiful children you bore Anni.'

Anastasia looked proud. She loved it when her children got her compliments.

'And I'm sure you will too, Vivi.'

Vivian looked solemn for a second. Her honey-blonde hair was tied back in an elegant ponytail and her huge bright-blue eyes were spaced far apart. Pale and ethereal looking, she was totally different to her darker, sharper, more sinewy elder sister, who had brown eyes like their mother. It made Vivian feel even sadder. She couldn't remember the woman Anastasia was always told she looked like. Vivian gripped her father's hand, grateful she was here next to him.

'Thank you,' she almost whispered, as she gave his hand a squeeze.

'Why don't you bring this mystery man of yours over?' Walter asked. 'It would be nice to meet him.'

'A man?' scoffed Anastasia. 'I thought darling Vivian was too busy for romance.' The thought of her sister finally having a boyfriend and no longer pining over the Joubert boy piqued Anastasia's interest and she raised an eyebrow.

Walter waved a hand.

The huge doorbell chimed and Vivian's heart raced, full of hope. Perhaps he was coming. Perhaps he was finally ready to officially stand by her side.

'I don't know why you're so coy, Vivi,' Walter interjected. 'I take each person at their own value, I don't judge based on their name or background.' As he said this, he knew it not to be true. If Vivian were dating a Kivvi, perhaps, Walter imagined it might be problematic. 'Nor should people judge you or your brothers for being Steinherrs,' Walter said, somewhat unsurely. They all knew the Steinherr name could carry as much contempt as it could kudos.

A man in a suit, tie undone, clutching a bunch of flowers, walked into the dining room.

'Hey, who's judging?' he said with a shit-eating grin.

Chapter Four

Emme eked out every step towards the doors, nervous about the upcoming introduction. Further down the platform she saw a woman reprimanding her children for something. Or was it her husband she was telling off as he approached the group and crouched down to greet his children? Either way, she looked pissed off.

Oh dear, Emme thought, recognising the man Cat had pointed out on the train from the Zoom call. And as she looked at the woman properly, she recognised her auburn hair and alabaster skin, that had shone so perfectly under the ring light of their video call. She was Alexia Harrington, Emme's new boss.

Oh dear, Emme thought again, as the woman noticed her approaching. Her tense face morphed into a forced showbiz smile with prim red lips. She had the look of a faded Hollywood star, her Rita Hayworth waves pinned perfectly off her face; telltale creases where her Botox stopped at her nose. She looked like she was going to either burst into tears or burst into song.

'Emmeline!' She outstretched her arms awkwardly. 'Welcome to Kristalldorf! How was your journey?'

The two little redheaded children stood either side of their mother, expectant to meet the woman who had the nerve to be replacing their adored Jenny.

'Mrs Harrington, Alexia, lovely to meet you,' Emme said as she went to shake her hand. Alexia was so fragrant-looking, Emme wondered if she should curtsey, but she took the outstretched gloved hands and let Alexia squeeze hers.

'Lexy, please. Did you meet Bill on the train?' She nodded towards her husband.

'Bill,' he said, outstretching his gloved leather hand.

They both shook their heads and Emme smiled affably.

'Nice to meet you,' she said.

'This is Harry, and this is Bella. Our munchkins. Darlings, give Emmeline a big Kristalldorf welcome.'

Lexy pushed her children with a palm on each back as they shuffled nervously forward and Emme got down to her haunches.

'It's so wonderful to meet you two in real life,' she said, looking each of them in the eye. 'Aren't you both gorgeous?'

Despite her childcare qualification, and that brief stint in the States, Emme hadn't had much experience in the past ten years, apart from her five-year-old nephew and niece, Zack and Zara, who she loved enormously. But what she lacked in experience she tried to make up for in planning. In the Zoom call earlier in the week Emme had gleaned all manner of clues about the children. Bella had a *Paddington 2* film poster on her bedroom wall when Lexy gave a brief video tour. So now she opened her bag and pulled out two cuddly bears.

'These are for you,' she said. 'I got them from actual Paddington station.'

Bella gasped as she took hers, clutched it and beamed. Harry looked a little disappointed.

'What do you say to Emmeline, Harry? Bella?'

Lexy waited for her children to say something charming and grateful, but it was taking longer than any of the adults found comfortable.

'You can call me Emme actually, no one calls me Emmeline,' she whispered mischievously to them, pretending to let them in on her secret.

'Thank you,' Bella mumbled shyly.

'Paddington's lame,' Harry said, so quietly, it appeared no one else seemed to notice, but Emme did a double-take.

'That's quite some suitcase!' Bill Harrington said, deftly changing the subject. Perhaps he had heard too.

'Grab a yumbo out the front and go ahead,' instructed Lexy.

Bill nodded.

'I'll follow on foot with Emmeline – Emme – and the kids.'

'Ooh, what's a yumbo?' Emme asked, perhaps overplaying her excitement.

'Oh, they're little electric cars that zip around town. Kristalldorf is carless, don't you know?'

'It keeps the air clean,' Harry said, flatly.

Bill looked like he had quite fancied the walk after sitting on two trains for hours from Zurich to Bloch, and then to Kristalldorf. But he clearly knew better than to argue with his wife right now.

'Can we get the yumbo with Papa?' Bella asked her mother, through lispy lips.

'No,' her mother said firmly. And that was the end of that.

The first fulsome snowflakes of winter were falling on the town, now shrouded by an inky navy sky.

'Perfect timing!' Lexy Harrington said, as if she had just pulled a giant lever and switched them on herself.

As Lexy, Emme and the kids walked from the train station, Kristalldorf unveiled itself like a hidden gem. The glow from the street lamps gave the town a timeless warmth as the peaks at the head of the valley turned from white to silver in the moonlight. The most iconic of them all – the Silberschnee – was obscured by cloud as Lexy, Harry and Bella led the way past wooden-fronted shops selling expensive watches, skiwear, tourist trinkets and chocolate. Most of them were closing, although the restaurants that peppered the centre of town were open, with staff setting tables and furnishing chairs with sheepskin blankets. In the distance, a centuries-old church chimed 6pm.

Tucked behind the shopping street was a warren of wooden huts and chalets, their sloping roofs bearing the weight of the first rising snow. Window boxes were tightly packed with geraniums, gamely fighting the chill to reveal their distorted colours to the twilight. Nestled between these were antique wooden storage barns, that looked as if sheep might be asleep inside as they had for centuries. Emme wondered how these structures endured, neighbouring such smart glass-and-wood shops and boutique hotels.

Past the church, they crossed one of several footbridges that linked the two sides of the town over the wide and flowing river, its roar drowning out Lexy's wittering. Emme could almost smell how pristine the water was, as she tucked her hands in her pockets. Passers-by heading towards the centre all nodded and smiled at Lexy and the children in their featherdown coats, snow boots and bobble hats. Emme felt woefully underdressed and cold in her decade-old hiking boots and the ski jacket she had borrowed from Lucille. She already knew it wouldn't cut the mustard.

Emme had winced at the fluoro orange and turquoise monstrosity and wondered how her sister had ever worn such a thing. Now she felt self-conscious walking alongside the very polished Lexy, bucking the local trend for featherdown in a Victoriana wool coat.

As they walked, Lexy pointed out the children's favourite bakery, the closed ski train station that took villagers to the slopes in three minutes, the riverbank path to the school and the direction of the town's best pizza restaurant.

'Obviously Kristalldorf looks *much* more spectacular in the daylight . . .' she said, almost defensively.

'I think it looks beautiful now,' Emme replied, trying to soothe Lexy's nerves, as well as her own.

The wealth in Kristalldorf was immense but understated. And it was quiet, save for the odd electric bike whizzing past, or the sounds of a distant après-ski bar, where a chorus of 'Take on Me' was muffled by all the wood and the weather in between. Cowbells rang on the hills behind the buildings, which were hardly high-rise.

Nestled between a pretty chalet and a small wood-fronted hotel was a set of wide but winding steps, where Emme could already see Bill up ahead at the top, the yumbo having dropped him at the base of the steps, her enormous case over his shoulders like he were participating in a survival challenge on a game show. A strategically placed light at the top of the steps illuminated him, as if he had won first place, and the children raced each other to see who would take silver and get to their father first.

'Careful!' Lexy called after them.

Emme breathed heavily. The thin Alpine air teamed with the ferociousness at which these steps were coming at her caused her to pant slightly.

'Quite the thigh workout living here,' Lexy said, glancing back at Emme, who was embarrassed by her lack of fitness. 'You'll have glutes of steel by Christmas,' she said.

Emme could almost hear the woman clench her pert buttocks as she kept an eye on her footing in the dark, while Harry and Bella chatted to their dad.

'I got the part of the Sugar Plum Fairy, Daddy!' Bella declared.

'That's wonderful, darling . . .'

'I scored two hoops – that's like goals – in basketball today.'

'Well done, buster.'

Emme reached the top step out of breath and took off her coat.

'Won't miss you in the dark!' Bill quipped, flatly, as he leaned on the handle of Emme's suitcase, a bead of sweat glistening on his jaw in the light of the building. *Their building* by all accounts. It had Chalet Stern hand-painted on the side in an elegant script.

'Gosh, thank you, sorry my case is so heavy . . .'

Bill leaned casually and waved, as if to say don't worry.

'You can carry it down when you leave!' Lexy said with a laugh.

Bill looked at his wife pointedly and the laughter stopped.

Emme smiled a little awkwardly.

Lexy tapped some digits into a keypad next to the door before a heavy-sounding lock was released and the front door pushed open with ease. 'I'll give you all the codes you'll need,' she assured Emme. 'We share this door with three other families, although two of them are away at the moment, and Mr and Mrs Muller keep themselves to themselves.'

They walked into the building entrance, which had stone heated floors and smelled of clean laundry. A tumble drier whirred in a low hum off an adjoining room.

Bill rolled Emme's case to the elevator and fluffed Harry's hair in the reflection of the lift's shiny doors.

'What's this then?' he said playfully, ruffling up his son's fringe. Harry batted him away affectionately.

'We'll all fit . . .' Lexy assured Emme, jabbing a button by the doors, which opened straight away. 'Top floor,' she said, trying to conceal her pride.

Of course.

Chapter Five

'Son!' Walter beamed. 'I wasn't expecting you!'

He threw down his white linen napkin, stood up and opened his arms for a wide embrace.

'I'd have made it in time for dinner if you didn't insist on eating at this ridiculous hour,' Lysander replied, hugging his father.

'Happy birthday, Dad,' he said, patting his father on the back, then handing him the bunch of flowers.

Anastasia and Vivian exchanged a look as if to gauge whether the other had known about their brother's surprise visit. Neither clearly did. Anastasia's children looked up and beamed at their uncle. Dimitri cleared his throat, stood up, and shook his brother-in-law's hand.

'Zander!' Vivian smiled, as she stood and wrapped her long arms around her brother's shoulders.

He squeezed her back. Anastasia stayed seated, almost bemused by the entrance.

'Kiki,' Lysander nodded.

'Hi, honey,' she said, blowing her stepson a kiss.

Lysander was tall, with salt and pepper hair and grey-blue eyes, and he spoke with an American accent, after two decades in the United States as a top-brass lawyer, living in a very gorgeous pied à terre overlooking Central

Park. At weekends he retreated to an oceanfront house on Fire Island with his wife and son. He was rarely ever in Switzerland any more.

'Is Blake coming?' Orfeas asked keenly.

'No, Meg and Blakey couldn't make it, buddy – Blake has school and Meg is *snowed*.'

I bet, thought Anastasia. Her sister-in-law was always overwhelmed by the latest gala event or fundraiser she was planning. She seemed to live for charity. Whether it was for botanical research, music therapy, Haiti or Gaza, she was often at The Pierre or The Plaza, hosting or speaking at a dinner or a black-tie ball. Fundraising was a full-time job for that Real Housewife of New York City.

'What a surprise!' Walter seemed to visibly relax for the first time that evening. What a timely visit. He really could use his son's counsel right now.

'Well I wouldn't miss Pop's seventieth, not for the world,' he said.

Lysander turned to his baby sister.

'What's this I hear about you having a new fancy man, sis? Are you finally over the Joubert boy?' he teased her.

Vivian smiled sweetly to conceal her annoyance and sat back down. She wasn't being coy. In fact, tonight she had been hoping to reveal him as her new boyfriend. After years of cat and mouse, lingering and longing, she felt that perhaps they might be able to make it official with his appearance at dinner.

Anastasia finally stood up to kiss her brother on each cheek.

A reverent butler entered the dining room, already carrying a spare chair, followed by maids carrying china. They set a place between Vivian and her father, and Lysander sat down seamlessly as the chair was put in place.

'This is such a wonderful surprise, *you'll* come with me to the Borromeo wedding tomorrow!' Walter declared, as if it was his best idea ever. 'You don't mind, do you my love?' He said it with barely a glance in Kiki's direction, and didn't notice her looking affronted. Anastasia and Vivian both bristled internally. They knew about the Italian society wedding of the year, and were rather surprised not to have been invited. Vivian was less bothered than Anastasia: she had a busy weekend with all the people in town for the mountain marathon and most of the hotels were at full occupancy. Anastasia would have quite liked to have gone. It would have given her a reason to escape the dreadful drudgery of a weekend with Dimitri and their children.

Anastasia and Vivian both knew Walter was invited alongside a plus one, for Kiki. Now their father was giving up Kiki's spot for their brother.

'Sounds like a hoot,' Lysander said, with a broad smile.

Chapter Six

'Welcome back to Chalet Edelweiss, Catalina.'

Cat was unpacking in the smallest bedroom, a cosy single room in the loft that had a skylight view of the Silberschnee's peak. Lumi Kivvi was leaning on the frame of Cat's bedroom door. She didn't often mix with the help, but she did look after them, and she had been devastated for Cat when her beloved grandmother had passed away suddenly, insisting she fly straight home for the funeral and paying for her ticket.

'How was it?' she asked, her blue eyes jumping out from the soft edges of an elegant silver-blonde bob.

Cat smiled wanly. Despite the hideousness of having to say goodbye to *Abuela*, she *had* caught up with cousins, seen friends she studied with at culinary arts school in Buenos Aires, and sought inspiration in the new restaurants of Palermo, San Telmo and Recoleta, getting fine dining ideas she could serve to the Kivvis (Lumi would appreciate them, even if Viktor and Mika didn't). The trip had also been a circuit breaker for Cat. A chance to draw a line under a toxic affair that had gripped her for most of the past year. Cat had been thinking of her ex-lover as she idly folded her underwear away.

'It was OK, thank you,' Cat was grateful, both for the concern and for the interruption.

'How's your mother coping?'

Lumi was a thoughtful boss and a thoughtful mother. She had been a nurse when she met Viktor in Helsinki twenty-five years ago, and had had three children with him: Aapo was twenty-four and an Olympic fencer who lived and trained in Paris. Mika was nineteen, and could mostly be found bumming around the chalet getting stoned. And young Stella, at fourteen, was still boarding at a very exclusive private school on the banks of Lake Geneva.

Three children, all born five years apart. Lumi had given the past quarter of a century to her family, getting back into the difficult baby years each time just as she thought she was coming out of them. It was only in the past few years that she had spent more time on philanthropy, putting the interest on her husband's billions to good use while he continued to take over the planet, one elevator and escalator at a time.

'My mother is coping well, thank you, ma'am. She was glad to have me home.'

'Well, it's good to see you looking so well. Take your time easing back into things here, although we did miss your summer rolls – oh those rolls!' Lumi rolled her eyes heavenwards. Cat was excellent at fusing any cuisine. Argentinian steak sliced into Vietnamese summer rolls and flavoured with mint and holy basil. Hearty pork knuckle and cider stews from central Europe given a North African twist with apricots and cinnamon. French stews and fish soups served with homemade American-style corn breads. Cat dreamed of food, when she wasn't dreaming about her lover. Fortunately, she'd returned to a kitchen that the maid had fully stocked.

'Is it just you and Mika for dinner tonight, ma'am?'

'Yes, Viktor's in Helsinki but he's flying in late tonight for the Borromeo wedding tomorrow.'

'Of course.' Cat folded the remainder of her clothes. 'I was thinking perhaps steak with salsa verde and truffle-cooked chips. Is that good for you? Or would you like something lighter tonight?'

'Cat that sounds wonderful – it's good to have you home,' Lumi said, as she smiled and breezed away.

Chapter Seven

Bella and Harry hadn't had a chance to get a word in while their mother was doing the tour, and Emme had wanted to ask them a ton of questions.

'The lift's very fast.'

'It's a new build, just before the pandemic.'

'I mean, no one buys Siberian larch now because of, *you know*, so this is Swiss pine and proud!'

'The doors are oak of course . . .'

As they walked through the heavy – oak – front door, Emme marvelled at the view through the glass windows of the landing area that led down the side of the chalet. Through it the village twinkled under snow and lights, clouds danced across the rising moon.

'It's beautiful!' Emme gasped.

'Oh it's even better from our balconies, isn't it children?'

Harry and Bella were still tugging on their father's jacket, asking him what he'd brought them back from the city this weekend.

'Did you get me Lego, Papa?' Harry asked. His Paddington bear was long since squashed into Lexy's bag, although Bella still clutched hers.

'Daddy, will you be able to see my show?' Bella pleaded. 'It's next month. In Thun!'

Lexy was still focused on the tour, not allowing distractions to derail her.

'Now there are two types of people in Kristalldorf – those who leave their doors unlocked and those who have digital entries – some people are less protective of their property . . .'

'Crime is non-existent in Kristalldorf,' Bill said, as if he were the superhero responsible.

'Well, *that's* not true!' Lexy snapped, loadedly.

Bill looked flustered as a strained unspoken tension rose and Emme looked from husband to wife, wondering what the issue was.

'The point is, no one uses keys . . .' Lexy said, punching a number into a digital keypad below a video screen. A gem on her right hand sparkled pink.

'The code is 1212,' she said. 'Our wedding anniversary . . .' Emme thought that was a bit rudimentary; easy to crack. Lexy must have read her mind.

'But it works on facial recognition too. And there is video recording on this door . . . no sound, but it stores images in the event history for thirty days,' her face dropped, as she gave her husband a flustered sideways glance.

Emme marvelled at the tech. The double lock on her flat door in Balham was so archaic it only worked if she leaned into the door at a very precise angle.

'Is there not video entry on the downstairs door?' Emme asked.

'No. Privacy laws or something,' Lexy muttered, and hastily rearranged her features to a smile. 'But you type in 4-1212 there. Our apartment number followed by our code. We'll get your face scanned when you've unpacked and I'll set you up with the BUZZ app on your phone. Bill's not interested but I'll need you to keep track of my parcels.'

The thick door swung open onto an enormous home that just happened to cover one floor – the top floor. The rich wood décor was lifted by light and large open spaces, filled with plump taupe sofas scattered with textured cushions of fawn, ecru and mushroom. Sheepskin blankets hung over the sofa backs and luxurious handwoven rugs sat under the modern coffee table. The expansive living room was adorned with exposed beams, and huge floor-to-ceiling windows framed panoramic views of snow-kissed evergreens, just about visible in the valley moonlight. The scents of pine and aged timber filled Emme's senses.

Lexy, Bill and the children kicked off their shoes and put them in a sleek cupboard to the right of the door, and Emme followed suit before following Lexy into the main living space.

'Swiss engineering,' Lexy cooed as she pressed the button on a remote control, and one of the window panels slid open, creating a seamless segue between the opulent interior and the breathtaking landscape. 'The indoor/outdoor flow here is *very* well thought out.'

'Jesus, woman, you're letting in an Arctic blast!' Bill snapped. Emme didn't like the way Bill spoke to his wife, as an icy waft made the atmosphere even tenser.

'Relax, Bill,' Lexy said through an acid smile. 'It always takes Bill a few hours to adjust to the temperature being ten degrees colder up the mountain,' Lexy derided. She didn't speak to him that nicely either, but Lexy was in full showing-off mode. And the sliding panoramic window *was* impressive.

'Erm, hands!' Lexy commanded in a singsong voice. The children washed them at the slick kitchen sink then nimbly escaped to their bedrooms. Bill ambled off to the fridge to have a look at its contents.

Lexy closed the sliding door, but stopped short of drawing the cream curtains. The twinkling lights of the view were too impressive to shroud.

'It's beautiful,' Emme said.

Lexy tapped a sensor pad on the sidewall triggering ambient lighting to cast an intimate glow over the room.

'Gustav, turn on the fire.'

Emme looked around – *who was Gustav?*

A small light glowed orange on the sideboard, then an electric fire roared into life.

'Gustav. He's *our* Alexa.'

Emme's eyes widened. It was certainly more impressive than the Victorian plumbing and rattling radiators back home.

Bill wheeled Emme's suitcase down a wide hallway, Lexy and Emme following. Lexy pointed out the children's bedrooms, a family bathroom with a white free-standing bath sitting atop dark slate tiles, brushed nickel hardware and a thick grey bubble mat. Emme's guest room was modern yet cosy, without a trace of the nanny who had left just days before. Bill deposited Emme's case in her room and swiftly left.

'That's our office, and that's our room round the corner . . .' Lexy said, but didn't go as far to show Emme somewhere that was obviously out of bounds.

'Wonderful!'

As they walked back down the hallway, Emme poked her head around Bella's bedroom door.

'Want to show me your room?' she asked.

Bella shook her head.

'No,' she whispered, looking down at her plastic pony.

'Bells!' Lexy admonished, who was lingering over Emme's shoulder.

'That's OK,' Emme said. She admired a girl with boundaries.

'Come on, everyone must be hungry . . .' Lexy flapped, as they headed back to the large open-plan kitchen and dining room.

Now she mentioned it, Emme had noticed the faint smell of fried food and spices emanating from the kitchen area. On top of a thick, engineered wood worktop stood a stack of cardboard boxes with KK embossed on them in a silver circle.

'Our maid delivered dinner,' Lexy said. She might look like a Stepford Wife but Alexia Harrington didn't cook. Fortunately she didn't expect her nanny to either. She had said in the Zoom interview that cooking duties would be limited to breakfasts, packed lunches and the odd heated *flammkuchen* or pizza after school because Lexy was a supporter of the KristallKit dinner service that most people in Kristalldorf without a live-in chef subscribed to. Lexy selflessly supported KristallKit because she had done the PR for the brand during its launch phase, and its owner, Samuel Sommar, one of Kristalldorf's most prolific and dashing businessmen, was someone Lexy would do anything to stay in with.

KristallKit was the first client of Lexy's when she decided to go back into PR and set up her own business from the Alps.

She carefully opened a corner of one of the boxes.

'Ooh, Thai,' she said, with a self-satisfied smile. Emme helped Lexy carry the boxes to a wood-and-steel dining table, already set by their maid before she had left for the evening. Emme placed the boxes in the centre, among the floral centrepieces and plates without cutlery, that made the room look all rather staged.

Chapter Eight

After dinner, the Steinherrs retired to the drawing room for post-prandial drinks and jollity. The mansion was unusual in Kristalldorf in that it was made from stone and marble rather than the usual wooden structures around the town. This gave it a slight fairy-tale look.

From any of the mansion's many balconies you could see the stunning peak of the Silberschnee, and on the other side of the river, the Anna Maria hotel, glimmering in glass. Over the decades, Walter had been furnished with lucrative offers to buy the land he owned on the opposite side of the river: it was prime real estate, furthest from the train station in the quietest corner of the town. But Walter would never sell.

Nanny Iris had been instructed to put the children to bed, and the butler was preparing drinks for everyone. Negronis for Walter and Lysander, Pernod on the rocks for Anastasia, a pineapple daiquiri for Kiki, and sparkling water for Dimitri, who always stopped at one glass of wine with dinner. Vivian, who was planning on returning to the hotel after her father had turned in, drank a coffee.

The head maid entered with the large birthday cake Vivian had procured from the most elegant bakery in Kristalldorf, and she started a shy ensemble of 'Happy birthday to you . . .', which Lysander, Anastasia and Kiki made louder.

Kiki rubbed her husband's back as he blew out a solitary candle, then kissed his balding head. He tried not to wince.

'Happy birthday, baby,' she beamed, as if she had arranged the whole shebang.

'Goodness! All of my children here!' Walter exclaimed. His children looked at each other nervously. '*Almost* all of my children,' he corrected himself.

'Does anyone know where Caspian is?' Anastasia asked.

'I had a message from him, from Portugal, a few weeks ago,' Lysander said, but neither sister asked much more. Vivian was internally horrified that Caspian hadn't been in touch with their father on his seventieth birthday.

'Liezel, get the forks with the shells at the end,' Kiki ordered quietly. 'They're much nicer.'

Much tackier more like, Anastasia thought. She wished Kiki weren't there. This was a rare moment three out of four of the siblings were in the same room with their father and she wanted to broach the issue of Seven Summits. She didn't want Kiki to be party to these family discussions, she didn't want outsiders there, and although Dimitri was an outsider too, as legal counsel to the Steinherr business, he would need to be in on the conversations.

The maid returned with a new set of cake forks.

'These ones, ma'am?' she quietly asked.

'No!' Kiki scoffed. 'Do I have to do everything myself?' Kiki marched out to the kitchens, the maid chasing her hurriedly.

Anastasia saw her opportunity.

'Papa, look, while we're all here . . . I've been thinking.'

Lysander turned around, negroni in hand, interest piqued.

Vivian sipped her coffee from a Louis XIV chair.

'Seven Summits,' she stated. 'What's your plan for them, because I have some amazing ideas –'

'No business tonight, Anni!' Walter held up a hand. Vivian looked at her sister, bewildered. What did she want to do with Seven Summits? She hadn't shown much interest in the Anna Maria since their father gifted it to them, so why go for Seven Summits? At least ask about managing the Silberblick, given she seemed to spend more time having secret meetings in room 204 of that hotel than she did at the Anna Maria. Anastasia obviously felt more than comfortable in the Silberblick.

'Let me enjoy my birthday, dammit,' Walter said with a half chuckle, but it had enough bite to shut his daughter down.

Anastasia swirled the ice cubes in her Pernod, looked into the fireplace, and wanted to scream.

Chapter Nine

'I'll get water,' Emme said, opening a few cupboards and finding a glass jug.

'Tap is fine,' Lexy advised, although Emme had assumed that and was already at the pristine sink, where there wasn't a watermark in sight. 'Purest water in the world.' Again Lexy said it as if it were something she had engineered. 'Darlings!' Lexy called, which felt for show more than anything. 'Dinner's getting cold!'

Emme brought the jug to the table. Looking at it, all set with charger plates, plates, napkins and glassware, as if *Harpers* or *Architectural Digest* were coming to shoot, you would think it was a place for conviviality and hearty cuisine. But something jarred with Emme. Lexy Harrington looked too much like an actress to be genuine. This home looked too much like a show home for it to be warm. The spicy scents of dinner came from a cardboard box. She glanced at the fridge – there were no rudimentary pictures on it like at her sister's house: hand prints of the twins, notes, meal planners and magnets from faraway places. There were no accidental crayon marks on the meringue cream walls, beautifully framed by taupe and tobacco-coloured toiles and curtains. Perhaps Lexy didn't like clutter.

What did feel warm, though, was the heating underneath the polished parquet floor, which invited barefoot exploration, only not when the family were home. Emme felt on edge so far in Lexy's company, and hoped her nerves would settle.

'Let's eat before it gets cold, then I'll give you a tour of the wider building, and give you the rules,' Lexy said, as she removed the lids from the takeaway boxes.

'The rules,' Emme repeated, careful to sound keen.

'There's a spa in the basement . . . it has a plunge pool, sauna, steam – a few workout machines . . .' she said, wittering as she plunged serving spoons into pad thai, nasi goreng, jasmine rice and Asian greens. 'Although there won't be much time for spa-ing – that's rule seven!'

'Of course not,' Emme said amiably, wondering how many rules there were.

'Kids!' Lexy shouted, a little more snappily. 'Bill!'

'Sorry, I was in the bureau,' he said, as he walked down the ample hallway, scooping up Bella as she came out of her room. Bill had taken his tie off and his contact lenses out, and put on a pair of glasses – he looked hotter with a child under his arm, Emme thought. Less uptight.

Lexy ignored them and carried on talking.

'I work part-time now and with Bill in Zurich, I need you on hand every day, which is rule one I suppose!'

'Of course,' Emme said, proffering a spoonful of pad thai to Bella, who looked at the food with suspicion. Or was she looking suspiciously at Emme?

'Weekends you'll have some time off – we tend to do family things, don't we darling?' Lexy said hopefully to Bill. Again, something felt off-kilter to Emme, like she were watching a show. Or was Emme just feeling cynical after Tom and Chrissy's beautiful wedding? She'd wanted to be happy for happy couples but she felt so bruised and sore having watched Tom marry Chrissy.

Bill nodded benignly.

Harry came out of his bedroom with a tablet in his hand and curled his nose up at the dinner.

'No iPad at the table!' Bella said, and Emme wondered which rule number that was. Bella clearly liked to boss her older brother around just as Lexy liked to boss their daddy around. Bill removed the device from Harry's clutches and placed it on the kitchen island before sitting down to eat. As they started, Lexy wittered about the daily comings and goings, the schedules.

Clearly Bill had no interest in the logistics of running this family, he just paid for it with his banking job in Zurich. Emme privately wondered whether the weekdays would be more enjoyable without him around, or whether she would crave his return on Friday nights.

'In fact, tomorrow we have a wedding, in Italy,' Lexy said, as she handed everyone chopsticks.

'Borromeo,' Lexy added, before taking a small bite of a gyoza dumpling, leaving a theatrical pause for Emme to be impressed or ask more questions. Emme filled the kids' water glasses. Her sister always seemed to do that with the twins.

'Bill?' Emme asked genially, proffering the jug.

'I'm good, thanks.'

Lexy already had a glass of something sparkling, and she carried on, fizzing and bubbling away, almost as if she were talking to herself.

'It's on the lake, not far over the border,' she said, before remembering. 'Oh Bill, we mustn't forget the present!' She turned to Emme. 'I always buy the present months in advance, then forget to take it with us.'

Bill glanced up with a furrowed brow as he chased an edamame bean around his plate with his chopsticks. It went flying across the table and hit his wife on the hand.

'Bill! My ring!' she snapped, protecting the pink-red jewel on her right hand. Emme looked up.

'He got it for my fortieth,' she smiled pompously. 'It's a ruby – 1.1 carats, from 1910.'

Emme showed interest, her eyes wide as the jewel glimmered. 'Bill bought it because it matches my hair but, goodness Bill!' she scolded him as if he were one of the children.

'Jesus Lex! An edamame bean is hardly going to take out a rock like that!' Bill shot, throwing down his chopsticks.

Lexy looked startled and a frosty air set its veil over the dinner table.

Emme looked out of the vast windows onto the balcony, pretending she hadn't noticed the tension. Steam bubbled up from the hot tub outside. It looked very pretty out there, Emme thought, as she searched for a distraction. Fairy lights coiled around the balustrade and Emme wondered if it was a seasonal thing, or whether they were there year-round.

She tried to lift the mood and focus on the joy of being in a beautiful home, her home for a season, where she could escape the happy newlyweds and regroup. She was not an eighteen-year-old working a summer in America, who hardly even knew herself. She was a competent, confident twenty-eight-year-old executive assistant who was usually very good at calming a stressed woman. She could defuse this.

'Whose wedding is it?' Emme asked with a charming smile. Weddings were the last thing she wanted to talk about since Tom and Chrissy's one week ago. She winced internally.

'Oh, she's the daughter of a client of Bill's – a count – she's marrying a very boring Italian industrialist.' Lexy said it as if it were a curious match. 'And she's awfully plain, despite the parents' best efforts.' She looked at Emme, almost conspiratorially in her tone. 'Just goes to show sometimes even the best nose job can't save you.' Lexy giggled, wrinkling her own very pretty, very tiny nose.

'What's a nose job?' asked Bella thoughtfully. She looked up at Emme, as if only she would tell her the answer.

'Don't worry, darling,' her mother said, brushing the question under the carpet. 'Their hospitality though is something else: the count always gets Ducasse to finalise his menus, and white peacocks roam the gardens of the island mansion. It's very pretty . . . even if the poor bride isn't.'

'Christ, Lex!' Bill scorned. He nodded pointedly towards Bella as if to say *not appropriate* and Emme imagined Lexy often spoke without thinking too much. Emme didn't think they were appropriate things to say in front of little girls or little boys, but the comment certainly helped her get the measure of Lexy Harrington.

'The biggest surprise was all four of us are invited, but Bill is a trusted confidant of the count.' Lexy fluttered her lashes rapidly and wiped red lipstick from the corner of her mouth. 'We leave on the first train tomorrow, back Sunday afternoon in time for dinner. Ready for . . .' she left another theatrical pause, 'ski school on Monday!'

The children's faces lit up and they gasped.

'Ski school?!' asked Harry. In the winter months, skiing was also on the curriculum for the children of Kristalldorf.

'Yeth!' Bella said making a fist in the air.

It was early November. The first flakes were falling in the village tonight, which meant it would be abundant on the mountain, and a new season was officially underway. Between November and March, the children attended ski school for two hours after lunch every day: pivotal learning for any child growing up in the Alps. Ski school was their favourite time of year, until it lost its lustre somewhere between Christmas and February, when the tourists made the slopes a little too crowded and the novelty had gone.

'Does ski school really start on Monday, Mummy?' Harry asked, a serious concern on his freckled face, just to be sure.

'Yes, darling,' Lexy said. He too punched the air with a little fist, a little more gung-ho than his sister, whose smile had returned to a frown. She remembered that one day she might have to get a job inside someone's nose. She pulled on her mother's pristine blouse sleeve.

'But what if I'm too big to do a nose job, Mummy? Surely I won't fit.'

Lexy looked confused by her daughter but continued talking, gyoza dumpling balanced on her chopsticks like a gymnast on the beam.

'Perhaps use the time we're away to acclimatise. The air is different here, you might feel light-headed. Have a look around, get your bearings, make yourself familiar with the rules.'

Emme smiled in agreement. She looked back to the balcony and the steam trailing up from the plunge pool. It looked like a serpent, weaving its way up against the starry Swiss sky. *What a pristine place*, Emme thought, although the tension in the Harrington home slightly took the edge off the mountain idyll.

Chapter Ten

Vivian walked into the Anna Maria shortly after 11pm and glanced over the guest manifest, to see whether the check-ins had all arrived and whether there had been any manoeuvring with bedrooms. Rich people always wanted to know they had the *best* room, so every day there was some juggling and ego smoothing between the concierge and head of housekeeping. When Vivian could see that everything was in order, she went to see the restaurant manager, Henrik, whose staff were tidying away for the night, and asked him how the evening's service went. All seemed satisfactory. No curveballs, no allergy incidents, no complaints.

'Excellent Henrik, thank you,' Vivian said.

They didn't get many complaints, the Anna Maria was the newest and coolest hotel in town, although some high rollers could be prickly. Viktor Kivvi brought friends in for dinner a few weeks ago, and it felt more like an inquisition than a relaxed social.

'You know no one eats ceviche for dinner in Peru, it's a lunch thing,' he'd said, looking at the evening menu with disdain.

'I don't want sourdough, can I get a basket of granary bread? In rolls.'

'Oh, you stock the Du Kok wine now? I heard it's supermarket standard.'

Viktor's business associates laughed.

'No sir, it's exceptional,' Vivian replied. 'Mr Du Kok's master vintner recommended this one himself when he visited. Said it was the best bottle they'd ever produced.'

Viktor Kivvi didn't like being corrected.

'Well, he would say that, wouldn't he?' he jibed, a little patronisingly, as he thumbed the wine list and ordered a French Bordeaux.

The man knew nothing about hospitality, but Vivian had greeted him and his guests personally and smiled when he made each and every dig.

The old families of Kristalldorf, the Sommars, the Herwegs or the Kochs, wouldn't have behaved like that in her restaurant. There was rivalry of course, but also respect among the founding families, those families who made Kristalldorf what it was: the most deluxe ski resort in the world.

Tonight there had been no big-name visitors to speak of, said Henrik. Mostly runners carb-loading ahead of the mountain marathon on Sunday, and that suited everyone fine. Runners didn't ask for much, except pasta, rice and a good night's sleep.

Everything was in order. Everything was in check.

So why did Vivian feel so out of sorts as she went into her office behind the reception area and switched on the table lamp? In the glow of the light she tried to look at the laundry expenses: housekeeping was coming in way too costly at the moment, and she tried to decipher how to trim the bills without cutting on quality.

Was it the surprise visit from her brother that niggled in the pit of her stomach? She was usually over the moon to see Lysander. To hear about New York. To hear how her nephew was getting on. Perhaps it was the ease with which her father had switched Kiki as his plus one for Lysander, when he wouldn't do that for her or Anastasia. But Lysander lived in New York and Vivian and Anastasia lived in the same mansion as their father, so of course he wanted to spend more time with his faraway son. Was it Caspian's lack of attendance at his father's birthday? He could be so selfish like Anastasia. Was it the sense that her father was holding something back? Was there something wrong? Perhaps it was that he was now seventy, and she wondered how many years they had left together. Then she realised, as she thought through all her options, that the sense of doom was down to her new boyfriend. Last night in bed she had invited him to join the family for Walter's birthday dinner. He hadn't said yes. But he hadn't said no either, before plunging into her for another round of intense and magical sex. Had that been evasive? Was he even her boy-friend anyway? They still hadn't put a label on it, which frustrated her as much as labels seemed to frustrate him.

Vivian called him. No answer. He never answered. She always had to leave a missed call for him to call her back.

'*Scheiße*,' she said, as she stared at her phone. Why was he keeping her at arms' length when he had confessed that he was falling; when she had told him that she was going to tell her father? Perhaps she should get out now, before she fell too deep. But she already knew it was too late. He was too damn hot and she was too damn hooked.

Chapter Eleven

Anastasia sat in the ornate wing-backed chair, looked at her nails and felt totally and utterly bored. Walter and Kiki had retired for the night and the children had long since been put to bed. On the other side of the opulently framed fireplace, Dimitri was chewing the fat with Lysander while they watched the flames crackle. Although they came and went as they pleased, all the adult children lived in the Steinherr mansion, or stayed there when they were visiting from the US or, in Caspian's case, between surf trips. It was a given that in a small town like Kristalldorf, they would live in the family's immense mansion.

After covering American politics and Lysander's latest cases, Anastasia stood up and yawned performatively.

'All this legal talk is such a bore,' she said, with a wince. 'I'm going to bed.'

Dimitri looked up at his wife to ask if she wanted him to come to bed too. He didn't even speak before she answered his question out loud.

'Don't be silly, you boys stay up all night if you want, I need my beauty sleep.'

'Night sis!' Lysander said with a smile, giving her hand a brief squeeze as she walked by.

Dimitri rose to kiss his wife goodnight but she was

already out the door. She didn't care for him to come near her. She didn't care much for his company at all.

Anastasia was coming through a particularly wild patch when Dimitri arrived in town thirteen years ago; even wilder than her teen years breaking out of boarding school. She was twenty-four and partied out after doing ridiculous amounts of coke and living it up with every count, prince or rock star who'd blazed through Kristalldorf. Dimitri Diamandis, with his decent looks, own wealth, and quiet, nurturing manner, was just what Anastasia needed. She knew she already had a job for life in any one of her father's hotels if she wanted, although her work ethic wasn't that of Vivian's, but on falling in love with Dimitri she realised that perhaps she should try being a mother. Maybe that was what she was craving. Stability that had been stolen from her when her own mother died when she was just seven. Dimitri was fifteen years older, the son of a Greek shipping tycoon and a highly respected lawyer. After a huge wedding in the Alpenrose, and three children in quick succession, Dimitri had served his purpose. Sex with him was boring and functional, his libido was almost non-existent and at fifty-two he wasn't ageing well. Fatherhood had made him lose his hair at an alarming rate, and suddenly his kindness came across as dullness to Anastasia. Since Ophelia had been born eight years ago, they had sex infrequently, and Dimitri didn't seem to mind.

Motherhood really hadn't excited her in the way she'd hoped either. She loved her three children, of course. She loved the perks of having a Greek island for the summer thanks to her father-in-law, but she would have preferred it if she could go there on her own. At least Nanny Iris travelled with them everywhere. And in term time the children were usually at boarding school.

Anastasia continued down the hall to her and Dimitri's grand bedroom and slumped back onto the bed without even taking off her boots.

As she stared at the elaborate ceiling rose that held a chandelier, she plotted her next move.

Since motherhood hadn't inconvenienced Anastasia much, she had enjoyed the perk of hospitality cosplay that comes with Daddy owning a portfolio of hotels. She had been the head of sales and marketing for all the hotels in the group, before realising she didn't like number crunching. She had been the head of banqueting before realising she liked eating caviar more than discussing the margins of it. And she had been the head of human resources, before realising that people weren't really her thing. Anastasia had been eyeing her father's three chalets in Seven Summits that currently sat vacant yet incurred large weekly cleaning bills. They could reap revenue and be exclusively hers: she could handle the management of Snowbell, Aster and Orchid: the rentals, the bookings, the staffing. She could hold events there. Fashion shows and salons. Cultural gatherings. Taking them on would also give her a constant rotating escape in this small town: a place where she wouldn't have her baby sister knowing her every move.

So it was highly inconvenient last Christmas, when Walter gifted his daughters the Anna Maria and said they could co-manage it. Why assume she yearned to co-own a hotel with Vivian of all people? Anastasia wanted Seven Summits. If she made them a success, perhaps her father would see her as the right heir to take over the Steinherr empire when the sad day came. Yes, yes, everyone knew Vivian was a workhorse, but surely Anastasia was the *face* of the business.

As she looked at the chandelier she remembered it was Friday night. Her lover would be back in town. She picked up her phone and dialled a number she had promised she would stop calling, a number she couldn't resist.

'I need to see you,' she purred. 'Usual place, usual room.'

And within minutes she was heading back down the sweeping staircase.

'I'm just off to the hotel,' she said, peering into the drawing room – Lysander and Dimitri were now smoking cigars by the roaring fire.

Lysander was surprised.

'Now?' Dimitri asked, puzzled.

'Yes, there's some business I need to attend to . . .'

'OK, don't work too late,' Dimitri advised.

'I won't,' Anastasia said, leaving the mansion, wrapped in her long fur coat, with nothing underneath except a see-through net negligee. As she stepped into the cold night her nipples tingled as she gave a furtive look at the Anna Maria on the other side of the river and carried straight down the left bank, towards the Silberblick, which was managed by a discreet German who was so terrified of Anastasia he never queried her regular use of room 204. She didn't like to conduct her affairs right under her sister's nose. It wasn't good for business or family.

Chapter Twelve

When Emme turned in on her first night in Kristalldorf, just after Bill had popped out for a beer, Lexy instructed her there was no need to get up at 6am to say goodbye to the family, and she airdropped her 'the rules', which were in addition to Emme's terms of employment, although there was some overlap she realised, as she read them in bed.

Rule one: Be on hand every day to look after Harry and Bella, unless time off has been pre-arranged. You can have weekend days off on request, and Christmas Eve and Christmas Day, as per your contract. As agreed with the agency, we need you over New Year.

Rule two: Get the children to school, all playdates and activities with fifteen minutes to spare, as per your contract.

Rule three: No overnight stays out of the chalet unless previously agreed, and no one is to stay here in your room.

Rule four: No shoes in the apartment. There is a discreet shoe cubby by the front door.

Rule five: No iPad or devices at the dining table or during any meal or snack time. Including your own devices.

Rule six: Take delivery of parcels and packages and
   leave them on the oak sideboard by the door. I
   do most of my shopping online.
Rule seven: No spa while on duty.
Rule eight: Don't use the laundry room after
   10pm, it upsets the neighbours.
Rule nine: Don't let the children nap – we want
   them tired in the evening.
Rule ten: Always wash your hands and the
   children's when returning home – cleanliness is
   next to godliness!

Emme committed the rules to memory, wondering whether 'cleanliness is next to godliness' was a joke, and as she drifted to sleep, she was grateful that she had the weekend to settle in before her nannying duties started in earnest on Monday. She had made it. From the heartache of watching Tom marry Chrissy to a remote Alpine beauty so far removed from it. Emme had kept her cool – declaration aside – she had found a new job, and she had moved to what felt like the most picturesque place on the planet. It was daunting and it was exhausting, but she felt proud of herself as she slipped into a deep and heavy slumber.

In the dark and confusion of the early morning, Emme heard the hushed tones of a family on a mission to make their train and the reassuring clunk of luxe locks, but the fatigue of the past week and waking up somewhere new made her fall back asleep as soon as the family had gone.

*

At 10am Emme woke, got up, tried to work out how to use the futuristic-looking coffee machine, opted for tea instead, and walked around the apartment, comforted by the warmth of the parquet floor. She pulled open the curtains to the balcony and marvelled at the hot tub outside, and the view beyond that. The glorious Silberschnee, so crisp and close it looked like if she stepped out onto the balcony, she could touch it. Yet it sat at the other end of town, beyond pretty wooden rooftops covered in a smattering of snow, the church spire, and all the beautiful buildings that hugged the Glanzfluss.

She took a photo of the view and hovered her thumb over her phone, poised to send the picture to Tom. Things didn't seem real if she didn't share them with Tom, and she was desperate to let him see the vista she was looking at right now. How beautiful it was. How much she wanted him to be in Kristalldorf with her. But they hadn't spoken since he and Chrissy went on honeymoon, since he said a stilted and interrupted goodbye to her the morning after the wedding, so her pride stopped her.

Emme didn't fancy braving the hot tub when the outside temperature read almost zero on the thermometer by the balcony doors, plus it might look a little indulgent if any of the neighbours saw the new nanny was already in the hot tub. So Emme settled on the interior tub in the family bathroom and turned on the taps. As the bath ran, she decided to call her mother and give her a video tour of the apartment.

'Oh goodness, look at that!' Marian said.

It was bigger than the entire Eversley home in Purley. Emme told her mother she had arrived safe and well and everything was fine – beautiful in fact – and that the children were lovely. Marian still didn't seem convinced that going from executive assistant to nanny was the right thing for Emme right now, but Emme had said too many times in the past week that the two jobs were probably more similar than anyone would know. Emme then called her sister Lucille who was on her way to the Kids Club at the cinema in Croydon, and gave her a quick 360-degree tour.

'Lucky cow, blue sky in November? It's stunning!'

'It's freezing.'

'Well it's pissing down here . . . at least you've got sunshine. And that view. Jesus, Em, it looks fake!' Emme stood on the balcony in her pyjama shirt and angled the camera so the Silberschnee sat behind her shoulder.

'It is beautiful,' Emme concurred.

'What's the family like?' Lucille asked.

'Oh you know . . . minted.'

'I bet. And the hot dad?'

'What?'

'The dad. You said he was a bit of a silver fox on your call.'

Emme suddenly felt self-conscious. What if they could see her? Hear her? The video security at the front door that connected to an app called BUZZ was pretty high-end. Surely a family like that might consider security inside too. Emme walked back into the apartment, closed the sliding doors behind her with the remote control Lexy had shown her last night and looked up to the corners of the rooms, the worktops and the appliances.

No visible cameras.

'Not my type,' she joked. 'But they're very nice, really

lovely kids.' Emme said it with a performative self-awareness not unlike Lexy, before Lucille said the film was about to start and they hadn't even bought popcorn yet.

'Go! My bath will be ready anyway. Speak soon.'

Emme didn't know why but she closed the bathroom door before undressing and stepping into the bath. She plunged under the comforting suds and watched the steam curl lazily from the water's surface, filling the bathroom with a dreamlike haze. All the stress and tension of the wedding, her confession to Tom, the big move to the mountains, came to a head, and Emme closed her eyes and surrendered to the comfort of the bath, the velvety bubbles clinging to her contours like a caress. She stretched out her toes. The tub was so large she could extend her legs out straight, and parted them a little, stroking the soft triangle between her thighs, finding the button that she knew would help her relax further.

She thought of Tom. A sigh escaped her lips. She tried to succumb to her own touch but the thought that filled her imagination was of Tom and Chrissy, naked, entwined together. Chrissy pinned down and exhilarated. Tom leaning over his new wife. On a sun lounger with the Indian Ocean breeze making their skin tingle.

'Fuck!'

She wanted so badly to make her own body tingle, but the thought of Chrissy, her face as she reached a climax and waves of pleasure rolling down the man Emme loved, was enough to put her off. She frowned. Wiped the suds from her brow, and decided to make this bath functional.

*

After she was dry, Emme put on her warmest clothes and Lucille's turquoise and fluoro orange coat and set out to explore Kristalldorf, taking the stairs down to the ground-floor entrance rather than the elevator. She passed the empty apartment on the third floor, and a name sign that read 'Glock & Grebe'. Then past 'Muller' on the second floor – the other couple who lived there year-round. There wasn't a name by the first-floor apartment door but on the post boxes outside she could see a man called Tomas Edstrom owned that apartment.

As Emme pondered who her neighbours might be, she retraced her path from last night, down the steep, wide steps to the carless road, where bicycles and yumbos passed her. She wound down the zigzag path to the Glanzfluss, which was roaring and gushing as it cut its path from the glacier to the valley. Emme crossed a bridge, figuring that if she made her way back to the train station, she would be in the centre of town.

Orientation was easy in Kristalldorf. The entire town was framed by the iconic silhouette of the Silberschnee, draped in snow and guarding the town like a stoic sentinel. In front of the mountain, Emme could see flashes of green meadows staving off last night's melting snow between the houses and buildings that obscured them; the river Glanzfluss cut through the town like a silver ribbon, bubbling with glacier water.

Emme drank in the faces of all the people she passed. Skiers clunked through town in snow suits in a kaleidoscope of colours, their boots thudding as they made their way to the ski train or the gondola, each heading out on the two main exits up to the peaks. Locals tended their shops, sweeping the cobbled pavements outside, straightening displays of snow globes, chocolates and trinkets. Shoppers weaved in and out of the more luxurious boutiques: watches, jewellery, designer fashion brands. Emme was already getting a handle on those shops she would frequent and those she wouldn't. Though she could always look longingly in the windows of the numerous designer boutiques.

As Emme glanced up she inhaled the scents of pine, chocolate and coffee, permeating the wooden facades of the cafés, some of which had outdoor seats with a sheep-skin on each chair, so coffee lovers could take in the view of the Silberschnee with their arabica.

Then she saw it: a supermarket bag made of paper. Then another. Then another, being carried by people coming from a small side street. Emme laughed to herself. This pretty town had curated itself so perfectly, even the super-market was hidden in a quad behind the more palatable shopfronts of Läderach, Lindt, Bogner and Patek Phillipe.

Emme explored the side street and found the discreet entrance of a deceptively large supermarket, branded Migros, and stepped inside, fascinated. Emme always loved a foreign supermarket. When she and Tom had been back-packing in Australia, or on holidays closer to home, they had loved going to local supermarkets and seeing what treats they could fill their baskets with. In Kristalldorf, the supermarket was as pristine as the streets outside it, filled with the aroma of freshly baked goods.

This place, Emme thought, before stopping at a wall full of chocolate bars that looked like vintage postcards, their wrappers were so beautiful. Continuing along an aisle of meats and cheeses, she wondered if it might be a nice touch to cook for the Harringtons tomorrow on their return: Bill had mumbled that he missed Yorkshire pudding the most when Emme asked them how long they had lived in Switzerland, so cooking a roast for them might be a good way to ingratiate herself. For now she settled on buying herself a beautiful bar of Cailler chocolate.

Back outside, Emme continued to the furthest point of town, the closest she could get to the Silberschnee without going off course. Where the road turned to trails, she stopped outside an impressive-looking modern hotel called the Anna Maria, with glass balconies all facing the mountain. Emme took in the view of the mountain from the street and imagined what it might be like to stay there. How rich she would have to be; how lucky she was to be paid to enjoy this scenery.

Pods glided overhead, coming from the gondola station on the river's edge. On the other side of the river stood a mansion that looked like something out of a fairy tale. Emme stopped as the road came to an end, looked, and listened. Pretty posts marked out the routes for various hiking trails; sounds of cowbells became more apparent, ringing from the foothills. The river bubbled and the soft whirr of the cable car gave a sense of calm. Emme imagined this must be beautiful in all seasons, and almost wanted to wish her time away to spring, to see what the view looked like then – with lush fields and wildflowers, she imagined. Emme leaned on a wooden post, took a photo of the Silberschnee's iconic peak on her phone, and planned her next move.

As Emme wound through a side street back towards

the church, she passed a pretty apartment building with dark wood balconies and flower boxes lining them. Each waist-height balustrade beam had a love heart cut out of its wood; each flower box was vibrant with hellebores, violas and pansies in lilacs, pinks and creams. Emme was just marvelling at how beautiful a simple block of flats could look when she saw a semi-naked woman rush out onto the balcony of one of the first-floor apartments. The woman wore a white shirt, a thong, and a mischievous smile. Her long legs and lustrous brown hair made her look like a supermodel, but given all the beautiful people Emme had walked past this morning, several women in this town looked like supermodels. They probably were.

The woman was clutching ice-white sneakers and a large coat. She leaned back against the wall. Her breathing heavy, her eyes alert. Her long, tanned limbs started to shake in the cold as she listened to what was going on inside.

Shit. What's happening?

Emme listened too. Another woman was shouting from inside the apartment, in what sounded like German. Then English. Emme looked to the balcony doors, and back to the woman leaning against the wall. She had a small smile of triumph at the corner of her mouth.

A tall man came out onto the balcony, and he was so handsome that Emme slunk back into the shadows with a gasp.

It's him!

It was the man with the aviators from the airport. The man whose presence in the darkness of the shuttle was so immense and enigmatic Emme had done everything she could not to look at him. Now she couldn't help herself.

The man's skin was tanned and his shoulders broad: each line and sinew told tales of pursuits played out under the sun. He had dark brown hair, sun-kissed bronze at the ends, that licked his neck like treacle. He had full lips, a strong nose and judging from his underwear, which was all he was wearing, a huge cock. His semi-erect penis seemed to throb through his white, tight, Calvin Kleins, no doubt having just withdrawn from the woman standing on the balcony with the mussed-up hair and the mischievous smile.

The man too seemed equal parts bemused and panicked, as he kissed the woman passionately and expeditiously, lovers stealing one last kiss, as he held her hand and helped her climb over the side of the balcony with a giggle, stroking her bottom in its thong as she went.

The woman shouting from inside spilled out onto the balcony: as tall and leggy as the first, but her mane was honey blonde. She berated the man in a mixture of German and English, which he responded to in English, his protestation and lies voiced in a soft South African accent.

'Genuinely, no one's here! I was just thinking about you baby, that's all,' he said, gesturing to his hard-on, which seemed to be holding on.

'Then why did you just rush out here?'

'I needed to cool off,' he said, looking down.

'I heard someone!'

'No baby, it's just me and the TV. And . . . well, I was thinking of you when you came crashing in.' The man pouted.

The woman softened a little, looking at him with drunk-in-love eyes.

'It's only you now, I swear.'

Big fucking liar!

Emme narrowed her eyes and opened her mouth in outrage. What was this guy like?

He leaned in and spoke platitudes, kissed the woman's neck and flattered her, until she started to soften. As he did so, the first woman with the Bambi legs hid at the side of the building, half listening, fully invested, as she slipped her trainers on, wrapped herself in her long coat and put on huge sunglasses. She walked off towards the town, hugging her body tight.

'Come on baby, you're just too much, I'm hard for you day and night,' the man said, as he looked at the blonde in utter awe. She was gorgeous too. Jesus, what did they put in the water here? The woman pouted. And allowed the man to press his full lips to hers. He held her face and slipped his tongue inside her mouth, pressing his cock into her skintight caramel trousers.

'Oh,' she sighed, looking like those long legs of hers might buckle. He pulled her in some more, putting a palm on each of her buttocks and pressing her towards him. His muscular shoulders enveloping her, her back now to the street where Emme watched, rapt. Shocked at the gumption of the man – and his lovers – in broad daylight.

The man, who had managed to convince one woman that he hadn't just been inside another only minutes earlier, locked eyes with Emme over his girlfriend's shoulder.

Emme wanted to frown. But she was also more turned on than she'd been in weeks.

Chapter Thirteen

Walter and Lysander stood on a terrace in the middle of a small island in the middle of an Italian lake and watched the bride and groom having their photographs taken by what looked like an entire *Vogue* entourage. White peacocks weaved among the guests who sipped Louis Roederer and a string quartet played Vivaldi.

'Edoardo doesn't look well.'

Walter observed his friend, the father of the bride, having his photo taken with his family. His expression was one of pride and nerves, his skin pale, his grin stilted. Maybe it was the pre-speech nerves. Walter remembered them well from Anastasia's wedding thirteen years ago in Kristalldorf. Lysander's wedding had been less pressure, as Megan's dad did a wonderful speech at long floral trestle tables on a beach in The Hamptons.

At best, this wedding would go in the society pages of *Tatler* or *Hola!* At worst, a small photo in the European gossip rags, and only because Dua Lipa was being flown in as the evening entertainment, rumour had it among the younger guests.

'Probably thinking of his legacy – handing it all over to that chancer,' Lysander said, nodding to the groom, whose teeth were too white to be natural.

'Edo's no fool!' Walter said in his booming voice. The two men stood side-by-side watching the families being directed under the red-orange foliage of larch and azalea. Walter wore a suit made by his tailor in Zurich; Lysander wore Armani. Both clutched their champagne flutes to their buttoned chests. 'And nor am I . . .' he added, turning to his son.

'What's up, Dad?'

Walter tried not to become irritated by his son's Americanisms. He dug deep to remember that Lysander was schooled there. He had married an American. Hell, he'd probably lived over there longer than he ever lived in Switzerland by now, so he tried to go easy. He wanted to talk to his son about succession, without letting him know he was ill.

'I might start slowing down a bit, I need to be thinking about *my* legacy. Who's going to take over, when I die.'

'Jesus, Dad! Weddings sure make you cheery.'

'I'm seventy now –'

'Seventy and a day. And I'm pretty sure you'll be working until you're ninety-nine, at least!' Lysander tried to lighten the mood.

Walter gave a rueful look.

'Your sisters aren't taking to the Anna Maria like I thought they would.'

'What do you mean?'

'I gifted them the hotel to see if they could pull together, but it's only driving them further apart.'

Lysander gave his father a doubtful look.

'Didn't you gift them the hotel to see who would come out on top?' He said it with fond remonstration.

Walter shook his head and tried to ignore the barb.

'Well it's not working.'

'They were both working at midnight!'

'Vivian was, Anni, I don't think so. Vivian didn't see her there last night anyway . . .'

'Oh, I thought she –'

'You know how she struggles to stick with any one thing, how flighty she can be,' Walter explained.

'Right . . .'

'I suppose I always knew Vivian would make a better go of it, but I hoped Anastasia would learn from Vivian's focus and drive. All I've done is pit them against each other. Even more.'

'So why don't you give Anastasia a different hotel to run?'

Walter shook his head.

'Too risky,' he said. Anastasia really didn't stick at anything for very long. He couldn't trust her with another major role in the business. Not on her own.

A make-up artist jumped in to powder the mother of the bride.

'What about you, son? How would you like to take over?'

Lysander almost choked on his champagne and put a fist to his mouth while he recovered.

'Dad!'

'What?' Walter looked puzzled.

'I can take a deposition from an ex-president but I know nothing about hospitality. Even Anastasia knows more than I do!' Lysander said it with a sardonic laugh.

'But you're my heir. Have you never considered coming home?'

Lysander let out an exasperated sigh.

'Home is New York.'

He tried not to hurt his father's feelings, although it irritated him, that for a clever and powerful man, he could be so stupid sometimes: marrying Kiki in Las Vegas after an exceptional night at the blackjack table was one of his most foolish moves. And now this? Offering him the business when it was so stark he wasn't the right choice.

'I've always known there's a job for me in the business if I want it, but I never have, Dad, I'm sorry but you know this. It's why I went into law.'

Walter shook his head but stopped himself short of saying it out loud: why had his sons failed him?

He looked across at Viktor Kivvi, chatting to the head of a French luxury goods empire and his Colombian social-ite wife. It gave him small comfort to know Viktor Kivvi didn't seem to have obvious successors either. One of his sons ponced around with a fencing sword while the other bummed around Kristalldorf as if he were still fifteen. And the daughter really was just a child.

'So what am I to do?' Walter asked, feeling a little dejected.

'Dad, it's so obvious. Vivian. She eats, sleeps and breathes the business. She's a wonderful host and a fair boss. She's too kind for anyone in town to double cross, so people don't mess around with her. It sounds like the Anna Maria is doing wonders, whatever you think.'

'It is, it is . . .'

Lysander looked across at his father, a little disappointed by his everyday sexism.

'Come on Dad, I'm your first-born son but that does not mean I'd be the right person to run the business. Seriously.'

Walter and Lysander paused as they watched Lumi Kivvi glide across the terrace in a long silver dress to join her husband and his group. She furnished her husband with a glass and he looked irritated by her in response.

Walter nodded, as if he were conceding a game of chess.

'I know. I just wanted to check with you, that you're certain the door is closed. It's my dream for you all to take it on. Even Caspian, in his own way . . .'

'Sorry, Dad. And it really is obvious. If you want to get things in place, I think Vivian is your woman. It won't be easy, but perhaps you can carve out a different role for Anastasia. She seems so . . . frustrated with everything.'

Walter nodded and took a sip from his glass but curled his nose up at it. He preferred Laphroaig Scotch whisky to Louis Roederer.

'Is everything OK?' Lysander had the feeling his father was holding something back. He remembered Walter's string of infections last winter, but he didn't seem to have had one for a while. And his mental cognition seemed tiptop, even if his mood had been a little grumpy of late. 'Is there something else on your mind?'

Walter looked across the terrace again and felt a lurch.

'Yes. There is.'

'Well, is it anything I can help with?'

'Yes. Get me out of my marriage, will you?'

Lysander breathed a sigh of relief; finally his father was seeing sense.

Chapter Fourteen

Emme sat outside a bakery enjoying a chicken and avocado baguette in the chilly sunshine. She could not stop thinking about the man from the balcony. The man from the airport. The arrogance of him. His burning gold-brown eyes, boring into her while he hugged the woman he had just cheated on. Making Emme complicit. Finding it funny.

The arrogance!

She wondered who the brunette was. How long the blonde had been put-upon. She thought about what the man might be like in bed, and tried to push that thought to the back of her mind. She was getting frustrated now.

Was Tom the only decent man out there? He had always been respectful of his dates and girlfriends, and treated them well. Emme had been on plenty of dates and seen guys too. Dates that had turned into sex and Sunday lunch, theatre trips and dinners, but neither of them had ever had a serious partner until Chrissy. Tom would never cheat on Chrissy like that dirty dog on the balcony.

Emme's heart sank again, as she looked up at the church and the bells rang 3pm.

Time to go back to the apartment.

She needed to unpack, she needed to settle in.

*

Emme wound through Kristalldorf and up the hill, getting hotter with each step in her fluoro coat and multitude of layers. The man on the balcony had stirred something inside her. The image of his hard-on in his boxers made her feel flustered. She thought about the empty apartment, and wondered whether to spend her first Saturday night watching a movie, or perhaps she would have another bath and finish herself off. That guy. His molten eyes. His electric smile. His cock.

Inside the apartment, Emme finished unpacking, familiarised herself with the schoolbag station, the fridge and list of all the foods the kids liked to eat, and looked over the notes she had made. Harry goes to bed at 8pm; Bella at 7.30pm. Bella likes to listen to audiobooks; Harry needs ambient music and sounds of nature to drift off. Harry is a fussy eater; Bella is more gung-ho. After rereading her notes Emme settled down to watch some TV, except she couldn't find the TV, let alone work out how to turn it on.

A loud buzz sounded from the system by the front door and made Emme jump.

Shit.

She looked at the video screen by the front door but couldn't see anyone. She opened the door. No one. It was someone downstairs, she could hear chatter on ground level. They'd probably pressed the wrong button. Emme closed the door and continued her hunt for the TV – Lexy had said the children were allowed to watch cartoons when they had performed their ablutions so there must be one. The door buzzed again and Emme tentatively pressed the button with a microphone symbol on it.

'Hello?'

'Hey!'

Emme recognised the voice.

'Cat?'

'Are you gonna let us in or what?'

Emme wasn't sure where friends stood in the Harrington house rules. Lexy and Bill didn't allow overnight visitors of course, but they hadn't specified whether the nanny was allowed to have friends over. But it wasn't like she'd invited her, or planned a party or anything.

'Emme?'

'Sorry. I'll buzz you in, come up!'

Emme pressed what she thought was the button to release the downstairs door but she couldn't hear any movement. The buzzer on the intercom sounded again.

'Still here!' Cat chimed.

'Shit, sorry. How's this?' Emme tried another button with a key on it, opened the oak front door of the Harrington home again and leaned over the balustrade. The intercom inside buzzed again.

'Still here . . .'

'I'll come down!' she said, cursing as the door swung closed behind her, before remembering she didn't need a key.

Deep breath.

It was OK. Lexy had told her the upstairs video entry recorded without sound. Emme still had a chance of being Mary Poppins and not Mary Pottymouth.

Emme hurried downstairs, giving her reflection a cursory glance in one of the stairwell windows as she went. She fluffed her soft chestnut hair. It was usually glossy and smooth but looked a little frizzy in the altitude. Why was she worrying? Cat wasn't one of these women who had to have their hair blow-dried to perfection that she'd seen around town.

As she reached the ground floor a nervousness fizzed in her stomach. She definitely hadn't expected to see Cat at Chalet Stern only a day after meeting her.

'Hey Catalina!' she said, as casually as she could. Next to her stood a beautiful man with rich brown hair that bounced in curls on top of his head and a sweet, shy smile.

'Please,' she frowned. 'Call me Cat!' Then she remembered her manners. 'This is Tiago.'

'Nice to meet you,' Emme said with a smile, and beckoned them in.

'My family are away . . .' Emme said cautiously, as she led them up the stairs.

'Yeah, the Borromeo wedding. The Kivvis are there too. Everyone who's anyone in this town is there today.' She let out an acerbic giggle.

Emme punched in the code and let them all in.

'Well this is a nice surprise, thanks for coming by.'

Cat strode in confidently and looked around the capacious living room. Tiago looked dreamily out to the balcony, as if the Silberschnee were luring him. Emme tried not to sweat that they hadn't taken off their shoes.

'It's T's only night off, like, probably all season, isn't it?' Cat turned to him.

Tiago nodded, his face earnest as he ate an apple he'd brought.

'So we're going out . . . you coming to party?' Cat looked to the corridor beyond Emme's shoulder to check the kids weren't about.

'Yeah, erm, I don't know, I was going to . . .' she trailed off. She was going to spend the evening trying to find the bloody television.

Tiago returned to the kitchen area and jumped up to sit on the thick worktop; Cat examined the appliances.

'Nice . . .' she said appreciatively, gliding a finger along the Gaggenau oven. 'Clearly never used.'

Emme smiled as if to say *that's about right,* but also had a feeling that house guests sitting on the kitchen surface, banging their trainers together like balls in a Newton's cradle, might be frowned upon. Emme thought it might be a good idea to go out as soon as they could. She looked at the clock on the slick oven, almost 5pm.

'So what's the plan?' she asked with a new sense of enthusiasm. She was here to start a new life, and she needed to push herself out of her comfort zone.

'Well Tiago can get us dinner at the Steinherrhof . . .'

Emme thought this was presumptuous, but noted Tiago nodded genially.

'Then there's live music in Down Mexico Way.'

'Perfect. What do I wear?' Emme was mentally going through her wardrobe.

Cat turned around, appraising Emme. She was wearing jeans, a white T-shirt, and a thick Breton-striped rollneck jumper. Cat and Tiago wore jeans and ski coats. Emme thought they made a cute couple, all chocolate eyes, off-duty snowboard wear and beautiful olive skin.

'You're fine,' Cat concluded. 'It's very casual here.'

'OK great, I'll just grab my purse and a lip balm.'

Chapter Fifteen

Under a velvety, dusky sky, Walter looked out across the lake and took a deep breath. It might be his imagination following the diagnosis, but he could feel a sharp pain in his back, like a knitting needle was searing through him and radiating outwards. The pain was inconvenient. The constant infections had been inconvenient. They were stopping him from thinking clearly, and he had to have his wits about him today – he had a hunch today was pivotal.

Lysander had gone to get them another drink but had been distracted by an old polo-playing friend, and Walter Steinherr was alone, on the terrace, when he heard the voice of an angel in his ear.

'They're cutting the cake and you're missing it . . .'

He turned around to see Lumi Kivvi, wife of his nemesis, radiant, a shawl over her long silver dress to ward off the bite of the evening.

'Lumi.' Walter breathed her name as if it were a blessing.

Lumi's cheeks flushed, and she glanced around.

'I was just looking for Mika, have you seen him?'

Walter shook his head. Lumi thought Walter looked tired, and a little confused. She couldn't know from his grumpy demeanour that this was the happiest he had felt in weeks.

'How are you, Walter?' she asked with candour.

'Desperate. I need to talk to you . . .'

Lumi laughed gently, belying her shock.

'Why now? We've barely spoken in the decade since I moved back to Kristalldorf!'

'I'm sick.' Walter said in a tone that grabbed her attention.

Lumi stepped back, a horror washing over her radiant features. Of course. That's why the old man looked so tormented.

'What's wrong?'

'Oh, nothing serious!' Walter backtracked with a wave of a hand. He didn't want to guilt Lumi into engaging with him. 'You know, just the idiosyncrasies of old age. You're still a spring chicken but I'm seventy now.'

'I remembered your birthday.'

'You did?'

'I've always remembered,' Lumi shrugged.

Lumi Heikkinen had been a young nurse travelling through Europe, when she tended to Anna Maria Steinherr at the Hospital of the Sacred Heart in Bloch. Lumi had done stints of nursing in Gothenburg, Hamburg and Stuttgart before stopping in Switzerland, because she fell in love with the Glanzfluss valley. When doctors told Anna Maria that her cancer was terminal, Anna Maria and Walter asked Lumi, Anna Maria's favourite nurse at the hospital, if she would care for her privately at their home up the mountain in Kristalldorf. So that Anna Maria could spend her last days close to her four young children; so that she could die at home.

Lumi didn't hesitate. She moved into one of the staff

rooms at the Steinherr mansion and gave Anna Maria unwavering palliative care. She got to know the children over the course of three months, and held them tight that horrific day Anna Maria died. When Walter asked Lumi to stay on, to offer some consistency and care for the children, and offered to pay her handsomely, she accepted.

In the months after Anna Maria's death, Lumi tended to the children by day and played cards with Walter in the evenings. Soon they fell in love. Forbidden, treacherous love. And after a night of passion on the bearskin behind the locked study door, Lumi realised she had to go. Their relationship had come too soon for anyone to be happy for them; and even more importantly, at twenty-five she was too young and carefree to take on Walter's four children.

Lumi fled Kristalldorf and went back to Helsinki, broken hearted. She took on a nursing role at the University Hospital there, secretly hoping that, with time, Walter might come for her. He never did. Lumi never returned. Until after she married Viktor Kivvi and had children of her own, and moved to Switzerland for the advantageous tax breaks. They settled on Kristalldorf after Lumi had said how stunning – and exclusive – it was. For ten years, Lumi and Walter had circumnavigated each other on the social scene – managing nothing more than polite smiles at charity galas and balls – smiles which became frostier after Walter stitched Viktor up with the Seven Summits deal. Walter's children hadn't remembered Lumi was the nurse who got them through their worst of times. But now, thirty years after that passionate night by the fire in Walter's study, they were alone in each other's company again.

*

'Well I have never forgotten a thing,' Walter said proudly. He wanted to stroke the contour of Lumi's cheek, the curve of her breasts held beautifully in her shimmering dress – she must be fifty-five now, and she dazzled – but he couldn't. She was a married woman. Married to his nemesis. Viktor would always be Walter's nemesis, for reasons he didn't know.

'You clearly forgot your senses,' Lumi laughed, 'because you got married in a chapel in Vegas. Of all places, Walter!'

Lumi tried to mock him, but Walter could see she still cared.

'You know how reckless I am; you know how I love playing cards . . .'

They both remembered their long nights and long conversations over poker, baccarat and *trente et quarante* in the Steinherr mansion.

'You know how I loved *you*,' Walter added, clutching Lumi's hand. And she felt completely undone, for the first time in decades.

Chapter Sixteen

First stop for the newfound friends was the sleek and bustling restaurant within the Steinherrhof hotel, where Tiago led Cat and Emme to a quiet booth and low-key instructed them to each grab a plate from the buffet. It was an unspoken rule in Kristalldorf that the workers procured freebies for their friends wherever they could. As Emme surveyed the spread of meats, potatoes, remoulades and salads, and Cat whispered that the buffet cost 150 francs per plate for those who paid, she realised that this option was better than the noodles she'd grabbed at the supermarket on her way home.

'Fill your boots!' Cat said with a wink.

A waitress with a name badge reading 'Camilla' came over and chatted to Tiago and Cat in English with a Scandinavian accent, and furnished all three glasses with white wine from a bottle labelled Du Kok Estate in a pretty scrawl.

'They don't mind us doing this?' Emme asked Cat in a hushed voice.

'No man, Tiago is the concierge/night manager here – he does the same for Camilla on her days off.'

From the way Camilla had fluttered her lashes at Tiago, Emme wondered what else he did for her.

As they tucked into their plates of hot meats and cold

salads, Emme drank in a feeling of self-satisfaction as she took a large gulp of South African white. She liked the camaraderie among the workers and this place was beautiful, even if it was a mindfuck. She'd been in Kristalldorf precisely twenty-four hours and already she was dining for free with new friends. She rose a little in her seat as she felt proud of herself for making the leap. Perhaps she could get over Tom and Chrissy.

Three glasses of wine and two plates of dinner later, Cat threw her napkin on the table and made a declaration.

'Let's head to Down Mexico Way, the guys will be starting.'

At a small corner halfway between the train station and the church, the sound of Eagles covers spilled out onto the street. A man came outside to light a cigarette. Tiago greeted him with a firm handshake and the two started talking in Spanish or Portuguese, Emme couldn't work out which.

'Is there live music every Saturday night?' Emme asked, as Cat held the door open for her.

'There's live music *every* night.' Cat said proudly. 'This is my friend Will's band. He's British.' She said it as if that meant Emme might know him.

'Oh, cool.'

Cat and Emme had to pass the band and a small dancefloor to get to the bar and the seating area, and the place was already half full. The singer raised a hand to Cat between chords on his guitar and Cat waved back, and leaned over to kiss the keyboard player once on each cheek, then punched the drummer on the arm from his tiny spot squeezed in between the edge of the stage and the bar. The venue looked like it didn't know quite what it was. It had a Mexican name but nothing about the interior looked Mexican. It was all mirrored walls and elegant tables. A group of men were sharing a bottle of Dom Perignon at the bar. A bunch of tourists, still in their ski clothes, were downing pints raucously. A group of young people in their early twenties were playing drinking games. The clientele seemed pretty male-heavy, which Emme found odd.

'You grab that table before those guys do and I'll get us a drink. What you having?' Cat asked cheerily.

Emme really didn't care, she just needed another drink. As she suggested wine, she took a remaining table and was relieved to spot a group of middle-aged women sitting with their husbands at a table near the back of the bar. The women wore rollnecks and pearls, their helmet hair from the day replaced by coiffed bobs.

She settled into the plush banquette behind a round table, took off her garish coat and looked up. Cat was stopping to chat to everyone she encountered on the short distance to the bar. A happy happenstance to have befriended her, Emme thought, as she looked at Cat's warm and animated expression. She'd hit the jackpot with this one.

Tiago slid in next to Emme.

'Sorry, just chatting to my brother,' he said in a thick accent.

'Oh your brother lives here too?'

'No man, all the Portuguese here are my family.'

He gave a sweet smile.

'Ah that's lovely.'

'Well, we have to look out for each other, huh.'

He nodded over to the group of men drinking champagne by the band. Their uniform wasn't skiwear or cargos, it was neat shirts and V-neck jumpers. Some of them wore their cashmere slung over their shoulders. And then Emme saw him. The man from the balcony. Tall and captivating with collar-length hair that ruffled around his face, he was unmissable. From the conversation he was leading, Emme could tell he commanded any room he was in. He had a rugged masculinity and an irresistible aura about him, which annoyed the hell out of Emme. She thought about the hard-on in his boxers as he chatted with his comrades, just as the band struck up the opening chords of 'Sex on Fire' by Kings of Leon.

Emme could not take her eyes off him. His tanned jaw. His dazzling smile. That cock.

What a dog.

Cat came back with a bottle and three glasses.

'*Pedí vino*,' she said, and Tiago nodded but furrowed his brow. 'You don't want it, *cariño*?' she asked.

'Nope, I fancy a beer . . .'

'Sorry I took so long,' Cat apologised. 'My buddy Carla works behind the bar . . .'

'No problem, I was just enjoying the view . . . You must know everyone in this place!'

'Kristalldorf is a *very* small town, and everyone is coming back for the season at the moment, so there's loads of people to catch up with. I'm in the minority of workers who stay year-round.'

Cat filled two of the glasses and placed the bottle down firmly.

'So who is everyone?' Emme asked, although there was only one person she wanted to know about. She was intrigued by the man who looked like an Argentinian polo player but had a South African accent when he was appeasing his girlfriend. It was as if his gravitational pull was so intense she could not take her eyes off him. Surely Cat knew the guy. Did everyone feel like this about him, she wondered? Two women *definitely* did, judging from this morning.

Cat pointed in the wrong direction for Emme's liking.

'They're instructors. Ski and snowboard. They come from all over . . .'

It was hard for Emme to drag her gaze away from balcony man to a bunch of dishevelled twenty-somethings with matted hair and tan lines around their eyes.

'Carla, Johann and Enno work behind the bar. The band are Will, Yannick and Lydia, she's Aussie . . .' Cat looked around. 'Those guys at the next table are from out of town – I'd say Emirati or Greek, I don't know them . . . those guys, I don't know . . . but the women look like they need a good fucking . . .' Cat gave a mischievous laugh as she nodded to the coiffed women with the pearl necklaces.

'I don't know any of the rich tourists who come to town – apart from Elton John and the European royals – I only know the loaded locals, and I have to be a bit careful what I say, in case they're friends with my bosses.' Annoyingly, Cat hadn't touched on the circle of men drinking champagne at the end of the bar near the band, who had now been joined by a squat woman with smiley eyes.

'Most of the workers come down later because they're, well, working.'

'How about those guys?' Emme said, taking a sip of wine and nodding to the man from the balcony.

'I don't know about most of them, but the guy talking is TDK.'

'TD what?'

'TDK.'

Emme thought Cat might be talking in text speak and tried to think what Dominique's teenage daughter might text her mother from exchanges she had been privy to.

Too damn kissable?

'TDK! Everyone knows TDK, even the out-of-towners. He's kind of . . . notorious,' Cat said cryptically.

Emme winced internally. Notorious wasn't good. But she already knew he wasn't a good boy.

'What does TDK stand for?'

It sounded like a virus. He looked as dangerous as one. His smile had the squat woman in a tizzy.

'Tristan Du Kok. The son of . . .' she trailed off. 'Long story. He's a wine importer. Owns the Vitreum hotel. Sort of. Although he knows cock-all – pardon the pun – as you English say, about the hotel industry. Biggest playboy in Kristalldorf.'

That much Emme did know.

'Not so big that he's at the fancy Italian wedding?' Emme asked curiously.

'Hmm . . . I'm not sure he'd be welcome. He's ruffled a few feathers.'

'Oh really?'

As if Emme wasn't intrigued enough.

'Are you single?' Cat asked with one arched eyebrow.

Emme nodded.

'Seriously, of all the guys in this bar, Tristan Du Kok is *not* the guy to go for. And he's fucking one of the Steinherr sisters . . .'

Emme wanted to tell Cat about the balcony incident,

but held back for some reason. Maybe she knew retelling it would reveal herself.

'Who are the Steinherr sisters again?' Emme probed.

Cat looked a little apprehensive suddenly.

'Remember I said on the train, the guy who owns most of this town, my boss's *enemigo* . . .'

'Wasn't that the name of the hotel we ate at?'

'Yes. The Steinherrhof. It's one of many. Ernst Steinherr made this town. His grandson Walter is the biggest land-owner in Kristalldorf today – owns five of the best hotels in this place. His daughters Vivian and Anastasia . . .' Cat looked around to see if they were in the bar, but of course they wouldn't be; if they weren't at the wedding in Italy they would be in one of their own hotels. 'They help run this town, and one of them is fucking Tristan . . . more fool her.'

'Oh right.' Emme wanted to know more. This whole town seemed to have a story.

'There are two sons too. One of them lives in New York, the youngest brother, he's cool – but he bums around the world, he's a surfer, surfs on Daddy's money.'

'Nice.'

'I know, right? While the women keep the family business booming. Although I'm not actually sure what Anastasia does . . .' Cat's features hardened. 'Doesn't always talk nice to people; she has a knack of making people feel shit . . .'

Emme thought about Chrissy. Chrissy had a knack of doing that. Or was it just the way she talked to Emme? With polite disdain.

'Vivian is cool, works hard. They're one of the wealthiest families in Kristalldorf, and there are a few. Not wealthier than the Kivvis, but the Steinherrs are old money. They built this town – they didn't buy their way into it.'

'Impressive.' Emme still couldn't take her eyes off the man she wanted to get back to. He was throwing his head back in laughter.

'And one of the sisters is going out with him?' She nodded back towards him. Cat didn't answer.

Emme watched him run his fingers through his hair.

'Is he from a local family?' She had guessed from his accent he wasn't.

'No he's South African. Mummy owns a huge vineyard outside of Cape Town. Du Kok Estate supplies most of the hotels and restaurants around here, he mostly imports his own stuff of course. Makes a *killing*. . .' Cat trailed off as she narrowed her eyes and pondered him. 'Really Emme, of all the guys in this place, he is not the one to turn your attention to.' Cat put a kind hand on Emme's arm, sensing her budding obsession.

'Oh I know that already!' Emme laughed her off, trying not to show what she was feeling inside.

The smash of a glass distracted them – coming from the group of ski instructors, and most of the people in the bar glanced over quickly to see what had happened.

'Whey!' cheered the debauched group.

'He is gonna regret that in the morning!' Cat said to Tiago, motioning to the instructor drinking beer from his own ski boot.

Emme was still looking at Tristan.

Cat and Emme soon got through their bottle of wine and Emme bought another, sobering up slightly when it came to tap and pay for it. She'd have to slow down on drinking at these prices. Or do what Cat said she did mostly, and let foolish foppish tourists chat her up and buy her drinks.

The covers band – The Cheeky Blinders – played the opening notes of 'Mr Brightside' and Cat led Emme to the dancefloor. Emme was feeling hot and heady, now in just her white V-neck tee and jeans, as they danced with other revellers – more tourists, more workers arriving after their shifts and greeting Cat with a kiss or a slap on the back. Emme was having a great night. And as she danced she felt the gravitational pull of Tristan Du Kok, still drinking with his group between the edge of the dance-floor and the bar. Surveying the room from his cocksure stance. Emme raised her arms, she felt giddy. She had the sensation of someone watching her, of her performing; the wine and the newness of the place giving her false confidence.

As if he'd be interested in me!

Emme almost scoffed to herself.

I need water.

Any reason to get closer.

She left Cat dancing to a Lady Gaga cover and squeezed through the now-packed bar, deliberately taking the path that would bring her closest to Tristan Du Kok.

'Excuse me,' Emme smiled as she made her way through.

You're so ridiculous, she thought to herself.

He's so fucking hot.

She thought about his huge cock and how beautiful he looked in his boxers, ripped, panicking and laughing. How many times had he had sex today, she wondered, as she caught his eye. He smiled. She gave a small smile back, slightly embarrassed that he might read her thoughts. She wanted to put her face into his neck as she passed him. Or would she smell the scent of yet another woman's legs wrapped around him?

Tristan made way and created a pathway for Emme with his arm, letting her through to the bar, her hot arm brushing his shirt. Shots tingled through her skin, all the way to her chest. She felt sensational. Did he recognise her? From the knowing look in his eye, yes.

The gall of him.

Emme nodded briefly as she passed him, and he held her eye.

The gall of me, she thought, mischievously.

Deep breath.

'Good evening,' he said, seemingly having broken away from the conversation he was in. Rude.

'Evening,' Emme replied, as they locked eyes.

Urgh, he does this all the time!

'Quite the spot of bother you were in earlier,' Emme said, falling into her own trap.

He leaned in and smiled.

'I saw you, spying on me.'

Emme flushed red.

'I was not!' she protested. He leaned closer.

'Wanted to join in?'

The arrogance of the man. Emme felt both outraged and utterly transparent.

'Oh please! You're so disrespectful.'

It annoyed Emme. He annoyed Emme. She could see why women were climbing over balconies for him and that's what pissed her off the most.

The man held his hands up in submission and smiled. Such a sexy smile, he was ridiculous.

'Sorry, you just seemed a little . . .'

'A little what?' Emme challenged him, almost aggressively.

Tristan pondered and settled on a word.

'Enchanted.'

'Enchanted? Get over yourself! I was trying to work out how to tell both those women what a creep you are!'

Tristan threw back his head and laughed. His eyes crinkling at their sun-kissed corners.

'I can't buy you a drink then?'

Emme levelled him with a look.

He's taking the piss out of me!

Of course he was. This tall, beautiful man who smelled of cedar, citrus and sex was taking the piss out of her, just a girl from Surrey in jeans and a white T-shirt, nothing special. Not a long-limbed glamazon in a thong. She didn't even wear thongs, she wore regular M&S knickers or big booty SKIMS because that's what felt most comfortable.

'I got it,' Emme replied snarkily, leaning over the bar and asking Cat's friend Carla for a glass of tap water, and hoping Tristan Du Kok, with his bottle of Dom Perignon and his massive hard cock, couldn't hear.

Chapter Seventeen

Emme woke up at almost midday with a terrible hangover. Despite her encounter with Tristan Du Kok at the bar sobering her up somewhat, she danced for hours with Cat and Tiago, plus Will, Yannick and Lydia, once The Cheeky Blinders had finished playing. They moved on to a basement nightclub and had a great night. Cat had taken a phone call and dashed off at midnight, but Tiago assured Emme Cat was OK and had made sure Emme got home safe. She had crawled into bed at 2am with nineties Europop ringing in her ears and a pint of water on the bedside table. She'd loved the night, but woken feeling wobbly about the decision she'd made to move to the mountains and become a nanny. Whether she was up to the job. Whether she could fit in. She was so out of her comfort zone, she wondered how the hell she would be able to stick it out until the end of the season.

Emme lay in her comfy bed, looking at the ceiling, wondering what the hell she should do. She wanted to talk to Tom. She wanted to ask Dominique Henry for her job back, but she couldn't bring herself to do either of those things, so she showered, got dressed and went for a walk, passing Mr and Mrs Muller on the stairs, down the wide steep steps from Chalet Stern to the path and back into the village to get ingredients to make the Harringtons a Sunday roast. Emme made the best Yorkshire puddings, and coming home to a full roast dinner might help Lexy Harrington calm down, she seemed so jittery and uptight on Friday night. It would also help soak up Emme's hangover.

She returned to the supermarket down the side street, and the first person she saw was Tiago, unpacking boxes of grapes in the fruit and veg aisle, wearing an orange T-shirt with Migros written on it. She had forgotten he worked here as well as a hotel. *Poor guy must be shattered,* she thought.

'Hey,' she said, gently nudging his arm with hers.

Tiago turned around, dark, expressive eyes lifting.

'Oh hi, how are you?' his Portuguese lilt was melodic and slow.

'Yeah, pretty tired, thanks. But –' she looked around and winced for him. 'Poor you, how's your head?'

Tiago shrugged genially.

'I'm OK.'

'Great night last night!' Emme said. 'Thanks for getting me home.'

Tiago nodded, and continued to unpack plastic boxes of grapes.

'No problem.'

'Where did Cat disappear to? Did she have to work early?'

'Yeah . . . Cat man . . .' Tiago winced.

'What? Did you two have an argument?'

Tiago looked puzzled.

'Erm, no . . .'

'Oh, are you two not a couple?'

'Me and Cat?!' Tiago laughed.

99

'Oh, sorry.'

'No, she definitely didn't go home with *me* last night . . .' Tiago said it with a raised eyebrow.

Emme looked at him guardedly.

'The only friends with benefits thing we do is when I get her into the Steinherrhof for dinner or she gives me Kivvi leftovers.'

'Oh right, sorry, I just assumed . . .'

'No . . . she went off with . . . well, it doesn't matter, none of my business. But she was *chapada* as we say in Portugal.'

Suddenly Emme felt flushed. She had a bad feeling.

'She'll be prepping dinner for the Kivvis very hung over right now. Naughty girl.'

What had happened? Emme didn't really want to think about it. So she focused on her own dinner.

'Speaking of which, can you point me in the direction of a chicken?'

'Sadly I can point you in the direction of every fucking thing in this supermarket,' Tiago said with a laugh, guiding her without touching her, delivering her to the fresh meat and poultry. 'Is there anything else I can help you with, madam?' He said it with a smile and a twinkle in his huge eyes.

'No thanks Tiago, that's great.'

Emme had time to kill before starting dinner, so she decided to stop for a coffee and read her book in an outdoor café she came across in a secluded little sun-trap terrace. The terrace was framed by wooden logs with flower boxes placed on top, all bursting with stoic winter blooms in pretty pastels. She thought reading in the fresh air might help soothe her hangover as she took *The Secret History* out of her bag and ordered a latte from the kindly waiter with a bushy beard.

As Emme waited, she closed her eyes, raised her chin, and invited the sun and sounds of birdsong to replenish her. She could feel vitamin D working its magic in the salve of fresh November sunshine on her skin. She'd started a new job in the prettiest place she'd ever been to in the world, and she hadn't even had to work for the first two days.

Emme was just thinking about the call Cat had taken before hurrying off and wondered what drew her away so compellingly, when her rumination was interrupted by a South African accent. Her eyes darted open and her hackles rose as she tracked him, Tristan Du Kok, the total dog, asking his companion, the blonde from the balcony, which table she wanted to sit at. The woman wore large sunglasses and a prickly smile. As she shrugged her shoulders her lustrous ponytail swung. Tristan took a nearby table, his back to Emme as his girlfriend took off her thick jacket, her cream jumper revealing rosebud nipples. The waiter came out with Emme's coffee and greeted them as if they were royalty. Tristan rose from the thick wooden bench and pressed the waiter's palm, his checked trucker jacket rising up his broad back to reveal his Calvin Kleins above his jeans. Emme couldn't help but look at the sliver of golden skin at the small of Tristan's back as he ran his fingers through his hair and chatted to the waiter about the quality of the snow the mountains had been gifted this week. The woman was politely aloof, as if she were elegantly grieving, as if she *knew* about the other woman on the balcony. She was clearly desperate to be left alone.

I would like to be left alone with him, Emme thought, surprising herself.

'I'll get your coffees,' the waiter said amiably, as he brought Emme's over to her. She willed Tristan not to turn around and see her, lest he think she was spying again.

Tristan Du Kok and the blonde talked in hushed tones Emme couldn't hear as she tried not to watch him stroking her arm as if he were consoling her. They looked like they were making up after an argument. He certainly seemed less jocular than last night. But the way his manly, tanned hand squeezed her arm tenderly filled Emme with a misplaced jealousy, reminiscent of all those feelings of Tom and Chrissy. Only this was more intense, more reckless. Nosier. Emme wanted to know *everything* about this couple, who were so beautiful. She pictured them having make-up sex that was both impassioned and languid.

After not being able to focus on her book, nor able to hear the quiet conversation, Emme finished her coffee, left a five-franc coin on the table and stood to leave. She needed to get the roast in the oven before the Harringtons could put up a resistance to her gesture. It would certainly ease her guilt at having a wobble this morning. Of wondering how she might stick it out and not cut and run. Except she realised then that something else could keep her in Kristalldorf.

Emme picked up her groceries bag and walked past the couple, hoping he wouldn't see her.

'Hey,' Tristan said, almost saluting Emme, clearly recognising her from last night. The blonde looked disinterested and sad.

Urgh.

Emme felt equal parts irked and thrilled, but did what everyone else seemed to do in this town.

'Hey,' she replied, not quite smiling, before walking away, cringing about her embarrassing coat, fully aware that Tristan's eyes were on her ass.

Chapter Eighteen

Cat caught her reflection in the door of the opulent La Cornue oven as she wiped it clean. Seeing her face, usually round and optimistic, made her feel deplorable after her midnight tryst. Two midnight trysts in a row. Both so misjudged that Cat was furious with herself for going back for more.

On Friday night, after Anastasia had summonsed Cat to the hotel, she waited for her on the bed in a see-through black negligee. She was an absolute vision. Cat had dropped her bag and crawled straight onto the bed. She couldn't resist. She parted Anastasia's legs and dotted her tongue up the inside of her calf, her thigh, teasing and tantalising until she reached her lover's pussy. She pushed the negligee up over Anastasia's washboard stomach, still tanned from a summer spent on a Greek island, and darted her tongue over her yearning clitoris. Anastasia groaned.

'God I missed you,' Cat almost cried. She hadn't even taken off her coat before making Anastasia come. Then it was Cat's turn. Anastasia finally peeled off Cat's clothes and made her sit on the edge of the bed before wrapping her legs around her and writhing on her until she went crazy. Their hard nipples felt electric against each other, until Anastasia pushed Cat back, lay alongside her, and finished her off with insatiable strokes. Anastasia and Cat spent two blissful hours, reacquainting, re-exploring, kissing every part of each other's naked bodies, hardly saying a word, until Anastasia said she needed to go. Wrung out and reset, it was only after Anastasia had left and Cat was dressing, that she realised Anastasia hadn't even asked her how Argentina was. How the funeral had been.

Of course not.

On Saturday night Anastasia summoned Cat again, bored to tears playing Monopoly with Dimitri and Orfeas in the mansion. And Cat was drunk enough and just the wrong side of reckless enough to dash off – before Tiago could talk her out of it – and hurry over the river to the Silberblick. Its dark decadent décor luring her in with every step. She went up to their usual room. Room 204. Just as she had the night before, yearning for Anastasia Steinherr's electric orgasms. Only Saturday night had a bite.

Cat couldn't shake her agitation, lying like a darkness under her desire. She had called it off when she left for Argentina. She knew she could never really have her. Mrs Diamandis. A Steinherr. Lady of the mansion with a husband who could give her the world and three children Cat had no interest in getting to know. Argentina could serve as the circuit breaker she needed. Yet like a fool, she'd fallen straight back into bed with her.

On Saturday night Anastasia awaited her lover again, this time no negligee. Her naked body had a gentle sheen. Cat took off her clothes while Anastasia pleasured herself, then she crumbled onto the bed and kissed her. It felt different only twenty-four hours later. The power play had returned. Cat's resentment had resurfaced. No matter how hard she tried, circling Anastasia's delectable wetness with her fingers, then her tongue, nothing worked. Something was awry for both of them. Anastasia was usually insatiable – she could come three or four times in one of their clandestine meetings. When she couldn't tonight, when she flinched a couple of times as Cat darted her tongue in and out of her, Cat felt rejected.

What was she playing at? Desperately trying to pleasure a woman who hadn't even asked her how she was? A woman who did anything to get what she wanted. The most selfish – most beautiful – woman Cat had ever known.

Cat sobered up fast.

'I'm going to go.'

Anastasia didn't protest. She didn't offer to make Cat come – a little courtesy for breaking up her night with her friends. She watched her go, and Cat went back to the Kivvi apartment, cried in the shower, then cried herself to sleep.

Now her head throbbed and she felt the familiar shadow of self-loathing as she wiped the ornate oven door. Lumi Kivvi walked in wearing an elegant dress. She smelled of Dior L'Or and wore delicate Graff diamonds in her ears.

'We're taking a chopper to Le Rosey. Stella's recital.'

Viktor walked in behind her, putting cufflinks on. Viktor rarely came into the kitchen and always looked uncomfortable when he did. 'Then Viktor's going on to Tokyo – do you have everything darling?' she said to her husband, noticing his tie was a little wonky. She straightened it; he looked agitated by the assistance, but still she finished the job.

'Will you get off me, woman!' Viktor barked at his wife.

Cat noticed Lumi looking somewhat hurt.

'Do you not want dinner tonight?' Cat asked politely, shifting the focus. She almost didn't want the night off. What if Anastasia called again?

No.

'We'll eat in Geneva before Viktor's flight, I'll be back late tonight, I won't need supper but Mika might, he's staying home.'

Teresa the maid bustled around behind the Kivvis and Viktor's Finnish assistant Benjamin came in and said it was time to go. Lumi pulled a loose thread off Viktor's shoulder.

'Will you stop fussing!' he snapped, and walked off to consult Benjamin. Lumi, always calm and patient, let his temper waft over her like a gentle breeze.

'Cat, when I'm back from the recital, why don't we start going through the Christingle menu?'

Thank god.

Cat could legitimately spend the afternoon trying out recipes and ideas, alone in the Kivvi kitchen.

'Whenever you're ready, ma'am.'

The annual Kivvi Christingle in December was always a chance to showcase her chef talents to the town, and she loved it. The thought of a focus perked her up.

Chapter Nineteen

Vivian Steinherr strode through the dining room of Avocet, Anna Maria's restaurant named after their mother's favourite bird, and was tugged on the arm by an American diner with ruddy cheeks.

'Miss,' he said in an entitled tone. Vivian stopped on her heel and turned. The man was dining with his wife and another couple, and they looked to be in their sixties. Vivian couldn't remember seeing them before, so assumed they weren't hotel guests. While Vivian didn't appreciate people tugging her on the arm, she still stopped with a smile.

'Yes?'

'May I speak to someone who knows about wine?' the man asked, rather patronisingly, assuming Vivian wouldn't know much about anything. She was just a waitress, there to take orders and look pretty.

Vivian widened her eyes with enthusiasm and took a deep breath.

'Well, I'm the hotel owner and manager,' she said, getting her barb in, 'so I can tell you a little, but I'll just find Michael our sommelier, he's on shift this evening, and he's *fantastic*.' All four of the diners looked up and smiled at Vivian. Her game face was charming.

'Oh, thank you kindly . . .' the man said, a little flustered, as Vivian cut a striking path through the restaurant. Michael was probably advising diners at another table. Vivian scoured the sleek dining room but couldn't see him. She had popped out for an hour and come straight back into a meeting with a tech company who were going to improve the online booking system and make it more user friendly. This was the first time she'd been on the floor during that evening's service. Vivian did usually like to meet guests and diners every few hours, to take a walk, get away from her desk, and chat to the clientele and staff. She couldn't see Michael, but Henrik the restaurant manager was talking to head waitress Mia-Mary near the cutlery storage drawers. Vivian slid into their conversation deftly and authoritatively, despite them looking like they were speaking in hushed tones.

'Is Michael around? I have a guest asking for some wine advice . . .'

Henrik and Mia-Mary glanced at each other. Mia-Mary looked nervous.

'What is it?'

Vivian looked between the two of them before Henrik spoke in quiet fury.

'He's gone home.'

'Is everything OK?'

Mia-Mary shook her head.

'Anastasia – Mrs Diamandis . . .'

'It's OK, Henrik, you can cut the Mrs Diamandis with me,' Vivian laughed.

'Anastasia . . . she fired him.'

Vivian's face turned from genial smile to confused fury.

'She what?!'

'She fired him. She fired Michael.'

Mia-Mary nodded, her eyes sad.

'What? When?'

Henrik looked at Mia-Mary, who seemed to have witnessed the exchange and had just been talking him through what had happened, although it still made no sense to either of them.

'This afternoon,' she said, meekly, scared that she might be next.

A rage rose through Vivian, but she was acutely aware that the customer was still waiting for advice on which bottle of wine to choose.

'Why?' she demanded under her breath. Mia-Mary shrugged, and before she could even attempt an answer, a furious Vivian said, 'Don't worry about it.'

She strode back to the table and put on her prettiest of smiles, using every fibre of her being to repress her anger and fight the fire in hand.

Vivian was seamless in her ability to put on a good front. It was what made her such a natural in hospitality. She always had been good at smiling her way through a shitstorm. Vivian the firefighter. Vivian the peacemaker. Vivian the people pleaser.

'I'm sorry sir, our sommelier is otherwise engaged but would you allow me to advise you?'

The man looked happy to be favoured with Vivian's attention, especially now he knew who she was. He nodded.

'Are you looking for a white or red?' She looked to the group, who agreed a white would suit their dishes.

'We have an excellent 2019 Chardonnay from Piemonte that Michael our sommelier brought in recently, or a sublime Chenin Blanc from the Du Kok Estate in South Africa . . .'

As Vivian reeled off her suggestions she smiled, a disarming, charming smile that belied the fury within.

The man looked at his party, impressed, and back at Vivian.

'We'll go for the South African, thank you, dear.'

Chapter Twenty

'Oh, to have proper roast potatoes, how do you do it Emmeline?' Lexy asked as if Emme was a clever puppy who had just performed a trick.

The Harringtons had got back from Italy just an hour ago, to the smells of roast chicken, roast potatoes and stuffing. Bill had taken Bella off for a bath in the hot tub, and Harry had wailed because he wanted bratwurst for dinner again.

Apparently he only ever wanted bratwurst for dinner, even when he got to dine at society weddings, five-star hotels, Michelin-starred restaurants, or on the KristallKit concierge food service. Lexy had shared this with Emme as if to say *you know what kids are like*, as Emme prepped the veg, but she didn't really. Her own niece and nephew always seemed grateful with whatever dinner was put in front of them. After the way he'd discarded his Paddington bear and now this, she was starting to get the impression that Harry seemed like a bit of a bratwurst himself.

Now the kids were showered, bathed, and sitting at the table with their parents and Emme, while Lexy reflected on a wedding that would be the talk of the region – as was the fact that Lysander Steinherr was back in town. That part delighted Lexy especially, as if Lysander Steinherr were Ryan Gosling.

Now Emme was sharing her tip for the perfect roast potatoes:

'Par boil for six minutes, drain, fluff them up, add a little flour and roast in hot olive oil!' Emme smiled, thinking about all the roast dinners she and Tom had shared: in the kitchen of her Balham flat, or his flat in Dulwich; or at a thousand pubs in between, while they read the Sunday papers and played boardgames.

Then it hit her like a ten-ton truck. Emme had never felt so dowdy, talking about her mother's perfect roast potato recipe while the blonde glamazon from the café was probably back in Tristan Du Kok's apartment, coming down his schlong. At least that exquisite image had nudged Tom out of her thoughts. Perhaps this *was* the distraction she needed.

'They're really very good . . .' nodded Bill, looking at his plate as if it were a mirage in a desert.

Emme looked at Bill, the harangued husband. He had caught the sun at the wedding. His blue eyes jumped out against his silver hair and he looked nicer in his Sunday lounging gear than he did in his stuffy work suit. Tomorrow he'd be heading back to his Zurich bolthole for the week, and Emme's job would begin in earnest.

Get stuck in, she thought, relishing that she could start work proper and forget all the noise in her head. But while Lexy returned to wedding gossip – this time the bride's Givenchy wedding dress – Emme smiled and nodded, and thought about how, only streets away, across the river, that damn man from the airport – Tristan Du Kok and his roguish grin – could be distraction enough to keep her occupied here in the mountains.

Chapter Twenty-One

Lysander Steinherr, whisky on the rocks in hand, looked at the portrait above the fireplace. It was a curious thing and he had always hated it. For some reason, his father had commissioned an artist to draw a family that didn't ever exist. Walter and his children had sat for the artist when Lysander was fifteen, Anastasia was twelve, Caspian was eight and Vivian, as blonde and angelic as a cherub, was six – and the artist had left a gap for their mother, which he later painted in using a wedding photograph of Walter and Anna Maria. The artist had deigned not to put the children's dead mother in her wedding dress at least, but it made for a very unsettling family portrait, which only Walter enjoyed looking at. Wives two and three, Mechthild and Susan, both despised the portrait of course. Kiki thought it quite funny. Fortunately, it was such a part of the furniture in the Steinherr mansion that no one really seemed to notice it any more. It was just there.

Lysander looked up and actually studied it for the first time in years: the proud patriarch; the sad children; the haunting figure of the mother, only her top half visible behind the progeny she couldn't have known at that age, a loving arm around her family. Lysander gently muttered, 'What the fuck,' to himself, as Anastasia sashayed in.

'How was the wedding of the year?' she asked, with an acerbic bite.

Lysander turned around.

'Oh, hi.'

His sister approached and proffered her face so he could kiss her on each cheek.

'Oh you know, usual society wedding.'

His vagueness pissed her off.

'Is that all?'

Lysander grinned and shrugged.

'Erm, the dress was . . . nice? And you must have heard about Simon Le Bon and the Heimlich manoeuvre already?'

Anastasia rolled her eyes and removed a large clip-on earring as she approached the drinks trolley and examined the bottles.

'Where's Dimi?' Lysander asked.

'He's taking a bath,' Anastasia said, as if bathing were a weakness. 'Nanny Iris took the kids back to school and – where's Dad and Kiki?' Anastasia looked around, as if they might be hiding behind the door. 'I looked for her to see if she wanted to join us for a *riveting* game of Monopoly last night,' Anastasia said sarcastically, 'but she wasn't here.'

'She went shopping in Milan, stayed over . . .' Lysander raised an eyebrow.

'I guess it's tiring spending our inheritance,' Anastasia said, as she took off her other earring.

'You don't need to worry about that.'

'Don't I?' Anastasia scrutinised her brother.

Lysander was very aware he might be breaking his father's trust, and it wouldn't be prudent for Anastasia to know about it yet, so he deftly changed the subject.

'Anyway she's back – they've gone for dinner at the Kristall Palace, I didn't fancy joining them.'

'You and me neither,' Anastasia said querulously.

'Anyway, what about you sis? What's turning you on at the moment?'

Anastasia picked up a bottle and paused. It would have been nice for Lysander or the butler to fix her a drink, but if she must . . .

'What?' she asked, defensively.

'Well it's not shopping, and it's not the Anna Maria . . .'

Lysander felt a little guilty about the conversation he'd had with his father about succession. He had nudged him towards Vivian, when Anastasia would be so hurt. But looking at it through his lawyer's lens, truths were truths. Vivian would be a much safer pair of hands for the Steinherr portfolio.

Anastasia sighed as she poured herself a Pernod and added ice from the bucket with silver tongs.

'You seem . . . not yourself sis. What would make Anastasia Diamandis happy?'

She took a large sip and strode elegantly to the fireplace with the freakish family portrait above it, before turning around and hesitating for a second.

The butler walked in.

'Another drink, sir? Madam?'

'I have one, thanks . . .' Anastasia said crisply, raising her glass.

'I'll take a negroni thanks, Kristaps,' Lysander smiled.

'Make that two,' Anastasia commanded, as she took another large sip of her Pernod.

'Very well,' the butler bowed, as he retreated to the kitchen, where a more abundant bar was stocked.

'Go on . . .' Lysander said, encouragingly.

'I want to take on Seven Summits . . . the three vacant properties.'

Lysander slumped back in an armchair and took the last slug of whisky from the glass still in his hand.

'I have so many exciting ideas for them and they're just sitting empty. Why did Father buy them if they were just going to gather dust?'

'To stop anyone else having them,' Lysander shrugged. 'You know he has this weird obsession with Kivvi.'

'Then wouldn't it make sense to piss him off more by making a killing out of them? Think of the wasted revenue!'

Think of the fun I could have in them.

'Maybe it pisses Kivvi off more to know that Dad doesn't even want the revenue.'

'But I could do so much with them!'

Lysander nodded, as if to say tell me more. He noted his sister's face was more animated than he had seen it all weekend.

'I could hold salons, creative events, worldwide launches. Dior and Gucci shouldn't be doing shows from Seville, London or Edinburgh over Switzerland! Chanel shouldn't be faking Swiss scenes at shows in Paris. They could be doing shows here, in Kristalldorf! If I could just get in and have a closer look . . .'

'What about the Anna Maria?'

'Oh please! You know Vivian and I can't work together. And she's completely taken over anyway . . . But those cha-lets, Zand, they could get ten K a night, at least! And it's not like Papa to waste a money-making opportunity. Why did he buy them just to leave them barely used and vacant for the best part of a decade?'

Lysander did wonder why his father's spite ran so deep.

'Anyway, talk about cutting off your nose . . .' Anastasia lamented.

'So why don't you tell him about your brilliant ideas?'

Lysander felt bad that Walter was thinking of leaving the running of the empire to their baby sister when, perhaps, Anastasia could do something brilliant with the Seven Summits properties. Perhaps their father could carve up the business: leave different hotels and properties to different heirs, rather than leave it all to Vivian and cause immense upset. Perhaps Lysander could find a way to manage certain elements from overseas. What if Vivian got the hotels, Anastasia Seven Summits, and he got the mountain train? Maybe even Caspian would want in – he wouldn't want to bum around surfing forever, would he?

'If only Papa would listen to me . . .' Anastasia lamented. 'He's so distracted at the moment. I don't know if it's turning seventy, or . . .' she scrunched up her face, '*Kiki*. But he's so hard to talk to these days.'

Lysander had noticed at the wedding. His father had seemed agitated. Troubled.

'What does Dimitri think?'

'Oh you know, Dimitri goes along with anything I want,' she said, with disdain.

At that they were interrupted by an angry voice shouting from the hallway.

'Who the fuck do you think you are? Where is she?'

It was Vivian, fuming, entering the room with the butler behind her, carrying a silver platter with two negronis on it.

'Miss Vivian . . .' he said, following her trail, trying to slow her down.

Anastasia and Lysander looked at each other, Lysander stood up. Vivian's pretty, sweet face was contorted into a livid scowl. Anastasia stood upright, on guard next to the fireplace.

'What?' she said, features defiant.

'You fired Michael, the best sommelier in the canton – dammit the best in Switzerland – why?'

Vivian was jabbing a finger at Anastasia, who had never seen her calm sister lose her temper like this.

'OK Vivi, don't get your bloomers in a twist.'

'How dare you!' Vivian roared.

Anastasia leaned back, alarmed.

'What's with you and Michael anyway?' Anastasia derided, looking to Lysander for a laugh, but his face wore an expression of concern.

'Michael's son has leukaemia – he's in the hospital. He works like a donkey at the hotel, with the loveliest manners and the best knowledge . . . And you fired him, for what?'

Anastasia pursed her lips.

'The wine was corked.'

'What?' Vivian almost gasped.

Lysander gently shook his head.

'My wine, I was dining with Dimitri at lunchtime and my wine was *corked*.' Anastasia said it as if it were a heinous crime. 'We should *not* be serving corked wine in a Steinherr hotel.'

Lysander winced.

'So you just fired him? For something that completely wasn't his fault?'

'Well I called him over and I didn't like his attitude.'

'You didn't like his attitude, so you just fired him? In front of the staff and other diners?'

'I didn't like his attitude!' Anastasia repeated, obstinately. 'He looked surly and a little – hangdog – for my liking . . .'

Vivian raised her voice in a way none of her siblings had ever heard.

'He probably looked a little "hangdog" because he's been spending nights in the hospital in Bloch with his kid!'

Anastasia shrugged.

'I didn't know that! All I know is what's in front of me, and he works in my hotel, and I didn't like his attitude when I told him the wine was corked.'

Lysander interjected.

'OK, this isn't good, Anni you can't just –'

Quick as a flash, Vivian picked up a cut-glass tumbler from the butler's tray and flung the contents in Anastasia's face.

Anastasia gasped. The alcohol stung her eyes.

'Viv . . .' Lysander said quietly.

'I don't like *her* attitude,' Vivian said, a righteous rage making her voice almost wobble into a cry, as she walked out of the lounge and out of the mansion, slamming the huge grand front door behind her.

Chapter Twenty-Two

Under the sparkling Omega Constellation clock at Kristalldorf station, Bill Harrington boarded the train that would take him back down the mountain to Bloch. At Bloch he would make his connection to Zurich, where he would spend the evening in his bachelor pad. Increasingly, Bill was going back to work on a Sunday night rather than a Monday morning, to get away from the tension of Lexy more than anything. He'd lied to her and said the first train on Monday was just too crowded, it made the working day in Zurich too stressful if he'd been on his feet since 5am, and Lexy hadn't seemed bothered. *Lexy.* He pondered his wife. He knew she was as vulnerable as she was showy, and a part of him almost pitied the desperation with which she socially climbed.

Sitting on the train he felt a slight pang of guilt – she'd be devastated if she knew the real reason he wanted to get back.

All the seats were window seats on this train, and Bill sat down to appreciate the panorama, even though it was almost dark. The only luggage he carried was his attaché case, having managed to make his life in Zurich as separate and independent to his life in Kristalldorf as possible. In his city apartment, Bill had all the suits, shirts, underwear and pyjamas he needed for the working week. In Kristalldorf his wardrobe was full of chinos, sweatshirts, thick jumpers and mountainwear, plus a couple of tuxes for galas, balls and events. He didn't need to carry anything between the two homes, apart from his laptop, phone and wallet.

As Bill set his attaché case down on the seat opposite and the mostly empty train pulled out of the station, he pondered the weekend. The mad wedding; a rare family weekend trip to Italy and a moment for him and Lexy to relax, although that was harder because the count had invited the kids too. And the pressure of the wedding, and making such an impression on everyone, seemed to stress Lexy out even more. Still, there was the good old-fashioned English roast dinner, cooked for him by the new nanny.

As Bill felt the pleasure of that in his stomach, he pondered Emme. She seemed OK. A bit pretty for his liking, but in a peachy, sexy, fresh-faced way. And Jesus, did she make a mean Yorkshire pudding. The kids would warm to her eventually, when they had got over all the upheaval of the past ten days.

And then he thought about *her*. And what the hell had happened. And how Lexy had gone mad. But Bill Harrington just couldn't get Jenny Jones out of his head.

Chapter Twenty-Three

It was Monday morning in the Harrington home and Lexy was hurriedly putting her earrings in as Emme pulled the kids' backpacks out of a discreet cupboard in the spacious corridor.

'So the code for their ski locker is also 1212 – our –'

Wedding anniversary? Emme remembered, as Lexy said it again.

Lexy gave Emme a prim smile. 'It's behind the InterSport shop, by the ski train, yes?'

'Yes, 1212, got it.'

Before bed, Lexy had bombarded Emme with all the vital information she needed for your average winter school day in Kristalldorf, even though Emme had already noted their routine down: The school day begins at 8am. Bella likes hummus in her pitta, Harry likes bratwurst (of course). They have yogurt (Bella will eat any flavour; Harry can be a little more selective . . . Emme wanted to ask if there was a bratwurst flavour around here). A packet of crisps each and a banana or apple, cut into slices, that Harry probably won't eat. Oh, and drop a Mini Babybel in their backpack front pocket for snack time. Oh, and don't forget fresh water in their bottles.

'Did I mention the tap water here is the best in . . .'

'Best in the world,' Emme had said, perhaps slightly forcing her own smile.

'School is on the other side of the river, behind the church. The kids will show you . . .'

Emme had already checked it out on Google Maps and done a walk through over the weekend. 'Pick them up straight after their lunch at 1pm.'

Lexy's barrage of instructions had continued in the morning, her voice getting higher and shriller by the minute.

'Ski school runs from 1.30pm to 3.30pm. The children meet Cedric outside the ski train station on this side of the river.' Lexy said that Emme could either go up with them and ski or have a coffee on the mountain while they have their lesson, or she could meet them off the train at the end.

'Obviously they get more ski time if you meet them mountainside . . .' Lexy said loadedly, as she swiped her phone frantically. 'Bloody thing!'

'Everything OK?' Emme asked cheerily.

'Damned Credit Suisse app. Honestly this country, it's so contradictory!' Lexy jabbed a finger at the screen. 'State-of-the-art tech and it's telling me to go in branch to pay money in.' As Emme watched Lexy's brow furrow she thought her boss was rather contradictory too. One minute praising Switzerland proudly and the next bemoaning the archaic banking ways of the canton.

'Oh dear,' Emme smiled. 'Want me to do it for you?'

Lexy grabbed her coat.

'No, don't worry.' She shook her head and looked at her watch. 'This country can be so pernickety. Bill earns over a million a year and this is *rented*,' she said with a mixture of horror and hurt. Emme looked confused.

'Why's that?'

'Foreigners can't easily buy. It's *very* closed doors.' As she said it her breathing got more rapid.

'Oh right . . .' Emme said, as she zipped up the backpacks. There was little chance she'd be staying in the canton beyond the ski season, let alone wanting to buy here. Not that she'd ever be able to afford it.

'Kids, are you ready? Teeth cleaned?' Emme asked, trying not to raise her voice. She wanted to show she was the cool, calm nanny, even if Lexy's flapping was making her feel flustered.

She scanned the living room, where she'd put the kids' things on the sofa. Their bags looked good to go. Pencil cases, water bottles and packed lunches as instructed, and a separate kit bag each. No shorts and plimsolls in Kristalldorf: here in winter, kids packed ski suits, ski socks and helmets for PE.

'Where is your office?' Emme asked, hoping the reminder would get Lexy out of the way. She knew from the Zoom interview that Lexy Harrington was the go-to PR person in Kristalldorf, but she didn't know where she was based.

'Walter lets me have a little office in the Alpenrose. Most of my work is for the Steinherr Group hotels. I've started doing little bits for the girls at the Anna Maria. And I do a couple of spas and restaurants. I did Du Kok Estates wine for a bit. I can't do Vitreum though or it would be a conflict of interest. I do the KristallKit for Samuel Sommar too.' She gave a saccharine smile. It wasn't her fault she had a smug smile, or maybe she was actually bragging. 'Now, before I go . . .' Lexy measured her tone as if she were about to say something really important.

She handed Emme two plastic cards, one in each hand, as if they were made of gold.

'Lift passes. Do. Not. Lose. Them. They go in the thigh pockets on their ski suits, the barriers let them through, but they can't take them to school – I don't trust them – so give them to the kids at the start of their session – zip them in, and collect them at the end.'

'Of course.'

'And here's one for you . . .' she said, as she magicked a third one from her trouser pocket. 'It's in the name of Jennifer Jones but no one will check. No one will remember her anyway.' Lexy raised an eyebrow as if she hoped it wasn't a name people would remember. Not after what she'd done.

'Guard it with your life,' she said with a crocodilian smile. 'They cost a fortune.'

Noted.

Emme smiled as Lexy bellowed out a harangued and hurried goodbye to her kids and left, not a second too soon. Emme stood for a moment, taking in the calm after the tornado, staring at the front door, utterly perplexed. The woman hadn't kissed her kids goodbye, she was in such a flap. What was this crazy bubble she had moved to? What had Jennifer Jones done to leave so suddenly and be replaced so swiftly?

Emme spun on her heel. Get the kids to school. With fifteen minutes to spare as per the rules. Then perhaps she could sit down and take the madness of this crazy beautiful place in.

'Come on kids!' she called keenly. 'Coats on! You need to show me your school!'

Harry and Bella came out of their rooms, and opened the hidden cupboard door to get their coats, scarves and mittens. They were young but seemed surprisingly independent.

'Ready to give me the tour?' Emme asked eagerly.

'Yes!' Bella replied. 'Jenny loved taking us to school!'

'I bet she did.'

Chapter Twenty-Four

'Kristaps, will you call the helipad and charter a chopper to Geneva?'

'Of course, sir.'

'And have Timo waiting with a yumbo in ten minutes,' Walter Steinherr instructed as he ate a bowl of natural yogurt and berries. Kiki had got him on a health kick soon after they married, and he just about tolerated the stuff. Fat lot of good it was to him now, he thought. He should go out on a high, eating all the foods he loved. Be with the woman he loved.

The butler nodded and walked out reverently.

'Want to accompany me to Geneva, Dad?' Lysander asked. 'Do a nice circuit in the chopper?'

Walter shook his head.

'Erm, no thank you, I have a meeting this morning,' he replied somewhat sheepishly.

Lysander drank orange juice and looked very smart for a man who was about to take a helicopter over the valley and a flight across the Atlantic. Dimitri was already in his office in the Alpenrose hotel across town and Anastasia was out getting an early-morning massage.

'Ooh, I miss New York,' Kiki oozed, longingly, wrapping her tongue around a melon ball as she lingered on her stepson. Lysander looked away sharply as he drained his glass, and Kiki turned to her husband. 'Darling, it's been too long. We haven't been to New York for what, three years?'

Lysander remembered the visit. Kiki had flirted with him then, too.

'We should take a trip to visit Zand, Meg and Blake!' Kiki thought she might be able to tag one of her trips to the West Coast onto it, after Walter had returned home. She liked LA. She imagined being there with Lysander, not Walter, and introducing him to her Bel Air friends, as she sized him up again across the table.

Lysander felt his stepmother's gaze.

No thank you, he thought.

'Yeah, Meg and Blakey would love to see you Stateside, Dad?'

Walter frowned, as if his mind was elsewhere, but he was very much thinking there would be *no* trip to New York with Kiki. Which reminded him. Business.

'That bit of American law you were going to look into . . .' Walter said, not all that cryptically. 'I would like you to check the ramifications please.'

Lysander nodded cautiously. His father and Kiki had married in Las Vegas five years ago, when Walter was on a high from high rolling. They'd only been dating for three months and he was completely smitten. They'd met when Walter, single for years after his disastrous divorce from Susan, was playing blackjack in Monte Carlo with a group of associates, and Kiki was the croupier. He'd never seen a croupier look so polished and powerful. Her white-blonde hair was slicked back in a short bob, her blue eyes and pretty nose gave her a prudent wisdom. She was statuesque and muscular. Walter was surprised to learn Kiki was from the United States. Even more fascinated to know she had worked in Las Vegas. Walter Steinherr had never been to Las Vegas – there had never seemed much point when he had Monte Carlo, Malta, Baden-Baden and Venice on his doorstep, but it was an itch that had always tickled him.

Over three months Walter wooed Kiki with dinners on the French Riviera; or he'd fly her to one of his hotels in Kristalldorf where they'd have dinner and take a room. When they had sex it was unlike anything Walter had known before. Kiki's blowjobs were dynamite.

People raised eyebrows in Kristalldorf to see a pneumatic croupier on the arm of Walter Steinherr, but she wasn't with him for his money, not that they knew that. Kiki had business plans of her own, and leaving the casino would free up her time to develop them. Plus she wasn't immune to Walter's chivalrous reverence.

When Walter whisked Kiki to Las Vegas for his sixty-fifth birthday three months later, he asked Kiki to marry him. No plan, no prenup. They had a driver take them to a little chapel and an Elvis impersonator did the honours. It gave Walter a small thrill to know his children would be horrified.

Now Walter wanted out, he was starting to panic. He had wanted a wife to look after him in his old age, not to go off shopping with girlfriends in Milan, Mykonos and Mexico.

Lysander had started to panic. His father lost more than he should have in his divorce to Susan; he did not want to see another chunk of his inheritance portioned off to an angry woman, who right now was undressing Lysander with her eyes. It would be even worse if his father died while they were still married. As it stood, with Walter wavering over his children's inheritance, Kiki would be getting a lot more than she deserved.

'Of course, Dad, I'll look into it as soon as I'm in the office. Is there anything else you need?' Lysander was thinking more like care packages and Hershey bars than Nevada divorce law.

'Yes, um, Seven Summits.'

Kiki looked up.

'What about it?'

'I'm thinking of selling.'

Lysander put his glass down and cleared his throat.

'Do you think that's wise? I – I know Anastasia had some ideas for it.'

'Anastasia has a hotel!' Walter scoffed. 'And she doesn't seem all that interested in that!'

'You want to sell them though? I thought you were adamant –'

'I'm thinking of putting them on the open market. See what I get for them. Kivvi will come running of course . . . begging like the bleating goat he is.'

'Dad, I can't easily action that kind of thing from New York. You'll need Dimitri on it.' Lysander winced, thinking of how devastated his sister would be.

'Dimitri does whatever job I entrust him with!'

Lysander felt uneasy. He couldn't help thinking that there was something his dad wasn't telling him. He'd been melancholy and reflective at the wedding and was planning to blindside Kiki with a divorce. Now he was finally considering selling the properties that had caused the most discord between the two biggest family empires in town for the past ten years. Plus he looked a little lost in his grand chair at the head of the breakfast table.

Lysander's gaze met Kiki's again. If only he could talk to her about his father's wellbeing. As she looked back at him and continued to lust after him over her lemongrass shot, Lysander mentally shut that conversation down.

Chapter Twenty-Five

Rush hour in Kristalldorf was frantic. Hotel and shop workers whizzed past on sleek E-bikes and weekenders headed from their hotels in yumbos to the train station. Those who worked in Zurich, Geneva or Bern had long gone, on the first morning train, or the very rich chartered choppers from the helipad. For those who remained, there was a definite sense of being locked in: the workers, the hikers, the skiers, the property owners; and the rest of the world shut out, so everyone could go about their business in the Alpine idyll.

The air felt especially cold today, the first real bite of winter, and it would be even more so up on the mountain.

Emme slunk into her snood as she held hands with a child on each side of her and cut what was looking like a now-familiar path down the steps to the road, then down to the river and crossing it towards school.

At the square near a grand hotel with a horse and carriage outside, with a traditional fondue *stube* opposite, Emme peeled off to the side street that looked like it headed into the valley wall, where other children were walking with their parents, nannies and governesses.

'Harry's in a big class – there are twenty-two children!' Bella gasped, as if it was a shock to her.

Yeah, try going to school in the UK, kids.

'But there are only thirteen children in mine!' She said it proudly, as if it were her own personal achievement.

'Lucky you Bella! Lucky both of you, look at this, your school looks wonderful!'

Harry scowled at his sister.

'Yes but my teacher is nicer. My teacher is a man.'

Emme squeezed both of their hands in hers to signal that there would only be harmony on this walk.

'I'm sure both your teachers are *lovely*,' Emme said. 'Is this the right entrance?'

They nodded, and Emme looked at the small playground, gated by wooden poles. There wasn't much space in town for a school, but it certainly looked perfectly formed with pristine play equipment, a basketball court and a large sandpit for the little ones.

'Tie my shoelaces!' Emme heard a princely voice demand, coming from a little boy across the playground.

'Nooo, *you* tie your shoelaces Arjun, you know how to tie your shoelaces . . .'

'I will not.' A boy in a duffel coat and glasses stood with his arms folded and his left foot pushed outwards. Emme and the children observed him.

'That's Arjun, he's in my class,' Bella said, with an eyeroll that made Emme smile back conspiratorially.

'Well if you won't tie your shoelaces you'll just have to trip over and bump that lovely big nose of yours!' the woman said. The boy waited, in deadlock. Standing his ground, nudging his foot out further, until he realised he wasn't going to get his way.

Emme watched aghast, glad the woman hadn't caved in. This town didn't need any more entitled men in it.

'Now, if you're finished, I suggest you go in.' The woman's pretty face was stern.

She caught sight of Bella in her peripheral vision.

'Bella, Harry, good morning!' the woman said, then turned to Emme.

'Ahhh, you must be the new Jenny!'

'That's what it says on my lift pass,' Emme replied with a grin.

The woman had beautiful dark skin and a northern British accent. Finally, another young British woman. Perhaps she could help Emme navigate this weirdness. And she obviously knew Jenny, which was intriguing in itself.

'I'm Cassie, Arjun's nanny.' She extended a hand and Emme shook it. Cassie had polished make-up, impeccable hair and a beautiful cream down coat. Emme felt terribly shabby again in her hand-me-downs, but Cassie had an energy that was warm and real.

'Hi, I'm Emme.'

The bell rang and the children went rushing in. Emme was heartened to hear Harry say to a friend, 'She's our new nanny,' as if this were a positive thing. Perhaps she and Harry were going to be OK. He hadn't been particularly nice to her since she arrived, but at least he hadn't spoken to her the way Arjun had spoken to Cassie.

'Nice to meet you Emme-not-Jenny.' Cassie released her hand.

'Bye kids! I'll pick you up for ski school!'

'Bye Arjun!' Cassie called. 'And fuck off if you think I'm getting on my knees to tie your shoelaces,' she added behind a stage smile. Emme gasped, then laughed.

'Is he like that all the time?'

'Yes. Gets it from his father. He is a *huge* man baby. The little shit sits on a special cushion in class like it's a throne.'

Emme crumpled her face.

'And the teacher allows that?'

'Mummy and daddy contribute *a lot* to the PTA.'

Cassie tossed her lustrous mane and rewrapped her caramel-coloured scarf.

Emme cleared her throat and plucked up the courage to ask Cassie if she wanted to go for a coffee. She seemed lovely, and perhaps coffee with Cassie would give her some answers as to what had happened to Jenny. Emme couldn't help thinking it was strange no explanation had been given as to why she left, or why there were no traces of her predecessor, ski pass aside. Not that it mattered, but Lexy Harrington and her rules were a little unnerving, and any insight might help.

'Drat, I'd love to, but I have to go down to Bloch to pick up some actual *bloomers* for Arjun while he's at school.' Both women stifled a giggle.

'Do Amazon not deliver to Kristalldorf?' Emme asked.

'I know right?! His mother ordered them from an old-school department store over *an hour* away!'

'Oh dear,' Emme offered. 'Maybe at pick up, when they've gone to ski school?' she suggested.

'Oh Arjun doesn't do ski school, he doesn't like snow.'

'He lives in Kristalldorf and he doesn't like snow?'

Cassie gave a look as if to say *I know*.

'I have to take him home after school, but maybe tomorrow morning, after drop-off?' Cassie said with a dazzling smile.

'That would be wonderful,' Emme beamed.

Chapter Twenty-Six

At the departures gate at Geneva airport, Lysander Steinherr looked at his watch. It would be 5am in New York, but the man whose name he scrolled to in his phone always slept with one eye open, and he answered with just one ring and a gruff:

'Who's talkin?'

'Rico! It's Zand Steinherr here . . .'

'Hey, Mister Steinherr, how you doin'?'

Rico was an Italian American from Hell's Kitchen who was the most reliable man in town when it came to getting the dirt on a dodgy politician, finding out who was schtupping who they shouldn't be, or getting secret paperwork pertaining to unlawful developments at City Hall. Rico had found unscrupulous ways to help Lysander Steinherr win big cases over the years, and Lysander always managed to find legitimate ways to use that information.

Lysander didn't beat around the bush.

'I'm calling from Geneva airport with a sensitive favour . . .'

'All favours are sensitive with me,' Rico reassured him.

'Great – well can you do a deep dive into Kiki Bouffon Steinherr? She's, er . . .' Lysander looked around at the people sitting at the departures gate.

'I know who she is,' Rico said steadfastly.

'There has to be something from her past. Her employment history is documented, no gaps, but I'm particularly interested in what she did before she was twenty-one.' Lysander had already looked into Kiki's employment when his father married her, and her stories about Monte Carlo, Vegas and Atlantic City had all tallied. 'I know you'll do great.'

'I'm already looking into it, boss.'

'Great. Usual rate, usual fee. But if you can find something watertight that gets my dad out of alimony, then I'll double it.'

'Thank you sir, I'll get on the case.'

'Thanks Rico.'

'No problem, have a great flight.'

Lysander ended the call, turned his phone onto airplane mode and walked up to the gate, Swiss and American passports in hand. He knew that by the time he was back at his desk in Midtown Manhattan there would be a manila envelope furnished with salaciousness. No woman could have fought off that many hard-ballers without having an interesting story along the way.

Chapter Twenty-Seven

As Emme weaved back through the high street she lingered on what Lexy had said that morning. This place was contradictory and bizarre. Some elements of Kristalldorf were state-of-the-art: the facial recognition entry Lexy had now set her up with, swipe cards for the ski lift, adverts she was walking past that looked like they might be holograms. While others were antiquated. The Omega clock at the main train station might be studded with diamonds, but it was analogue. The horse and cart waiting to ferry guests on the cobbled stones outside the Grand Hotel Sommar on the square.

This place is endlessly confusing.

Emme thought of Cassie and already sensed she would be a handy ally in navigating Kristalldorf; how she would be able to ask her questions she couldn't ask her boss.

As Emme walked past the train station she noticed the Steinherrhof hotel beyond it, and idly looked through the windows, not expecting to see Tiago behind the desk, but pleased that she had. He looked up, smiled and waved.

'Hi!' Emme waved back, miming a question as to whether she should go in and say hello.

'Of course!' Tiago mouthed, nodding, so she walked in under the heavy old-oak frontage, through swish glass doors that glided apart with ease.

Tiago, wearing a suit, looked surprisingly sharp compared to the boy who laconically ate an apple on her boss's kitchen counter.

'Good morning,' Emme said, as she approached the front desk. The reception area was empty. Norah Jones oozed out of hidden speakers.

'Hey, how's it going?' Tiago asked with tired, smiley eyes.

'Good thanks – it's quiet here!'

'Most of the guests are skiing already, good dump last night,' he said, as he rubbed his eyes. They chatted for a few minutes about Tiago nearing the end of his shift.

A colleague of Tiago's walked past in a neat uniform.

'Good morning,' she said in English with a French accent.

'Good morning,' he smiled back.

'So you've come for the spa, miss?' Tiago asked with a wink.

'Oh . . .'

Emme looked around. Rule seven: no spa-ing while on duty. Was she technically on duty while the kids were at school?

'Erm, I don't have a bathing costume,' she whispered.

'Well that doesn't matter,' Tiago answered with a wry smile. 'There's an over sixteens area. Attire not necessary.'

Emme blushed.

Tiago waved his arm.

'Just kidding. The Germans like that space the best. We have a little gift shop through there, selling swimwear. If you want to choose something?'

Emme panicked about the price and Tiago, reading her mind, gave a brief shake of his head before his colleague, wearing a name brooch that said Magali, joined him behind the desk. Magali familiarised herself with the computer and looked at the handover notes.

Tiago widened his eyes encouragingly, as if to say *this is your last chance, my shift ends soon.*

'Well, I do have a few hours and I did really want to use the spa today . . .'

Tiago outstretched his arm.

'Of course. Come with me.'

He walked round the desk and led the way to the gift shop, pushing an olive hand through glossy black curls, leaving his hair sticking upwards. Inside, a prim woman was unpacking stock.

'Jessica, Miss Emme is going to choose a bikini, I'll charge it to her room.'

The woman nodded as she placed cuddly marmots, each holding a Swiss flag, onto a shelf. Emme looked along a rack of bikinis for sizes that might fit.

Shit.

A mink bikini cost 2,000 Swiss francs, which would be almost that in sterling. She slid it along and looked for something cheaper, something more practical.

She flew through the rack, worried that if she took too long, Tiago might be rumbled.

'Just bring it to the front desk when you're ready, and I'll get your towel, robe and locker key,' he said, with a nod and a small bow.

Emme smiled gratefully and looked at the swimwear, all high cut, string ties and tiny triangles, and settled on a silver metallic one. It was still 300 Swiss francs, but was the cheapest in her size.

She motioned to Jessica that she was taking it, who nodded and said, 'Have a nice day,' in an American accent. Clearly Jessica trusted Tiago too. Or did they all do it?

Emme took the bikini back to Tiago on reception, who removed the tags and handed it, along with a towel, flip-flops and robe, to Emme, and walked her in the direction of the lift. As he pressed the lift button and they waited, a long-legged woman wearing tight black jodhpurs, boots, a black polo neck and a fur coat stormed into the hotel with such fervency it was as though a gale had blown in.

'You!' she barked at Magali on the desk, as she whipped off her black Gucci sunglasses and gave a piercing look. It was the woman from Tristan Du Kok's balcony, the first woman who'd clutched her coat with a wicked smile. Emme couldn't take her eyes off her as she waited with Tiago by the lifts.

'Yes, Ms Steinherr,' the receptionist said reverently.

'Have you seen my father?' she asked, accusingly, envelope clutch under her arm.

'No, ma'am, but I am just starting my shift.'

The woman tossed her glossy chestnut hair back over her shoulders.

Tiago turned his back to the two women on reception, glad to be otherwise occupied with the arrival of the lift.

'Anastasia Steinherr,' he whispered to Emme. 'Her family owns the hotel.' He returned to his regular speaking volume. 'Spa is in the basement. I'll charge this all to your room. Have a nice day, miss.'

'Thank you!' Emme mouthed as the lift doors closed. Tiago would probably be gone and sleeping by the time she was done.

'*De nada*,' he replied. And as the lift closed on his smiling face, Emme wondered why the hell Tristan Du Kok's Steinherr sister girlfriend would have to hide from another woman on the balcony.

The pool was ambient-lit and totally empty, the water serene and flat, changing colour on rotation thanks to the underwater lights. Green to purple to blue to red. It was begging to be dive-bombed into. Emme looked at her reflection in the mirrors as she tiptoed along the pool's edge. The tiny metallic bikini wasn't what she would ordinarily choose, but she felt pretty good in it. The string cut flattered her petite curves, and the shine of the little triangles made her nipples just about protrude through the fabric. She thought of Tristan Du Kok pressing his hard-on into the blonde; the tenderness with which he comforted her in the café. Didn't Anastasia Steinherr care that Tristan Du Kok also slept with someone else?

Dammit.

She decided to leave the pool and explore the outdoor space, where there was a quad clad in cedar, with a sauna and steam room off to one side, and a plunge pool in the middle. The cold blast of Alpine air would do her good, but it was so freezing outside, she bypassed the swing chair and went to the sauna room which, again, was blissfully empty.

Emme hung her robe on a hook outside the door and entered the small piping-hot steam room. Almost instantly she felt a moistness on her forehead; beads of sweat on her top lip. She placed her towel down on a top slat and lay on top of it, hoping no one would come in and ruin her peace. What a few days it had been. And here she was.

A freebie in a plush spa, all thanks to the new friendships she was forming.

She closed her eyes. Still she couldn't shake the thought of Tristan Du Kok. First taking Anastasia from behind. Then sliding his cock into the blonde after she'd left. How beautiful they all were. How soft his lips and manly his rhythmic thrust might be. Emme felt sensations she hadn't felt in years; sensations she craved to feel with another man.

She thought of her last fling, Leo, a friend Tom had fixed her up with, from a covers band he and Leo played in called The Right Stripes. Leo was a drummer, but he was a clumsy lover. His hands wandered erratically and nervously. He didn't put his hands on her the way Tristan had the blonde. Leo hadn't made her come once. She had only been with him to test the waters. See if it would rattle Tom. See if she could take her mind off her best friend. It had fizzled out after three weeks.

Emme closed her eyes and tried to breathe against the stifling air. She imagined she were riding Tristan's enormous cock. His strong thighs holding up her petite curves. She would fit more neatly onto him than either of his leggy lovers.

Emme's hand wandered. The metallic shimmer of her bikini bottoms almost pulsating with the heat from her clitoris. She knew that if she touched herself now, she would come quickly. But what if someone walked in?

What if he *walked in?*

Oh god, she wanted him so badly. To feel what those women had. Surely she'd hear someone come in before they saw her? Her hand slid down and her fingers made that first exquisite touch. She imagined Tristan's thick lashes and cocky smile as he walked into the steam room, pushed aside the V of her bikini bottoms, and gently teased his tongue into her.

Emme moaned, pressing harder. The fantasy of Tristan, scooping her up and lifting her off the bench, his hands clasped under her buttocks while he guided her onto his throbbing cock. Him standing; her legs wrapped around his waist. The sensation of him inside while he thrust. They changed positions, Emme on her tiptoes, Tristan caressing the curves of her arse.

Oh my god.

She was so close to coming.

And then she was suddenly interrupted.

My phone!

It was ringing in the pocket of her robe, just on the other side of the door.

Shit.

She was so close, but something could be wrong with the kids, it could be the school, who had her number now as the first port of call in an emergency. She had to answer it.

Emme got up and felt light-headed.

The rush of cold air from the courtyard felt both shocking and invigorating at once.

She grabbed her phone before it could ring off, not even stopping to see who was calling.

'Hello?'

'Emme.'

The voice sounded distant.

'Oh. Tom.'

Her heart raced.

There was a silence as Emme wrapped one arm across her body and looked at her goosebumped skin. She pressed her brow into her plump white robe to dab away the sweat, then swiftly put it on.

'Everything OK?'

She walked back inside to the pool area, where she found an empty lounger. All the loungers were empty. She could talk freely. She could still feel the wetness between her legs.

'Yeah, I just wanted to . . . erm, check in on you.'

'From your honeymoon?'

'Yes.'

There was another pause, and all she could hear was the sound of her heart sinking.

'How are the Maldives?'

'Beautiful. Just beautiful.'

'What time of day is it there?'

'It's late afternoon, I'm about to have a sundowner. We're about to have sundowners . . .' he sounded guilty.

Emme's fantasy and her frustration at being cut short from it made her feel bold.

'Why are you calling Tom?' she took a deep breath. 'To rub it in?'

'Rub it in?'

'Yes, that you're in the Maldives and I'm freezing!'

'No! No . . . I wanted to, erm, say hi. See how you're getting on in Switzerland. I've been wanting to make sure you're OK. I've been thinking about you . . . about what you said to me. The night before.'

'Please Tom, let's not – I shouldn't have. I was speaking out of turn.'

'You weren't, it was very . . . brave.'

Emme chewed her lip and searched her brain for a response.

'I don't really want to talk about it. It's fine. I've moved on.' She knew she hadn't, of course, she was just trying to make this call less excruciating. Although she did find her mind on Tristan Du Kok again and felt another fleeting flash of excitement. But who was she kidding? Tom was the love of her life. And he was on honeymoon with someone else.

She let out a sigh, lay back on the propped-up lounger, and examined her legs stretched out in front of her. The gulf between them made Tom sound nervous, she could tell that even from his breathing.

'I'm fine, really, you're not all that, anyway . . .' Emme joked, hollowly.

Tom gave a meagre laugh. Sounding relieved that she was joking, but as though he desperately wanted to talk to her about it. He hadn't realised she was moving to Switzerland so soon and it was obviously not the goodbye he wanted.

'Well I suppose . . . I just wanted to see how you're getting on, with your new life in the mountains.'

Emme wriggled her toes, still a shade of peach sorbet from the wedding.

'It's great, thanks.'

When she thought about it, perhaps it was. She had only been in Kristalldorf one weekend and she was in a luxe and empty hotel spa, courtesy of a friend. 'Really, you don't need to worry about me. I've actually had the best weekend, the family are really lovely . . .' OK maybe that was pushing it – the mother had a carrot up her arse, the dad was weirdly vacant and the boy might take time to warm up to her, but it could be worse. 'I've made some friends already . . .' She thought about Tiago upstairs and his kindness. Of Cat and her exuberance. Of Cassie and her wit. 'And I've even been dancing.'

'Dancing? Already?' Tom tried to sound excited. 'Europop?'

'Yes!' Emme softened. 'Well Europop and American covers. They love a covers band out here.'

'Cool! Maybe The Right Stripes can do a gig out there?'

'Yeah maybe,' Emme said idly.

'You didn't cheat on me with "99 Luftballons" did you?' Tom's chuckle fell short. It was Tom and Emme's party piece: at any twenty-first, thirtieth, engagement party or wedding they had ever been to, Tom and Emme would do the *Just Dance* routine to '99 Luftballons' by Nena in perfect harmony. Full of laughter, usually to rapturous applause and everyone saying they made the cutest twosome. Except they didn't do it at Tom and Chrissy's wedding.

The tone of her voice landed somewhere between warmth and carelessness. She tried so hard not to care.

'No, no balloons . . .'

Tiago walked through the spa door, in his coat, looking for Emme.

'Look, I have to go, I'm meeting a friend,' she said, quickly.

'Wow. Yes. Of course.'

'And you have sundowners. Go have one for me yeah?'

'Yes, sur—'

'And give Chrissy my love.'

'Will do.'

'Buh-bye.'

Tom was halfway through saying goodbye back when Emme hung up, flipped her phone over, and tried to stifle back her tears.

Tiago was already walking towards her, his gaze firmly on her face. Was it her imagination or was he making a concerted effort not to look at her body? She liked him all the more for it.

'Hey, I'm finishing my shift, just wanted to check everything was all OK with you?'

He looked odd standing next to a pool in a suit and ski coat.

Emme nodded, her eyes glassy and sad.

'Great, there's pastries and juices through the chillout room there. Help yourself.'

'Thank you, Tiago. This is *just* what I needed. I owe you a drink.'

'Hey, no problem,' he said, walking away with a wave.

Emme clutched the back of her phone on the lounger, and realised her hand was trembling. From talking to Tom. From her moment in the sauna. From envisaging Tristan Du Kok fucking the woman upstairs – and Emme's burgeoning desire to know everything about him.

Chapter Twenty-Eight

In the fifth-floor penthouse of the Steinherrhof hotel, Lumi and Walter lay entwined on the bed, a tussle and bustle of sheets around them, a satisfied glow on the face of Mrs Kivvi.

'Oh Walter! What have we done?'

It had been thirty years since their passion on the bearskin in front of the fire in Walter's study.

The sex was still fiery, deep, loving and illicit.

'We've done what's needed to be done ever since you returned, Lumi.'

'But what are we going to do?' she trailed an elegant, manicured finger along his liver-spotted arm. His skin bore the hallmarks of age, but he was no less of a lover than he had been that night. More daring and free perhaps.

'We are going to have a wonderful time. Make up for all those years wasted.'

'But how? This would break Viktor!' As Lumi said it, she wondered if Viktor would even care. Increasingly, he had been speaking to his wife as if she were staff or a waitress — and he never spoke nicely to them. Apart from his assistant Benjamin. He seemed to have more time for Benjamin than for his wife of twenty-five years.

'How are we going to manage this?'

Walter sat up, now slightly indignant. They were not children, running around behind their parents' backs. He owned this town, and dammit if he and Lumi wanted to be together, they of all people would be able to make it work. He lay back with a sigh.

'We're not teenagers, Lumi. We're not stupid. I did not wait thirty years to mess this up now. We will have our own channel to each other – I'll get you a phone – we will meet up whenever we damn well want.'

As Walter shifted his position against the plump pillows, Lumi noticed a violent-looking bruise on his back, dark blue and ample, as if an elephant had kicked him in the liver.

'What's that?' she asked, disturbed, smoothing her palm down his back.

'What's what?' Walter gruffed, remembering. 'Oh, I, er, I had a bit of a mishap on the slopes . . .'

Lumi studied him. She didn't believe him, and gave him a look as if to let him know.

'It's fine. Really.' He leaned over to kiss her neck again, with a slight wince. She wasn't convinced he was telling her the truth.

'And what about your wife?'

Lumi was surprised by how much it had stung when the news got out that Walter Steinherr had a new wife. And a croupier at that! When Lumi had moved back to Kristalldorf, Walter had been recently divorced. Available, even though she didn't ever imagine she would be with him again. And she didn't really want to, after the business with Seven Summits. But time had softened her.

'Irrelevant,' he said dourly. 'What about your husband?' he asked, with a devilish twinkle.

A flash of guilt washed over Lumi's kindly face.

'Walter . . . please . . .' she said. Perhaps this was all a terrible idea.

He clasped her hand and sought to reassure her.

'You don't think I waited for you, but I did. All those lonely years, in my marriages, in my solitude. I thought about you, I dreamed about you.'

Lumi looked at him, concerned for a second that he was confusing her with Anna Maria. With that time in his life. Her blue eyes penetrated his.

'When you waltzed back into town ten years ago, I knew we'd be together again. Kiki was just a . . . a distraction. I was scared I could never have you. But . . .'

He leaned over her and she surrendered again, her long silk chemise riding up.

'Oh Walter!' she said, in the tangle of their passion, and stretched open her legs deliciously.

Chapter Twenty-Nine

Harry and Bella had come out of school buoyant, excited for the first lesson of the season. It seemed half the class were heading to the ski train on the other side of the river. Emme had worked out there were two ways to get up to the slopes. One was the fast and slick ski train from the centre of town, on the Harringtons' side of the river which cut through the mountain in minutes. She didn't know it was owned by the same man whose hotel she stole a bikini from this morning, but that was by the by.

The other way to get to the slopes was from the gondola station at the end of the valley path towards the Silberschnee, by the Anna Maria hotel. There, cable cars glided quietly and graciously, luxurious pods with heated seats, rising up the mountain with the best view of the valley. Ski school's meeting point was at the main ski train station in town, where the masses would clunk through a short tunnel in ski boots and pile into train cars, damp with melted snow, and that's where Emme, Harry and Bella were due to meet Cedric.

Emme and the kids arrived along with the post-school crowds and located the Harrington locker with a little help from Bella, before Emme helped the children into their salopettes, boots and helmets. She crouched down and zipped their ski passes safely into their trouser pockets.

'OK, can you see where –'

She didn't need to finish her question.

'Cedric!' the children chimed, as they ran up to a man in a blue ski coat and salopettes. He wore a woolly hat over curls and had a matted beard. Something about him seemed familiar.

'Hey kids! Good summer?'

It was November, hardly the end of summer. But this town seemed to operate in two seasons: "summer" and "the season" – which ran from November until Kristalldorf Sessions, the music festival that took over the town in early April. That's how long Emme had committed to stay for now. Who knew beyond that? The Harringtons spent much of the summer travelling: Bill couldn't take all of July and August off unlike Lexy, so he would join his family for the odd week in Majorca, Capri or Rhodes. During Emme's call with the agency, they said the previous nanny had stayed with the family over summers so that Lexy had help on holidays, and that was an option to consider if it all worked out well. However it worked out, Dominique Henry had agreed to give Emme a sabbatical until the end of April, and by then she would know what to do.

'We went to Australia!' Harry said.

Emme looked at them, surprised. She didn't know that.

'Oh wow, you are lucky.'

'I held a koala!' lisped Bella.

Cedric seemed pale and a little distracted.

'It did a poo on her arm!' giggled Harry.

'Everything alright?' Emme said, cocking her head to get a good look at Cedric.

'*Oui*, yes,' the instructor nodded earnestly. His leathery cheeks making him look older than his years.

'I'm "the new Jenny",' Emme joked, but Cedric didn't seem to find it funny. Maybe it wasn't. 'Emme,' she held out her hand but he glanced away.

This guy needed to go to charm school, rather than teach ski school, Emme thought, but the kids seemed enchanted.

'Skis?' Cedric asked, as enthusiastically as he could muster.

'They're in the locker,' Emme said, 'I'll just grab them.'

The children put on their ski gloves and Harry idly kicked his sister's schoolbag down a step.

'Hey!' Bella objected. She was very protective of her *Encanto* backpack.

As Emme returned she noticed Cedric looking towards her, but he still wouldn't meet her eye as he took the skis from her.

'Are you coming up on the train?' he asked.

'I have to get my own skis sorted first, but I'll meet you, if you tell me where?'

Cedric explained where to meet, but looked like he could barely remember the way himself. Did Lexy really let this guy go off with her children? Should *she*?

'OK, Zita Café at 3.15pm,' Emme confirmed.

She picked up the schoolbags from the floor to put them in the locker. 'Kids, have a wonderful time, I'll see you up the mountain at the end of your lesson.'

Harry and Bella trudged off with Cedric, to the thudding sound of ski boots and poles clonking along the spongy floor of the tunnel to the mountain train, along with all the other excited children.

Chapter Thirty

Cat leaned against the marble island of the kitchen in her chef trousers and a grey V-neck T-shirt making notes. Notes about flavours. Notes about the canapés in front of her. Notes about drinks and concoctions. Notes to distract her from the very person who had suddenly appeared in the doorway like a mirage. Seeing Anastasia Steinherr, a lithe silhouette, her legs coltish, as she leaned against the frame in tight trousers, boots and a fur coat, was so alien, Cat did wonder if she was going mad. Instead she gasped.

'What are you doing here? Lumi isn't home and Viktor is in Tokyo.'

'I came to see you.'

'How did you get in?'

'The maid, I said I wanted to see you.'

'Here?!' Cat looked through the doorway beyond Anastasia nervously, in case Teresa or Gerard might be listening. 'I'm at work.'

Anastasia pouted like a child. Her lips were long and full. Cat couldn't help but remember the best of times kissing them.

Anastasia took a big look around the room, drinking in the details before she walked in nonchalantly, placing her purse on the vast kitchen island. The Kivvi kitchen looked part chef's kitchen, part Tiffany New York. It had pale cream walls and a palatial La Cornue range oven with duck-egg-blue vaulted doors and ornate handles. Above the white marble worktop streaked with elegant black wisps hung a large oven hood in the same pale blue shade as the oven doors. Anastasia certainly admired the room as if it contained precious jewels. She tossed her hair and pulled her most demure of faces, before levelling Cat with a look.

'I wanted to apologise.'

'Apologise?' This was most unlike Anastasia. Cat didn't think she'd heard her apologise for anything.

'For bad sex, the other night.'

'Oh.'

Cat's hopeless gaze was torn between her lover and the doorway.

'I was spent. From the night before,' she quickly clarified.

Cat blushed and looked down. The Montblanc pen in her hand was shaking. She let it drop. Anastasia approached with careful, panther-like steps. Cat got weaker. Someone could walk in on them at any time.

'Friday night was a dream. Saturday I got greedy. I was too tired, too stressed, I shouldn't have called you, I'm sorry.'

Cat had hated how different it had been to the night before. The prickly way in which Anastasia flinched when Cat touched her – she wondered if she had been sleeping with her husband again. It had filled her with an uncomfortable, jealous rage on the walk back to Chalet Edelweiss.

Cat smiled appreciatively, but stood firm.

'Look, I can't go on like this,' she said, returning Anastasia's gaze with a weary look. 'I told you when I went back for the funeral . . . it has to end. I can't handle it. It's such a mindfuck.' *You're such a mindfuck,* she thought. 'It's over.'

Anastasia approached the island, almost purring.

'It can't be,' she whispered. 'I care so much.'

Cat shot her a look and lowered her voice to an angry hiss.

'Care? You didn't even ask me how the funeral went.'

Anastasia looked taken aback. Cat could be so sensitive, but now wasn't the time to point it out. She put her hand to her chest, to show her concern.

'It's just a power trip with you, it's all about how quickly I'll come running after you've clicked your fingers. You don't care.'

'I do care,' Anastasia pouted.

Anastasia walked around the island and approached Cat from behind. She opened her fur coat and pressed her body into Cat's back.

'Please,' she whispered into Cat's ear. Her breath was sweet. 'Let me show you.' She peppered kisses onto Cat's neck. Cat leaned her head away, trying to fight it but only offering Anastasia more skin. She felt weak at the knees. She could feel Anastasia's hips pressing into her bottom, she felt Anastasia's hand slip down into the waistband of her chef's trousers, lowering into the lace sheath of her knickers.

Cat groaned, with one eye still on the kitchen door.

'Please,' she protested longingly.

'I want you so much,' Anastasia said, before trailing her tongue up from Cat's collarbone to behind her ear. Cat supressed a groan.

'Too risky.'

'Let me make it up to you . . .'

Anastasia started circling Cat's clitoris with a manicured, bejewelled finger as she continued to dot her neck with kisses. Cat could feel her wetness building on Anastasia's tantalising touch.

'I want to eat your pussy. Take me to your bedroom.'

Anastasia ran her free hand along the shiny kitchen counter, appraising the finesse of the finish. 'Or maybe I'll have you here.'

'They could be back any time now . . . the staff are here.'

'Please, let me make it up to you,' Anastasia continued to circle, and Cat's legs almost buckled as her breaths got heavy. She had to lean onto the counter to stop herself crumbling. Anastasia's touch, the sensation of her kisses, it was pure bliss. Cat closed her eyes and rolled with the pleasure.

'Ah, Mrs Diamandis,' the butler said, as he walked into the kitchen with the dry cleaning.

Cat opened her eyes and shoved Anastasia back with a jolt.

'Gerard!' Cat said, in a fluster, as he paused, a pile of luxurious coats and dresses slung over his white-jacketed arm. Gerard was impeccably mannered and impeccably tactful.

'I was just here doing a tasting,' Anastasia said, flashing a supermodel smile and nodding to the canapés on the worktop. 'While I was waiting for Lumi, who I understand is out.'

Gerard looked up with a bemused yet professional smile.

'Yes, ma'am, can I pass on a message for when she returns?' He wanted to spare Cat her blushes as she put an apron on over her clothes and smoothed it down.

'It's fine, I'll be in touch again.'

'Very good,' he said, poised as if he were waiting for her to leave.

Anastasia put her moist finger between her teeth as if she were thinking, but it was just a way of teasing Cat, who shot her a look.

Why the hell had she come?

'The basil crème was just exquisite chef,' Anastasia said, as Gerard held the kitchen door open for her with his free hand.

Cat watched Anastasia sashay through it, into the living area, and couldn't help noticing how much she was studying the décor of Chalet Edelweiss as she saw herself out.

Chapter Thirty-One

It took nearly the entire ski lesson for Emme to get back to Chalet Stern and try – and fail – to locate Jenny's skis. They hadn't been in any of the cupboards and they weren't in the family locker back by the ski train station. Emme didn't want to disturb Lexy at work so she rushed to the ski hire shop next to the mountain train, where it was taking a painstakingly long time to hire skis, boots and a helmet.

The man checked her height and weight, asked what level she was ('pretty much beginner') and asked her how long she needed the skis for.

'Oh I don't know. Just a couple of days until I work something out.'

The man took a little too long with his screwdriver, setting the bindings.

'Please, how long is it going to take?' Emme cursed herself for not taking Cedric's number. She thought it was enough that he had hers down as the emergency contact. She didn't think she would be the one throwing a curveball today. Emme *hated* being late.

'You're from London, right?'

Emme sighed, what did that have to do with anything?

She watched the man with black eyes sort her skis slowly, biting her tongue so he didn't slow further.

'Where are you from?' she asked, trying to place his accent and relax into a smile.

'Egypt. Alexandria is my home. Mo Salah is my king,' he said. Emme smiled, genuinely this time. She noticed the Liverpool FC crest on his fleece top.

'Nice.'

It worked, he got a little faster with the screwdriver.

'All done,' he said. 'That's . . .' he pressed some numbers into a till. 'One hundred and seventy francs please.'

Shit.

'Great – thanks!'

'Keep your helmet with you but there's a locker room downstairs you can leave the skis/poles/boots in at the end of the day,' he said. 'You can leave your shoes down there now if you want?'

'Great, thanks,' Emme said, handing him her trainers as she typed in her PIN to pay and rushed out.

Snooty London woman, she imagined him thinking.

Snooty London woman, he thought, as he watched the beginner skier rush out. He hadn't even had a chance to show her how to clip them on.

Chapter Thirty-Two

Cat had only just recovered from her surprise visit from Anastasia when Lumi Kivvi returned from running her errands in town.

She walked into the kitchen, her cheeks flushed, clutching a box of Läderach chocolates, which she set on the kitchen island and encouraged Cat to try.

'My goodness you *have* to try the pistachio truffle Catalina, here . . .'

There was a buoyancy and an optimism about Lumi that Cat found comforting. Lumi was a calm counter to her chaotic thoughts about Anastasia, although she worried whether Teresa or Gerard might inform their boss of the surprise visit.

Cat picked up the confection wrapped in green and white paper and opened it, grateful for the distraction. She placed it in her mouth.

'*Madre mía,*' she exclaimed, eyes rolling heavenwards. 'Amazing.'

'Aren't they?'

Lumi had a glow about her, but Cat would never have guessed why. That three hours ago Walter met her at the door of his Steinherrhof penthouse clutching a huge box of *tartufi* for the woman he'd waited thirty years to be with again. That they'd had an indulgent soak together in a vast bath tub to wash away the guilt.

'Have another,' Lumi said.

'I mustn't, ma'am, I have lots of tastings today.'

'Oh yes! Can we sit down and work through the Christingle menus? Goodness, it's only a month away . . .' Cat had never seen Lumi look so excited about planning the Kivvi Christingle. She didn't know a thrill shot through her, that this might be the year that Walter Steinherr might finally deign to come.

Cat smiled. Going through the menus was precisely what she wanted to do. Cooking was what she loved most. Since she could remember, in her grandmother's kitchen in Bariloche, Cat made *asado*, *chimichurri*, *empanadas* and *alfajores* . . . graduating to more sophisticated dishes such as blue cheese macarons, artisan bread with ash butter, carpaccio with celery puree and egg yolk on morels mash when she moved to Buenos Aires for her culinary arts degree.

'Yes I've been tinkering and have some ideas I picked up when I was home.'

'Well fire away, Catalina!' Lumi leaned on the island, her eyes sparkling as she listened intently to Cat's suggestions of caviar, pickled cucumber and chicory; *chicharrónes* with cumin, chipotle and red cabbage; mini lobster rolls with lemon aioli; salt hake *brandades* and olives; chicken Caesar sourdoughs.

'And now you remind me, ma'am, that pistachio truffle flavour would go exceptionally well with a blood orange and cardamom miniature sponge I've been trialling.'

'Well there's plenty more where those came from,' Lumi said, her cheeks flushing a deeper shade of crimson, as she gestured to the box.

'Oh I make my own, Mrs Kivvi,' Cat said proudly.

'Of course you do.'

Cat continued to make notes while Lumi got herself a glass of iced water from the huge industrial refrigerator and pulled up a stool at the island.

'Actually, I could do the blood orange macarons Miss Stella loves so much. What do you think about that?' Cat asked.

'I think this is going to be our best Christingle yet!' Lumi positively glowed.

Chapter Thirty-Three

The walk through the station and down the tunnel to the ski train was peppered with the clunk of heavy plastic boots as people made their way off the mountain. At the barriers at the end of the tunnel Emme swiped her ski pass and boarded the train that was already waiting. Emme couldn't face walking a step more than she needed to, she already felt a blister coming on from the heavy ski boots. In her cargos and coat – she was no better dressed for skiing than she had been for the spa that morning – she lamented her crap gear as she saw chic European women in sleek fur-lined one-pieces and mirrored ski goggles walking past her through the tunnel. She really would be better prepared next time. Perhaps Cat might know of a second-hand forum for workers to buy and sell clothes. There must be loads of it going around, and she didn't really want to spend all her salary on skiwear she was only going to use for a few months.

The train was mostly empty on the way up and travelled at high speed at a high incline, through a dark tunnel where Emme's ear popped at the roar, until it came to a stop at another set of steep steps that each lined up with a door and gate to the train. Emme got out and felt miffed she had to clunk up all these stairs to get to the exit, heavy skis and poles over one shoulder.

It all felt like such an effort, until she walked out of the ski train exit and saw the captivating view. The white snow dazzled her eyes, but in front of her, the iconic Silberschnee glimmered in the sunshine, crisp and close and the focus for all the skiers whizzing past. A woman in a houndstooth check ski suit and silver helmet whizzed by at lightning speed, so close, she nearly took Emme out.

'Out of the way!' a child bellowed, coming from her left.

'Fuck!' Emme cursed, stepping back fast. She didn't realise the ski train exited onto an actual ski run – whose idea was that? She looked around for Cedric, Harry and Bella as she clunked awkwardly on her boot heels to a terrace where people were sitting at wooden tables. Rows of skis were propped up on wooden racks to the side of it, while skiers ate late lunches of schnitzel and chips; hotdogs and onions; leek and potato soup.

Emme leaned over a terrace wall and asked a woman smoking a cigarette if this was the Zita Café.

'*Nein*, this is Schneehütte,' the woman replied.

An American woman overheard as she clicked her skis on and told Emme she had to take the ski lift to get to Zita.

'Don't get off at the first one, stay on to the top.'

'Top?'

Shit.

Emme thought she *was* at the top. It was already 3.15pm. Cedric and the kids would be waiting and she didn't have his number. Surely he'd call her?

Emme had only ever been skiing once, with Tom in Colorado, and he'd had to haul her on and off the chairlift – but watching the lines of people postprandial and merry, lining up their skis and plonking their bottoms on padded seats, she hoped muscle memory might kick in. All she had to do was put her skis on first, she realised, as everyone else had.

Emme thrust her poles into the snow and leaned on them while she repeatedly tried to get a boot to lock into a ski. After five attempts she almost cried.

'Jesus!' she called out, desperate at being late. An instructor with another group saw her struggling and cleared the snow that was obscuring her ski bindings with the end of his pole.

'Now try . . .' he said, holding out an arm for her to lean on. 'Stamp down until you hear a click.'

It took three more attempts until the first boot locked into place. The other clicked in on the first attempt.

'Thank you,' she said, utterly grateful and terribly nervous. The instructor and his group were heading to the chairlift too, and he gave Emme a hand by holding out his pole for her to take. He dragged her and propelled her forward in front of his group.

'Line up!' he bossed, telling her to go and stand next to a couple and a child who had just moved forward and formed a line behind a blue stripe marked out in the snow. Rows of seats were coming around a carousel, and Emme tried to emulate the other passengers alongside her, watching their timing for when to sit.

She plonked down onto the seat which propelled the four of them off the ground and up into the air.

How does the kid do it?

How do Harry and Bella do it?

We could all fall off and plummet to our deaths!

Emme wanted to scream, this felt so unsafe. The child along the row could easily fall forward, and the gap between the snowy mountain and the soaring seat was only getting wider.

'The barrier!' the man in the group called to her along the seats, part in panic, part in anger. Emme was unwittingly obstructing it, and the man wasn't able to pull it down.

'Oh, sorry!' she said. Embarrassed and relieved. She moved, and the man brought a barrier down over their heads in front of them. Still, it didn't feel very secure. The child could slip under it easily.

Emme tried to take in the stunning view. Pristine untouched snow underneath them. Slaloms to the left and right. She felt petrified.

At the first station the family alongside her lifted the barrier and glided off with a polite nod that Emme read to be *good luck* and she continued to soar. She placed the barrier down this time, pleased with herself that she knew how to, and looked at her watch. It was almost half past three. She really hoped Cedric hadn't thought she'd messed up and gone down to the village to meet her. If she stayed on, would this chair take her down or did she have to ski it? She looked at the tiny figures below her, making tracks in the glimmering snow. The quiet of the journey, the gentle sound of skis cutting through snow, gave a strange and unsettling peace. Everyone looked like they knew what they were doing.

Fuck.

Emme looked at her watch again as she saw the summit ahead. She didn't have time to not get this right. A sign on a grey steel column illustrated that now was the time to lift the safety barrier up again, and she pushed it back with such might it clattered up with a bang above her head that almost made her cower.

How did people get off this thing? She tried to remember how Tom showed her. Emme hadn't had a chance to look at the people in front, at their technique. If she looked back to ask the ski instructor on the chair behind her, she'd miss her moment to get off. Was he even still there?

She put her skis out in front of her, legs stiff, throat tight, and stood, but her legs were shaking, and one tip crossed over the other as she tried to get off.

I'm not ready!

Emme was pushed off, and with each inch she moved, the tips of her skis seemed to get more entangled, as if a magnetic force was driving them together.

'I can't!' she bellowed into the howling breeze. A man smoking a cigarette waited for her to fall in a heap. She was conscious of the next chair swinging round, and how she needed to get out of the way fast.

'Miss!' the instructor who had helped her at the café shouted as she lay supine, as if she didn't know they were about to land on top of her.

'Move!' yelled a woman in his group.

The man operating the chairlift extended a ski pole for Emme to grab onto and practically dragged her out of the way just in time for the instructor and his charges to glide off, one of them tutting as they went.

'All OK?' the chairlift operator asked, his accent sounding Italian.

'No,' Emme said, letting him pull her up to her feet. She had no clue how her skis had stayed on.

'I hate this,' she muttered, to herself more than anything. She brushed the snow off her jacket, which really wasn't warm or waterproof enough for this high altitude. 'But thank you.'

'*Prego*,' he said, as he took another drag of the cigarette that seemed to balance on his full lips.

'Zita Café?' Emme asked, in a strange accent that sounded slightly Italian yet slightly German. The man pointed his ski pole to a building concealed by his hut. It was a small café with chairs on a sun deck and a Swiss flag billowing in the breeze.

Then she saw Cedric and the kids, larking around on their skis outside the café.

Thank god.

Cedric was throwing mini snowballs for them to hit with their poles like baseball bats. He seemed much warmer, much more fun with just the kids, which was a relief to Emme. She stopped and smiled, they looked happy. Maybe he was just better with kids than adults, and that's why Lexy liked him. Still, she was over twenty minutes late, so she used her poles to get across the flat and slushy end-of-day snow to retrieve them.

'Emme!' they said in unison, buoyed by a fun first ski session.

Emme smiled and waved.

'Hey!' she said, turning to Cedric, who seemed less flaky than he had earlier. 'I'm so sorry I'm –'

Cedric stood taller and prouder. Perhaps all instructors thrived on the mountain. He removed his goggles and put them on his helmet, and Emme realised his ski suit was different – now black instead of blue – as she felt the blow to her stomach.

'Oh. It's you.'

Her face dropped. Her heart raced.

'What are you doing here? Where's Cedric?'

It was Tristan Du Kok standing in front of her, his dazzling smile lit even brighter by the reflection of the snow. His nose was tanned with a subtle smattering of dark-brown freckles from the sunshine. She looked at the children with concern. 'You were meant to be here at three fifteen,' Tristan replied.

'Cedric was sick!' chimed the children.

'I saw sweetcorn in it and everything!' gloated Harry.

Bella scowled at her brother.

Emme was completely flustered, even looking at Tristan Du Kok stirred a passion and a rage in her. She tried to measure her face.

'Why didn't he call me?'

'Because he was 3,500 metres up a mountain and he said you were down in the village. I was up here.'

'But you're not an instructor – are you?'

'I have been,' Tristan answered blithely.

'Jesus!' Emme exclaimed.

Lexy will kill me, she thought. Then she remembered where she recognised Cedric from. He'd been one of the very drunken party of ski and snowboard instructors in the bar on Saturday night, drinking beer from his boot. No wonder he looked peaky. 'That was one hangover . . .'

Tristan shook his head and put a finger to his lips.

'Yeah, maybe it's best you don't let on to Lexy,' he said.

'Why do you care?' Emme asked.

'Cedric is a buddy.'

Emme didn't think the guys in cashmere jumpers mingled with the instructors drinking shots off an old wooden ski.

'And I was just checking out the conditions for heli-skiing

but it's too windy, so when I saw he was in a state, I sent him home and said I'd finish his lesson.'

Emme scowled.

'We've had a great time haven't we kids?'

'Yay!' they both cheered.

Tristan unclipped his ski helmet, took it off and ruffled his collar-length hair.

'Do you know this man?!' Emme asked the children sternly.

'Yes he's a friend of Mummy and Daddy,' Harry replied.

'Great,' Emme said flatly. At least that was something.

'Old family friends. Lexy's family, the Brighams, used to holiday with us in Botswana.'

'Nice,' she said acerbically.

She looked at Tristan, desperately annoyed, desperately trying to conceal her racing heart. Tristan rummaged in his pocket and picked out two five-franc coins. 'Kids, why don't you go buy a hot chocolate each and Emme and I will come follow you in a second.'

The way he said *Emme*, with his deep South African accent and warm smile, felt like liquid amber, with a sting. How did he know her name?

The kids, she concluded. The kids had yelled her name.

'Yes!' they cheered, their eyes lighting up. Harry took the two coins and they propped their skis and poles up against a triangular wooden stand and trudged off inside. Tristan looked at Emme, his golden-brown eyes piercing. She flushed red. She felt completely inadequate and utterly exposed. She took off her rented helmet and put her mittens inside it as if it were a basket.

'Cedric could have called me,' Emme lamented.

'Seriously, he was puking all over the place. He couldn't even think straight, let alone wait for you. He reckons it's alcohol poisoning – I say ski instructors can't handle their booze.'

Emme rolled her eyes.

'You said you were one . . .'

'Exactly. *Was*. I did a couple of seasons in Aspen when I was a kid, but I know too much about fine wine to guzzle drinks from a ski boot.'

Oh please.

'I'm Tristan by the way.'

Tristan dug his pole into the snow, took off his gloves and extended a hand. It hung between them, before Emme placed hers in his, large, warm and confident. She remembered where those hands had been and pictured them on the blonde woman's waist.

'Emmeline,' she said primly, as he wrapped his fingers around hers. Perhaps it was the famous foehn winds whipping up over the Alps, but a shiver ran down her spine.

He released her hand and ruffled his hair, which smelled divine, and not of hired ski helmet like Emme's.

'You're new in town, yah?'

'Yah . . .' Emme replied, feeling silly for emulating him. Jeez what was with this guy? What was his pull?

'Yes, I'm from England. Just here for a season,' she elaborated.

Suddenly Emme didn't want to seem like another worker. She didn't want to keep looking young for her age. She wanted to look like a glossy woman, like all the women skiing in their Moncler suits and Gucci helmets. Or like Anastasia Steinherr, with her slick wardrobe and long mane.

Not some girl in hand-me-down winterwear. She wanted to tell Tristan about all the things she enjoyed about working in London. The theatre trips and the ballet. The art and the restaurants.

'Nice, I love the UK.'

'I'm from London, I work in the City. I'm, erm, just taking a career break, looking after the Harrington children.'

'Yah, I heard about the previous nanny's dispatch . . .' Tristan had a glint in his eye.

Oh god don't tell me you fucked her too.

Emme shrugged.

'You're friends with both Lexy and Bill then?'

'Everyone's friends in this town,' Tristan replied cryptically, before revealing a little more. 'When I was a kid, Lexy used to make me dress up and be her stooge for her shows and rehearsals and stuff. She's much older than me of course.'

'Of course,' Emme said, trying not to look Tristan up and down, but she gauged he was a good ten years younger than Lexy Harrington.

'So how long have you been here?'

She didn't want to ask him questions, his ego was clearly already massive, but how the hell does a wine importer from South Africa end up on the mountain?

Then his arrogant air dropped a little, he looked warm and genuine.

'Eight years. My father and I came skiing and . . . well . . . we never left.' He looked at Emme with a sadness, and then down into the snow, where he stabbed his ski poles.

She itched to know what made him sad; what made him tick. His face was so handsome. His jaw twitched.

'It's a beautiful place, Kristalldorf,' Emme said, softening. Tristan looked up, his eyes flashing with a sad intensity. 'Shall we?' he said, pointing to the warm café interior. *The kids.*

'Yes.'

Emme looked down at her skis, not knowing how the hell to get the things off. Tristan suddenly slammed his foot on the binding at the back of her boots, making her jump.

'What are you doing?' she snapped, flustered, thinking he might have broken them. 'I have to pay for them if I break them!'

'Erm, helping you out of your gear . . .' he said with a wink, and held out his arm.

'Oh, thanks,' she said begrudgingly, as she bent over, picked them up and propped them against the rack next to where Harry and Bella had placed theirs.

In Zita Café Harry and Bella were sitting at a table by the window, each clumsily spooning and slurping a hot chocolate. Trollies were stacked up with trays of plates, empty glasses and half-eaten food. It very much looked like the end of the day.

'Would you like a hot wine?' Tristan asked.

'God no, thanks. I need to get the kids back down, tea-time, homework, piano, bath . . .' she clunked over to the children in her godawfully uncomfortable boots, looking back to see what Tristan's were like. Black, shiny, expensive. Less painful, she imagined. He was watching her walk and she scowled at him before turning back to the children.

They were giggling about something, licking hot chocolate off their top lips.

'Come on, we need to get you two home.'

'Hmmm, this is yummy!' Bella said, as she swirled hers with a spoon and a little went on the table. 'Try it!'

Emme stopped, touched. That was a nice offer from Bella, but the hot chocolate had melted marshmallows in it and looked pretty disgusting from this angle.

'I'm OK lovely, but that's very kind of you to offer, thank you.'

'You're not having any of *mine*,' said Harry with a smile. 'Come on finish up . . .'

Emme felt very aware of Tristan, his huge presence, lingering behind her.

'Can we ski with Tristan a bit longer?' the children asked.

'I'm afraid not, the slopes will be closing soon. And we need to get you home for your piano practice – your mother will be worried if we're not back soon.'

Emme thought of the camera doorbell, knowing that Lexy would be aware of all their comings and goings on the BUZZ app on her phone.

'Oh,' they sulked.

'TDK!' bellowed a posh British man with a thick head and a large royal-blue ski suit. 'Wondered when I'd bump into you!' The man with the pink face guffawed and clunked his way over.

'Lawrence! Long time no see my friend . . .' Tristan said as the men gave each other a hearty embrace and patted each other on the back.

Urgh. Emme winced internally. Posh twats backslapping. The last thing she wanted to be around.

Emme took the kids by their hands and led them out to their skis.

'Come on, you'll see Tristan another day I'm sure . . .' she said. If he was such a good friend of Mummy and Daddy, perhaps she would too.

Outside, Emme and the kids got their gloves and skis on, and looped their poles around their wrists.

Which way down?

Tristan was coming out, still chatting to his friend, who was lowering his goggles and about to set off.

'You need a hand?' he called. Emme looked over her shoulder to check he was talking to her.

'We'll be fine,' she waved him away. What was it with this guy and why did he irk her so much? He hadn't been bad to her. He had made a path for her when she tried to get to the bar. He had helped Cedric out and watched the kids. It looked like they had a great time learning from him too.

'Right kids, can you show me the way back down to the ski train?'

Emme hadn't expected to be going to the top of the mountain today, but she knew she had no choice but to ski back down to the mountain train stop she had come out of. If the kids could do it, she could remember how to, right?

Harry and Bella looked puzzled. Wasn't *she* the one to get them home safe? They said nothing. 'That way I assume?' she pointed to the slope.

'Yes,' Bella lisped, unsurely.

The kids lowered their ski goggles from the top of their helmets to their faces, reminding Emme to follow suit, then she watched them propel themselves, off the top of the slope.

'Not too fast, don't go off without me!'

Harry and Bella plopped down the slope, disappearing

temporarily while Emme edged herself to the precipice. She could not lose these children on the mountain on her first proper day in the job, but the bright red and fluoro pink coats of Harry and Bella reappeared like fluorescent dots in the distance, and they were getting smaller.

Shit.

The slope seemed far steeper than it had from above in the chairlift, but she had to get to the children. Emme was gaining speed and felt frightened. She tried to remember what Tom said, when they went skiing in Wolf Creek. Not as fancy as Aspen but she'd spent two days building up the courage to go down a blue run and under Tom's tutelage she had managed — although not loved — it. She placed a pole on the snow to try to slow herself down but it dragged behind her. Were it not for the loop on her wrist, she would have lost it.

'Kids!' Emme yelled. 'Stop and wait!'

Fuck.

Emme remembered a tip Tom had given her back in Colorado. One he reminded her of the morning after the wedding, while Emme was helping Tom's father and sister take down the flowers and decorations in the church. She had just told him she was moving to the Alps for a season. He'd only got wind of her plan to become a nanny two nights ago and now she was moving to Switzerland. Tom laughed and asked if she were serious. Emme tried not to cry, and he realised she was.

'Wow Em, that's wild. You don't even like skiing.'

'I'm going to learn to love it,' she said, puffing her chest out a little.

'We're going to miss our flight!' Chrissy urged from the

church doors, sunglasses on, Mulberry bag slung over her elbow. Tom ignored her, and looked at Emme, a lingering sadness behind his hungover eyes.

'Remember: always ski into the mountain.' He diffused the tension with a conspiratorial smile.

'Tom!' Chrissy snapped again. 'Oh, hi Emme,' she said, noticing Emme clearing up the detritus of her wedding.

Now she remembered his words, while she was whizzing, losing control, reaching a perilous speed. She wished Tom were here now. Or did she?

Always ski into the mountain.

What did that even mean?

The dots of the children were getting smaller. The light was fading. It was heading for 4pm on a Monday in November, Lexy would be checking the BUZZ app and fretting.

'Kids!' Emme bellowed.

Suddenly the piste got narrower and even steeper, with skiers flying past from behind Emme on both sides.

Seemingly everyone was trying to get back to the village before the slopes closed. Emme was sweating. She felt both boiling hot and freezing cold, as she hurtled now, towards the piste's edge.

I'm going to break a bone.

I'm going to plummet over.

I can't see Harry and Bella.

'FUCKKKKKKKK!'

Emme threw herself to one side in a violent thrust, which took one of her skis off as she came to a halt. Her errant ski teetered on the slope's steep edge.

'Shit shit shit!' she threw her poles down in frustration

but they wouldn't come off her wrists. She started to cry. At least she had stopped hurtling at a frightening velocity. And she didn't appear to have broken a leg. She could move. She sat up and narrowed her eyes. She could see Harry in red and Bella in pink, now motionless dots at the bottom of the piste – they were waiting for her, thank god.

I have to get to them.

Yet she knew there would be another three or four pistes after this one. Some steeper, perhaps.

'Hey!' she bellowed, raising a pole, checking the kids knew where she was. Harry raised one back. 'Wait there!' Emme shouted in her loudest voice. She looked up – the mostly empty chairlift continued its gentle hum. Chairs coming up, chairs going down. She was shocked to see one of the chairs had a couple in it, casually heading downwards. She didn't know you *could* go down in the chairlift.

Fuck.

Emme sobbed as she tried to stand, wondering how she would retrieve her delinquent ski. Her face was cold, she had snow down the back of her neck and the overpowering smell of other people's sweat in her ski helmet made her want to be sick.

'Fucking hate this,' she snarled to herself.

'Well perhaps you'd let me help you then . . .' said a calm, low voice.

Oh god.

Emme looked up at the silhouetted figure, a halo from the low sun forming behind him. She nodded gently and stifled her sobs.

'You don't know how to ski?' Tristan asked.

Emme shook her head, knowing how ridiculous and downright dangerous she had been. 'I'm a little rusty,' she said quietly.

It was embarrassment after embarrassment with this guy.

'Hey, don't worry!' Tristan said, with a wave of his gloved hand. 'I'll get you down . . .' He held one of his ski poles out for Emme to cling onto and pulled her to her feet. One booted, one with a long Salomon ski attached. 'Wait a sec – stand into the mountain so you don't slide down on your bottom or on one ski.'

Ski into the mountain.

Tristan put a solid hand on each of Emme's shoulders to position her, showing her what Tom meant with just one electric touch, as she stood perpendicular to the slope.

'Stay there,' he said, then glided over to her wayward ski, picked it up and put it over his shoulder, before gliding back to Emme like the Milk Tray man.

Emme frowned. She really didn't need to be rescued. Except she did.

'Look, I seem to be everyone's Plan B today, but I'll get you down the mountain whether you want me to or not. But you need to listen to me, yah? It's quite dangerous.' He gave her a piercing, almost disapproving stare. Emme had no choice but to nod.

Tristan positioned her ski in place next to her boot and put her hand on his shoulder.

'Lean on me,' he said. 'And press hard.'

She stamped onto the ski with vigour and it clicked into place.

'First things first, do you know how to brake?'

Emme winced.

'I think so . . . do I cross my skis at the front?'

'Jesus, lady!'

'Lady?' she scowled. He'd forgotten her name already.

'Jesus, *Emmeline*. If you cross your skis at the front you'll get tangled and fall over. Which is dangerous. So cut the attitude and listen, we need to get back to town.'

Emme nodded.

'Stand sideways, if you stand facing down, whoosh, you'll slide down, out of control. So first things first, always stand perpendicular to the mountain. And cut your skis into the snow to make a little shelf.'

'Got it,' she said, rooted to the spot.

'Now I'm going to show you how to brake without falling over, and hopefully how to move without falling over, right?'

Emme nodded.

'Put your goggles back on,' he said, placing them on for her, softening with a patience that made him seem even sexier.

She almost couldn't look at him for fear of flushing red, grateful for the shield to her eyes.

'Imagine your feet are French fries right now, two long thin chips I think you call them.'

Emme nodded.

'That's how you go. When you're facing down the mountain, parallel legs will give you speed.'

'What if I don't want speed?'

'That's what I'm telling you. To slow and stop, make your feet into a triangle shape, like a slice of pizza. Bring your toes together but do not cross skis. And keep your heels apart. Got it?'

'French fries, go; pizza, stop. Got it.'

They heard Bella calling something up, the kids must be bored and freezing.

'OK, I'm just going down far enough to check the kids are OK and know to wait, then I'll pull myself back up and come to you.'

Emme thought about Tristan, his physicality, and hung her head.

Not now.

'Don't go anywhere, yah?'

'No chance,' she smiled with some irony.

Tristan whizzed straight down the slope to the kids while Emme gathered herself, taking long and measured breaths towards the Silberschnee to try to calm her racing heart. She didn't move an inch, apart from to crane her head to see Tristan heaving back *up* the mountain, part skiing, part stepping up into the slope. He looked like he was fighting a force. She could almost hear his grunts of effort, defying physics and gravity as he tested every muscle in his strong body to get back to her. She felt guilty now.

'You OK?' he called up.

'Yes,' she conceded. It was her ego that was bruised more than her body. 'Thank you,' she said, as he reached her.

He said nothing, but wiped his brow between his helmet and the top of his ski goggles. She was relieved she couldn't see his penetrating eyes right now.

'Are they OK?'

'Yes, bored, but they're waiting.'

'Oh god . . .' Emme panicked a little.

'It's fine. Look I'm going to cradle you down. You need

to stand between my legs, keep your toes pointing in and your heels out – but don't let your skis cross, got it?'

'Got it.'

'We'll start to the side and then I'll gently turn us, the important thing is not to panic. Relax and go with me.'

Emme let out an uncertain whimper. She hated the feeling of being out of control. She just wanted to be back in the village, to be in the Harringtons' warm apartment, although something about Tristan was starting to calm her as he stood behind her, framing her in their stance, his skis outside of hers, his shoulders curled and his arms cradling Emme's body.

'Tuck your poles in.'

'OK,' Emme said, suddenly feeling honoured by his touch.

'We're not going to fly, we're just going to take it slowly. Focus on your toes and I'll do all the rest.'

If this wasn't so terrifying it would be glorious. The Silberschnee was tinged almost pink as the sun was getting low over the opposite ridge; the view was beautiful. Tristan smelled beautiful – she could feel his breath on her neck – but the tension and fear ruined the mountain idyll. Emme's knees were locked to the point her thighs burned. Her fists gripped her redundant poles for dear life.

Tristan enveloped her and guided her down, turning slowly, as they snaked towards the kids waiting at the bottom. She almost didn't want to reach them, she yearned for their closeness not to end. She wanted to take in the view for longer, for Tristan to press closer into her back, so she could feel what the women on the balcony could feel, but he didn't, he kept just the right amount of distance needed to safely steer her down to the kids, who were bored and bemused, waiting at the bottom.

'Finally!' Harry said.

'Are you OK?' Bella asked.

'Yes, thank you,' Emme smiled.

'Right, kids, go in front of me now, but not too far ahead,' Tristan commanded, as he guided them down two blue slopes and three nerve-wracking reds, until they got back to town.

'Oh, no ski train?' Emme asked, confused, when they reached the village.

'The ski train is long closed. We had to ski all the way back to Kristalldorf.'

'What, they don't wait for everyone?'

'No, Little Miss London, the last train is the last train. Then it's on you to get down. Or me,' he joked, softening.

Emme realised how catastrophic it could have been.

Her phone rang.

'Shit, it's Lexy,' Emme said, hurrying to answer it.

Tristan smirked a little, again ruffling Emme. This wasn't funny.

'Everything alright?' Lexy asked.

'Yes, yes, we had such fun at ski school, we're still in town, but just heading back to the apartment now.'

'Oh great, I worried they'd skied off to Italy or something.'

'No no, we're just heading back now.'

'Great. KristallKit is being delivered at five pm, so make sure you're home then. I'll be back shortly after.'

'Wonderful, see you there,' Emme said, panicking a little. She would have to hurry.

*

Tristan took off his boots and put on a pair of Zegna lo-tops he'd stashed in his small backpack, while Emme and the kids trudged to the locker. Tristan walked over, boots slung round his neck, skis and poles on his broad shoulders.

'I've gotta go, but ski safely on the mountain next time, right?'

Emme nodded knowingly, and swallowed her pride. She knew she needed to get some ski lessons, fast.

'Thank you. You totally bailed me out. Twice.'

Tristan turned to the kids. 'Watch out for that one, yah?' he said, thumbing Emme. 'She's trouble!' He looked back to Emme and winked.

Is he flirting?

Bella giggled.

Then Tristan leaned in to Emme and lowered his voice a little.

'Hey, if you want to catch up some time, I know you like hanging out around my apartment.'

Emme inhaled quickly. Shock, outrage and embarrassment all rolled into one.

'Knock on the door and join us next time.' He smiled a knowing smile which screamed mischief.

In one fell swoop he'd ruined it all. Emme was mortified.

'I do *not* want to be in your throuple, thank you very much,' Emme hissed, under her breath. Tristan favoured her with a lingering look.

'Hey, your loss,' he smiled. 'And you're welcome,' he added, as he walked away without turning back.

Chapter Thirty-Four

By the end of Emme's first week in Kristalldorf, she was becoming familiar with the kids' routine and getting used to her new role, yet tired enough that Bill returning from the city for the weekend felt like having a little respite. Lexy had told Emme that she might not be called upon as much at weekends while the family caught up, although she had offered to take the children to a screening of *The Polar Express* at The Grand Hotel Sommar and Harry had almost seemed to like her when she said he could have sweet *and* salty popcorn mixed together. She'd made a friend in Cassie after they went for a coffee after drop-off and another on Sunday morning, and they had graduated to friendly WhatsApps. And she had deliberately not walked past Tristan Du Kok's balcony again.

On Sunday night, after everyone had gone to bed, Emme googled Tristan Du Kok but found nothing, apart from a few Instagram and LinkedIn profiles of men who clearly weren't him and a page about Du Kok Estate wines, with a contact number in Stellenbosch but no photo of the man himself.

Work had been so busy for everyone now that the season was getting started that Emme hadn't had a chance to social-ise with either Cat or Tiago since that first weekend. But on the Wednesday of Emme's second week in Kristalldorf, when Lumi and Mika Kivvi had decided to eat out at the local pizzeria, Cat messaged Emme to ask if she fancied impromptu drinks.

'Mind if I pop out for an hour or two?' Emme asked Lexy, as she sat looking at her laptop. Lexy stopped to think, and concluded that as she didn't want to go out and the children were already asleep, that would be fine.

'Of course!' she said, as if it had come naturally to her.

'Thanks,' Emme replied, feeling weird having to ask permission to go out at twenty-eight when she had lived mostly by herself, in a flat she owned, since she was twenty-two, but such was the job she had sought out.

Emme grabbed her coat and put on a slick of make-up, just in case. Then headed to Down Mexico Way to meet Cat.

'Are they here every night?' she asked, as they walked past The Cheeky Blinders and slunk into a booth on the edge of the dancefloor, opposite the band.

'They rotate with a few other bands, Deja Groove and the Clone Tones – a few solo guitar players/singers. Will sometimes does solo nights. But they all play the same four or five venues. There's music every night of the season.'

The season. Emme wondered what Kristalldorf might be like in summer.

'What are you having? It's my round . . . I think.'

The last time they were out, in the basement club with Tiago and the band, Cat had got a round in just before she took a call and took off.

Emme was relieved to remove her hideous coat: underneath it she was wearing a royal blue jersey top with pouffed ruched sleeves, light denim jeans, and patent black platform brogues. It was the smartest outfit she'd packed.

'G&T please, *amorcita*,' Cat replied, checking her phone.

Emme grabbed her purse just as Tristan Du Kok walked in with a group of associates. He was wearing a pale shirt with the sleeves rolled up and a cashmere jumper slung over his shoulders, charcoal chinos and the same cream Zegna trainers he'd put on at the end of their skiing session last week. He looked sharp yet casual. Emme's heart raced and she slumped straight back down. Although she wanted to meet Tristan's trajectory, she needed to get her head together first.

'What's up?' asked Cat, looking between Emme and Tristan. They watched the group settle, standing at a high table near the bar, as Tristan beckoned Johann from behind the bar for table service. That's how high rollers rolled.

'Oh, nothing . . .' Emme said, unconvincingly.

Tristan ordered for the group and glanced up, seeing Emme and Cat at their table.

'Urgh,' Emme protested.

'What?!' Cat said, hitting her on the arm.

Tristan swaggered over, his hands in his trouser pockets, a knowing smile at the corner of his lips.

'Have you recovered?' he asked Emme with a smouldering grin.

Cat looked between the two of them.

'Recovered from what?!' she said, an eyebrow raised. There was not much that went on in Kristalldorf without Catalina Sosa knowing about it. Her inky eyes widened. 'You two have met then?'

Emme blushed. Tristan cleared his throat into a balled fist.

'Oh, erm, I had a little mishap on the mountain last week.' Emme blustered. 'Tristan went down on – with – he went down with me. Had to get me and the kids back to town.' Emme was so flustered, she was only making things worse for herself.

'Oh, did you?' Cat said, looking at Tristan with a sparkle in her eye.

'I did,' he said with a self-satisfied smile. He turned to Emme. 'Have you had any lessons yet?'

'Actually, I have,' Emme said proudly. She'd eventually located Jenny's skis and boots and by happy happenstance they fitted. Only yesterday, while the kids were at school, Emme had a lesson, and it was a good first attempt.

'Cedric?' Tristan asked, with a raised eyebrow.

'God, not Cedric!' laughed Cat. 'What a disaster! Did you see him that night? He was fucking Sandrine round the back of the Silber Stube, I was surprised he could get it up.'

Emme and Tristan looked at each other and winced, Cat detecting their shared familiarity.

'Not Cedric,' Emme said. 'Milla.'

'Oh, Milla's great,' Tristan said appreciatively, and Emme couldn't help but bristle. Was he sleeping with her too?

'Who are your friends?' Cat asked, Emme feeling relief to shift the focus from her pitiful skiing ability.

'Oh I'm showing some wine buyers around town, on a sampling trip. Easier and more central to fly them here than to Cape Town.'

'Nice,' Cat said.

'You girls should come on over, say hi,' Tristan said before turning on his heel. 'Better get back to them.' He saluted and walked away.

'"You girls"?!' Cat mimicked. 'Please! How offensive.' She turned to Emme, waiting for her to concur, but she looked flustered and flushed, which made Cat double-take.

'Seriously, "girl", forget about him.'

'What?'

They watched the barman settle two bottles of Dom Perignon and a round of glasses on Tristan's table, before Tristan nodded for him to deliver a third to Emme and Cat.

'He is a notorious playboy, actually a fuckboy. A messed-up one at that.'

The barman approached with a tray.

'Bottle from TDK for you two,' he said, with a wry smile.

'Oh, we couldn't possibly,' said Emme.

'Thanks,' Cat cut in, already pouring it. 'Come on, *cin cin*!' she said enthusiastically, corralling her into raising their glasses to Tristan: a shy smile from Emme; a sarcastic one from Cat. He looked back and nodded.

Emme took a sip and placed her glass down thoughtfully.

'What do you mean, "messed up"?' she asked.

'You don't know?'

Emme stared at Cat with an 'obviously I don't' look on her face.

'About Tristan's dad?'

Emme shook her head as she observed Tristan and his group. There were three men and one woman, all dressed for business, not après-ski, and they seemed to hang on Tristan's every word.

'Charles Joubert – Tristan's dad – caused loads of mayhem, even before he arrived in town. He won a hotel from Walter Steinherr at the blackjack table in Monte

Carlo – you know Vitreum? The most incredible hotel in town? On the hill?'

Emme had seen a hotel, shimmering and seemingly unreachable above town.

'Then he came to town to gloat and take over the hotel, with Tristan. Seven or eight years ago . . .'

Eight, Emme remembered from the mountain. Cat continued.

'They spent a few months ski touring. Pissing people off in town. Walter tried to buy Vitreum back, it was obvious Joubert knew nothing about hospitality. Made him a real nice offer, but he insisted on running that hotel, and running it badly.'

'Then one day, Charles Joubert went missing. Tristan was the last person to see him, over by the Teufelsgletscher. He says he heard him fall down a ravine, but he didn't see it. It was all over the news.'

'Shit!' Now the mournful glaze in his eyes made sense.

'I mean, people go missing in the mountains. There are avalanches, or skiers get lost and show up days later. But when someone is worth five billion dollars and they're out skiing on the ravine with their son, and they disappear without a trace . . .'

Cat seemed to relish the sharing of this story, but something about it felt uncomfortable to Emme as she watched Tristan deep in conversation. This was his dad Cat was talking about.

'Tristan "cooperated" with the police,' she said making air quotes. 'Showing search and rescue where he last saw him. Getting his own team of ski tourers out there. But nothing. No trace except for Daddy's jacket, hanging on a rock.'

'Shit.'

'Tristan did a good job getting Vitreum back on track, but when a court declared his dad dead three years later, Tristan decided to sell it – to Alexey Stognev, not Walter Steinherr – and start importing his mother's wine over here.'

'Did they ever find a body?'

'Nope. But the rate global warming is going, I reckon he'll show up. As the glacier retreats, more than ski poles are being discovered. I reckon that's why Tristan's hanging around. It's not like he needs the money from wine sales.'

'Oh no. Poor guy.'

'Poor guy? Poor little rich guy. Some say he *pushed* Daddy into the ravine – he was a bum until then, like Caspian Steinherr, surfing and skiing his way around the world, trying to pretend they weren't who they were. But, you know, that rumour seems a bit crude.'

'Shit . . .'

'Tristan Joubert changed his name because of the press intrusion – to the name of his mother's family wine empire – probably worth another five billion. Watch your back, Mama!'

Emme scowled.

'That's horrid Cat!'

'I'm just kidding. He's made good on it. He sells a shit-load of bottles. He made Du Kok Estate one of the most prestigious brands here – and look at the wines we have on our doorstep! The French and Italians don't like him much. His mother visits once a year.'

Emme shook her head.

'Wow, five billion dollars . . .' she thought about Tristan's apartment building. Pretty expensive, she imagined, but not billionaire fancy, like the Anna Maria or the fairy-tale mansion opposite it on the other side of the river. Maybe Tristan the surfer bum was still there; maybe he liked to slum it a little. Maybe he wanted to hide his wealth – or how he came about it.

'Seriously. He's sexy, but he knows it. And he is toxic. Avoid him like the plague, *nena*.'

'Anastasia Steinherr already knows all this then, I guess . . .' Emme mused.

Cat's champagne went down the wrong way and she coughed into her glass.

'Are you OK?' Emme asked, patting Cat on the back.

Cat put her drink down and tried to regain her composure.

'Anastasia? You know her?'

'Yes, I saw her, half naked, running out onto Tristan's balcony when another woman turned up. Then pashing with him before climbing off.'

Cat frowned.

'You did? When?'

'Like, the Saturday before last. It was my first day here. Anastasia Steinherr, looks like Cindy C, right? I saw her in the Steinherrhof a few days later, being a bit of a bitch if you ask me.'

'Right . . .'

The colour drained from Cat's face as she shook her head.

'You said Tristan was dating a Steinherr sister?' Emme was confused.

At that moment the tall blonde with the rosebud breasts, the blonde from the balcony, the blonde from the sun-drenched café terrace, walked into the bar and straight towards Tristan, kissing him warmly on the lips before greeting his associates.

Now Emme felt ashen-faced as a surge of envy rose through her body, as she watched Tristan put his palm on the small of the woman's back.

'That's the Steinherr sister I *thought* he was dating,' Cat said, with an anger that took Emme by surprise. 'That's his girlfriend Vivian.'

Chapter Thirty-Five

Lysander Steinherr sat at the desk in his expansive corner office at Manhattan's most prestigious law firm, and looked out at the traffic on 8th Avenue. Taxis. Buses. Couriers.

'What have you got for me?' he asked, with intrigue, down the phone. There hadn't been a manila envelope waiting on his desk, as he'd expected. In fact, Rico had been unusually slow in getting back to him on this. It had been nearly two weeks.

'That's the thing, boss. She's clean as a whistle.'

'Really?' Lysander rubbed his smooth chin and looked at the family photo of him with his wife and son on the desk. Megan was clean as a whistle. She wore white dresses to the polo and had an all-American-girl smile. Blake was tanned with dirty-blond hair and a toothy grin. The three of them looked like they'd popped out of a Ralph Lauren ad. But Kiki?

'I spoke to her former boss at the resort in Vegas. Accurate, professional, she had outstanding guest services . . . An exceptional employee, they said.'

Lysander remembered a comment his father made, when he got back from Vegas, Kiki now his wife: when his children protested at the shock news of their nuptials, he'd said his new wife was highly respected in Vegas, as well as Monte Carlo, and they would extend that respect to her in Kristalldorf too.

'Shit,' Lysander said. 'What about Atlantic City?'

'They couldn't remember her that well, so I did a historical dig into HR: never late. Never sick. A highly reliable croupier by all accounts. I spoke to a roommate from around that time. No dirt.'

'And before then? She must have started earning before she was twenty-one . . .' Lysander said, suspicious. Surely a woman that seductive knew her currency from a young age.

'Good at school. Decent grades. Favourable yearbook reports, if nothing spectacular. She worked at a farm shop in Cherry Hill out of school. She was Miss Hoboken 2007. Honestly, boss, I can't find nuthin'. Dad is a mechanic, mom is French – it's how she works in Europe – and she works the cash register in a pharmacy . . . I mean obviously she married up, but there ain't no dirt on her.'

'Dammit.'

Lysander clicked his Cartier pen frantically and frowned. Surely there had to be something?

'I mean, I'll keep lookin', boss, but I can't find something if it ain't there.'

'OK thanks, Rico, appreciate it.'

Lysander hung up and looked out of the window. He was too good an attorney and too honest a man to fabricate anything. Maybe his dad would just have to pay off another wife.

Chapter Thirty-Six

On Emme's third weekend in Kristalldorf, the Harringtons asked if she'd like to spend the Saturday on the slopes with them.

'We're going to Monte Rosa, we might even ski into Italy today, what do you think, Bill?'

He looked up from his newspaper and rubbed his eyes.

'Yes dear.'

'What do you think Emme?'

Emme wasn't convinced Lexy wasn't asking her for the childcare.

'You know what, I won't thank you,' Emme said, graciously. 'Unless you need me?'

'No, you're fine,' Lexy said primly.

'I need to make some calls home, I might go for a swim.' She didn't want to spend a potential day off with her wittering boss. Plus she wasn't ready to ski in front of the family yet. She'd had two lessons with Milla now and her turns were still pitiful.

'I might check out a spa.'

'Oh, the one at the Steinherrhof is wonderful! Sooo relaxing,' Lexy cooed.

Emme didn't say she'd already been.

'Great, thank you.'

*

As Emme weaved through town, she wondered if she might like skiing more if she had some better gear. It would be foolish to wait until February to buy ski clothes, and she wanted to finally get out of her sister's garish hand-me-down coat. It was just too embarrassing.

Emme bypassed the Bogner boutique on account of it having a velvet rope across the open doorway, and went into an equally exclusive but ever-so-slightly more welcoming boutique that sold a mixture of brands. If she was going to finally buy a ski jacket and trousers, they needed to be nice enough to feel good in, but not break the bank. Emme chose gloves to replace her woollen mittens and a decent enough helmet which she knew she could have bought at Decathlon for a fraction of the price back home, but a helmet was no good to her at home, and she needed one now. *Fuck it*, she thought, as she picked up a lilac Goldbergh two-piece and tried the jacket and salopettes on, just for fun.

A shop assistant with voluptuous lips and poker-straight hair admired Emme in the mirror of a rather open changing room area.

'It's stunning with your colouring,' she said.

'Thanks,' Emme mused, admiring herself in the mirror. The lilac did suit her golden-peach skin tone. She dared to dream, before carefully peeling off the jacket. She handed it to the assistant and stepped out of the salopettes as she wondered what cheaper suits the store might have.

'And of course the jacket can be worn around town, not just on the slopes,' the assistant said.

Emme was tempted, but they were so expensive. She was just handing the salopettes to the assistant when someone made her jump.

'Suits you,' said a familiar voice from the shop counter. Tristan again.

'Christ!'

She thought she was the only customer in the boutique, and now she was standing in just the caramel-coloured base layers that hugged every curve and contour of her body tightly. She felt exposed and awkward and put her forearms across her breasts to try to conceal herself.

Tristan was tacit in his admiration, throwing her a *don't on my account* glance.

The shop assistant looked over, delighted.

'Tristan!' she said in a singsong voice, holding the lilac ski suit over her arm as she went to kiss him on each cheek.

'Muffie, how are you?'

'All the better for seeing you . . .' she said.

This was the guy who slept with his own girlfriend's married sister, as Cat had explained to Emme. She wanted to hate him, but he was just so bloody dazzling; his smile so warm and sexy, she felt so seen under his appreciative gaze, that her shoulders dropped and she felt instantaneously relaxed.

'What can I do for you, Tris?' the assistant asked, coquettishly.

'I need four helmets please, Muffs, I'm taking my wine buyers skiing – and of course they came to the mountains without any gear . . . nor any idea for that matter . . .' he winked at Emme. And she felt it to her core.

'Of course, what sizes?'

Tristan pondered his group.

'I'd go one XL, two L and one small please. Actually make the small helmet special; she's from New York and it'll be a nice touch.'

Muffie picked up a white Louis Vuitton helmet with matte white embossed flower motifs and interlocking LV logos on the front, which Emme had been eyeing. At 2,000 Swiss francs, she'd chosen an Oakley one instead.

'Is this good?' Muffie asked.

Tristan took the helmet and stroked it, impressed. He rubbed his thumb over its smooth shiny surface.

'Would you wear this one, Emme?' he asked, proffering it.

'Hmm . . .' Emme replied.

He swaggered over to her, helmet in hand, so she could see it up close.

Emme caught the twinkle in his eye, and something about the way he approached her, the way his eyes fell on her pert breasts, gave her a thrill. He was a player, but maybe she could play him too. She was still aware that she was in her caramel SKIMS, which made her look practically naked.

'It's pretty cool, yeah,' Emme said casually, eyeing it, while Tristan couldn't take his eyes off her.

Tristan broke the tension to glance back to the till.

'Great, I'll take three of the black Monclers for the men and the white Vuitton in small.'

'Very good,' Muffie said, as she started to gather the stock. 'I just have to go to the basement for the XL. Don't go anywhere!' she joked.

'I won't.'

Tristan looked back at Emme. Cocksure and flirtatious. She met his gaze and rose on the balls of her feet clad in ski socks.

'You know,' he said, slowly. 'On the mountain . . .'

'Yes?' Emme lifted her chin. The atmosphere between

them was electric. She had never felt so mischievous. She had never felt so turned on.

'You know how I wish it really ended?' He edged closer.

'Tell me . . .' Emme arched her body towards his as Tristan put the Vuitton helmet down on the chair and placed his hand on Emme's hip. Stroking the contour of her arse, he then drew a circle on Emme's stomach before sliding his hand into the waistband of her SKIMS. She couldn't believe how much she wanted him. How little she cared that anyone might see through the shop window, or come in through the door. She inhaled quietly and ecstatically, letting out a gentle moan as she felt Tristan's finger press her pulsating pussy; Emme felt her heart racing out of her chest.

'Here you are!' Muffie said with blithe obliviousness as Emme and Tristan quickly pulled apart. 'One extra-large helmet.'

'Wonderful, you're an angel,' Tristan said sincerely, returning to the counter.

Emme pulled her clothes off the chair, put them on as quickly as she could, and brought the gloves and helmet to the till. She knew the Goldbergh coat and salopettes were beyond her budget.

Tristan opened his wallet and took out his gold card. 'And whatever the lady is buying,' he said, gesturing to the lilac two-piece Muffie had placed on the counter.

Emme gasped, already flushed pink.

'No really, I couldn't.'

'Yes, you could. I insist. That Louis Vuitton helmet would look gorgeous on you too.'

'I can't, it's too much.'

'Really, it's nothing, it would be my pleasure,' Tristan

said with a shrug, piercing Emme with the intensity of his gold-brown eyes.

Why me?

She wanted to hate him for being such a playboy, for not being Tom, but Tristan's touch had been so exquisite, she was lost for words.

'Really,' he said again with such assurance Emme knew protesting was pointless.

'Well . . . thank you,' she said, equal parts grateful and embarrassed. Tristan handed his card over to Muffie, who rang it all through while Tristan and Emme fucked each other with their eyes.

'All of it?' Muffie asked, a slight huffiness in her voice.

'Yes,' Tristan answered, still favouring Emme with a penetrating look. She couldn't take her eyes off him either, the strength of his gravitational pull more powerful than a lifetime of crushes rolled into one. The sensation of his touch still lingering between her legs.

Tristan broke first when the card terminal beeped.

'It needs your face ID,' said Muffie.

Tristan obliged.

'Can you have my guests' helmets sent to the Anna Maria please, Muffs? I need to meet a business associate at Vitreum.'

'Of course,' she said efficiently, as she wrapped Emme's goods in tissue paper. Her flirty tone had turned to something a little more put out by being the third wheel in this transaction, but still, TDK was spending a small fortune in her store. She had to be polite.

'Thank you,' Emme said, with a grateful nod. 'It really is too much.'

'No problem,' Tristan said with a warm wink. 'Call it a welcome to town gift,' he added, flashing that come-to-bed smile of his. He put his wallet away. 'Have a good day!' he said, as he saluted the women and left them both utterly undone.

Chapter Thirty-Seven

Later that evening, Vivian Steinherr was talking to her restaurant manager, Henrik, on a sofa by the fireplace when she saw Tristan walk through the Anna Maria entrance and approach the front desk. A small thrill lifted her fatigue after a long day, but fell again when she realised he had seen her, but chosen to pretend he hadn't. He'd been evasive all week, cancelling a dinner date on Vivian's day off on Monday, and on Wednesday when she'd joined him and his wine buyers in Down Mexico Way, she'd felt a shift. He was polite and nurturing in front of the group, who were all staying at Vivian's hotel, but when they were alone back in Tristan's apartment, they hadn't even made love.

'Excuse me for a minute will you, Henrik,' Vivian said.

'Of course, I'll be in the restaurant if you need me,' he replied, as they both got up.

Vivian walked over to the front desk in her delicate cream sweater, navy trouser suit and Gucci loafers. Her wardrobe was more understated than her sister's: Victoria Beckham or Isabel Marant tailoring by day; Tom Ford and YSL for evening. Clothes hung from Vivian beautifully, although she hid her figure more than she should. Around her neck she always wore a delicate Bucherer necklace: a gold cross set with a single diamond that had been her mother's. It sat on her decolletage beautifully.

'*Grüezi!*' she greeted Tristan eagerly. She waited for him to kiss her but he didn't. 'Is no one seeing to you?' She was one part annoyed that the desk had been left unattended; two parts happy to see him alone. She wanted to hug him, to wrap her arms around him. For her legs and hips to be locked around his again. But something about him was unsettling her tonight – it had unsettled her all week – as he rubbed his left hand through his hair and almost leaned back from his position, resting his right forearm on the front desk.

'Hey,' he said, smiling, businesslike. 'I'm just checking some ski helmets were delivered here, to my group.'

'Oh I don't know, I'll have someone check.' Vivian leaned against the desk on her left arm, unwittingly mirroring Tristan. She touched his hand lightly, then backed off.

'You OK?'

'Yeah, I've just been meeting an associate.'

Vivian didn't like it when Tristan was vague. They both knew everyone in this town, so if he said 'associate', it would only arouse her suspicions. 'Associate' sounded like a fob-off. Vivian didn't like being fobbed off. She still couldn't get the sound out of her head from a few weeks ago, when she dropped in on Tristan's town centre apartment one Saturday morning. She could hear music. She could hear laughing. She could hear moaning, she was sure of it. Vivian was nice but she wasn't a walkover.

'Which associate?' she asked forthrightly.

'Stognev. Up at Vitreum,' Tristan said, defensively.

It irked Vivian that he hadn't taken her to Vitreum. Her father had built that hotel before losing it to Tristan's father in a card game. The least he could do was take her up there, make her feel welcome. Why was he holding back? Why was he keeping her at arm's length? She knew Tristan wasn't always the cocksure man he appeared to be. The first time they had finally made love after years of longing, in the penthouse of the Anna Maria one sultry night, he had said something about not being good enough for her. At first Vivian thought it flattery, but as she dwelled on it during quieter times in her office, or by the fire at the Steinherr mansion, she did wonder if Tristan had imposter syndrome. He was from new money, and relatively new in town compared with the Steinherrs, Sommars or Herwegs of the world. He was under immense pressure to make a name from his mother's vineyard, rather than be shackled to his father's disastrous foray into hospitality with Vitreum, or the question marks around his disappearance. It made Vivian cut him some slack when he had been evasive in recent weeks, but now it was starting to smart.

'Oh right,' Vivian said, knowingly. 'Haven't seen him around town for a while.'

'He's been in the UAE.'

Vivian didn't want to talk about Alexey Stognev; she didn't like that Tristan was the only person in town who didn't mind doing business with the man. He was the least agreeable of all the hotel owners, and she suspected, like many, that Vitreum was a front for his more nefarious revenue streams. Vivian tried to forget that Tristan had sold her father's beloved Vitreum to Stognev and not back to the family. She wanted to forget business altogether. She wanted to drink Pinotage with Tristan and talk about their days. To be naked with him again. It had been over a week since they'd made each other come. Another factor to incite her suspicions.

'Hey, do you want to grab some dinner tonight? Fabrice is starting his shift soon, he can cover things here for a couple of hours.'

Vivian trusted Fabrice far more with the hotel than she did Anastasia, who hadn't set foot in the Anna Maria since Vivian rehired Michael the sommelier with a grovelling apology and a 5,000-franc bonus for his stress.

Vivian looked around, still agitated that no one had come to reception, so she rang the bell sharply.

'Er . . .' Tristan hesitated.

The Anna Maria's day manager hurried from out the back.

'Nora, where have you been? Mr Du Kok has been waiting for too long – he's wondering if you took a delivery of ski helmets?'

'Yes, I took delivery myself, about an hour ago. Concierge then delivered them to the correct rooms.'

'Great, thank you,' Tristan said.

Vivian noted that Tristan was speaking to the day manager in the same businesslike tone he was using with her.

Tristan ran his finger on the shiny surface of the front desk in circles, seeming to be doing anything he could to avoid looking at Vivian.

What is wrong?

'What do you say?' she said breezily. 'We could go to 1865? The new chef from Peru is meant to be *incredible*.'

Tristan gave Vivian a grave look.

'I have to take the group out for dinner, and actually I was going to take them to 1865.'

'I could join you?' Vivian said, trying not to sound too desperate, her wide blue eyes losing hope with every second.

Nora shuffled some papers.

'Hey, can we have a chat, in your office?' Tristan asked.

Vivian's gaze turned steely as the penny dropped. He was about to dump her. And it was not going to happen in her office, behind closed doors, where she would have to sit and pick up the pieces working alone late into the night. The least he could do was have the courage to own it.

'Let's go to the bar,' she said, and strode off ahead, grateful that there were enough people there, enough background noise and music, for her to be dumped unnoticed; for her to keep her cool. In public, Vivian was very good at putting on a brave face. She had had to all her life.

She stopped at a high table by the vast window and didn't even bother sitting on the stool. If they were going to do this, they could do it like one of the stand-up meetings she favoured. Fast and efficient.

Still, a part of her hoped she'd read it wrong.

'What's up?' she asked, coolly. Tristan looked at her, his eyes pained.

'Viv, look, I, er . . . I think it's best we . . .'

'Oh please!' she scoffed. 'So predictable. Who is she?'

'What?'

'Meeting "Stognev" up at Vitreum? Sure.'

'I was! He was asking my advice about the heliport thing . . .'

'Oh please! Then why didn't you say?'

Tristan shrugged.

Her patience for the sad boy who lost his daddy down a ravine had worn thin. If she listened to her heart, she already knew he was going to break it. She had pursued Tristan Du Kok for years: in friendship she had listened to his stories about his father, about their sometimes difficult relationship, and about how much he missed him. She in turn had confided her dreams of taking the Steinherr name beyond Kristalldorf, beyond Switzerland. She had told him of her desire to have a family and be the mother she didn't remember having. As they progressed to friends with benefits, she clung to the audacious hope that the motherless woman and the fatherless man might beat the odds given his reputation and be something more. But he hadn't even had the manners to come to her father's birthday dinner.

'You're so full of shit!' she gasped, as quietly as she could. 'I know there was someone in your apartment that day.'

'No!' Tristan lied, so convincingly he almost believed it himself.

'At least if you're dumping me for her, have the decency to tell me who she is.'

'No, I just think . . . you're an *incredible –*'

'*Unglaublich,*' she said, shaking her head in disbelief. 'Do I mean nothing to you?' She looked at him. Didn't he *feel* it, how incredible it was when they were making love?

Tristan looked uncharacteristically pallid.

'Viv, you mean *the world* to me . . .'

'Oh please!' she scoffed.

A waiter came over with a tray.

'No thank you,' Vivian said, before he even had a chance to open his mouth. He swiftly walked away.

'You do. Which is why I think it's best we're friends.'

Tristan looked resolute, and Vivian fought back tears.

'I swear Vivian, you're the smartest, most beautiful woman in the world. But you're my friend. You have been since I arrived in town. When everyone was pointing fingers at me, you didn't, and I treasure you too much because of it.' He swallowed so hard his Adam's apple bobbed. 'And if we keeping doing this,' he waved his finger between the two of them, 'I will keep hurting you. I don't want to hurt you.'

She shook her head and looked out of the window, to the Glanzfluss, to the fairy-tale mansion on the other side of it, in which she felt so lonely.

She looked back at Tristan. Tall, so handsome, so sexy. Why did he make her feel like she wasn't enough for him?

'Go fuck yourself,' she said quietly and angrily, as she walked away. She had a hotel to run.

Tristan stood at the table on his own, his hands in his pockets. He was glad not to have seen Vivian's crying face. Her crying face usually undid him. Her anger he could take. But he had no choice. He could not stop thinking about the English woman in her caramel-coloured underwear. Her pert breasts and silky clitoris. Her inquisitive eyes and no-nonsense normality. She reminded him of the girls he dated before his name was notorious. When he could surf or ski around the world in anonymity. She was finally giving him a conscience. Making him want to come clean. And he couldn't treat Vivian Steinherr the way he had been for a second longer.

'Are you early or am I late?' asked Shivam Masrani, one of Tristan's party of wine buyers, as he strolled into the hotel bar, hands in his pockets, hair slicked back on this thick head. Tristan tried to unscramble his thoughts and put on his best smile.

Chapter Thirty-Eight

Walter sat at the large executive desk in his office, whisky in hand, ruminating on succession. The grandfather clock belonging to his own grandfather Ernst ticked melodically in the corner of his capacious study, an acute reminder that he was on borrowed time. The mansion was quiet. He didn't know where Anastasia or Dimitri were, but imagined they probably weren't together. Vivian was at the Anna Maria. Kiki had gone to Lapland, taking a group of children with cancer to meet Father Christmas.

'Wouldn't that be better in December?' Walter had asked.

'Some of them might not make it to Christmas, Walter,' Kiki had said with a levelling look. Walter conceded, although he was still a little sore. He wanted out, but he had pride. He hadn't married Kiki so she could swan off here, there and everywhere. He had wanted a wife to take care of him in his old age, and she had at first. But her shopping trips and treatments and altruistic trips with sick children soon took priority over her husband, although she wasn't to know he had cancer too.

Which reminded him. The issue of an heir. Lysander had ruled himself out and suggested Vivian. Caspian seemed so hellbent on shunning the business his ancestors had built, affording him a life of travel and surfing, that he was out too. But what about Anastasia? He had to consider her, and she had experienced more facets of the business than any of his children. But she had never stuck at any of them. He had thought that gifting the Anna Maria to both daughters would show Anastasia the work ethic and staying power that this business took, if she were to work with Vivian up close. Perhaps she was more like Caspian than any of them had realised. A drifter.

But Anastasia's biggest currency was her beauty. Both his daughters were beautiful of course, but Anastasia was classically so: glossy, symmetrical and sumptuous in her style. Perhaps she could be the figurehead of the Steinherr portfolio, representing the business on the world stage, if the girls did decide to spread their wings, while Vivian kept everything running.

Who was Walter kidding? With that solution, both daughters would feel hard done by.

He swirled the ice cubes in his cut-glass tumbler of Scotch, but the dilemma only made him feel sad. He didn't want to feel sad. Time was short and pleasures were few. Exhaling a gruff sigh, Walter opened a side drawer of his desk and took out a Cartier box. He placed it on the dark-green leather surface of the desk and opened it. In it sat a white-gold, emerald and diamond panther bracelet. It was a little ostentatious for Lumi's classic style but he was feeling impulsive, and he suspected she would love it if she knew it were from him.

Walter rang the bell for his butler, who was at the study door within seconds.

'Yes sir?'

'Arrange delivery of this please. To Lumi Kivvi at Chalet Edelweiss.'

'Certainly sir. Any card to go with it?'

'No, that's all.'

It was an audacious move, but Walter was feeling more and more reckless by the day.

Chapter Thirty-Nine

There were two *apotheke* pharmacies in Kristalldorf, which rotated late-night opening during the ski season, to cater for all the tourists' blister, pain relief and knee-support needs.

Emme had made it to the Leben *apotheke* in the centre of the village by the skin of her teeth before the kindly pharmacist switched off the lights at 10.05pm. Lexy Harrington had had a crisis when she realised her favoured skin moisturiser had run out, just as she was taking off her make-up.

'You can use some of mine?' Emme said, proffering her moisturiser. The kids were in bed and Bill was watching a Jack Reacher movie. Lexy frowned. There was clearly no way she would put Clinique on her porcelain skin.

'Would you be a doll and pop to the pharmacy? They stock Dr Levy serum there . . .' Lexy fawned, her own face taking on the appearance of a sweet, porcelain doll. Lexy was in her bath robe, white towel wrapped in a turban on her head, having spent the evening trying to cling onto her youth.

Emme jumped at the chance. The kids were asleep, the chalet felt claustrophobic, and she hadn't been able to stop thinking about Tristan's exhilarating touch in the boutique earlier. She needed the air. So Emme found herself picking up Lexy's 230-franc tube of Dr Levy moisturiser in the nick of time.

Emme was about to head back to the apartment when she thought *fuck it* and decided to extend her walk a little. Make Lexy wait. Emme needed to walk and mull over just how *right* that had felt in the clothes store, when she knew he was so wrong. So she pocketed the skin serum and wound through a backstreet and down a tiny alley whose wooden-beamed huts and small stone houses almost touched overhead. The street was shrouded in darkness and silence, except for distant music coming from a nearby bar.

A couple walked past, wrapped up and giddy, and the man reminded her of Tom. She considered Tom, and how it hadn't been him she was yearning for in the boutique this afternoon. The woman smiled at Emme as she rested her head on her partner's shoulder. Emme smiled back as the couple passed.

The silhouette of another figure appeared at the top of the alleyway, backlit by the lamps of a busier street behind him. A long shadow approached and the figure edged into a locked hut's doorway to make way for Emme. It was only as they were almost side by side, strangers in the dark trying to avoid touching, that she realised the man was Tristan.

'Oh.' Emme said, stopping in her tracks and relaxing a little. 'It's you.'

Tristan narrowed his eyes to focus.

'Hey,' he said, softly but assuredly.

Their bodies were close; encased by the cobbled street and its buildings. The air was crisp and cold, carrying the faint scent of pine, snow and Tristan's musky fragrance. He was wearing his grey down jacket and a scarf; he carried his gloves, as if he were just about to put them on. He looked stunningly sexy.

Emme felt a jolt ripple through her body. She gazed into his eyes, caught in a slice of moonlight.

'What was that about earlier?' she asked with a smile, but something about Tristan looked haunted and her eyebrows knitted into a frown that mirrored his. 'Everything OK?'

'Yeah, yeah, busy night,' he said, pointing his thumb over his shoulder behind him. 'Just dropped my buyers back after dinner.'

Emme pictured him at dinner, enchanting his wine buyers, wondering if he'd lingered on their encounter in the boutique. She hadn't been able to get it out of her head.

'What about you? What are you up to?' Tristan asked, warmly.

'Just running an errand for Lexy,' Emme smiled, silently acknowledging how demanding her boss was. Tristan recognised it in all Emme didn't say.

'Yeah, she used to make me run errands for her.'

Emme was surprised.

'Really?'

'Yeah, like I said, she used to boss me around when I was a kid.' He rolled his eyes. 'On holidays in Africa.'

Emme still couldn't imagine their families being entwined. Or Tristan doing anyone's bidding. She took the serum out of her pocket and waved it.

'Well, I got her face cream, so now she can get her beauty sleep.' Emme said it wearily. She didn't want to talk about Lexy. She had been gifted a chance encounter with this sexy – conflicting – man who made her feel a million things all at once.

They locked eyes until Emme broke the beat.

'You know, you didn't need to buy me that stuff,' she said, wondering if it was a little problematic. This was not *Pretty Woman* and she was no one's whore. But god, she fancied Tristan, shrouded in the shadows.

'I know,' he said, gloves in his left hand, as he pushed his hair back with his right.

'But I wanted to.' He shrugged and smiled. 'And you wear it well.'

The night was thick with anticipation as Emme and Tristan found themselves edging closer, the moon drawing them together like the tide being pulled to the shore.

He looked at Emme, and she felt the pent-up passion of his gaze.

'I want you,' he leaned in and said, breathily and blatantly.

She smiled. She *felt* it, although she wasn't sure why he wanted her.

She arced her body as he met her with his, almost proffering her neck. Tristan took the cue and kissed it, pressing his full lips from her collarbone up to her jaw.

Emme let out a hopeless breath. She didn't want to be another conquest but her legs were trembling, that delicious wetness from earlier rising inside her again, until she turned to face to him and he cupped her cheekbones with his hands.

Fuck it.

Emme rose on the balls of her feet and their breath mingled, then their lips, then their tongues.

His kiss was as gentle as it was passionate, their bodies pressing together feverishly as their embrace got faster and more frenzied. Their hands drew to each other's hair; Emme felt Tristan's hardness in her abdomen as the world beyond the backstreet faded into oblivion as if they were the only two people on the planet.

Emme broke for air and let out a groan as Tristan went back to her neck, now ravaging it as he pushed her into the wooden doorway and his hard-on grew bigger. Emme breathed frantically. She remembered what his cock looked like on the balcony. How beautiful it was sheathed by his boxers. She remembered how softly he'd circled her for a few stolen seconds.

'We can go back to mine?' he suggested.

Then Emme remembered the women. Sisters.

This is crazy!

She pulled back and shook her head. She could feel the coldness of the building's exterior behind her. The warmth of his strong, hard body in front on her.

'No,' she said, flustered. 'I can't.'

Tristan studied Emme to see if she was serious.

'OK,' he said, respectful disappointment filling his smile.

Another couple entered the alley, two male friends talking through tomorrow's skiing schedule, and Emme and Tristan hurriedly and instinctively hugged each other tight, shrouding their faces into a secret embrace so as not to be recognised. The men passed and they released each other from their cocoon.

Emme took a deep breath.

'Want me to walk you home? If you are going home . . .'

'I am. And I don't. But thank you,' Emme said, before walking away, utterly confused.

Chapter Forty

On Sunday morning the Harringtons went to Thun to see Bella perform as the Sugar Plum Fairy in her winter dance show. The journey would take the best part of two hours each way, plus the show itself and dinner. They'd be gone for hours.

After they'd left, Emme went back to bed and lay on her side, watching reels, reading the news on her phone, doing anything to stop her thoughts turning to Tristan. She lingered on the kiss in the tiny street. His soft tongue. His growing hardness.

It had been steamy and it had been flattering. Tristan clearly wanted her, and although she couldn't work out why and didn't want to be another notch on his bedpost, it had been the kiss of her life.

Emme didn't imagine she'd get the opportunity to kiss him again, but if she did, she pondered whether Tristan might just be the tonic to help her get over Tom. He was certainly distraction enough.

She couldn't think even long enough to focus on her fantasy. She was too flustered. So she got up, showered, and called Cat to ask a favour.

'Can you spare a few hours to come skiing with me?' Emme asked, as she paced the apartment in her thermals. She was getting better at skiing and thought going out with a friend and not a teacher might be a more fun way to improve.

'Damn, I can't – Mrs Kivvi wants to do a tasting. The party is only two weeks away and I'm elbow deep in the kitchen. It's kind of a big deal. I could maybe come up late afternoon and join you, if you're ready to go out by yourself.'

Cat's comment bolstered her. Maybe she was ready to go out by herself. She'd had another lesson with Milla and was gaining confidence every session.

'No problem, don't worry, I'll try myself. I can just about turn!' Emme joked. She had mastered turning right to left across the slope but was struggling with left to right.

Cat laughed.

'Hmmm, be careful! Maybe go to KristallKinder, the nursery slopes . . .'

It was midday by the time Emme got through the tunnel, on the ski train and onto the mountain. Her ski map of Kristalldorf showed her where the kids' ski park was, and it was a good idea of Cat's to suggest heading there so she could build up her confidence. Emme started on a very gentle, short incline, alongside a class of what looked like toddlers they were so small, and with each short run Emme gained confidence and remembered, she could do this. And she could do it on her own.

She decided to head to the slopes proper and even found her fortitude faced with the chairlifts. The quiet from above was eerie sometimes, when a chairlift stopped high over a piste and people on it waited for it to restart, but Emme got used to worrying less about why they were stopping – some idiot probably got tangled up in their skis disembarking like she had her first time – and she started to get used to whole notion of skiing. Dare she say it, she was even starting to enjoy it.

During one still moment as the chairlift stalled while she was on it, Emme watched the skiers below, trying to learn from their techniques, their snaking figures and turns. She watched a group tracking down a gentle blue run. A man with a black-and-white helmet snaked while four nervous skiers followed his trail. He waited for them to catch up on a flat right underneath the stationary chairlift. On the other side of a cluster of pines, deer footprints revealed animal adventures. Two snowboarders flew down and ended up tangled, laughing in a heap on the ground. A child who must have been no older than six whizzed down, beating her parents to the bottom. The guide with the black-and-white helmet pointed to the majestic peak of the Silberschnee, the mountain that everyone seemed to gravitate towards, and Emme followed his finger. Cat had boasted that only the people of Kristalldorf got this exceptional view. The Swiss and the Italians who lived on the other side of it only saw a shadowy, less majestic peak.

Emme listened to the guide, his loud commanding voice cutting through the quiet stillness of the air under the stationary chairlift.

'Silberschnee means "silver snow",' said the indisputable South African accent.

Tristan.

'But personally, I would have named it the Rosaschnee, as it looks more pink.' The four tourists, wearing their new helmets, all gasped.

'Yes!' said an American woman in the same white

embossed Louis Vuitton helmet as Emme. 'I see it!' She sounded enchanted.

An Irish man spoke.

'Is it always pink?'

'No sir, and it's really barely pink now. Later in the day you get what we call "alpenglow" – it only happens at the right time, in the right conditions.'

'Wow,' marvelled the woman.

'It hits best just after sunset, or just before sunrise, when the sunlight has no direct route to the mountain, and it's reflected off ice crystals and particles in the atmosphere. It's mild now, but if anyone wants to get up super early with me tomorrow, we can.'

The novice group looked less enthusiastic at the prospect of skiing in the dark.

But Emme wanted to go with him.

Tristan looked up as the chairlift started up again, and recognised Emme from her new lilac outfit and white helmet.

'Hey!' he waved a pole skyward.

She waved a gloved hand, as casually as she could, somewhat embarrassed to be caught by him again, concerned he was going to think she was following him or something.

'Want to join us?' he called up helpfully. 'They're all newbies!'

'No, it's OK thanks!' It was so dismally embarrassing skiing in front of him the first time, even though she had improved, she didn't want to have to do it again.

At the top of the chairlift Emme glided off it feeling rather proud of herself for managing it, and thought that if

Tristan's party of beginners could do that blue slope, so could she, especially if she heeded the technique and the advice of Tristan and Milla in her head. And she did it. Cautiously so, but she managed to snake down the mountain, making S-shaped turns both to the right and the left, and feeling proud of her control, even if her knuckles were white in her gloves clutching the poles. She even noticed Tristan's tracks, his figures and turns, and followed them, feeling they were a safe bet – knowing that he was nothing of the sort.

Emme got to the bottom and wanted to punch the air she was so pleased with herself, but instead she took a selfie to send home. She sent it to Cat too. Emme in front of the Silberschnee, turning pinker by the minute. This place was so fucking Instagrammable.

As Emme put her phone away, Tristan's group lapped her and he skied over to her, almost kicking snow up in a fan. He stopped with a smile and put his goggles onto his helmet. His brown eyes gleamed in the light. The secrecy of last night's kiss making them both smile.

'Wow, you've come a long way! Blue slopes on your own!'

'Thanks.' She wasn't sure if he sounded patronising or proud of her, but she settled on the positive.

'Want to join us for one last loop?'

'I'm OK, I should get back to town.'

'Come on, show me how far you've come.'

They held each other's eye as the largest man in the party, a wine buyer from India, slammed into the back of Tristan and he in turn almost knocked Emme off her feet.

'Yeesh!' Tristan said, looking a little annoyed, his strong

brow furrowed as he held Emme tight with both arms, almost in a clinch. 'Are you OK?' he asked.

Emme nodded.

'Yes, thanks.'

Tristan shook his head then remembered his manners. The buyer, Shivam Masrani, was the sommelier to a Maharajah in Maheshwar, and he had a lot of money to spend on Du Kok Estates.

'Careful now,' Tristan said, politely but sternly enough to let the man know he was a liability.

Masrani had been the clunkiest skier of the group. Shivam gruffed a little while Tristan untangled his ski tips from Emme's.

'One more slope?' he asked the group as he stood up.

Everyone nodded.

'Great, we have an extra skier in our party – this is Emme from London. Emme, this is Kelly, Shivam, Justin and Patrick.'

The wine buyers smiled and nodded hellos, as they all shuffled themselves into the queue for the chairlift. The chairs were four people wide, so Tristan instructed the four wine buyers to take the first chair, and he and Emme waited for the next. As they waited, her heart pulsed. They were about to be alone, in the air, for five whole minutes. More if the lift stopped again.

As much as Emme didn't want to like him – this dog who slept with his girlfriend's married sister – the thought of being on her own with him, riding the peaceful panorama with him, was thrilling, especially after last night. She wanted her thighs to touch his on the chairlift. For it to stop so they could talk forever. He was so sexy, she had never physically fancied someone with all her body like she did Tristan. Not even Tom. With Tom it was pure, deep, friendship and love. She could picture being married to Tom, creating a family with him – but Tristan stirred a lust in her that she had never known. And he wanted her too. She could have fucked him.

I should have fucked him.

'Quick Wolfie, slide in!' said a father to his son, as the next chair scooped them up and lifted them skyward.

Damn.

Emme was sitting at one end of the chairlift, next to her was Tristan, then the little boy was nestled between Tristan and his father at the other end. Emme and Tristan looked at each other, their faces close, both feeling obvious disappointment not to be alone.

They sighed and smiled at their luck.

Why am I falling for this? Emme asked herself, as Tristan pressed his thigh against hers. She felt it. Electricity from his body to hers. Making her wet, even under all those layers of underwear, thermals and salopettes.

The dad fussed over his son. Tristan broke the tension and leaned into Emme.

'You've done well, you've really progressed.' This time he didn't sound patronising, he sounded genuinely impressed.

'Thanks. Although I confess I've had a few more sessions with Milla now.'

Tristan nodded.

'It shows.'

'I've even started to enjoy it,' she added, laughing. Emme looked at his lips and had to look away. She wanted to taste them again. She wanted them on her nipples so desperately.

'Look, Daddy! The mountain is pink!' the boy said.

'I heard what you said to the group about the alpenglow.' Emme said quietly. 'I'd like to see it one day.'

Tristan leaned in closer.

'I'd like to show you.'

Their lips so nearly met, but it was time to get off.

At the top Emme couldn't have been more disappointed at the four eager faces awaiting them, but together they all snaked down the slope again, and Emme felt a surge of envy when Tristan guided Kelly, putting his hands on her hips to help her lean and turn. Even though she knew he wasn't looking at Kelly the way he was looking at her. The chemistry was intense. Being near him was intense. If she'd been alone with him on the chairlift, they would have kissed again for sure. The knowledge of it felt thrilling.

'Right guys, let's bypass this chairlift, go down the next slope, and take the cable car all the way back to town, yah? You need to see the famous diamanté gondola . . .'

'A diamond what?' Patrick asked.

Emme had heard about the diamanté gondola – kitted out with padded, heated seats. And because it was sponsored by a jewellery brand, the interior was studded with sparkling gems.

Only in Kristalldorf.

'Only one in ten of the gondolas is diamanté, but the others are pretty plush too . . .' Tristan explained.

'Next slope is a trickier blue, some say it should be red, but I think you've got what it takes.' He looked to Emme and nodded. Emme wasn't certain, but Tristan Du Kok seemed to have a knack of making people feel competent and capable enough to achieve anything.

It took them a while – Shivam almost cried at the steepest point – but they managed to get to the bottom of the slope and the top of the gondola cable car station that would take them back to Kristalldorf.

'OK, skis off, and skis and poles in the rack on the out-side of the car!' Tristan instructed, as the gondola swung around the carousel slowly enough for him to help each member of the party put their skis in the rack outside.

'It's a diamanté one!' he said, as if he had arranged it, and he ushered the buyers in one by one, holding their hands to help them in as the gondola moved around a carousel. Just as Emme went to embark, Tristan put an arm across her body.

'Wait,' he whispered. She looked at him just as the doors seamlessly closed on the wine buyers.

'What?'

'We'll see you down there!' Tristan shouted to his group, who were all too awestruck by the diamanté gondola and the view of the Silberschnee from it to notice they'd been deliberately separated.

Tristan put Emme's skis next to his on the external rack of the next gondola and ushered her in, then he followed. Making himself big so no one else would want to join them.

'No diamonds,' Emme jovially pouted, then smiled.

Tristan approached her.

Both of them prayed no one would enter their cable car in the next few seconds.

'Doesn't matter . . .' Tristan shrugged casually.

The doors slammed behind him and they both felt the thrill.

'You're the only jewel I can see.'

Whether it was to exorcise thoughts of Tom or because her body was yearning like never before, there was no question about what was going to happen next. Emme felt sensational; her body tingled.

Tristan pressed a button next to the door and moved over to Emme. She could see his hardness in his black salopettes. She looked from his crotch to his face and raised an eyebrow. He was smiling back. He had the sexiest smile she had ever seen.

'How long do we have?'

'Long enough to make you come,' he said, confidently.

Tristan held Emme's face and they gazed into each other's eyes before slipping their tongues into each other's mouths. His kisses were even more electric in the daylight. Slow at first but soon their exploration was fast and frenzied. Emme broke away.

'But what about?'

She nodded to the wine buyers, all marvelling, unaware, at the peak.

'I've put the window tint on. We can see out the front but they can't see in – and they won't even know why.'

Emme pressed herself against Tristan and felt his hardness against her, rubbing her in just the right place.

She couldn't slide off her jacket and salopette braces fast enough, as Tristan unbuttoned the poppers at the waist of her new lilac trousers. They continued to kiss feverishly as he rolled down her trousers, SKIMs and knickers, and stroked her wetness with his finger.

'Oh my god!' she groaned. She so wanted him to finish what he'd started in the shop.

He slid his finger in his mouth to taste her and groaned

himself, before slumping to his knees and parting her with his tongue.

'No time,' she said. 'I want you inside me.'

Emme lifted Tristan's jacket and unbuttoned his ski trousers, feeling his rock-hard cock tethered inside.

'Oh my god,' she gasped as he silenced her with another kiss and she stroked the long velvety contours of him as she released him from his Calvin Kleins.

'Do you have a condom?'

She was not going to let this fuckboy inside her without one.

'Yes . . . yes . . .' he said, grappling one from his trouser pocket.

He tore off the condom wrapper and expertly rolled it onto his cock, while Emme smoothed her hand along its hardness just to check it was all in place. She was so wet, she couldn't wait. And then she felt it. Hard and warm and moving deep inside her. Slowly at first while she opened up, then frantically as she rocked, her pulsating body vibrating with the hum of the gondola.

Tristan pushed her base layer top up and then her bra to reveal her breasts. He kissed her sweet nipples and seemed in a rush to get to know every curve of her, he wanted to make her come fast, and he could feel it building.

Emme was flushed and breathless as she rode him, pulling his face back up to hers and kissing with increasing intensity.

'Oh god!' she cried, as he thrust deeper; she rode him harder, until she bit his lip as she came, faster than she ever had, with a raging, helpless moan that surprised her. All the stress and tension of the past few months rolled through her body and down this beautiful man's cock. She turned to face the Silberschnee as she rode the wave of her most exquisite orgasm ever, pressing her cheek against Tristan's as they both looked out at the mountain's pink peak.

Her body shuddered in bliss.

'Oh my god,' she sighed again, kissing his face, his perfect face. It was the most electric and intense sexual experience of her life. Tristan looked at her in awe.

Emme raised herself up and off him and flipped over, her knees firmly placed on the heated seats as the ground was getting closer. They could make out the figures of people who had decided to ski all the way down back to the village. Faces emerged into sight as Tristan plunged into Emme from behind and with just a few delectable strokes, unleashed himself inside her with a groan.

With only seconds to spare, Emme and Tristan had their clothes on and zipped back up as the gondola doors dramatically opened. Emme stepped out reborn.

'Well that was a little bit special!' said Kelly the New Yorker. 'Did you get diamonds?' she asked Emme.

'We had it all,' Emme said, cheeks flushed, as she looked to the gondola behind. To her relief it was empty. But if there had been people in it, they would have seen Tristan Du Kok fucking Emmeline Eversley, all the way home.

'Right, dinner!' Tristan said, as they stopped outside the Anna Maria.

Not here, of all places, Emme thought. She really didn't want to risk seeing his girlfriend.

She wanted to go home and have a shower. The Harringtons would be home from Thun soon and she didn't want to look as flustered as she felt right now.

Shivam, Kelly, Patrick and Justin thanked Tristan for a wonderful ski lesson, and they all agreed to reconvene at 8pm for their final evening dinner.

'Want to drop your skis and boots at mine?' Tristan asked Emme. 'Less distance for you to carry them?' he said it neutrally, as if he were helping out an old friend.

'Oh it's fine, I can put them in the Harringtons' locker when I pass it. Thanks.' They stood hesitating for a second, safeguarding their secret.

'It would be nice to do that again some time . . .' Tristan said, disarming her.

'It would.' She smiled. It didn't have to be weird, this didn't have to be anything. Emme needed the fun, the release of another man, to remind her that she was wanted and needed. The sting of Tom's marriage would soon fade if Tristan looked after her like that. And then Emme leaned in to kiss Tristan goodbye, and he backed away.

Chapter Forty-One

'I won, I won!' Bella said as she ran into the apartment clutching a trophy. Emme had to steady herself so the child wouldn't send her flying.

'Well done sweetie, let me see it!'

Bella had already thrust the award into her face, so close that Emme could see her reflection in the metal.

Lexy and Harry closed the door behind them. Bill had gone straight back to Zurich from Thun, while the rest of the family changed onto the Bloch train, and then headed back up the mountain to Kristalldorf.

Emme leaned back and examined the trophy.

'I didn't realise it was a dance competition!'

'It wasn't but I got a special award for doing my best,' Bella lisped proudly. Harry scowled a little as he skulked to his bedroom.

'Well that's wonderful,' Emme said, giving Bella a hug. 'Well done you.'

Lexy hung their coats in the cupboard and let out an exhausted breath.

'Has the KristallKit arrived?' she asked hopefully. 'The kids are pretty hungry . . .'

'Yes, I put it in the fridge but I didn't check if it's one that needs cooking or re—' Emme stopped short when she realised Lexy was staring at her curiously. 'Either way, I'll put the oven on . . .' Emme said, self-consciously.

'Everything OK here?' Lexy asked, a cocktail of suspicion and intrigue in her arched auburn eyebrow.

Emme was fresh out of the shower and wearing lounging trousers and a jersey top, her damp hair combed back and her face make-up free, but had Lexy recognised that telltale glow?

Emme touched her cheek self-consciously.

'Yes, yes fine, I just went skiing . . . beautiful conditions up there,' she said, flushing pink. 'It was so cold I needed a really hot shower when I got back.'

It had been a long and luxuriant shower, washing Tristan away. As she'd lathered suds into her breasts, her taut tummy, her crotch, she'd replayed every thrill of it over and over.

'I bet,' Lexy said, as her sage eye lingered over Emme. 'Did you go with friends?' She was onto something. She could smell it.

'I went on my own,' Emme replied, proudly. 'Cat and Tiago were busy.'

'He's a pretty boy isn't he, Tiago?' Lexy was following a dead lead.

Emme hadn't really noticed, but he had clearly caught Lexy's eye whenever she was in the Steinherrhof.

Lexy opened the fridge and took the KristallKit out of it with the simple instructions.

'Gosh, I am sooo shattered,' Lexy said. 'What have we got? Please let it be quick . . .'

'I can do it . . .' Emme offered.

'Oh good, thanks,' Lexy said, sliding the boxes along the worktop to where Emme was leaning. 'It's been a long day.'

Emme looked at the instructions. Chicken tagine, jewelled couscous and flatbreads. All pre-cooked, it just needed warming.

'It won't take long.'

Emme busied herself reading the heating instructions on the KristallKit's boxes as Lexy picked up *Vanity Fair* and went to the lounge area with the large, inviting sofas. She yawned.

'Oh, before I forget: Bella needs to rest after today, so I think I'll cancel Cedric's lesson tomorrow and tag it onto another day. Maybe the Saturday of the Kivvi Christingle – I'll be having my hair and nails – ooh.' Lexy stopped when she spied a white Louis Vuitton ski helmet on the sofa, in just the spot she was about to slump into. 'Whose is that?' she said excitedly. She dropped the magazine and picked up the helmet, inspecting its smooth surface; her eyes lit up with avarice as she thumbed the LV logo.

'Oh, it's mine,' Emme said, a little embarrassed.

'Goodness!' Lexy smiled, icily. 'Didn't they pay you well in the City!'

Chapter Forty-Two

'Why did you sleep with Tristan Du Kok?' Cat asked Anastasia, as they lay naked on the bed of room 204 of the Silberblick. Cat thought back to that night on the same bed, the night after their reunion. Insatiable Anastasia, lying on the bed spent. She was tender and she couldn't come because she'd already fucked TDK several times that morning. But then what did Cat expect? She already knew what she was capable of. Mrs Diamandis was a married woman who Cat already knew wasn't faithful. She was a spoilt bitch who could summon her whenever the desire took over. She was heiress to both a hotel fortune and her husband's family shipping empire. Cat knew what she had been getting into.

Cat thought back further, to last New Year's Eve, at a party at the Steinherrhof. The Kivvis were away in the Caribbean, so she was helping Tiago, working a party Anastasia and Dimitri were hosting for friends in the private dining room. The hotel manager Pietro had bragged that they had Viktor Kivvi's personal chef working for them that night, hoping it would get back to Walter, who was with Kiki at a party in Monte Carlo.

That night, Anastasia had made a beeline for Cat. Flattering her behind the scenes. Complimenting her on her exceptional palette. Locking eyes with her as she cleared the plates. Following her to the cloakroom and confessing to Cat that she was so intrigued by her she wanted to make her come against the fur coats and ski jackets belonging to their friends. Cat was mesmerised and didn't stop to ask *Why me?* when Anastasia slipped Cat her phone number at the end of the night. She was paralysed with passion. She wanted to do it back to Anastasia, a million times over, and over the course of the past eleven months, she had.

And here they were again, facing each other, wrapped loosely in sheets having enjoyed a beautiful stolen hour of Sunday afternoon sex that Anastasia had begged Cat for. Cat had a few hours off between going through the Kivvi Christingle tastings with Lumi and a dinner she was scheduled to cook that evening, so when Anastasia texted her '204?', their code for their rendezvous, followed by begging, flattery and dirty talk, Cat responded with a thumbs up. She agreed because she wanted to look Anastasia in the eye and ask her what the hell she was thinking, sleeping with the man her own sister was dating. Another treachery against her husband. Another treachery against Cat. Plus it was a chance to say goodbye to her for good. But not before tasting her one last time.

Cat felt surprisingly calm about it, as if she had resigned herself to not liking Anastasia very much. If she didn't like her, perhaps it would make it easier to walk away. She was in lust with Anastasia, nothing deeper. The woman was stunningly beautiful.

Anastasia rested her cheek on her closed palms, on her pillow, looking at Cat.

She shrugged.

'He's hot, isn't he?'

She didn't seem to feel much remorse about it.

'But what about your sister?'

'Oh that's dead in the water. She's just obsessed with the idea of him. Anyway she's even more obsessed with that *fucking* hotel, she'll bore Tristan to tears if she hasn't already.'

Cat frowned, her disapproval clear, if calmed by the sensational orgasm Anastasia and she had reached together.

'It was just a one-time thing anyway.'

'It was?'

Cat studied her.

'One thing led to another . . .'

Cat knew she was lying.

'On a Saturday morning? The night after you and I had —'

'Shhh . . .'

Anastasia silenced Cat with a slow and sumptuous kiss.

Cat pulled back.

'Why are you here?'

'Well, firstly, this is my father's hotel . . .'

Cat gave her a look.

'You know what I mean . . .'

Why did Anastasia desire her so much? She could never understand it.

Anastasia propped herself up and pushed Cat's shoulder gently so she rolled onto her back. She lowered the white sheet that enveloped her.

'Because I'm crazy for you,' Anastasia said, nuzzling into Cat's neck with a kiss. 'Your pussy . . .'

Cat groaned. Anastasia continued to dot kisses down Cat's decolletage, to her breasts, rounded and buoyant from blissful passion. 'Your talent . . .' she said, sucking one nipple with a gentle flick. Cat opened her legs out again and stretched her toes. 'You're an artist.'

Cat blushed.

'And you know what I want to do?'

'What?' Cat teased.

'Next time, I don't want to fuck you in Papa's hotel.'

Next time.

Cat wasn't doing very well at ending it.

Next time.

'Where do you want me?'

'I want to make you come in that kitchen of yours.'

Anastasia rolled on top of Cat and paid attention to her other nipple, circling it with her soft tongue.

'First course, on the worktop,' she said, not breaking eye contact as she sucked, then lowered herself down to Cat's belly button.

'Second course . . .' she kissed her stomach. 'On that beautiful Persian rug in the entrance.'

Cat groaned.

Anastasia went lower.

'Third course, dessert . . .' her face was level with Cat's pussy. 'I'll go here,' she dotted her tongue onto Cat's clitoris, making her arch her back. 'In your bedroom.'

'*Dios mio* . . .' Cat sighed.

'I want to see where you sleep.'

'*Sí,*' she whispered breathlessly, trying not to think of the ridiculousness of Anastasia in her bedroom; in her small staff quarters, when she slept in a mansion.

Anastasia slipped her tongue in a circle then stopped, and raised her head.

'Even better, we can do it on Viktor's bed.'

Cat raised her head and looked down her body.

'When are the Kivvis next out of town?'

She couldn't conceive of this but Anastasia had paused between her legs. Was she serious?

'All of them?' Cat laughed. 'It's rare. And Aapo's back in town next weekend, staying for at least a week until the party.'

'That's a shame . . .' Anastasia pouted.

'Anyway, there are servants! I'd lose my job . . .' Cat was so reeled in, she wanted Anastasia to carry on; she wanted to press her head back down and make her stop talking.

Anastasia lifted herself up, back level with Cat, so their breasts were pressed together again.

'I'll get you another job.' Anastasia shrugged, plainly. 'I could get you a chef job in any hotel in town.'

'They're good to me,' Cat protested.

'*I'm* good to you,' Anastasia said, kissing Cat on the lips again, slipping her tongue inside her mouth, and tragically, they both knew she was lying.

Chapter Forty-Three

'The iPad's not working, Emme! It's stuck!' Bella complained, as she sat up from lying prone on the sofa. It was the last Friday in November and the kids were tired from ski school. Bella had been watching cartoons on the iPad and Harry was in his bedroom building Lego while Emme took a breather and looked at her phone on the sofa next to Bella. She had spent the week idling over Tristan Du Kok and why she hadn't seen or heard from him, and it left her full of regret. Not about what she had done. Sex in the gondola had been spectacular. She was regretful she hadn't bumped into him in this small town. Every night she had gone to bed she had thought of the delicious sensation of Tristan inside her. But the polite thing would have been for him to seek her out.

Emme had certainly sought Tristan out. She'd finally found his social media footprint since remembering what Cat told her: that he was called Tristan Joubert by birth. Emme had found the news stories. Charles Joubert had gone missing while ski touring in the Swiss Alps with his son Tristan. Both were competent skiers. Charles was believed to have fallen down a ravine near the Teufelsgletscher glacier. Tristan, then twenty-two, gave search and rescue accurate coordinates of the last known sighting, but Charles's tracking device was found elsewhere, in his abandoned coat pocket, hanging off a branch hundreds of metres away from where his son last saw him.

And now she was looking at pictures of Tristan Joubert again on Instagram: Tristan looking like something out of a Gillette ad: playing polo, rugby, surfing or heli-skiing. Tristan on safari. Tristan in a verdant vineyard. He looked younger and less refined, even more tanned, but he hadn't posted for eight years and his comments were turned off. As Emme ruminated on the screen and studied his beauty, Bella tapped her on the arm.

'It's stuck! This box is in the way, it won't let me watch!'

'Sorry Bells, let me have a look,' Emme said, taking the device. 'Why don't you watch the cartoons on TV while I fix this?'

Emme gave a deft clap and commanded Gustav to raise the television, and the vast flat screen glided upwards from a sideboard. How far Emme had come in less than a month.

As Bella settled to watch TV a knock at the door startled them both. Usually visitors buzzed on the downstairs main entrance first.

'You wait here,' Emme said, stroking Bella's hair as she got up. Emme put her phone on the console table by the large oak door and opened it, expecting to see a neighbour from the building, but aghast to see Vivian Steinherr standing eagerly on the other side, clutching a document file. Emme smoothed down her hair and checked herself. She suddenly felt terribly exposed.

'Oh! Hello.' Vivian smiled, not expecting Emme either, although she looked less furrowed than when Emme had seen her on the terrace café with Tristan; less prim than she had seen her that night in Down Mexico Way. Today she looked professional and cool, her game face on. Emme was relieved she wasn't angry and confrontational. Vivian couldn't know.

Emme glanced at the phone on the side in full view, grateful that the screen had darkened to sleep.

'Hi,' Emme said unsurely. 'Can I help?'

'Is Lexy in?' Vivian asked hopefully. 'I have a press release for her. I was heading to a meeting nearby and thought I'd drop the hard copy. It's full of my scribbles.'

Vivian looked beyond Emme for a second, and Emme wondered if she should invite her in. What was the Kristalldorf etiquette for your boss's boss calling by when you happened to have fucked their boyfriend?

'Lexy's at work, I think. She's not usually back until after five.'

Vivian rolled her eyes.

'Oh drat, I could have caught her at the Alpenrose!' She smiled as if she'd been silly. 'Never mind, I was passing – stairs aside.' Vivian joked, nodding in the direction of the steep wide sweep from the road up to Chalet Stern, although no staircase could beat her Bambi-like legs. 'Can I leave this for her?'

'Sure,' Emme said, taking the file. 'Would you like to come in?'

Emme really didn't want Vivian Steinherr to come in. She was wracked with guilt for the man they had both had inside them. And he had slept with her *sister* too.

'No it's fine, I need to get on . . . thank you.' Vivian nodded, as Emme's phone beeped and flashed up with a notification. Her face flushed red as she snatched up her phone in case Tristan was illuminated in all his Insta glory.

Phew.

A message from her sister, against the backdrop wall-paper of her niece and nephew. Emme tried to style out her panic as she pocketed her phone.

'Right then! Cheerio, I'll be sure to give this to Lexy as soon as she's home.'

Vivian looked a little cautious. Emme's reaction was odd.

'Great, thank you,' she said, as she turned away and elegantly bounded down the stairs.

Emme closed the door and looked across at Bella on the sofa, hammering a finger on the iPad screen.

'Bells, be careful!'

'I fixed it!' Bella said proudly as she squinted her eyes and peered at the screen. 'Pur-chase succ-sex-ful! Now can I watch *Bluey*?'

'Bella!' Emme said, more sternly, walking over to retrieve the iPad. 'What have you done?'

Emme took the screen and studied it.

'Oh dear. "Purchase successful. You now have 90 days' cover". Bella!'

The girl looked up with doleful eyes, as Emme scru-tinised the screen to see if she could undo the transaction. She pressed the back button but the screen went blank.

'Emme! Come and look at my Ninjago set!' Harry bel-lowed from the bedroom. And Emme was so surprised that Harry *wanted* to show her his Lego set that she handed the iPad back to Bella so she could get back to *Bluey*.

Down the hallway Emme poked her head around Harry's bedroom door. He'd spoken to her with disinter-est at best for much of the time since she'd arrived, but now she could tell from the look on his face as he sat on his knees, turning his Lego set on the plush carpet, that her approval meant something to him.

'Oh wow Harry, it's really cool!' she said, getting down on her haunches.

'So this is Zane's apartment . . .' he said, before tentatively giving Emme a tour.

After a few minutes and the onset of pins and needles, Emme looked at Harry's face, his auburn eyelashes sweeping over his eyes, and thought she might have finally cracked him.

'Ooh, can I have a play with this figure?' she asked, cautiously.

'No,' Harry said, swooping the ninja up off the floor.

'OK,' Emme said, pulling herself up to standing and circling her tingling ankle. 'I need to start dinner anyway, but great job Harry.'

Harry didn't say anything, but Emme could tell from his smile that he was proud of himself.

As Emme walked down the hall she took her phone out of her pocket to check the time, and ruminated on Vivian Steinherr's visit. She swiped up to awaken it and was confronted by Tristan's Instagram again.

That was close. She felt bad about Vivian, but Tristan was so intoxicating, her swirling feelings of passion had managed to overcome the guilt. She studied the screen as she walked into the kitchen. Tristan Du Kok and his father, smiling on a ski slope in Switzerland. It was the last picture he'd posted. He was handsome in his early twenties, but like the Du Kok Estate wines he sold, Tristan seemed to get better with age.

Where are you now, Tristan?

Chapter Forty-Four

Walter Steinherr was sitting at his grand wooden desk in his capacious study at the Steinherr mansion reading through papers, when a figure in the doorway made him start.

'Son!'

Lysander had been waiting, leaning against the frame. He hadn't wanted to make his father jump, and it felt strange the butler announcing him in his own family home, so he'd lingered for half a minute while he waited for his father to look up.

Walter took off his reading glasses and placed them on the dark-green leather writing surface, next to his pile of papers.

'It's only been . . . what . . . three weeks! To what do I owe this pleasure?'

Lysander gently shut the door behind him. He wore a blue shirt unbuttoned at the top, a navy blazer, and smart suit trousers.

'Is everything alright?' Walter asked, standing gingerly.

'Yeah yeah, it's fine Dad, but . . . well, there's been a development.'

Lysander embraced his father. Walter managed to hide the pain from the signs of his son's affection, pulsing through his spine, as he looked over Lysander's shoulder and winced. Walter carefully sat back down and Lysander casually slumped into one of the two huge studded leather armchairs facing the desk.

It was the chair Lysander had sat in when his father called him to the study for a talk before he went to live in the United States. It was the same chair he'd sat in when his father lectured him on striving harder at school when his grades were in doubt. It was where Lysander had sat when his father told him he needed to set an example to his siblings – to stop crying around the house over their mother and pull himself together. That was the first conversation Lysander remembered having in that chair. He wore a navy blazer that day too. Now the roles were to be reversed, and he would advise his father.

'Can I get you a drink?' Walter said, gesturing to a gold trolley stacked with cut-glass bottles, tumblers and tongs.

'No, really, I'm fine, look . . . is Kiki around?'

Walter's eyes widened. What news could it be if Lysander had to deliver it in person?

'No, she's in Milan, shopping with a girlfriend.'

Lysander raised an eyebrow sceptically. Ten days ago, Rico DeLuca had called him saying he'd done some more digging; he'd left no stone unturned and found something very interesting on Kiki Bouffon Steinherr. Lysander had spent the nine days since wondering how the hell to tell his dad. He had expected to find some dirt on Kiki in the depths of her past, but he hadn't expected to find present-day scandal, happening right under his father's nose.

'Do you have something?' Walter asked, hopefully.

'Yeah, it's kind of uncomfortable though, Dad . . .' he said, opening his blazer jacket and pulling out his phone. He opened a website featuring a statuesque beauty with a black shiny bob, naked except for heels, pleasure lighting up her face in all manner of tantalising positions. The name Eden Roque was emblazoned across the screen in a jolly font.

'Why are you showing me this?' Walter frowned, perplexed.

'Scroll down,' Lysander instructed, leaning across the desk to show his father how to. As he scrolled down Walter saw Eden Roque naked in clinches with women. Eden Roque with men. Eden Roque in threesomes. Eden Roque with cocks in her mouth. Eden Roque with her asshole on display. Eden Roque riding a beautiful black man. Eden Roque naked but for a Santa hat in Lapland. All while she eyed the camera coquettishly.

Why was Zand putting porn on his desk? Walter put his glasses back on and peered closer.

The woman's familiarity. The butterfly birthmark on her abdomen. The face of pleasure he knew too well.

'What the . . . ?' Walter said slowly, aghast, as he scrolled further and saw his wife on all fours on a beach. 'Kiki?' He looked shellshocked. He looked old. He looked up at his son in dismay.

Lysander walked an apologetic yet hopeful tightrope.

'I think that's your "out", Dad . . .'

Chapter Forty-Five

Emme had just waved the kids off with Cedric at the ski train and was walking along the high street when she heard Cat call out her name. She stopped in her tracks and smiled to herself before she turned around outside the Läderach shop, where the assistants were putting up their Christmas display.

'Hey!' Emme said. Cat was approaching, carrying her snowboard and a huge smile, and hugged her friend in greeting.

'Mad party Saturday – want to earn some extra cash?'

Emme could always use extra cash in Kristalldorf. A 500ml bottle of water on the slopes cost the equivalent of five pounds; and she wanted to be able to buy some new going-out clothes.

'What do you need?'

'The Kivvi Christingle is this Saturday and I need an extra pair of hands to serve drinks and canapés. Do you fancy it? I could get agency staff but it's a great way to get you in . . .'

Emme knew the kids had an extra ski lesson on Saturday morning and Lexy would be getting her hair and nails done, but she didn't know whether she'd be needed in the afternoon yet.

'The Harringtons bring their kids . . .' Cat said, almost reading Emme's mind.

Would Tristan be there?

Emme realised she wouldn't get an invitation any other way, she was just the help.

'I'd love to, thank you. I'll need to double check with Lexy, but I'll text you.' She pondered that her boss had been in a better mood this past week. Less on edge in the mornings. Less wittery at the dinner table. Hopefully she'd be fine with her taking this work.

'Great, thanks.'

'Tiago's helping too, bless him. He's taking a night off from the Steinherrhof and getting Camilla to cover his shift just to help me out.'

'Ahhh, he's a good guy,' Emme said.

'Yeah, sadly not *my* good guy,' Cat laughed, referencing Emme's mix-up when she first arrived in town.

'Hey, erm, is Anastasia going?' Emme asked, with sympathetic concern.

Cat didn't have the courage to tell her they'd already had amazing make-up sex when Cat had gone to end it there and then, that they'd been messaging each other still. 'She's been before, with her husband. Not always.' Cat said it casually, as if she were indifferent. 'Vivian sometimes comes too.'

Shit.

Emme still hadn't told Cat about her sex in the cable car with Vivian's boyfriend. Might Vivian and Tristan be there together? If so, it might be too much. But at least it would give her an insight.

'Their dad never goes to the Kivvi Christingle of course, but the daughters represent him.'

251

'How do you cope, seeing Anastasia there but not being able to talk?' Emme asked nervously.

'We only hooked up on New Year's Eve, at a party at the Steinherrhof. I was helping Tiago out then . . .'

'Will you be OK if she's there this Saturday?'

'I'll be better for it if you are,' Cat replied, pressing her palms together in a plea.

'I'll see what I can do,' Emme promised.

Chapter Forty-Six

It was the first Saturday in December, and the first thick snow of the season – the type to really settle, even in the village – was kissing the fantasy-like turrets of the Steinherr mansion and building fast. Inside, by the roaring fire of the study, Walter had called his children – bar Caspian, who was riding waves off Maui – for a family meeting before the Kivvi Christingle.

Vivian had been surprised her father wanted to go to the party, and had asked Lysander if there was cause for concern. His return to Kristalldorf so soon after his visit for Walter's birthday had caused Vivian further alarm. What was going on that she didn't know about? Lysander said he was in Europe on business and had decided to stay for the Kivvi Christingle, but still, Vivian was astute enough to know something was awry.

'What is it, Papa?' Anastasia asked, walking in, wearing a crimson Valentino gown. She was surprised to see Dimitri already sitting in one of the wing-backed leather armchairs opposite Walter's desk. 'Kristaps said you wanted us all together?'

Dimitri looked away.

Vivian was sitting in the other armchair, wearing a black Saint Laurent suit that made her look more willowy, more ethereal, than usual.

Lysander was perched on a leather studded Chippendale sofa, arms folded. Anastasia was alarmed that no one else looked surprised to be convened for a family meeting one hour before they were going to a party.

'What's going on?'

'While Zand's back in town, I wanted to talk to you,' Walter said. He had his steely, businesslike face on.

Vivian looked at her father, her blue eyes ablaze with concern.

'Where's Kiki?' she asked.

Walter stifled a glance in Lysander's direction.

'She's lying down. She has a migraine.'

'Oh.' Vivian looked sympathetic. 'I guess she's not coming to the party then?'

'No,' Walter said gravely. 'No, she won't be coming to the party.'

One hour earlier, Walter had served Kiki with divorce papers and asked how long her little side hustle had been going on. Over the past few days he'd done a deep dive into his wife's porn content. Eden Roque had been a busy girl, shooting in Ibiza, Mykonos, Bel Air, and of course, Milan.

'Did you use me for the jet-set lifestyle?' he asked, almost hurt.

'No Walter,' Kiki said kindly. It was most certainly not a side hustle or a hobby. 'I'd done it for a couple of years before you happened upon my blackjack table, I promise.'

Walter studied her.

'I've made my own – very good – money, for the past

seven years. It's high-end feminist porn. Beautifully shot.'

'Harlot!' Walter spat, and Kiki gasped, before retaining her cool.

'I promise I didn't seek you out,' she implored.

'And the sick children in Lapland?'

Her defiance dropped. There were no sick children in Lapland. She started packing her things.

'Well, what the hell's going on?' Anastasia asked, her chestnut mane tumbling over her breathtaking dress.

Walter sat back in his chair behind his desk.

'Just before Zand heads back to New York, and before I get any further down this road than I want to . . .'

Anastasia sat on the sofa next to Lysander and crossed her long legs.

'I want to talk about my exit strategy.'

The girls scoffed.

'Please!'

'Daddy . . .'

Lysander was silent.

Dimitri was almost robotic.

'I'm seventy now, I need a plan.'

'Please, Daddy,' Vivian implored. 'I don't like this talk.'

Lysander looked at her as if to say, *it's OK.*

'I need a plan for how our family business will continue to thrive, long after I'm gone.'

Vivian went pale. Anastasia frowned. Lysander looked thoughtful.

'What I've learned from three generations in this industry, is that hospitality always needs a figurehead. Conrad, Rocco, Bernie, Bill . . .'

Anastasia rolled her eyes. *All men,* she thought.

'The Steinherr portfolio needs a figurehead.'

Vivian listened intently. Dimitri gently nodded.

'And I think it's fair to say that neither of you have enjoyed running the Anna Maria together.'

A shocked and petulant expression danced across Anastasia's face; Vivian raised her hand while she spoke.

'Daddy it's not that I haven't enjoyed running the Anna Maria, I love it!'

Walter raised his palm to stop her.

'I need to put a sole heir in place, ready to run everything if – when – I die.'

Anastasia looked at her brother next to her, arms folded but relaxed, and the penny dropped.

'What?' she gasped, looking between Lysander and their father.

'He knows *nothing* about this business!' she scolded. 'He turned his back on being a hotelier when he went to New York to defend American sleazebags!'

Lysander shook his head and stayed calm.

'Wrong tree, Anni,' he mumbled quietly.

Dimitri squeezed the bridge of his nose.

'No, I'm going to put Vivian in charge as the Steinherr figurehead, to represent the family.'

Anastasia stood abruptly as she gasped.

'WHAT?!'

She stormed over to their father's desk and leaned one hand on the plush leather writing surface. She pointed her other hand at her sister.

'Why her?' she spat.

Vivian flushed a shade of flattered.

'Daddy!' she said wide-eyed, as pleasantly shocked as her sister was wildly so.

Lysander kept his arms folded and looked at his shoes.

'But what about me?' Anastasia's angry voice wobbled. Walter looked at his eldest daughter, equal parts vicious and beautiful, and his smile grew.

'My wealth will be left to *all* of you Anni. Even Caspian. But Vivian will become director of the Steinherr hotel group. You can take your pick of which hotel you want to manage.'

Anastasia shook her head, as if co-managing the Anna Maria with her dreary sister had been enough to put her off running a hotel at all.

'I don't want to manage a goddamn hotel!' she snapped, as if she was going to burst into tears any second. 'I just wanted –'

'No!' Walter bellowed, cutting her off again, which only added to Anastasia's frustration and fury.

'You have children Anastasia, Vivian doesn't . . .'

Vivian felt that cut like a knife. For a loving man he could be so clumsy. So steely.

'Vivian has more time to oversee everything. You can pick and choose, as you always have.'

'Yes but –'

Anastasia shook her head and suppressed her tears. She was so incredulous she couldn't get her words out. *She* should be the face of the Steinherr empire. How could her father show such favouritism, to wide-eyed naïve Vivian, who didn't even have the balls to fire substandard staff?

'Enough!' bellowed Walter, shocking the entire room. He had lost his patience to the point that now seemed as good a time as any to tell his daughters his other plan for the business.

'While we're at it, I'm going to put the Seven Summits chalets on the market.'

'What?!' Anastasia and Vivian both said in unison.

'But Daddy, I don't think they've appreciated at all in the past eight years. And you haven't made any revenue from them,' beseeched Vivian.

'You're just selling? Without consulting us?' spat Anastasia.

'The timing is right,' Walter declared.

Anastasia shook her head and watched all her plans evaporate. The events. The high-end hire. The fashion shows. The private suites for her to escape to and conduct her trysts. The ridiculous wealth the family could have made from them. Thirty thousand francs a *day*. And her father was probably going to sell them at a loss.

'Dimitri has drawn everything up . . .'

Anastasia shot her husband a look.

'I'm going to announce it to Kivvi at the party myself,' Walter said, defiantly.

Anastasia turned her wrath on her husband.

'You knew?'

Lysander and Vivian exchanged a look. Dimitri remained steadfast.

'I work for your father . . .'

'You're married to *me*!' Anastasia barked, and stormed out. Out of the study, out of the wing, and out of the mansion, slamming the huge front doors in her wake.

Walter glanced between Lysander, Dimitri and Vivian, looking a little bewildered.

'Well, that went well,' quipped Lysander.

Dimitri stood up, excused himself, and went to see if the children were ready.

'Daddy, I'm totally honoured,' Vivian said, with an apologetic smile. 'And I will make sure everything is OK with Anastasia, I promise. She can have any job she wants.'

Walter nodded, he knew it would all be fine in the end. He just didn't know when his end would be. Dr Blitzer had said months – a couple of years perhaps if he took the chemo he was refusing – but not much time.

'Right, let's go to this party!' Walter declared, sounding more jolly than Lysander could have predicted.

Chapter Forty-Seven

At 1pm Emme walked through swish automatic doors that looked like they might open directly into the mountain, but instead glided into a sleek lobby with several elevators, all of which were branded with the Kivvi engineering logo. Emme looked at the names above the lifts and pressed the one labelled Edelweiss, to a gleam and a ding.

In the lift she studied her reflection. Cat had loaned her a little black dress with a white Chanel-style collar and net ruched sleeves, which she wore with tights and black Ted Baker stilettos she had borrowed from Cassie, who was fortunately the same petite shoe size as Emme. Her hair was sleek, the top of her chestnut bob clipped out of her face with a black velvet bow, her skin and lips peachy and clear. She looked like staff, but she felt just about sexy enough that if Tristan were to be there, he would notice. Even if she couldn't compete with his girlfriend.

The lift wasn't moving and Emme couldn't see a single button to press inside it. No door closing sign. No internal button that read Edelweiss. She poked her head out and looked in the lobby again, and felt rather silly, returning inside to just her reflection looking around for clues.

A man entered the lobby with crates of champagne

flutes for the caterers, walked into the lift and nodded at Emme, still standing bewildered.

'Up,' he said in a gruff voice, and the doors glided shut.

Oh, Emme thought, realising she still had a lot to learn.

The lift doors opened onto a luxurious landing and the man indicated for Emme to leave first. She headed to a large modern door, which a maid opened immediately. Her outfit wasn't that dissimilar to Emme's, although she wore a white frilled pinafore over the top of her more staid black dress.

'Glasses!' said the man over Emme's shoulder.

'And I'm here to help Catalina,' Emme said.

'Go through to the kitchen.'

Emme entered the Kivvi chalet and looked around in awe. A baby Steinway sat on a Persian rug that looked faded but probably cost a fortune, while the walnut wood of the high-vaulted ceiling let the Swarovski chandeliers shine.

It was like the Harrington home on steroids. Vintage mid-century French armchairs sat atop plush cream rugs while sturdy timber and steel hardware fused the traditional with the modern. No wonder Lexy was so excited about attending this party. This was no red-and-white-checked cutesy chalet; no clichéd antlers on the wall. It was the most luxurious home Emme had ever stepped in, and considering she'd been living at the Harringtons' for weeks now, that was saying something.

'Whoah,' she whispered to herself, as she headed to the kitchen, which was buzzing with Cat shouting orders. Tiago was wearing a shirt and a bow tie, which Emme playfully tugged on each side. 'Looking sharp, Tiago,' she said, straightening it. His dimples sank as he smiled.

'Why thank you, ma'am,' he said, as if Emme herself were the Queen. Lydia from The Cheeky Blinders was also on hand to help, in a white shirt and short black skirt, her blonde fringe dipping into her soulful eyes, along with the Kivvis' head butler Gerard, who was getting very sniffy about the extra staff milling around his territory.

Cat looked up.

'Wow,' she said, appraising Emme. 'My dress looks better on you!'

Emme gave a quick and playful curtsey while Tiago laughed and Gerard scowled.

'What can I do?'

Emme examined the rows and rows of beautifully pre-sented canapés on baking trays covering every marble surface in the vast kitchen.

'Help me decant those three trays onto these slate boards please. Keeping uniformity in size and alignment. We have thirty minutes to go.'

'Sure thing.'

'T, do you have the napkins?'

'*Si jefa!*' he saluted. He had counted out stacks of forty little black square napkins and put them in piles on the worktop.

'The order of service is up on my chalk board there – that's the order of rotation,' Cat directed. 'Emme and Tiago, if you take the canapés out in rounds in that order, and keep coming back for more before you move onto the next canapé. It's very important you stick to that order.'

'Yes chef!' Emme said with a smile.

'Lydia and Gerard are already on drinks. Gerard, the frozen ice balls need to be left to the last moment, yes?'

He nodded quietly.

'Damn rosemary slowed down the freezing process,' Cat lamented.

'But they're so beautiful!' Lydia said, taking one out. A perfect sphere with a sprig of rosemary and a redcurrant inside each ball made for festive ice cubes; raspberries set in jelly and frozen would be going into the champagne.

'Put it back!' Cat said, half angry, half flirtatious, as Lydia returned the ice ball to the freezer. 'We need all the ice we can get. It's going to be busy.'

Tiago, Lydia and Emme exchanged mischievous smiles while Gerard continued to line up his glasses: champagne flutes, martini glasses, coupé cups, whisky tumblers and highballs for the children and the teetotallers.

Emme had an excited feeling about today.

At 2pm the party was under way, with Tiago and Emme circulating the canapés amongst the best and brightest of Kristalldorf's high society. The Kochs, the Sommars, the Herwegs.

'*Hej!*' said a cheery man as he sauntered into the kitchen. 'This all smells wonderful Catalina. You've excelled yourself.'

Aapo Kivvi walked with the elegance of a dancer and had the charm of his mother.

'Thank you,' Cat said, opening the oven to a roll of steam. 'Aapo, this is my friend Emme, she's helping out.'

Aapo walked over to Emme, who was placing chicken Caesar sourdoughs at jaunty angles in neat rows and held out a hand. He seemed rather formal.

'Oh,' Emme wiped her hands on a tea towel and shook Aapo's soft hand.

'Pleased to meet you,' he said.

His formality fused with friendliness made Emme laugh.

'Pleased to meet you too,' Emme said, then got back to her task.

'Anything I can help with?' he asked Cat. As busy as she was, she would never have said yes.

'All in hand, thank you Aapo, you enjoy the party. Find your sister and tell her I made her the macarons she loves . . .'

'Well that is news I would love to deliver,' Aapo said with a smile, as he bowed out and went in search of Stella.

The Harringtons arrived soon after 2pm, and Bill quickly got lost in conversation by the piano with Oliver Koch while Lexy sought out Emme in the kitchen to see some behind-the-scenes action.

'Here you are!' Lexy almost sang, as if she were Ginger Rogers making a grand entrance. Emme looked up. Lexy's Hollywood red waves and lips were polished – her glam squad had done a good job – and Emme felt pleased for her that she was where she wanted to be, although her presence made Emme feel flustered. Still, she did her best to stay polite.

'Lexy, this is my friend Cat,' Emme said, as she picked up the next rotation of canapés. 'She's the one responsible for the amazing food today.' Emme smiled, and raised a platter. '*Chicharrónes* with cumin, chipotle and red cabbage,' she said proudly. 'Would you like one?'

Lexy waved a hand and gestured to her figure-hugging dress that accentuated both her tiny waist and her rounded bottom.

Cat didn't have time for chitchat, especially with anyone who didn't appreciate the artistry of her food, so she kept her head down and barked orders.

'*Chicharrónes*, salt hake, *vamos*!' she called, and Emme took her cue to leave.

Lexy seemed to resent Cat's authoritative tone over *her* employee, but sauntered out of the kitchen and bumped into Formula 1 driver Oscar Goodall and his model girlfriend Touran, whose handbag Lexy fawned over at first sight.

'That is divine!' she simpered. 'You *must* let me stroke it!'

Emme and Tiago rotated in opposite directions with slate platters, Emme often stalked by Bella for canapés and hugs, and she kept a firm overview of every person she saw walk in through the grand front door. She noticed a bald man with his son and two daughters in matching dresses. She noticed a man who looked like an aging rock star, with a skinny scarf and a beautiful wife. She recognised a Bollywood couple she had seen walking the high street hand in hand – the wife had green eyes and emerald earrings that weighed down her earlobes. She recognised minor royals from their blue eyes and Hapsburg chins. She recognised Swedish pop star Frida Alm. She thought she saw David Hasselhoff and Elton John (not together) but she couldn't see Tristan Du Kok. As Emme weaved through the guests, offering food but keeping as low a profile as possible, she saw Vivian Steinherr enter on her father's arm. She looked incredible in a black velvet suit that draped off her languid body. How could Emme, serving canapés in a borrowed Chanel rip-off dress, compete with Vivian Steinherr? Of course Tristan wouldn't have reached out to her after their passionate, animal instincts took over in the gondola. He was an animal. And this beautiful woman was his girlfriend.

She shook her head and continued on her rounds, noticing a handsome man with salt and pepper hair following closely behind Walter and Vivian. Swedish pop star Frida Alm made a beeline for him.

'Lysander Steinherr, as I live and breathe!' she said, outstretching her arms.

'Frida, my darling,' he said in an American accent, as he squeezed her arm and kissed each cheek.

'Canapé?' Emme proffered, but they both ignored her.

'Do my eyes deceive me?' Viktor Kivvi said, clutching a glass of Japanese whisky on the rocks. 'Walter . . .' He couldn't bring himself to shake the man's hand, but he gave a cautious smile. 'Welcome to my home.'

'Viktor,' Walter said, nodding politely. Viktor looked almost thrown. Ever since he had moved to Kristalldorf and started the Seven Summits project, it had been met with obstacles, red tape and planning bureaucracy, all underpinned by Walter Steinherr, whose own projects and buildings seemed to rise seamlessly out of the ground.

What was the old curmudgeon up to, finally attending the Kivvi Christingle?

Walter looked at Lumi who shook her hair and gave her most gracious smile.

'Lumi,' Walter said, his voice almost like butter. 'And you know my daughter Vivian, I'm sure.' He proudly presented her, keeping a palm on her back.

'Hello,' Vivian said graciously, smiling and genial. Vivian kissed Lumi on each cheek, then shook Viktor's hand and gave him a judicious smile as if to say, *I haven't forgotten how rude you were in my restaurant.*

Lumi was always entranced to see Vivian up close at her party. The baby she knew had grown into an alarmingly beautiful woman. She wondered if Vivian might remember her loving touch as the motherless infant cried in Lumi's arms. Lumi's heart broke for a second, while Vivian felt the intensity and awe of her gaze.

'This is beautiful,' Vivian said warmly, as she stroked the shoulder of Lumi's powder-blue Oscar de la Renta gown. Her hand landed near Lumi's Cartier panther bangle. 'And this too!'

'Thank you,' Lumi said, shooting Walter a look. 'You look stunning, as ever.'

Vivian smiled modestly.

'And my son Lysander is here from New York . . .' Walter looked around. 'Over there somewhere.'

'Well, do come in,' Viktor said. 'Make yourselves at home.'

When Anastasia Steinherr Diamandis turned up alone in red Valentino and a fur coat, just gone 3.30pm, Tiago spotted her first. She snatched a flute of champagne from a tray Gerard was circulating with and knocked it back, placing the damp and empty glass on top of the Steinway. Gerard looked horrified and deftly removed the glass as the pianist played 'O Come All Ye Faithful' with a frown.

'Shit,' Tiago muttered to himself, wondering whether he should let Cat know, or whether she would be best not knowing from the sanctuary of the kitchen. Anastasia already looked half cut, and she looked like a woman on a mission.

'Lobster roll, ma'am?' Tiago said, proffering the slate.

'No,' she said.

'Well, will you let my colleague take your coat?' Tiago nodded to a maid, who came over with a plush hanger. Tiago realised that buying time was a bit hopeless when she'd just sunk a glass of champagne without letting it touch the sides. Anastasia took off her fur and almost dropped it at the maid's feet.

'Thanks,' she slurred, as she continued into the party with a bitter and predatory gait.

'Ah, there you are!' Dimitri said, looking at his wife with flaccid concern. Anastasia scanned the room with hooded lids, barely acknowledging her husband. 'Everything alright?' he asked, looking for someone carrying a tray of water.

Anastasia shot him a reproachful look.

'Mummy!' cried Ophelia, running over. 'There's a games room! Orfeas got to meet a grizzly bear on the VR!'

Anastasia looked at her daughter almost without recognition, but she patted her head.

'That's nice,' she said, with disinterest.

'Why don't you see if you can see the bear, sweetheart,' Dimitri said softly.

Ophelia smiled and ran off.

'Where's my father?' Anastasia spat at her husband. Dimitri looked around the vast open room, which was now full of the great and the good of Kristalldorf mingling over drinks.

'He was chatting with the Sommars last time I . . .' but Anastasia had stalked off before he could finish.

*

'Lysander it's so wonderful to see you back in town!' Lexy Harrington fawned in a fluster. 'How is New York?'

Lysander couldn't remember for the life of him who this woman was, but he responded to her questions and asked benign ones in return, so as not to give himself away. She kept talking about Bill this and Bill that – obviously her husband was someone important – and how she had been to New York several times with work when she lived in London.

'I *love* New York,' she cooed. 'It's electric!'

Lexy tried to ignore the fact that Lysander Steinherr was looking over her shoulder for most of their conversation, but he did pay a little more attention when she said how much she loved working out of the Alpenrose with his father and Dimitri.

'I'd say of all the Steinherr properties, the Alpenrose is my favourite,' she gushed. 'I didn't like Vitreum much anyway . . .'

During a pause in the canapé production, somewhere between the chickpea crostini and the beef sirloin teriyaki, Gerard insisted Tiago and Emme help do a sweep of empty glasses while he and Lydia continued to offer guests full ones. Emme looked to Cat for confirmation.

'You've got five minutes, *vamos*!' Cat called, as Emme and Tiago headed out with empty silver trays.

'I'll go this way and hit the games room and cinema,' Tiago said, his bow tie waning a little now. 'You go that way and do the study and lounge . . .' Tiago and Emme swept out in opposite directions, collecting empty glasses as quickly as they could so as not to mess with Cat's precise timings. Emme headed left, through the main throng to the library, where empties sat on Viktor Kivvi's desk and bookshelves. Harry Harrington was sitting on the study's plump leather sofa looking at the screen of the boy next to him.

'You having fun there?' Emme asked the boys as she swept up as many empties onto her tray as she could. Harry nodded vaguely, lost in the screen.

'Let's go back on the VR,' the other boy said, conversing with adults was *so* boring, so they ran out, bumping into a man in the doorway.

'Easy tigers!' said the familiar voice, sexy, deep and South African, which sent a shiver down Emme's spine. She turned around.

He's here.

The boys giggled and ran around Tristan, off to the games room on another floor. Emme steadied her tray on Viktor's desk and froze, as she looked up at him standing tall, and if she wasn't mistaken, slightly sheepish, in the doorway.

'Tristan . . .'

He walked in, gently, champagne glass in hand, a raspberry fizzing at the bottom of it.

'Hey you – I, er . . .'

For a supposed charmer he didn't have many words. He looked apologetic, which only made Emme want to get in there first.

'Hey, don't worry about it.'

Tristan looked confused.

'Look, I've been away, in Geneva, then I went to London . . .'

Talk of London suddenly made her homesick. She

wanted to be in London right now, and not here at a party with Tristan Du Kok looking sharp and beautiful in a suit – trying to make excuses for fucking her and running, even though she had done it too.

'Please, it's fine, I know how it is,' she looked over his shoulder, to indicate that she was cool about Vivian. She didn't want his pity and she would never say a word.

Tristan shook his head.

'Know how what is?'

'You and your girlfriend. Honestly, I won't mess anything up for you.'

Tristan got nearer, shaking his head gently.

'Mess anything up?'

'Yeah. I knew what I was getting into. You're a fuckboy!' She tried to give a laugh, but it came out slightly shaky. She hoped he didn't notice.

Emme remembered her vow to herself. Tristan was beautiful to look at. He might even help her get over Tom. The sex in the gondola was blissful. But she wouldn't do it again. She'd felt too guilty seeing Vivian on her doorstep.

'I'm single. It's over.'

Emme took a step back.

'Since when?'

'Since before we . . .' he looked at her blisteringly.

'What?'

For two weeks Emme had felt sensational yet treacherous, and yet there was no need. Still, she knew what Tristan was capable of. She'd seen it with her own eyes.

'I haven't been able to stop thinking about you,' he confessed.

Emme looked at Tristan's lips and wanted them so badly

again on her skin. What the hell was going on? Why *wasn't* he with Vivian Steinherr? Why was he interested in her?

Tristan drained his drink and took the raspberry from the base of the glass, licking the droplets off it and putting it to Emme's mouth. She parted her lips and let the sensation of champagne and the taste of the berry linger on her tongue. She took his thumb in her mouth and suddenly they were back in the gondola, his huge cock penetrating her from behind. She moaned softly as she sucked him, their gazes not shifting, their bodies drawing closer together like metal shavings to a magnet. They could do it again. She looked at his suit trousers, their bodies drawing together as he gently withdrew his thumb but pressed his hard cock into her little black dress.

'So why didn't you –'

'Oh Emme!' said a shrill voice from the doorway. 'It's *you* in here!'

Emme and Tristan drew apart quickly. She smoothed the bow in her hair; he put his free hand in his pocket.

Lexy Harrington was standing in the doorway, a showbiz smile suppressing her rage. She shook her empty flute accusingly, as if Emme had failed her.

'More champagne?' she suggested, saccharine with a bite.

Emme flushed red.

'Right on it . . .' she said, as she picked up the tray and gave Tristan the briefest of looks as she went on her way. Lexy put her empty glass down on Emme's tray as she passed her. 'I'll bring it over to you,' Emme said, her deferential tone just about overriding her annoyance.

*

Back in the kitchen Cat was plating up beef sirloin teriyaki and duck hoisin rolls onto slates while Tiago looked concerned.

'As the English say, she's hammered,' he said, almost apologetically.

'Who's hammered?' Emme asked, as she placed the tray of empties next to Lydia, who was stacking dirty glasses in the glasswasher.

Cat shook her head. She did not have time for this.

Tiago looked at Emme. 'Anastasia Steinherr, she's hammered. Avoid her with the drinks, she looks *muito bêbada*. She needs water.'

'Got that,' Emme said.

Cat tried to ignore the feeling of impending catastrophe and focus on her work.

'OK, Asian round is ready, *vamos*! Then we move on to desserts.' Cat clapped her hands twice.

'Yes boss!' Emme and Tiago chimed, stifling a laugh, but Emme's heart was still racing from having seen Tristan.

Mika Kivvi walked into the kitchen, eyes like pinpricks.

'Hey man, can I just get a bag of chips?' he asked Tiago.

'No Mika!' Cat snapped, and he retreated into the pantry.

Emme and Tiago headed out with the next slate platters, Emme only just remembering that Lexy Harrington was waiting for her champagne.

Fuck her, she thought.

Lumi exited an upstairs bathroom, where she'd been to reapply her make-up, when she saw Walter waiting for her on a landing, leaning against a balustrade.

'Walter!' she gasped, then put on her hostess smile. 'Can I get you a drink?'

'I can't wait any longer, I have to be with you.'

Lumi looked up and down the landing, and then over the balustrade at the party beyond the empty entrance below.

'I'm with my family,' she said, nervously. 'Stella's room is just along there . . .' she motioned down the hall as he clasped her hand. 'We have to keep things between us.'

'I know but –'

'Is Kiki not coming?'

Walter looked taken aback and realised it was the first time anyone had mentioned Kiki in the two hours since he'd arrived at the party. Perhaps their marriage – perhaps this Eden Roque business – could be swept under the carpet.

'No, no . . .' he said, looking a little weary. 'It's over, my marriage is over. When will you walk away from yours?'

'Ah, there you are!' Viktor said, looking up, and slightly irritated. What was Walter Steinherr doing upstairs in his home anyway? 'I'm about to say a few words.'

Lumi blushed.

'Of course, let's go.' She and Walter hurried along the landing and down the large floating staircase. Viktor waited at the bottom, eyeing them beadily, then turned on his heel as soon as Lumi reached him.

Walter grabbed Viktor by the arm, stopping him, which made him bristle. Viktor looked at Walter's hand until he removed it.

'Viktor, before you make your speech, there's something I want to tell you.'

Lumi's eyes widened in panic. She shook her head ever so slightly.

'I want you to know first . . .'

Lumi's heart raced. Viktor paused.

'I'm putting Snowbell, Aster and Orchid on the market.'

Viktor took a step back in surprise.

'What?'

It made no business sense at all. He eyed Walter suspiciously. Was that why he'd come this year? To gloat that he was selling them to someone else?

'And you can have first refusal.'

Viktor scratched his head. He couldn't believe it. This building had been his passion project and Steinherr had made it difficult for him at every turn. He'd convinced Stognev to double-cross him at the deeds stage, causing years of drama and discord between the three richest men in town.

'Really?' Viktor asked, not daring to believe it. And what was the catch? Would Walter ask for an eye-watering and insulting price?

'Market value – we'll get Umansky to come up with a fair price.'

Lumi's smile was full of a different kind of relief.

'Why now?' Viktor asked, candidly.

Walter looked to Lumi briefly, then back to her husband.

'An iron is eaten away by rust . . . so the envious are consumed by their own passion.'

Lumi looked at the floor. Walter's covert plea might just break her into a million little pieces.

Viktor narrowed his eyes in puzzlement. He didn't know if Walter was talking about himself or Viktor, but he was happy with the news, nonetheless.

'What can I say?' Viktor exclaimed, finally extending a hand.

Walter took it, and the two men broke their deadlock.

'A happy Christingle indeed!' Viktor said, shaking Walter's hand effusively before turning it into an amicable slap on the chest.

'Let's go, speech!'

Lumi and Walter walked two steps behind Viktor, knowing that with this gesture came a watershed moment. Nothing would be the same again.

When Anastasia burst into the kitchen, her legs almost buckled, she was so half cut.

Cat was filling blood-orange macarons with starbursts of basil-infused cream when she looked up in alarm at the noise.

'Here we are again!' Anastasia slurred, admiring the décor as if she was remembering it from a dream.

'*Calma!*' Cat snapped, levelling Anastasia with a look. Gerard and Lydia were filling glasses, and Gerard looked up, knowing what danger this might entail.

'Mrs Diamandis!' he fawned. 'Can I get you an elderflower fizz? Perhaps some water?'

Anastasia steadied herself with her palms on the island and took a few deep breaths.

'No.'

'What are you doing here?' Cat asked, as politely as she could. Lydia watched while she unsheathed balls of decorative ice and put them in two balloon glasses. Samuel and Karius Sommar had specifically asked for gin and tonics. Emme came in with another silver platter of empty glasses and placed it on the island, looking from Anastasia, whose head was hung between her shoulders, to Cat, piping bag in hand and furious.

'Are you OK?' Emme mouthed.

Cat nodded.

'Yes, desserts now, please,' she said, indicating a silver tray of chocolate mousse in delicate shot glasses, with a homemade pistachio truffle atop each one.

Gerard filled a long glass with ice and water from the filter tap and placed it next to Anastasia, who looked like she was trying to regain her balance.

'Here you are, ma'am,' he said, reverently.

'I said NO!' Anastasia bellowed, swiping the glass off the edge of the smooth marble surface, along with the silver tray of empty glasses Emme had just laid there. There was an almighty crash, which made everyone in the kitchen jump. Everyone except Cat, who continued to pipe with an unsteady, shaky hand.

'Hold off one second,' Lumi whispered in Viktor's ear, as she went into the kitchen to see what all the noise was about.

'Ah, Anastasia, is everything alright?' she asked, calm and fragrant, while Gerard got to work with the dustpan and brush. Lumi had noticed Anastasia, prowling around the party like a pinball bouncing from bumper to bumper, and she meant to mention it to Walter and ask if everything was alright, but she had been so preoccupied by his declaration, by the fact his marriage was over, by his decision to sell Snowbell, Aster and Orchid, that she hadn't had the chance to tell him.

'My husband's about to do a speech,' Lumi said, putting her palm on Anastasia's back. Anastasia's hands, weighed down by diamonds, seemed to grip onto the air above the kitchen surface.

She looked up with a slow and furious furrow, but Lumi Kivvi had a serene authority about her. Something about Lumi's voice reminded her of calm during turbulence, somewhere in the depths of her childhood. It wasn't comforting enough.

'Would you like a coffee?' Lumi asked, as if it was going to happen anyway. 'Gerard, get Mrs Diamandis a coffee and I will ask Teresa to see to this,' she said, nodding at the floor.

'Very well, ma'am,' Gerard nodded, clearing a few sharp shards away first.

'Macarons,' Cat said, handing Tiago a plate of her beautiful creations. 'Make sure you find Miss Stella first . . .' Cat added. Lumi met her eye with a grateful smile.

Gerard busied himself with the coffee, Lydia left with a tray of drinks and Tiago and Emme picked up the first dessert platters.

'I understand you and Catalina are friends,' Lumi said warmly, trying to distract Anastasia from whatever the hell meltdown she was having. 'Teresa said you called by to see her.' Anastasia looked up at Cat, slowly and deliberately, on the other side of the kitchen island, piping more ganache into macarons.

'Who's Catalina?' Anastasia said blankly, while the chef tried not to cry onto her patisserie.

Emme returned to the main throng and began another clockwise rotation with a tray of chocolate mousses in glasses, while Tiago went anticlockwise with the first rows of macarons. As she worked the room, Emme heard snippets of conversations. Bill Harrington was discussing hedge funds with a bored-looking Oscar Goodall. Mads Christensen was telling Frida Alm about the song he had written for the Danish Eurovision entry next year. Boutique hotelier Dirk Detzer was asking Dimitri Diamandis which Greek island was best to start with, as he had never been. And Lexy was fawning over Priya Kapoor's earrings and showing her the almost-as-ostentatious pink ruby on her right hand. All these conversations stopped when Viktor chinked a fork against a crystal glass and called for attention around the piano.

Where's Tristan? Emme thought, as she quietly continued to circulate.

'Ladies and gentlemen, may I have your attention please?' Viktor said, his small fuzz of tobacco-coloured hair in a whirl above his thinning pate.

The pianist paused 'Für Elise', and children started to reappear from the games room. Stella Kivvi shooed a few children out of her bedroom and down the stairs to the throng growing around the large open living space. Emme weaved quietly, silently offering desserts in delicate shot glasses. 'Where's Lumi?!' Viktor almost barked.

'Here!' she said cheerily, coming out of the kitchen, one arm around the waist of a swaying Anastasia Steinherr, who she deposited next to Dimitri, while Gerard deftly followed with a strong black coffee. Vivian shot Lysander a concerned look across the room. Lumi looked back behind her and beckoned Cat to come out of the kitchen and show her face, as was tradition during the speeches. Lumi always reminded Viktor to thank the staff. Cat put her tea towel on her shoulder and feigned a smile, despite feeling wretched on the inside.

Guests gave a little cheer as Lumi joined her husband at the piano and promised not to break into song.

'I'll leave that to the experts,' she nodded across the room, towards Frida Alm.

Viktor didn't laugh at his wife's joke, but paused to get his words together, looking at his impeccably shiny shoes for a moment.

'Good people of Kristalldorf, thank you for coming to our annual Christingle, and may I say they get more wonderful every year.'

Aapo had rounded up Mika and Stella and they stood close to their parents, while guests gave a grateful clap and cheer.

Lumi tapped the small of Viktor's back and he seamlessly thanked Teresa, Gerard and the team, and Catalina in the kitchen for her excellent catering. There was polite applause, and Cat gave a bashful nod. Emme and Tiago, silver platters in front of them as they passed each other, exchanged an amused look. They really were invisible today.

Viktor went on to thank the 'beautiful and damned' of Kristalldorf, to applause and laughter.

'This year is particularly special as I believe it's the first time we've had you here, Walter,' he said, even though he knew for certain that was true. 'It just goes to show what we can do when we come together,' Viktor continued. He raised his glass to Walter, across the room, who raised his glass back, although it was Lumi he was drinking to, not Viktor.

'So before we sing "Gaudete" together, I would like us to all raise our glasses: to old friends and new.'

Emme looked across the room and saw Tristan, in a corner near Cat and the kitchen. He saw Emme and raised his glass, giving a subtle, knowing smile. Emme flushed. God, she wanted to be with him. Had he really ended it with Vivian? She hadn't seen them interact once during the whole afternoon, so perhaps it was true. Emme felt the burning gaze of Lexy, her bemused smile boring into her as she saw the interaction between them. Emme put her head down.

'To old friends and new!' everyone cheered, before taking a sip and applauding Viktor and Lumi for their generosity. From across the room another fork chinked, this time on a china coffee cup. Everyone looked around to see who the next speech was coming from.

'Can I just say a few things?' Anastasia slurred.

'Christ, is she drunk?' Walter muttered to Vivian, who squeezed her father's arm.

Cat leaned back against the closed kitchen door, shielding her eyes, terrified of what was about to unfold.

'Of course!' Viktor said, intrigued.

Dimitri stepped forward and quietly whispered in his wife's ear.

'Everything alright?'

Tiago and Emme both stopped their rounds and looked at Cat. Emme edged towards her.

Anastasia ignored her husband and continued. Their children, who had migrated towards their parents, looked up at their mother.

'While we're kissing everyone's asses . . .'

Lumi frowned.

'Can we also raise a glass to my sister, Vivian . . .' The bitter tinge in her voice was palpable to everyone. Guests started to look at each other. Tristan drained his drink, placed the glass on the mantelpiece, and put his hands in his pockets nervously.

'Not only has my father decided to sell Aster, Snowbell and Orchid, which is *great* news,' she said sarcastically. 'I could have made them *amazing*,' she slurred as an aside. 'But my sister Vivian is taking over Papa's empire!'

'Anastasia!' Walter scolded, in a low and booming voice.

'Come on sis . . .' Lysander pleaded, as he walked across the room and looped his arm through hers. She flung it away angrily. The guests all felt the tension.

'I mean, he really doesn't trust me, does he?' Anastasia said, almost playing for laughs. Vivian burned red, wanting the ground to swallow her up.

'But you can't have it all sis . . .' Anastasia said, jabbing a finger across the room in Vivian's direction.

Vivian's gaze turned steely; a rash creeping up her pale cheeks. She shook her head gently, pleading with her sister.

'That man you've pined for, for what, eight years?' Anastasia looked around the room. Tristan took a step back.

'Where are you Tristan?' Anastasia bellowed, a bitter *come out come out wherever you are* challenge in her voice. Cat kept her hand shielded over her eyes and shook her head.

Emme's blood ran cold.

'He's here!' Frida Alm said cheerfully, reaching her arm up to point a finger above Tristan's head from where she was standing next to him.

Anastasia spotted him.

'Ah. There you are!'

Tristan levelled her with a look, a silent plea not to do what he knew was coming.

'I can confirm, after recent inspection, that Tristan Du Kok is one. Great. Fuck.'

The children – and most of the adults – in the room all gasped. Lumi put her palms up and tried to appeal for calm while Viktor looked at his friends in disbelief. Vivian saw red and raged.

'That was YOU scuttling off the balcony like a cockroach!' she shouted, launching herself into the middle of the room. Walter held her back by one arm, while her other pointed fiercely.

'How DARE you!' she looked between Anastasia and Tristan, whose hands were still in his pockets. Face sombre.

Tristan looked back at Vivian and made a silent plea of an apology, but she ran, tears filling her eyes as she charged out.

Emme headed efficiently towards the kitchen. Vivian's harrowed and hurt face had made Emme feel even more wretched for her strange part in it, and she wanted to get to Cat. She had to walk past Tristan first. He looked at her, pleading with her now. She shook her head.

'Not now,' she said under her breath, stopping for a second. There was so much she wanted to say to him.

'Not so fucking smug now!' Anastasia shouted from her spot, taunting her sister's trail.

'Fucking bitch,' Cat whispered to herself, shaking her head at the kitchen door.

'Mummy, what's going on?' Olympia demanded, looking up in shock.

'Bill, I think we should go,' Lexy said, her face contorting at the language her children were hearing.

'Carols anyone?' chuckled Viktor, quite amused that the Steinherr family fallout had been so beautifully delivered to him on a plate, while also hoping it wouldn't affect Walter's offer.

'Youuuuu BASTARD!' Dimitri Diamandis yelled, lunging across the room at Tristan Du Kok and landing one surprisingly well-placed blow to the right side of his eye. Tristan fell sideways, into Emme, in a smash and a clatter of chocolate mousse and glass.

'No!' Cat hollered.

'Stop that!' cried Viktor's assistant Benjamin.

Frida Alm screamed the loudest, but all the guests around Tristan were covered in glass and chocolate mousse.

Emme and Tristan had both fallen to the floor in a heap.

'ENOUGH!' bellowed Walter Steinherr, as Lysander, helped by Karius Sommar, pulled his brother-in-law and held him back.

'Go home, Dimi! Take the kids!' Lysander ordered.

'Calm please everyone!' begged Lumi.

And with that, the annual Kivvi Christingle was over.

Chapter Forty-Eight

Emme stood in oversized men's jogging bottoms and a sweatshirt, her feet bare on the cold tiled floor.

'Thank you, Tiago, I appreciate all of this.'

'It's nothing,' he smiled.

'No, really, I'm a mess.'

'Here, take my boots, they're big but they'll get you home. Wear thick socks.'

'Are you sure?'

'Don't be weird about it,' Tiago said with a shrug and a joke.

The heel of Cassie's borrowed stilettos had broken when Emme went flying.

Tristan had looked desperately at her, in their messy clinch.

'Are you OK?' he'd asked, his handsome brow brooding and bleeding.

Emme had nodded, and been helped up by Tristan, closely watched by Tiago and Cat, who admonished Dimitri Diamandis for hurting her friend as a consequence of his violent rage.

Although Emme had managed to hobble to Tiago's place in one shoe, the broken one in hand, she couldn't walk home like that. The snow had settled in Kristalldorf and she was grateful for the change of clothes as she looked around Tiago's humble apartment. It was the least fancy place she had seen since arriving: six Portuguese and two Mexican workers shared three bedrooms, but it was clean and warm and felt like the safest bet at the time. At least she had somewhere to go. Poor Cat was stuck in Chalet Edelweiss, picking up the emotional shards after Emme and Tiago had helped her with the physical ones.

Emme caught the thick balled-up pair of ski socks as Tiago threw them.

'Never made a more dramatic 100 francs, huh?' he joked.

Emme shook her head.

'Don't,' she said with a weary smile.

Now wasn't the time to tell Tiago or Cat that she had inserted herself into this ghastly mess a fortnight ago. It was all so fucked up.

'What's going on?' asked Nieves, Tiago's flatmate, as she walked into the apartment. 'My friend said there was a fight at the Kivvi party and –'

Nieves saw Emme standing in Tiago's clothes.

'Oh,' she said, intrigued. Tiago never brought girls home.

'Long story, I'll tell you later . . . but this is my buddy Emme, she was working there with me.'

'Oh really?' Nieves said, almond eyes full of intrigue.

'Wow, news really travels fast in this town!' Emme said, raising an eyebrow. She put on Tiago's socks and laced up his boots as Nieves slunk off to the kitchen with her grocery bags.

'Want me to walk you home?' Tiago asked.

'It's fine,' Emme said, gathering her purse, coat, and a plastic bag of clothes. She was dreading getting back to the Harrington home and hearing Lexy wittering about the drama they had all just witnessed. She was worried about Tristan and the state of his face. For a small guy, Dimitri Diamandis certainly packed a punch.

Emme opened her arms out and gave Tiago a hug.

'Thanks T,' she said. 'I'll wash these and return them.'

'You better had.' He said with a smile. 'That sweatshirt cost me fifteen euros.'

And he squeezed her back. Two outsiders in their strange huddle.

Chapter Forty-Nine

'How COULD she!' Vivian sobbed in a rage, as she stormed along the hallway of the Steinherr mansion, followed by her father and brother.

Nanny Iris hurried down the stairs to see if the children were back. Walter looked up at her. 'Prepare their bath, they will be back any minute. Kristaps, you had better prepare an ice pack for Dimitri's hand.'

The butler looked confused, but nodded and raced to the kitchen.

'Is everything OK, sir?' asked a maid as she came out of the kitchens.

'No!' Walter bellowed, and continued down after Vivian, who went into the plush lounging room, only because it was the furthest away from the front door, and slumped onto a daybed under a window. Night had already fallen on Kristalldorf, and the room was cosily lit.

Vivian threw her face onto the plump cushions and sobbed.

Lysander sat next to her and rubbed her back.

'The humiliation!' she sobbed. 'She was screwing Tristan! The slut!'

Walter didn't want to think of either of his daughters screwing anyone, so he retreated to the living room, its fireplace already lit, and fixed himself a drink.

He looked up at the portrait of his first wife and his family. He wanted to ask Anna Maria how the hell he was going to fix the mess between their daughters, but he heard the front door open again, and wondered if it were Anastasia. He was *furious* with her. For making a scene more than what she had done behind her sister and her husband's backs.

He walked into the ample hallway, its floor tiled black and white.

'Dimitri . . .' he said sharply. Walter was furious with him too. Honestly! The first time he had gone to the Kivvi's Christingle and his son-in-law – his attorney – had started a brawl.

The children stood around their father, their faces pale in shock.

Dimitri's thin hair, or what remained of it, was dishevelled and he had a swollen bloody fist.

'Go upstairs and find Nanny Iris,' Dimitri said, tepidly. The children went running up the mansion stairs, passing Kiki as she came down.

'What the hell are you playing at, brawling in public like that? With that man?' Walter scolded, towering over Dimitri, who looked like he might vomit.

Walter saw Kiki at the curve in the stairs, wearing a pink chiffon peignoir and fluffy mules and stopped.

'Are you still here?' he snapped.

Kiki observed Dimitri's swollen fist and dishevelled combover and gave a coquettish smile.

'Jeez, I thought *I* was in trouble.'

Chapter Fifty

It was almost 8pm when Emme punched in the code and let herself into Chalet Stern. She hoped the children would be in bed – Lexy and Bill put the kids to bed at weekends, to make up for all the days they didn't in the week, unless they were out for the evening themselves. But after the drama of the afternoon, Emme decided to buy herself a little more time by heading straight to the laundry room on the ground floor.

She opened the carrier bag with her tights, Cat's little black dress and Cassie's shoes in it, and examined the dress in the blade of moonlight that shone through the small side window. Chocolate mousse had got on the white Peter Pan collar.

'Shit.'

The room smelled of washing power; Mr and Mrs Muller's bedsheets billowed from drying lines across the ceiling in the dark, alongside the cloak that always hung there and no one seemed to own. A tumble drier whirred and offered warmth.

Emme put Cat's dress and her tights in a washing machine drum with some liquid and thought about the chaos of the party. Anastasia's outburst. How cruelly she had looked at her sister. About the screams when her husband punched Tristan. The smash of all the glass as Emme went crashing underneath him in a heap. She slammed the machine door to snap herself out of it but jumped when she saw a silhouette in the reflection of the washing machine door.

Emme gasped and turned around sharply.

Lexy was lingering in the doorway, leaning against the wooden frame, her arms folded. Her face was in the shadows. The suspended cloak looked like the grim reaper was watching them.

'You made me ju—' Emme was trying to brush off her scream.

'You be careful Emmeline,' Lexy said. Her voice was low and angry, at a pitch Emme hadn't heard before.

Water started to rush into the drum, which made her think she must have misheard. Lexy Harrington sounded threatening.

'What?'

'That man is no good.'

Emme scrunched up the empty plastic bag with the broken shoes and pulled it across her body. The long sleeves of Tiago's sweatshirt drowned her.

'I thought you were family friends.'

Lexy wouldn't know how Emme knew this; it seemed to have caught her off guard.

'He was a sweet boy, but greed got the better of him.'

Emme knitted her eyebrows together.

'Be wary of anyone who can break *three* hearts in one callous hit.' Lexy said it like a teacher, as if she were telling Emme off.

Emme quickly turned on the wall light, a button that worked on a timer, and saw Lexy's incandescent face illuminated. She looked Emme up and down, seemingly repulsed by the sight of her in a man's clothes. Tristan's, she probably assumed.

Emme stayed quiet, she felt as though Lexy was rage baiting her; that she was trying to get a reaction, and she didn't want to give her one.

'I saw you at the party. I saw him putting food in your mouth like you're another plaything.'

Emme blushed.

Lexy sounded demented.

Emme wanted to get out of there but Lexy was blocking her in.

'He's dangerous!' Lexy snapped.

'Dangerous?'

Emme walked towards Lexy, hoping her boss would move out of the way and let her get upstairs so she could have a shower and go to bed.

'And I don't just mean with women,' Lexy almost spat. 'Google Tristan Joubert's father, google Charles Joubert, and you might wonder what guilty secrets that boy holds.'

Emme finally broke.

'Why are you bringing that up?'

The women stood staring at each other as the timed light went out, and the room fell into darkness again.

Lexy didn't answer.

Emme felt claustrophobic, she had to get out of there, so she walked right up to Lexy, standing in the doorway and hoped she would let her pass.

The shard of moonlight now caught part of Lexy's face, and Emme could see a flash in her eye that looked so angry, as if she were considering her next move, that Emme felt somewhat scared.

Lexy broke the impasse and moved to one side, to enable Emme to go upstairs, but Emme turned right, out of the laundry room and out of the front door – she had to find Cat or Tiago. No, she had to see Tristan. She wanted to look him in the eye. She wanted to touch his face. He was wounded and right now he had no one. Wherever she went, she had to get the hell out and as far away as she could from Chalet Stern and Lexy Harrington's fury.

Chapter Fifty-One

It was tradition, after the annual Christingle, for the Kivvi family to retire to the cinema room of Chalet Edelweiss and watch a Christmas movie while Cat cleaned up the kitchen, and the staff cleared up the empty glasses, the half-eaten canapés and the napkin detritus, scattered all around the home. But not today. Lumi had sent Aapo, Stella and Mika ahead to choose the film, while Viktor's assistant, Benjamin, paced around Viktor's study flapping.

'How dare they!' Benjamin snarled.

Lumi looked at him. He was definitely exceeding his brief. Viktor looked out of the window, hands in his pockets; his crinkled forehead in waves.

'Peasants don't know how to behave so they resort to punching!'

'And you resort to name calling Benjamin?' Lumi said with a sage look of disapproval.

Benjamin seemed to have even more disdain for the locals than Viktor had. His strong views on immigration were conveniently forgotten when it suited his job to live nomadically across borders. Benjamin was the sort of nationalist to go on torch-lit marches with far-right friends on his weekends off in Helsinki; yet enjoy the trappings of Viktor's homes in Kristalldorf, New York and St Bart's.

He smoothed his quiff upwards.

'All I'm saying is these people have done nothing but make life difficult for you and your husband,' Benjamin said, curtly.

Lumi wanted to laugh at the irony.

'These *people* offered Viktor what he wanted on a plate today,' Lumi said, with a waning smile. 'The chance to own the entire building, which was his dream!' Her Oscar de la Renta gown felt heavy now, and she wanted to change into a house suit and get out of this stuffy office.

'Hmm, that is true . . .' Viktor said, looking out at the town with a self-satisfied smile. This entire development would be his, as it should be.

'Great!' Benjamin hissed, as his phone lit up. 'That's the press – now I'm having to do damage limitation . . .'

Lumi approached her husband by the window.

'Come, let's watch a film with the children . . .' she said soothingly.

'Give me a minute will you, woman!' he snapped.

'Fine.'

Lumi couldn't stand to be in the men's company for a second longer, so she went to change, passing staff cleaning on her way through. She remembered Catalina in the kitchen, and went to check on her.

Cat was wildly wiping down the pale blue oven when Lumi poked her head around the door.

'You'll take the colour off it at that rate!' Lumi said.

Cat looked up and stopped.

'Oh, hello Mrs Kivvi, is everything OK?'

Lumi didn't seem vexed by what had happened, but then she rarely seemed vexed by anything.

'Can I get you a plate of snacks for the cinema room?'

'No Catalina, we've all eaten plenty thank you, I just wanted to commend you for an exceptional menu today. You really did excel yourself.'

Cat smiled gratefully.

'Got a little dramatic with the desserts there . . .' Lumi said with some diplomacy.

Cat sighed heavily.

'That was quite a memorable one Mrs Kivvi, but you know what they say?'

'What's that?'

'If you're not living on the edge, you're taking up too much space.'

She gave a solemn smile.

'That's the spirit, Catalina,' Lumi smiled, and left the kitchen. Cat leaned on her forearms, on the impeccable oven top, dropped her head, and cried.

Chapter Fifty-Two

Emme knocked on what she hoped was the right apartment door, frantic and cold, still wearing Tiago's clothes under her lilac puffer. His boots had cut through the snow, leaving a trail from Chalet Stern to the building with the love hearts cut out of the balconies.

'Who is it?' said a gruff voice.

'It's me, Emme,' she replied, her chest pounding.

Tristan opened his apartment door, gingerly, and looked at Emme. His eye was swollen and bleeding. His bare torso cut. Soul music played through the stereo in the warmly lit apartment behind him.

'Jesus!'

Emme clutched his face in alarm, examining the damage more closely. She hadn't seen the extent of it at the time as, after helping Emme up and dusting her down, Tristan had shaken his head at the bemused crowd and walked out, pride and face both bruised. He hadn't realised until he got home that he had shards of glass jabbed into his left shoulder blade too.

'Are *you* OK?' he asked, examining Emme's worried face.

'Yeah yeah, none of it cut me . . .'

They appraised each other's faces as Emme put her hand to Tristan's split eye, to where Dimitri had landed the blow and cut his eyebrow with the edge of his Rolex. 'Oh no . . .' she groaned, before dotting it with three gentle kisses, the action coming naturally to her, knowing it was this softness he needed. 'Gosh, Tristan, have you put ice on that?'

He shook his head and winced, then opened the door wider to let her in.

Tristan's apartment was small, simple and homely. It had mid-century European furniture, a neat kitchen and functional curtains. It looked like a holiday rental rather than a billionaire playboy's bachelor pad. A fire roared from a small log burner. Al Green played through speakers while CNN rolled muted on TV.

In the low glow of a lamp, Emme sat side-saddle across Tristan's lap and gently pressed a checked tea towel filled with ice to his eye, cleaning it as she dabbed.

She'd discarded Tiago's boots and trousers and wore just a sweatshirt and her underwear. Tristan wore jersey joggers that showed the outline of his exceptional cock, his broad and tanned torso bare. Emme checked his shoulder blade for any last pieces of glass.

'What a mess,' Emme said.

Tristan put his hand on top of Emme's to slow down her movements at his brow.

'I'm sorry. Not my finest hour,' he said, stroking the curve of her thigh with his free hand.

'You didn't do anything wrong today!' Emme said defiantly, inwardly cursing the Greek man with the pointy face.

'No, but I did,' Tristan said, with some shame.

He certainly had. And Emme knew she was on a

precipice as she looked at him and wondered if she should have come. He had hurt Vivian and slept with her sister. But she couldn't not come. She had to see him tonight.

'Vivian seems really nice . . .' Emme said, regretfully.

'She is,' he winced. 'I shouldn't have messed her around.' Tristan sighed and leaned his head back against the wall. 'Maybe it was a fucked-up way of ensuring she'd hate me.'

Emme stopped dabbing his brow.

'Why do you want her to hate you?'

Tristan took a laboured sigh.

'Because she should hate me. I'm the son of Charles Joubert. My dad screwed her dad out of his most spectacular hotel. I twisted the knife when I sold it to the Russians.'

Emme looked at him, confused. He seemed to make life harder for himself. Is that what he was doing with her sitting across his lap? Getting involved with someone it could never go anywhere with? Someone who would inevitably hate him? She was the help who worked for his friends. Although now she thought about it, she hadn't seen him talking to Lexy or Bill either at the party.

'Vivian seemed willing to overlook it, but I know what my dad and I did caused Walter Steinherr heartache.'

'Did Walter approve of you two?'

'I never gave him the chance to.'

Emme studied his strikingly handsome face, his dark tousled hair pushed back off it. His thick straight brows sheltering an intense gaze.

'So you were being cruel to be kind? Come on . . .' Emme said, as if she was no fool. 'Were you not just being greedy?'

Tristan pierced her with a look.

'If Vivian's father *has* picked her to succeed him with the

299

Steinherr group, she can't run the business and date me, not in the shadow of my family.'

He looked unnervingly neutral about it, which made Emme feel cautious.

'So you want her but can't have her?'

God this guy is a headfuck, Emme thought.

Tristan took Emme's hand.

'I want you.'

He kissed Emme slowly and carefully while he adjusted his position, his elegant athleticism jarring with his sore shoulder.

Emme let Tristan gently slip his tongue inside her mouth. She raised her hands to his face, the cuffs of Tiago's sweatshirt caressing his jaw as she stroked him with her thumb. She felt his hardness grow under her.

'You do?' Emme teased, pressing down a little.

'So much. I am *fascinated* by you.'

They kissed again, then Emme pulled back.

How could she trust a guy she had seen lie so expertly? Why hadn't he got her number somehow? Called her from Geneva or London?

'Really?' she asked, as she put her hand on his cock, long and hard, rising in his lounging pants. He lifted her sweatshirt off with a wince of pain, then expeditiously removed her bra. She held his eye as her nipples were freed, level with his chest, as he stroked her breasts appreciatively. Emme groaned, before Tristan unwrapped the tea towel next to him on the sofa and picked up an ice cube. Without taking his eyes off her, he rolled it over Emme's decolletage, down to one nipple, then the other. She moaned as water from the ice cube ran down between her breasts, then he licked and kissed each nipple with a considered tongue.

'Oh Tristan . . .' she groaned. 'Can you . . . ?' she asked, wondering if he were up to it. She could feel a wetness in her underwear that she didn't want to put a stop to. He nodded as he lifted her gently and slipped his hand inside the lace of her knickers, pulling them down her legs. Emme was fully naked now, sitting across Tristan's clothed lap. She wanted to have him again, this time without hurry or haste. She wanted them to take their time and enjoy every second of the bliss that was about to come. She turned to fully face him and opened her legs to straddle him, while he raised them both off the sofa. Emme clung to Tristan's pulsating arms as he kicked off his joggers and put his hands on her waist, positioning her glistening pussy over his throbbing cock.

'Wait!' she gasped breathily. And he instinctively leaned, arcing their clinch so he could grab a condom from the drawer of the side table at the end of the sofa, before slumping back down so he could skilfully slide it on.

'God!' he groaned as he felt the sweet tightness of her. She moaned too, then she lifted his chin so his eyes were on her.

'Look at me,' she commanded in a whisper.

They were going to make each other come, and she wanted him looking at her intently, so there was no hiding. She groaned as she eased down him and felt his shoulders finally relax.

Chapter Fifty-Three

Anastasia Steinherr sat in the back of a limousine, half-way to Germany, huge Gucci shades covering most of her bleary face. It had been a fretful night in the Kristall Palace, before she crashed out across the vast bed in the penthouse there, still dressed in carmine Valentino. When she had awoken at 4am, fuzzy-headed but defiant, she had showered and had the Kristall Palace yumbo driver take her to the Steinherr mansion, where she silently changed and packed a bag of clothes before creeping out before dawn.

At the car port at the edge of Kristalldorf, she met a waiting limo.

'Where to, Mrs Diamandis?' asked the driver.

'The Black Forest.'

The six-hour journey to the luxury spa facility would give her enough time to send all the messages of regret and apology she needed to, and explain that she would be away for a while for some 'rehab'. She sent the first one to Dimitri, who had made such a buffoon of himself, he almost didn't warrant an apology. Fancy creating a scene like that! But she messaged him a few words to say sorry for the duplicity, and that she was going away for a while to work on herself.

As the driver wound through mountains and tunnels,

past lakes and medieval turrets, Anastasia sent a message to Nanny Iris to tell her to give the children her love and tell them she kissed them while they were sleeping (not true), and that she would write to them at school (which was true – handwritten letters were Anastasia's favourite form of communication). She didn't make any pledges about being back in time for Christmas, although she knew it would be on Nanny Iris's mind.

She didn't owe her father or sister an explanation right now – their treachery had been too much – but she sent Lysander a message, saying she was going away for a reset, and that perhaps with space in New York he could reflect and see things from her viewpoint.

She pondered Walter. What *was* going on with her father? He was making all these erratic decisions lately. From marrying Kiki, to now having chosen Vivian to run the empire over her. It felt like a dagger to the heart. He was probably about to have a baby with Kiki, he was behaving so wildly. Why wasn't she at the Kivvi Christingle anyway? The migraine seemed a little unlikely.

The thought of Walter and Kiki having a child repulsed her, as the car skirted Lake Constance. Perhaps that's what this was all about, although Anastasia had been intrigued to see a vast pile of Kiki's Louis Vuitton suitcases on the luggage rack by the front door as she left the Steinherr mansion in the dark.

She didn't feel any sympathy for Tristan Du Kok, although he had been an exceptional lay, on several blistering occasions. She thought about texting him, but decided he could wait.

As she looked at the sorry grey clouds gathering over

the long lake, she thought about one person she did perhaps owe an apology to.

Anastasia opened her messages to Cat and paused her thumb over the text box as she looked at the photo. A smiling face in ski gear. Wild black curls. A terribly sexy mouth that had done wonderful things to Anastasia's body. But what was the point now, Anastasia pondered. She had only pursued Cat last New Year's Eve because she could be a key to Seven Summits. If her father was selling the apartments, then Anastasia and Cat were done.

Chapter Fifty-Four

Emme woke in Tristan's arms to the sound of the bells chiming in the square for Sunday morning service. His naked body spooning hers like a Trojan warrior as she emerged from a blissful sleep. They had made love to each other, passionately and intensely on the sofa, then again in Tristan's bed in the middle of the night, and Emme already knew she was in too deep to question it.

'Tell me about London,' he whispered, realising from the sound of her breathing that she was awake. Emme rolled over to face him, her body curled in a foetal position, her knees almost to his chest.

She put her hands on his muscular, tanned arms.

'You've just been!'

'Tell me about *your* London,' Tristan said.

She pondered her London – a small flat in Balham and a job by St Paul's Cathedral – and imagined it would be different to Tristan's London. Flying in and flying out for whistlestop trips on his private jet. What was he doing in London last week anyway?

'The walk from the South Bank across the Millennium Bridge, to where I work, makes me think it's the most magical city in the world.'

Tristan looked at Emme like she was the most magical

thing he had ever seen in the world. Who was she kidding? He looked at every woman like that.

'Sounds amazing,' he said, enchanted.

'How well do you know it?'

'My dad took me on trips there. To the tennis. To the polo. I was just there to meet a business associate of my mother's . . .'

'Nice. Where did you stay?'

'A hotel in South Kensington, but I've never really seen the *real* London.'

'I should show you some time.' Even as Emme said it, she had a feeling it would never happen. She couldn't imagine Tristan at a gig in Camden, or strolling with her through Hyde Park.

'I'd love that.'

'Who were the business associates?'

'Guys who might be running the estate back in South Africa,' he said, looking a little cagey. 'We need new staff and this team runs an estate in the Napa Valley . . . and, well, they might be heading south.'

'What's your home like?' Emme asked. She had never been to South Africa.

'Beautiful,' he said, piercing her with his golden eyes. 'A different kind of beautiful to this. Rolling green fields and stunning mountain views, the best beaches in the world . . .' he trailed off. He didn't offer to show her.

'And Du Kok Estates? How long has it been in the family?'

'Three hundred years . . .' he said, proudly. 'My mother has been running it since her father died in the 1990s and, well, she made it go global. We were a boutique winery before then.'

'Wow, she sounds incredible.'

Tristan gave a rueful smile. He looked like he missed his mother.

'Yah, she is.'

Emme desperately wanted to ask him about his father. She hadn't forgotten Lexy's warning last night, but thinking of her now reminded her that she needed to get up and go home. She might be needed today.

She yawned and stretched out.

'I'd better go . . .' she said, looking at the clock next to the bed. Tristan's room was simple: a double mattress on the floor with books and an alarm clock next to it. He must be the only billionaire who didn't have furniture in his bedroom, Emme had thought, as they fell into it last night.

Tristan rolled on top of Emme and nuzzled her neck playfully.

'Can't you stay?' he asked, aching to make her come again. He pressed into her. She lifted her pelvis.

If only.

'I can't, I might have to look after the kids. I left in a hurry. And Lexy . . .' She pondered whether to tell Tristan how *weird* Lexy had been about him last night, and suspected it wouldn't go down well. The past few hours since the party had been so blissful, she didn't want to ruin them. 'Lexy is on my case at the moment. I need to get back.'

Tristan dotted kisses into Emme's neck.

'Really? Come on.'

Then Emme blurted it out.

'Yeah, she seemed to have an opinion about your dad . . .'

Tristan backed off, looking at Emme cautiously, before

jumping up. He pulled his white boxers from the floor and put them on.

'What did she say?' he said, an angry flicker in his eye.

'Not much . . .' Emme half lied. She could tell these were tricky waters to navigate. 'I know you said you and Lexy were friends, but –'

'I didn't say we were friends,' Tristan said defensively.

Emme wrapped the feather duvet around her and sat up.

'Erm, yeah you did. When we were skiing.'

'No I didn't,' he said, with utter conviction. 'I said everyone's friends in this town.'

Why was he being so weird? He had gone from hot to cold in seconds.

'Well, you'd better head back then. I need to shower anyway. Sort out my fucking face,' he lamented. He left the bedroom and went to look in the bathroom mirror.

Emme sat up in the bed, feeling baffled.

Is that it?

Didn't he want to know what Lexy had said?

She heard the hot water of the shower turn on.

Emme got up and walked around the apartment, looking for her underwear and Tiago's clothes. She couldn't find everything.

'Tristan, have you seen the joggers I was wearing?' she asked, as she poked her head around the doorway. He was holding them.

'Whose are they anyway?' he asked, as he almost flung them at her. A suppressed rage in his eyes.

Emme was startled – Tristan was obviously highly sensitive about his father, and she could understand why, but there was no need to be rude. She caught the joggers.

Jesus, she thought.

'Thanks,' she said sarcastically. As she got dressed, Tristan got under the shower and started humming – to shut out her noise perhaps – as she gathered her things and let herself out.

Chapter Fifty-Five

Lysander sauntered down the hallway of the Steinherr mansion, towel around his sweaty neck. He'd been running on an incline when the text from his sister came in. No apology for the shambles she'd caused at the party. Just a note to say she was taking off. Lysander had slowed the machine right down and wondered where she might be escaping to for her 'reset'. The Diamandis family island? Too cold in December. Perhaps the Caribbean. Either way, it was probably for the best, and made him itch to get back to New York. Meg would never cause such a scene at a society event. She would never shoot off and leave Blake for weeks on end. Meg was like apple pie; the golden girl of New York, and Lysander was ready to get back to her. As he walked up the hall in his gym gear, he saw Kiki standing by the gold console table next to the front door. She was scribbling a note under the shadow of a huge vase of white hellebores.

Lysander looked to the pile of Louis Vuitton suitcases on the gold luggage trolley with a sense of relief.

'Catching a train?' he said, trying to sound neutral, but triumph bubbled out of every bead of perspiration. He dabbed the towel on his face, lest he reveal his glee.

'Actually, Timo's taking me to the heliport . . .' Kiki

replied, with a self-satisfied smile. 'My luggage will follow in transit.'

Kiki wore a hat, a tuxedo dress and stilettos, as she placed earrings in her lobes and picked up her purse. She was certainly going out in style.

'Where are you headed?' Lysander asked.

'Milan,' she said tartly. 'Then maybe Bel Air. Who knows?'

'The world is your oyster,' Lysander said, somewhat patronisingly, which irked Kiki.

'You know I don't want your inheritance,' she said, levelling Lysander with a look. He didn't expect that. She tapped the edge of her envelope clutch into his chest to make her point.

'You did your little digging – you might have even seen my work . . .' Kiki raised an eyebrow.

'Well two million Instagram followers can't be wrong Kiki. Or should I say, Eden.'

She edged even nearer; she was as tall as Lysander in her heels, her lips lingered at his jawline.

Making him feel uncomfortable gave her a thrill.

'Did you watch me?' she teased in his ear.

Lysander breathed heavily.

She could sense the hard-on her stepson had for her, but she stopped herself from touching it in his gym shorts.

She pulled back.

'I make plenty of my own money.'

Lysander put his palms up.

'Hey I wasn't –'

Kiki cut him off.

'I did before I met your father, and I make even more

now. All your father did was afford me the time to work on my content. I don't need a single Steinherr cent.'

Lysander looked at her, almost in admiration, because he had no doubt she did make a lot of money. And with that, Eden Roque placed her clutch under her arm and strode out of the Steinherr mansion, as free as a bird.

Chapter Fifty-Six

Emme walked into the Harrington home, sad at Tristan's turn in tone and in desperate need of a change of clothes and a shower. She was crushed to see the family were all sitting around the table eating a late breakfast. She had hoped for some peace and some headspace.

'Did you go to a sleepover?' Harry asked, a perplexed crinkle in his ginger freckled face.

'Those are funny pyjamas,' Bella observed in a matter-of-fact way.

Bill looked up from his newspaper.

'Morning,' he said, cheerily.

Lexy looked like she might have a nosebleed and feigned a smile.

'Oh, Emme's home,' she said, behind clenched teeth. A silent *how nice of her* hung over the pancakes the maid had been in to make.

'Morning!' Emme said, as warmly as she could muster, her head held high, as she grabbed a glass of tap water and went to her room.

The slump hit as she got into her bedroom and closed the door, leaning on it behind her and shutting her eyes. She felt like a teenager who had stopped out illicitly, not a twenty-eight-year-old woman who had just had the most explosive sex of her life. What had happened to turn Tristan like that? Was he that sensitive about his father? What darkness was Lexy alluding to? The same nefarious motives as Cat?

'Fuck,' she said quietly, cursing herself for even mentioning Lexy's psychodrama.

Emme walked across the bedroom, sat at the dressing table and scrutinised her reflection in the mirror. She looked tired but not as bad as she'd feared. She was running on adrenaline and good sex. She leaned in and examined her slightly red eyes. She must have only had a couple of hours' sleep, such was the long slow passion of the night. She sighed, before there was a knock at the door, which made her jump.

'Yes?' she called, but Lexy was already standing in the doorway.

'Rule three. No overnight stays out of the chalet unless previously agreed,' Lexy stated, her arms folded. 'Is that crystal clear?'

Emme turned around and looked at her boss. She was wearing her Sunday casuals. Blue jeans restraining her ample bottom; a white shirt that hugged her small waist. Emme took a deep breath, trying to disguise her contempt. Surely Lexy's creepiness last night had led to extenuating circumstances.

'Did you need me last night?'

'Bella was sick.'

Emme's heart sank.

'Oh dear.' Emme wracked her brains. She had eaten a lot of canapés at the party. 'Is she OK?'

'She is now.'

She had looked it just now, cheerily eating her breakfast. Emme rubbed her temple.

'Sorry, it won't happen again.'

'Apology accepted,' Lexy said, turning on her heel. Then she stopped and looked back.

'Oh and what's all this about an expense from the iPad? I had a mystery hundred-franc bill from BUZZ, and someone bought a Netflix film.'

Emme ran her fingers through her hair. She just wanted a shower; to be alone.

'Oh, sorry, I meant to say . . .' Emme wracked her brains. 'I don't know about the Netflix one but Bella accidentally pressed something when she was playing on the iPad, I meant to follow it up . . .'

'So she's just using my credit card, and you're not noticing?'

'Do you not have a PIN to protect purchases?' Emme asked.

They both knew it was probably 1212, which both children would know too. Lexy didn't like being questioned. Her mouth shrunk to a lined circle.

'You should be monitoring them better,' she admonished.

Emme looked at her. She wanted to scream, but knew she was on a knife edge. Lexy was her bread and butter, her home. For now.

She stood up, rubbing mascara and sleep from the corner of her eye.

'Sorry. I will.'

Lexy paused, a supercilious expression on her face as she looked Emme up and down, still wearing another man's clothes. What was wrong with her?

'Do you want me to do something with the kids today?' Emme offered. She didn't usually take them out on their own on a Sunday, but she had to do something to offer an olive branch, or this was going to be unbearable.

'No,' Lexy said swiftly. 'We're accompanying Bill to Zurich today. To see the Christmas decs. Bella is just about up to it. But I want you back on it, with a clear head from tomorrow. Do you understand?'

'Crystal clear,' Emme said, with her own, forced smile.

Chapter Fifty-Seven

'Nice of you to meet me here on a Sunday, Günter,' Walter said, his shirt open, while his physician listened to his heart through a stethoscope against his saggy chest.

There was a silence while measurements were taken and assumptions made.

'Not at all Walter, anything for my patients.'

'It's just it's . . . rather difficult to see you discreetly at the moment, and I wanted to see how things are looking.'

The head offices of the Steinherr group, on the fourth floor of the Alpenrose, were rarely used at the weekend. If Walter had business to attend to, he'd do it at his larger desk in his study at home, and Dimitri rarely worked weekends, unless there was an issue. Lexy Harrington used the tiny broom cupboard-sized office, but never at weekends.

'How's the bone pain been?' Dr Blitzer asked. 'I can see some bruising here on your back, I'm not sure if you were aware of it . . . ?'

Lumi had pointed it out.

'Not great, but isn't that because of my age?'

'Hmmm . . .' Dr Blitzer said, analysing Walter's latest blood scores.

'You have stage three blood cancer Walter, but it does seem to be what we call "smouldering" at the moment.

It's when you flare up that we need to be on high alert. If infections become more frequent, as they were last winter when it was one after the other, we'll have to alter your treatment plan. By which I mean, consider a more robust and targeted approach.'

Walter nodded unhappily. He had shot down the suggestion of chemotherapy every time Dr Blitzer raised it.

'It might be wise to avoid crowds while we're monitoring . . .'

'Well it's too late for that,' Walter said, with a wry laugh.

'Kivvi Christingle?' Dr Blitzer asked.

'It was yesterday. I didn't see you there . . .'

'Madeline had a concert in Salzburg.'

'In which case, I am even more grateful for your time this afternoon. Thank you, my friend.'

Dr Blitzer put his stethoscope around his neck and packed up his medical bag. He knew fighting with Walter Steinherr was pointless. Walter knew the steroids he was on could tank his immune system – and still he'd partied. Pointing out the foolishness of living life while you were dying was moot.

'Until we have the latest biopsy back on the bone marrow, I would just relax Walter, sit and wait.'

He looked flummoxed. And old. Perched on his desk.

'I've never sat and waited for anything my whole life.'

'I know, but what I mean is, there is no point fearing this cancer. It will flare up at any point and worrying about it won't make that fact any easier. In fact, worrying might speed it up.'

Dr Blitzer had a way of delivering grave news both bluntly and kindly.

'Do I look worried?' Walter asked with a stubborn defiance.

Dr Blitzer gave a rueful smile.

'I still recommend you avoid crowds indoors while we go through the winter bugs, but I know you won't forget to enjoy yourself, my friend.'

Walter thought of Kiki, waltzing out of his life as Dr Blitzer prescribed another bottle of iron tablets. He thought of how her secret identity blindsided him. He had never been played for a fool until now; was age catching him off guard? Or was it the cancer? He thought of Lumi, who he ached to be with in his final months.

'Oh don't worry,' he declared. 'I intend to.'

Chapter Fifty-Eight

Showered, refreshed and in her own clothes, Emme walked around the apartment and wondered how the hell she was going to last there until April. The mood was tense at the best of times; and if Emme wasn't in Lexy's good books, it was going to be unbearable.

She got herself a coffee and reflected on her night. The drama of the party had fizzled away the moment Tristan had let her in, but she was worried about Cat, and decided to call her. She didn't answer, so Emme walked into town to get shampoo and conditioner supplies and something for lunch, then she thought she might call in on Cat to check she was OK.

Outside, the village was bustling. She could feel Kristalldorf was building up to peak season, with the streets getting more crowded with skiers and tourists every day. On the high street Emme saw Tristan outside a bakery, chatting to a bunch of ski instructors, snow falling into his newly washed hair. She couldn't see his face from her angle, to see how he was, and she didn't want to go over and say hi. He had been so cold and standoffish when she left. Was there a darker edge to the fuckboy than she could have imagined? Should she heed Lexy's warning? She glanced at him deep in conversation, holding court with the group, and remembered what Cat had said about Tristan hanging out with the ski instructors. It *was* weird that a billionaire wine buyer mingled with the workers. But then she was a worker too. Maybe he liked to slum it. Emme continued. She couldn't bear the thought of him being dismissive again.

Tiago was stocking sanitary towels when Emme bumped into him in the supermarket.

'Thank you so much for last night,' she said. 'I put your clothes in the wash . . .'

Tiago blushed.

'Hey, don't worry. You OK?'

'Yeah, I'm OK, have you spoken to Cat?' She was concerned for her friend after what had happened.

Tiago shook his head.

'I texted her but she's not answered.' He looked a little helpless.

'I called her but no answer either,' Emme frowned. 'Oh dear. Do you think she's OK?'

Tiago stopped stacking and leaned on his pile of crates.

'It was pretty brutal, the way Anastasia was in the kitchen.'

'I know. What a cow,' Emme concurred.

'Apparently she's skipped town,' Tiago said with a shrug.

'How do you know that?'

'Everyone knows everyone's business in Kristalldorf,' he winked.

Emme certainly hoped not.

'I was going to call in on her after here,' Emme said.

'She'll be OK,' Tiago said. 'She's a bad bitch, our Catalina.'

There was always something comforting in Tiago's tone, Emme thought as she squeezed his arm and headed to the checkout.

'I'll let you know when I speak to her,' Emme called back.

As Emme waited in line at the checkout, she picked up two Lindt chocolate reindeer for Harry and Bella from a display at the till.

'You shouldn't have,' said a voice in her ear. She looked round and smiled cautiously at Tristan.

'How's the face?' she asked. 'Looks like it's gone down a bit.' Despite her reservations Emme couldn't help but feel an urge to reach out to touch him but she managed to hold back. She shouldn't trust him, she shouldn't let him in.

'Look, I, erm . . .' Tristan looked around guardedly. 'Look, I'm sorry about this morning.'

He put his own supplies on the conveyor belt behind Emme's. Focaccia, cheese, salami and olives. 'I shouldn't have sent you packing like that . . .'

Emme narrowed her eyes. She shook her head gently. It wasn't OK, so she didn't want to say it was.

'Really, last night threw me – literally,' he quipped. 'And then this morning, about my dad . . .'

'It's sensitive, I get that,' Emme conceded.

Tristan cleared his throat.

'Are you working?' he asked.

'They've all gone to Zurich to see the Christmas lights.'

'Nice,' he said.

Her heart raced. She had never fancied anyone so fiercely.

'Want to go for a hike . . . ?' he asked, with flirtatious intrigue.

Emme looked herself up and down. She was wearing jeans and a leopard-print sweatshirt, her new lilac ski coat and trainers.

'I don't have my hiking boots on.'

'You're fine,' he said, sliding a glance down her body.

Emme paid and packed her goods, then Tristan did the same, placing his shopping in Emme's paper bag and scooping it up under his arm.

Presumptuous.

He slung his other arm around Emme's shoulder and she looked at him, puzzled. Floored by his public declaration, and somewhat self-conscious in case Tiago might see them. Anyone could see them. Tristan Du Kok with his arm around an English nanny. Tristan Du Kok with the waitress from the party where he had been punched in the face for fucking two sisters. Tristan Du Kok, the man who cut dodgy deals with Russian oligarchs. Tristan Du Kok, who Cat joked about killing his father on a hike through the mountains in order to inherit his billions.

The snow started to come down heavily, and as Tristan stopped outside the supermarket to put his gloves on, Emme couldn't help remembering Lexy's warning. She already knew Tristan Du Kok wasn't to be trusted, but was she physically capable of keeping away from him?

'Where are you taking me?' Emme asked, as he clutched her hand tighter and they wound along a trail away from the centre of the village. The brown woody path, which bounced underfoot, had turned white with the weekend's snow, and was hard to navigate in trainers. Emme lamented not going back to Chalet Stern to get her boots, and she started to get out of breath as they made their ascent above the town and the air got even thinner.

'You'll see . . .' Tristan replied cryptically. His playful sparkle, which had been missing last night and this morning, was now back.

Emme inhaled the scents of pine and fir, which felt crisp and exhilarating against the woodsmoke curl from a distant chalet below, and they chatted as they hiked. After about twenty minutes they stopped to take in the spectacular view of Kristalldorf from above, although ostensibly it was so Emme could catch her breath. While they were paused, she fired off another text to Cat to see if she was OK, and noticed a missed call from Tom. Now was not the time to call him back, so she raised her phone and took a couple of pictures of the spectacular scenery.

'It's beautiful,' Emme declared.

'I never tire of it,' Tristan said. He surveyed the view and Emme looked across at him in profile.

A deep boom sounded in the distance, bouncing across the valley like thunder.

'What was that?' Emme gasped, eyes wide.

The noise reverberated around the valley in a deep and foreboding rumble.

Tristan turned to her, his smile both penetrating and disarming her.

'Dynamite,' he said.

'What?'

'Emergency Rescue set off controlled explosions in the mountains. They do controlled avalanches to prevent catastrophic ones.'

It sounded eerie. A boom thundered again.

'I don't like it,' Emme said, hurrying behind Tristan. He squeezed her hand then put his arm around her shoulder and pulled her in. She felt breathless.

'We're almost there.'

Where?

A mountain deer galloped onto the path on the edge of the ravine, sending a fallen tree branch tumbling off the edge. Tristan froze as the deer stopped and looked at them. He put his finger to his lips and smiled.

'Wow,' Emme whispered.

Tristan nodded as the deer scattered off into the white pine forest. They continued around a curve in the path when a glass structure revealed itself like an iceberg in the ocean as they rounded the corner.

'Oh my goodness,' Emme said. It was the shimmering hotel she could see from the town whenever she looked up to the east side of the valley.

'Vitreum,' Tristan said, as if it were both a blessing and a curse.

Chandeliers inside the lobby blasted fractals of light around the building. They looked like they might reach the valley walls too.

'It's incredible.'

Tristan ushered her forward, their hands linked until he let her go, and she looked up in awe as if she had arrived in a magical palace.

She turned in a circle, looking around the lobby in astonishment.

'Good afternoon Mr Du Kok,' said a woman behind the desk.

'Good afternoon Nieves, any messages?'

'No sir,' she said with a smile.

The lobby was bustling with people buzzing off the same excitement of being there. Of staying at the famous Vitreum hotel. It had appeared in fashion shoots, *Architectural Digest*, *Forbes* and *Vogue*. It had been used in a James Bond film. The building was iconic in hospitality and architectural circles. Yet Emme had never heard of it until she moved here. She'd never imagined from Kristalldorf below that the sparkling glass hotel on the hill would be quite so spectacular up close.

'How did everyone get here?' Emme asked in awe. She hadn't seen a single soul on the walk up the trail, aside from the deer, a mountain hare and three marmots.

'There's a tunnel that goes off the square. The one next to UBS with the travelator?'

Emme had seen it.

'And from there, an elevator brings people up.'

'That's quite a ride!' Emme said.

'Come on,' Tristan said, still carrying their groceries, to a series of elevators that took guests up to their rooms. He bypassed three of them and went to the one that had just the letter P illuminated above the door. He swiped his watch against the call button and the doors glided open in an instant.

'After you,' he said, holding out an arm.

As the doors closed on them, Emme was reminded of their moment alone in the gondola, only this ride would be over in seconds.

The lift doors opened onto an apartment at the top of the building; sweeping views of the Silberschnee were so clear and crisp it almost didn't look real.

Emme was gobsmacked. The vast penthouse, with its luxe furnishing, capacious layout and impressive panorama was incredible, and so different to the cosy apartment in town, it made Emme even more acutely aware of all the different facets of Tristan.

'Oh my goodness,' she said, tucking her hair behind her ear. 'This is insane! And it's yours?'

Tristan nodded as he put the groceries down in a large plush kitchen with salmon-pink Italian onyx worktops under a huge copper pendant that looked more like an art installation than a light. In front of them was a sunken living room with a long thin lava fire and retractable window walls, firmly closed to keep the high flurry out. Emme walked to it as if she were a moth to a flame.

'It's . . . unreal!' she said, smoothing her hand along the glass wall, not quite daring to touch it lest she leave a fingerprint.

'You want a drink?'

Emme was distracted. It was like she was in a dream.

'Erm, yeah, just a sparkling water thanks.'

'Take your coat off, make yourself at home . . .' Tristan busied himself fixing the drinks and a platter of bread, cheese and charcuterie.

Emme put her coat on the low cream sofa and looked around the apartment, aware that they were dizzyingly high up – the penthouse was designed to give the illusion of floating in the clouds, and it certainly worked. The interior looked like something Emme had seen on *Selling Sunset* or *Buying Beverly Hills*, yet it had been plucked out of California and placed on top of a Swiss mountain.

'It's incredible!' she said quietly.

Tristan brought the glasses and a board of food over, set them on the coffee table, and handed Emme the sparkling water.

'Cheers,' he said.

They clinked glasses and he observed her for a second, before kissing her carefully on the lips. He winced as he leaned over.

She pulled back.

'Still hurts?'

'A little,' he said, clutching his shoulder.

Emme took a sip of her iced water and looked around. It all made sense now – the humble pied à terre in town felt more everyday and accessible than this stunning hard-to-reach space. But then hard-to-reach felt appropriate for Tristan Du Kok. She realised she didn't know anything about him, other than the very little he had told her, and a whole lot of gossip.

'Was this your dad's?' Emme asked, knowing he was so sensitive about it, but she didn't want to tiptoe around him now.

Tristan took an olive and nodded.

'He won the hotel in a card game,' he added sheepishly. Emme nodded gently, encouraging him to continue. She was desperate to hear *his* version.

'I used to live up here with my dad when we were in town.'

Emme took a slice of focaccia and looked at the snow whirling outside between Vitreum and the Silberschnee.

'Best view in the village.' He double clapped his hands sharply. 'Fire!' he added in a commanding voice, which startled Emme, then made her laugh when she realised. More bloody tech, she internally eye-rolled, laughing at the mad scenario she was in, and thinking, if only her friends could see her now.

The long thin fire at one end of the room lit in an elegant ribbon.

'Sorry to make you jump,' Tristan added wryly.

Emme laughed. 'It's OK. I am slowly getting used to Kristalldorf ways,' she said, although this penthouse was next level. She had no clue where televisions, fire or ice would appear from at any given moment. She looked back to the view.

'It is the best view in town. Does that not also make it sad for you?' Emme dared to ask. 'That you shared this place with your dad?' She turned back to Tristan, searching his face for clues.

'I guess. But I can't let this go.'

'Of course not.'

'I sold the hotel to Alexey Stognev on the condition I keep this as my home. But . . .' he looked around, a little embarrassed. 'I struggle to sleep up here, so I use it more as an office.'

'And sleep down in the village,' Emme said, joining the dots.

Tristan turned up the fire and Emme saw the sadness in his eyes. She crouched down and rubbed a hand over the navy jumper that covered his athletic, sore shoulder.

'We were up here the morning before he died.'

His hair flopped into his eyes and he pushed it away, along with a tear, on the palm of his hand.

'Look, you don't have to tell me anything – I shouldn't have said anything about Lexy . . .'

Tristan almost laughed.

'Yah, lots of people think I killed my father. I was with him ski touring that day. I was the lone son and heir. No body found. I know what they say.'

Emme felt guilty for having looked it up. For having given Cat's hypothesis any air time.

'He was a difficult man, but not so difficult I would push him down a ravine.'

'Of course not!' snapped Emme. 'I didn't think for a second!'

'Yes you did . . .' Tristan said, looking at her with his magnetic, troubled gaze, then back to the fire.

'So what happened? That day?'

Emme hadn't been aware of it at the time – deep in her studies and social life at twenty. But since Cat told her, she'd googled the coverage that popped up in newspapers all over Europe, the *Sunday Times* in South Africa, and small stories in the *Financial Times* and *Wall Street Journal*. All of them quoted canton police statements and said the search for Charles Joubert's body was ongoing, until a later story on the BBC said the case was being closed. From the haunted look on Tristan's face, it would never be closed for him.

'We were out skiing, we'd had a great day, great conditions. On the Teufelsgletscher glacier, but we both knew what we were doing. I was ahead, and then I heard a cry – a terrible cry. It was desperate . . .' Tristan swallowed hard, as he looked to the fire in bewilderment. 'I didn't see him fall, but I know he went down the Hexenfinger ravine. I heard that cry disappear and get further away. I heard a godawful thump and the silence. I hear it every night.'

He shuddered.

'Was he not wearing a tracking device?'

'It was in his coat, which was found miles away. I hadn't noticed him take it off.'

'And search and rescue couldn't recover the body?'

'No. You've seen choppers on the mountain, how hard it is to land on a piste. Only cavers could get down there, and they didn't deem it worth putting anyone else's life at risk.'

Emme smoothed her palm under Tristan's jumper, up over his spine.

'Cat reckons the mountain gives up its secrets. Maybe your dad will be found one day.'

'She's right. That's why I hang out with the instructors. They're useless drunks but they're the best for the job of searching for something in the snow. I pay them to see if they can find anything down there, or anything along the trails. In case there was anything I might have missed.'

'And that's why you stuck around here, looking for him?'

Tristan nodded.

'And the beauty of the place,' she added.

He nodded again, and caressed her nose with his thumb.

'You never know what's going to happen next here,' he said, quietly.

But Emme knew right at this moment. She kissed Tristan gently on the lips, he tasted of olive brine and musk. He took Emme's face in his hands, kissing her intently as she lifted her jumper over her head and freed her breasts from her T-shirt. Within minutes they were both naked on the bearskin rug in front of the fire, caressing every curve and sinew of each other's bodies. Tristan lowered his kisses to Emme's abdomen, to her pussy, to her clitoris, before she moaned exquisitely and rolled over, liberated on all fours while she arched her back and pushed her bottom towards him. Tristan had a steady hand on each hip, caressing Emme's peachy curves as he took her from behind with a solid, rhythmic power.

As she took his thrusts she looked out at the view with a smile. The length of him, his touch, the way he leaned down and kissed the skin on her tingling spine was so sensational, she had to bite her lip and try to think of something else to stave off her orgasm and prolong the joy.

She held off as long as she could, until Tristan Du Kok lay on top of her on the bearskin, the weight of his muscular body all streaming to one delicious point between her legs. She came with a roar as dynamite exploded and reverberated around the valley. Tristan followed soon after, legs paralysed as he filled Emme and they fell into a bruised and lovestruck heap.

When Emme woke from the post-orgasmic glow, the Silberschnee was turning pink in the panorama outside the window. The fire was low, and Tristan had put a blanket over them in their huddle. She looked at Tristan's Patek Phillipe watch, ticking quietly, remembering it from the airport shuttle. She groaned when she saw the time. It was almost 4pm; the Harringtons would be back from Zurich soon, she imagined, and today was meant to be her fresh start. Her heart sank. She didn't want to move from this spot. She didn't want to be Harry and Bella's nanny. She could feel Tristan's enormous arms around her; his velvety cosh pressing into her buttocks. She wanted to enjoy an extended holiday, not be a nanny in a tense household.

Then a thought struck her, which she said out loud, before she could stop herself.

'Do you know what happened to Jenny?' she asked, as she stroked the hairs on Tristan's arm.

'Who's Jenny?' he said softly, into her ear.

'The nanny before me. She left suddenly, it must have been at the end of October.'

Tristan was quiet, still half asleep. Emme rolled over to face him. She couldn't help thinking about Lexy last night in the laundry room, warning Emme off Tristan, as if she personally had lost something because of him.

Be wary of anyone who can break three hearts in one callous hit.

Had Tristan broken Jenny's heart? He had joked about 'the previous nanny's dispatch' that first day on the slopes.

'Look, if you slept with her, I can handle it. I'd rather know . . .'

Tristan looked like he was trying to remember a Jenny in his conquests. It made Emme feel a bit sick. He yawned and stretched.

'I don't know a Jenny,' he said. But Emme had seen him lie to a woman before; and she couldn't help thinking he was now.

'People are telling me not to trust you.' As Emme said it, she knew what she meant was, *I don't think I trust you.*

'Lexy's telling you not to trust me, right?' Tristan quipped. 'That's rich. I mean . . . Lexy Harrington is not the most reliable narrator, she's all over the place.'

But Emme couldn't stop pondering it.

'At first I thought Jenny had an affair with Bill, but now I'm wondering . . .'

Tristan was fast waking up.

Emme knew she risked him going cold on her again, but her curiosity was too much. Tristan rubbed his eyes and looked at Emme intently.

'Look, I didn't push my dad down a ravine and I swear I never had a conversation with this Jenny girl, let alone had sex with her.'

Tristan stroked Emme's cheek.

'Come on, it's not a crime to be a single guy and sleep with a woman. Or two.'

Tristan's tone was transparent and honest and Emme admired him all the more for it. 'I never professed that either Vivian or Anastasia were the love of my life, although I know morally, it was perhaps unwise . . .' He smiled. Emme threw him a theatrical frown as if to say *you can say that again*.

'I didn't sleep with your predecessor, I swear. And I've never lied to you about what I've done or haven't done, have I?'

'No but I've seen how easily you do.'

Tristan frowned.

'I'm an open book,' he said, and leaned in to kiss Emme.

'So what was this morning about?'

'You caught me off guard. I wasn't in the mood to talk about my dad then, but I've had some time. I thought about you. I wanted to bring you up here and show you.'

Emme looked at him and melted as they kissed, passionately, naked and entwined. She still couldn't believe this was happening so hard and so fast. Or what Tristan might see in her.

He pulled back.

'Look, I have to go back to Cape Town.'

Emme groaned.

'When?'

'Next weekend, for about a week, maybe ten days. See my mother. Go through some business stuff.'

Emme looked a little dejected.

'I'll be back for Christmas, and I would *love* to spend it with you, if you're around?'

Emme needed to have a conversation with Lexy about which days she was needed over the Christmas holiday. She had Christmas Eve and Christmas Day off for sure, and the thought of a Christmas reunion with Tristan was enchanting.

After luxuriating together under Tristan's rain shower, where Emme examined every beautiful mole on his body – and took his cock in her mouth – she got dressed, and Tristan led her by the hand towards the lobby.

'What about this week?' she said, as they exited the penthouse lift. 'I hate leaving it to chance to bump into you.' They kissed again, under the sparkling shards of the art installation in the centre of Vitreum's lobby and all the people milling around them.

Tristan broke off.

'Give me your number, yah?' he said, handing his phone over to her. She pressed her digits into it, and handed it back. 'And we have this week, I'm not flying until Saturday,' he smiled.

Emme knew as she said goodbye and walked towards the mountain lift, reborn and reset, that a lot could happen in Kristalldorf in a week.

Chapter Fifty-Nine

'My dear, you were excellent,' Walter said to his daughter from his desk in the large plush office on the fourth floor of the Alpenrose.

Vivian smiled, graciously.

She had just hosted the monthly business breakfast, for all of Kristalldorf's movers and shakers. A select group met monthly to talk about issues in the town, taking it in turns to chair the meeting, and today Vivian Steinherr had been at the helm. She knew her pride was at stake after the Kivvi Christingle last weekend, but Vivian did what she did best: held her head high, put on a smile, and ensured the board-room table was brimming with pastries, juices and artisan sausage rolls, all provided by Tomasso, the head chef at the Alpenrose. She led the meeting by talking about urgent business for peak season and Christmas, and asked all the hoteliers present to share room occupancy, so that everyone could get a handle on how busy the town, its hotels and restaurants would be, as it affected them all. Everyone was courteous and reported back. No one made a mention of her boyfriend sleeping with her sister and being punched to the floor by Walter's attorney.

Samuel Sommar had attended as usual, raising the issue of the lack of accommodation in town for the workers.

Oliver Koch wanted to talk about April's music festival, Kristalldorf Sessions, and said he had sponsored a new big top for the central venue. Walter Steinherr announced he wanted to freeze the ski lift prices for next year, which was met with raised eyebrows from Koch and Sommar. Walter had increased the Kristallpass price every year they could remember. And Alexey Stognev, who usually shunned the monthly business breakfast, asked about planning permission for a full heliport up at Vitreum, which the others had shot down.

'We can't be a carless village with two heliports chugging overhead!' Sommar protested. 'It's enough you have a permit for one helicopter to land up there! It's a protected wildlife area!'

Stognev looked surly, muttered something in Russian under his breath, and lamented wasting his time by coming.

Notable in his absence was Tristan Du Kok, who sometimes attended, but wasn't expected to today, given the brouhaha of the weekend. Viktor Kivvi never attended, because hospitality wasn't his game, and the founding fathers liked to keep it that way. Vivian would have liked Tristan to attend so the coward could look her in the eye.

The business leaders wished each other a happy Christmas season and scheduled to reconvene on 6 January at Grand Hotel Sommar on the square, and Vivian followed her father into his office for the debrief.

'Thank you, Daddy,' Vivian said, relieved it had gone well, relieved to be back in her MO as hospitality badass and not sobbing victim. 'I still want more women in hospitality in this town. Those guys are all so stuffy and stuck in their ways. Samuel aside . . .'

Vivian sat in the chair opposite her father's desk.

'Well, we're down one woman at the moment,' Walter said ruefully.

Vivian looked at him with her winsome gaze. She was furious at her sister, but still felt regret for their father.

'Have you heard from her?'

Walter shook his head.

'She's been in contact with Dimitri,' he conceded. 'She's gone to rehab, but I don't know where, or how long for . . .' he said sadly.

'Daddy, it's not your fault!' Vivian said, although she could see it was delicate for their father. She tapped the notepad she'd brought into the meeting but never used; she would write up the minutes from memory back at the Anna Maria. Vivian had an excellent memory.

'Any word from Caspian about Christmas?' she asked, hopefully.

Walter shook his head and looked out of the window. Kristalldorf was picture perfect from the office. Snow covered the village, and he could see Christmas decorations were being put up on the street below. If only he could have all his children home, he thought.

It might be my last.

'Lysander said something about Hawaii,' Walter said, wistfully.

'I'm going to get back to the Anna Maria,' Vivian said, 'I'll take a pastry but don't forget to have one yourself,' she said. She was worried about her father. He was losing weight and looking frail.

'Of course!' he said, humouring her.

She kissed him on his bald head and walked out towards

the elevators. As the doors closed on her she breathed a sigh of relief to have got through that first meeting when she had been so exposed. Her father was determined, but so was she. She'd got through the worst humiliation of her life, surely she could get over Tristan Du Kok.

Chapter Sixty

Emme rode Tristan like the stallion he was, shouting in abandon as her breasts moved in tandem with his thrusts and they both battled to time their orgasms to perfection.

'Yes! Yes! Yes!' Emme moaned, as she collapsed into a heap on Tristan's torso. His cock exploding in its sheath inside her. A shudder of pleasure ran through her body. This was unlike anything she had ever known, the sexual awakening she was finally getting at twenty-eight. It was raw and rapturous alchemy. Although she had a looming feeling it was coming to an end.

She held him tight and smelled her own sweet breath in his neck.

'Incredible,' he said breathlessly.

Emme had delivered the children to school, done some errands for Lexy, and gone to see Tristan in his town-centre apartment. He had been on a Zoom call to buyers in Japan when she arrived, and he let her in and said he wouldn't be long. She went into his kitchen and made them both a coffee, while he talked to three Japanese hoteliers, then Emme stripped off behind the laptop screen, taking great pleasure in seeing Tristan, his smile and sparkle back, hardening for her and desperate to get off the call. She took as much pleasure in the sexual liberation she felt as she did in how sexy she found Tristan. She had never felt so comfortable in her own skin and so desirable.

Now they were spent.

Ski school was about to finish for the term, and it was fast approaching 1.30pm, when Emme had to collect Harry and Bella.

Tristan lay on his back, his arms stretched out like Jesus on the cross.

'God, Emme,' he sighed. 'What have you done to me?'

She smiled. She still couldn't believe it. But you couldn't fake the passion between them, and she was loving it.

She dismounted him and went to get in the shower.

'Hey, I was thinking it would be nice to go out for dinner tomorrow night?' Tristan said, still lying on the floor as he heard Emme lather herself up.

'Really?' she said, delighted.

Out. Like a couple. No secret sex trysts in the middle of the day. 'Before my flight.'

Her heart sank. She really didn't want him to go. She didn't want to be in Kristalldorf without his distraction. And then her heart sank even further when she remembered.

'I have to babysit tomorrow night. It's Lexy and Bill's wedding anniversary.'

'Can't they get another sitter?' Tristan asked, getting up off the floor and poking his head around the bathroom door.

'They already pay me for this kind of stuff.'

'I'll pay them double to find someone else.'

'I don't think that'll go down very well, do you?'

All week Lexy Harrington had done everything she could to add chores to Emme's burgeoning list.

'Can you take Bella for a haircut before dinner?'

'Harry wants someone to watch his taekwondo training this week – I'd like you to do it.'

'Can you pop to Bloch to pick up some ballet shoes?' Popping to Bloch was a three-hour round trip.

Emme hadn't been asked to do these things until now. It was as if Lexy was *trying* to keep Emme away from Tristan.

It was 12 December tomorrow, there was no way she could get out of looking after the children while the most tense couple in Kristalldorf went out to celebrate their wedding anniversary.

Tristan looked at her in the shower, to check she was serious about not going out.

'But I'm going to miss you . . .' he said, admiring Emme's peachy ass.

'Sorry, I just can't. Lexy's busting my balls. Why don't we go for breakfast Saturday morning instead, before your flight?'

Tristan conceded, watching Emme as she continued to teasingly lather herself up. Seeing the way Tristan looked at her made her feel more radiant, more irresistible, than she'd ever felt in her life.

Chapter Sixty-One

It had been almost a week since the Kivvi Christingle and Cat hadn't received a single word from Anastasia. No apology for causing a scene that resulted in a heap of smashed chocolate mousse and glass all over the party she was catering. No apology for publicly telling the world she had slept with Tristan Du Kok when they had talked about it in bed and Anastasia had said it was nothing. No apology for pretending she'd never met Cat, and blanking her from just one metre away. Not even a compliment on the exceptional menu she'd crafted.

Cat heard on the grapevine that Anastasia Steinherr Diamandis had fled town and checked herself into rehab, but no one seemed to know where she was or when she was coming back.

Cat was still thinking about her when she took the elevator up to Chalet Edelweiss, armed with a bag of groceries. She planned a comforting goulash dinner for whoever was around this evening – the tender paprika scents of cooking could lift the saddest of spirits – and she needed the balm of something this evening. Cat and Emme had exchanged texts but Cat had wanted to lie low all week, such was her disappointment and personal shame.

As Cat walked into the apartment a florist was just

leaving, and Gerard was taking delivery of yet another bouquet. There had been a steady stream of floral arrangements in shades of blush, festive mulberry, soft lilac and even a few funereal white ones, which Lumi had raised an artfully threaded eyebrow about and smiled graciously on acceptance. The party hadn't been *that* devastating. All the offerings had arrived with handwritten thank-you notes for the Kivvis, and every surface in the chalet was now adorned.

'And still they send them!' Cat said, smiling sardonically.

'Actually Catalina, these are for you,' Gerard said, with a raised eyebrow of his own as he proffered the bouquet.

'Oh,' Cat said, silenced as she took the beautiful hand-tied posy of pink and white avalanche roses, Italian ranunculi and winter hellebores. Cat stopped herself from saying how beautiful they were out loud. 'Thank you.'

She took the bouquet in its water base and headed through to the kitchen with her groceries. No one ever sent Cat flowers. She placed them on the marble worktop, placed the bags down next to them and took off her coat.

Deep breath.

Cat opened the envelope, read the card, and welled up.

Chapter Sixty-Two

Emme sat idly looking at the television but not watching it. *The Holiday* was on, and the children were asleep. It was Bill and Lexy's eleventh wedding anniversary, and Bill had come back from Zurich an hour earlier than usual – a show of enthusiasm he was trying to muster – so they could have a few sundowners at the Kristall Palace before the table he'd booked at an Italian restaurant in the middle of town.

She thought she might text Tristan, to see what he was up to, but she didn't want to come on strong and she was seeing him for brunch in the morning anyway. She looked at her phone and hovered over the newness of his name in it; appraising his picture in a small circle when the name TOM LARNER flashed up, almost making Emme jump.

Shit.

Emme and Tom had exchanged pithy messages over the past month, but not many, especially not since she had first kissed Tristan. Was she really that fickle? Or was this crazy mountain bubble complicit?

Emme answered. None of this was Tom's fault. And actually, she had been a bad friend to him. Friends didn't just move overseas and not call each other.

'Tom!' she said, cheerily. 'How are you?'

'Emme, at last!' he said. 'I've been trying to catch you for ages . . .'

She really had been a bad friend.

'I'm so sorry, it's so full-on here,' she said, as she looked around the tranquil living room. Another lie. An audiobook was blaring from Bella's room so Emme went to turn it down. Bella was fast asleep so she tiptoed in and turned down 'Gustav' with three clever swipes before shutting the bedroom door behind her.

'How are you? How's London? How's married life?'

She wanted to sound as neutral and as normal as possible.

She was fine!

She was over it!

She had been having the sex of her life!

And that felt good.

'Yeah great – all fine here. We miss you at ConCore! I miss my bitch buddy . . .'

Hmmm, Emme thought. Tom was skirting something. Although they both worked together and enjoyed venting over lunch at Pret, ConCore wasn't what defined them. They had all manner of shared pursuits.

'Hey bitch away, any time,' Emme said, looking at the television. Jack Black and Kate Winslet were goofing around in a video shop.

'No, it's all good . . .'

Tom told Emme how he had seen Dominique Henry's PA in reception, getting a ticking off because she'd messed up a car booking. He also said he was going to Switzerland skiing with his team in February, and wouldn't it be funny if the trip was to Kristalldorf?

Would it?

346

Emme wondered. She tried to imagine riding Tom, on a stolen few days in the mountains – was it the town that made her horny or Tristan? But she couldn't picture it, because suddenly, the thought of being with Tom was all wrong. Maybe it would be different if she saw him.

'Hey, I was wondering . . .' Tom finally cut to the chase. 'Are you coming home for Christmas?'

'No – I'm here through to April. Why? Is everything OK?'

Tom was silent for a beat.

'Oh it's just . . . it would have been great to see you.' It seemed like a lifetime ago when they last spoke, from the poolside of the Steinherrhof spa.

'Yes,' she said, feeling conflicted.

'And there's something I need to tell you.'

'Oh right. Can't you tell me now?'

'It's better in person . . .'

Tom sounded cagey now for sure.

She's pregnant.

Emme groaned internally. Perhaps she wasn't over him. This obsession with Tristan was all just suspended reality.

She took a deep breath, which was interrupted by a shout.

'EMME!' Harry bellowed.

Emme gasped.

On the television, Jack Black sang the notes of the *Jaws* theme tune as he clutched the DVD box.

'What's the matter?' Tom asked.

'Oh, I have to go –'

'Emme!' Harry shouted again, sounding more scared than princely.

'Harry needs me –'

'Harry? Who's Harry?' asked Tom.

'I'll call you back.'

Emme ended the call and rushed to Harry's bedroom, just as he came out of it, sobbing. He saw Emme and ran into her arms, clinging onto her for dear life.

'Shhh, hey it's OK, I'm here . . .'

'There were monsters, and I wasn't allowed to look at them . . . and I feel sick . . .' Harry grasped for air between sobs.

'Hey, it's OK,' Emme said, rubbing Harry's back in her embrace. 'Sounds like a bad dream.'

'I feel dizzy.'

He rested his head on her shoulder.

'Shhh . . .'

Emme held him for a few minutes crouched in the hallway and then said she'd get him a glass of water and a thermometer, before leading him back to bed. She checked his temperature as the thermometer beeped.

'Hmmm, 37.4, a little on the high side but I think you're OK, buddy. Have another sip of water,' she said, passing him the glass from the bedside table.

'Will you sit with me?' Harry sighed.

'Yes,' Emme said, wedging herself in.

Emme sat propped up next to Harry until he fell back asleep and as she watched his eyes flicker, she realised how far they'd come in a few weeks. The boy who had disdainfully cast aside his 'lame' Paddington bear clearly needed her in his hour of need.

Emme was starting to drift off herself when she heard a gentle knock at the front door and opened her eyes. *Never a dull moment,* she thought.

Emme checked Harry's brow with her free hand and, reassured by its temperature, she carefully unlooped his arm from her waist so she could extricate herself. The knock sounded again. She'd left her phone in the living room so couldn't see who had got through the downstairs entrance and up to the front door on the BUZZ app.

'Coming,' she stage whispered, as she padded down the warm hallway.

Emme opened the door to see Cat on the other side of it.

'Oh, hey!'

'You're lovely,' Cat declared. 'Thank you.'

She got the flowers.

'Can I come in?'

'Of course you can, I've just got the little man back down as he was feeling poorly, but I think he's OK now,' Emme said quietly. 'Come in, I was watching *The Holiday* . . .'

'What's *The Holiday*?'

'Are you kidding me?' Emme said in mock horror.

'Come in and sit down, *there*!' Emme commanded. But not before Cat gave her a huge hug.

Chapter Sixty-Three

'What do you think of Emme?' Lexy asked, as she sawed into her bloody steak.

Bill looked befuddled and paused twirling his tagliatelle, fork frozen in his hand.

He considered his wife as though it was a trick question. Questions often were with Lexy.

He resumed twirling.

'Erm, the kids seem to like her.'

'Yes but what do *you* think of her?' Lexy seemed to be in a particularly combative mood despite it being their wedding anniversary.

'She seems less, erm, problematic than Jenny . . .'

'Jesus, Bill! Why can you never give a straight answer?' Lexy hissed, as she saw their neighbour Tomas Edstrom pass their table with a nod and a wave, so she faked a smile as quickly as a Christmas lights switch-on.

Tomas disappeared to the bathroom and Lexy returned to her questioning.

'Do you find her attractive?' she asked, as she gave a gentle flick of her tonged auburn mane.

Bill looked up, his mouth stuffed so full of pasta his words were incomprehensible.

'Pardon?' scoffed Lexy.

Bill swallowed.

'I said she's a pretty thing, but it's not my place to say.'

'Why not?' Lexy probed, as she mopped up her pepper-corn sauce with a last chunk of steak.

'Well, what does it matter if she's bloody pretty or not, Lexy? What corner are you backing me into now?'

Lexy leaned back, caressed her stomach and rolled her eyes, as if she were a petulant child.

'I just wondered if men think she's sexy. It's hard to tell when someone's looking after your children. It's hard to tell what people think.'

'What does it matter what people think? It doesn't matter that she's sexy, does it?'

Gotcha.

Lexy primly placed her knife and fork in a line on her plate and took a slug of red wine.

'You know, I don't think Emme does enough with the kids,' she declared.

'You don't? She always seems busy when I'm home with her.' Bill mopped a splash of ragu from the corner of his mouth with a white linen napkin and declared himself finished.

'Well, you're hardly home,' Lexy countered.

A waitress came to clear their plates.

'Everything alright with your dishes?' she asked, as she gathered the detritus.

'Top notch,' Bill said appreciatively while Lexy gave a brief smile.

When the waitress left, Lexy resumed the conversation, much to Bill's apparent chagrin. Why was he being so cagey about this nanny?

'Well, I think she's too busy with her social life. She's gallivanting around town too much when she should be helping out more. She should be teaching the children to read more fluently. She should be helping them with their German, for god's sake.'

'Does Emme speak German?' Bill asked, his eyebrows in a knot.

'I can't remember, but what's the point of a nanny who doesn't *enrich* the children?'

'They learn German at school,' he added idly.

Lexy looked around the restaurant, and she felt so agitated and uncelebratory that she wanted to cry.

'Look, what's the real issue here, Lex?' Bill cleared his throat and took a sip of beer from his tube glass. 'I know it's hard for you to trust after Jenny, but I promise the same thing won't happen again.'

And with that, Lexy felt a rage coil up her, flooding every vein. What was worse was that Bill would never know the extent of how his words stung.

Chapter Sixty-Four

On Saturday morning Cat decided to deep clean the kitchen and do an inventory of herbs and store-cupboard ingredients. She was feeling uplifted by Cameron Diaz, Jude Law and Emmeline Eversley from their impromptu movie night, although the awakening of Harry Harrington vomiting in his bed as the credits rolled had put a slight dampener on the warm and fuzzy glow. Cat was making a list of herbs and spices that needed restocking when Lumi walked into the kitchen, fixing a brooch to her cashmere sweater.

'Would you like lunch today, ma'am?' Cat asked keenly.

'No thank you Catalina, I'm meeting an old friend.'

'In which case, when I've finished this I might go snowboarding this afternoon. Would you be wanting dinner?'

Lumi pondered it.

'Hmmm, I'm not sure right now.'

Viktor had taken Mika with him to Helsinki, to try to ignite some interest in the business and make him useful. Lumi had already had texts from her son saying it was a disaster and that his dad was being 'a prick'.

Somehow, her son's pain rolled over her. She was too blissfully happy riding the wave of a rekindled love affair to worry about her young prince. He'd find his way. Young people always did.

'What do you want to do with your life, Catalina?' Lumi asked suddenly. Cat was taken aback. What was she meant to say? She didn't particularly want to cook for a family for the rest of her life. But she didn't want to bite the hand that fed her.

Lumi looked at her as if to say, *go on*.

'Well, erm, I would like to open my own restaurant one day.'

Lumi looked enchanted.

'Oh really! Where?'

'Who knows? Buenos Aires. Paris. Zurich. Here.' The idea was gathering pace. 'Argentinian traditions with a Swiss twist.'

'You do it so well,' Lumi conceded.

Cat stopped herself.

'I suppose you don't want to hear this, ma'am,' she said.

'I do Catalina. I think you would be wonderful. I can see it now.' She threw her cream coat over her shoulders and fluffed up her silver-blonde hair. 'It's not easy in this town, but I'm sure between us we'd have the contacts to do some research.'

Cat looked confused.

'Are you trying to get rid of me, ma'am?' she joked.

Lumi laughed.

'Goodness no, but I am not one to clip a young person's wings.'

Cat smiled gratefully. She'd never considered it as a real possibility. She didn't have the finance for starters. Where would she begin? But Lumi's faith lifted her spirits. There was more to life than a dead relationship.

'Have a lovely afternoon snowboarding Catalina. And if

I am back for dinner, I would love some of that Argentinian goulash, if there are any leftovers?'

'There are, Mrs Kivvi.'

With that, Lumi waltzed out, and Cat decided to hit the mountains. She hadn't been snowboarding all week, and she just knew that when she was flying, through powder and air, all the tension built in her shoulders would be left in the tracks behind her. Besides, she had a restaurant to think about. If Lumi could envisage it, then why couldn't Cat?

Chapter Sixty-Five

'Tristan, wait!'

Tristan stood under the rotors of the helicopter and Emme ran to him.

'I'm so sorry!' she said, as she reached his solid, sturdy body, and jumped into his embrace.

He picked her up and kissed her as she wrapped her legs around his waist.

Lexy Harrington had decided this morning would be the perfect opportunity to go to see *It's A Wonderful Life* at the Kristalldorf Picturehouse, with Bill and without the kids. 'You can watch them and fix some pancakes, can't you Emme?' she had said, icily, as she left, clutching her husband's hand. Bill looked like he didn't want to do much more than read the paper, but he had been told.

Emme's farewell brunch with Tristan had been scuppered. There would be no public dining experience for them, no first outing as a couple. No goodbye sex on the penthouse floor of Vitreum.

She had texted him frantically, asking if he could delay his chopper, but he had limited time to get to Zurich airport in time for his first-class seat to Cape Town. Even Tristan couldn't bend the timetables of aviation for sex.

'You made it!' he said, squeezing her tight. 'I'm going to miss you so much.'

'Do you know when you'll be back?' Emme asked, as he put her down and held her face.

'*Sir, wir müssen wirklich los!*' said the helicopter pilot, flicking switches and making his final checks.

Tristan, holding a large black Prada holdall, looked remorsefully at Emme.

'Next weekend, I hope. I'll let you know.'

'OK, go carefully,' she said, feeling overcome with the reality that she was going to miss him so much.

'I'll give Yolanda your best,' Tristan smiled. 'She wants to meet you!'

'Really?' Emme said, beaming. 'Well I'd love to meet her.' She felt a million dollars as she kissed him goodbye.

'I'll be in touch from Cape Town,' he said with one final, passionate kiss, before he walked away with a wave. He put on his aviator shades, turned back, and beamed.

Chapter Sixty-Six

One week before Christmas, a Thursday night, was the first evening in weeks that Emme, Cat and Tiago all had a rare night off together. They met in the bar of Hotel Europa, where none of them worked and none of them had any obligation to anyone, and they raised their Christmas cocktails to their own festivities, which were more sedate than the last time they had all been together, working the Kivvi Christingle.

'We should call it *los tres mosqueteros* Christmas party . . .' Cat said, raising a colourful cocktail.

'*Salud!*' Tiago added.

'Cheers,' Emme smiled, although her smile belied the knots in her stomach. She had been on the phone to Tristan several times a day, every day, over the past five days – she'd even met Yolanda Du Kok on FaceTime – a powerhouse of a woman with cheekbones to die for.

'OK, so here's a funny thing . . .' Tiago said, as they savoured their drinks and watched Will, Lydia and Yannick setting up a small acoustic set in the corner of the hotel bar.

'*Dime . . .*' Cat commanded. Tiago rubbed pink foam from his top lip and cleared his throat.

'So my roommate Nieves works up at Vitreum, and she swears she saw you up there Emme.' He turned to her, with molasses-sweet eyes.

Emme flushed red.

'Oh, you've been!' Cat said in surprise. 'Isn't it cool?! I mean . . . dirty Russian money aside.'

Emme shrugged. She could barely get her words out as she looked at Tiago, knowing that he knew. His eyes got even wider.

'*Merda*, so it's true?' He put his hand over his mouth in shock.

Cat looked between Emme and Tiago, wondering what the hell they were privy to and she wasn't.

'What's going on?' She hit Tiago playfully on the chest.

'I mean . . . I thought Nieves must have got it wrong but . . .'

'But what?!' demanded Cat.

Tiago looked at Emme and realised maybe she hadn't wanted anyone to know.

'Erm, I guess what happens at Vitreum stays at Vitreum . . .' Tiago backtracked.

Emme winced.

'*Hijo de puta*, what's going on?!' Cat banged her fist on the table, laughing in exasperation.

'Nieves saw right,' Emme admitted, turning to Cat. 'I was up there with Tristan.'

'Tristan? What the fuck?!'

'One-two one-two,' Will said into the microphone, with a flourish of a chord on the guitar. It was a well-timed distraction, as the friends all paused to take another sip from their drinks.

'I know, I know . . .' Emme groaned, returning to the elephant in the room. 'I'm an idiot, and I'm probably heading straight into my own train wreck . . .'

'Since when?!' Cat said with impassioned but affectionate incense. 'Why didn't you tell me on movie night?'

Emme thought back to that moment on the gondola almost a month ago.

'A few weeks.' She looked shyly at Tiago. She didn't really want to spill about that in front of him. 'I'm so sorry! But it's been incredible . . . and not what I planned. He broke it off with Vivian before anything really happened . . .'

Cat raised a doubtful eyebrow.

'Did the whole Steinherr double dip not put you off?!'

Emme curled up her nose.

Tiago looked a little shocked.

Emme stood firm.

'He's been calling every day from South Africa.'

'Why didn't you tell me?' Cat asked, looking half hurt.

Will finished tuning his guitar and welcomed everyone to the Hotel Europa bar and to the Cheeky Blinders band. He smiled over at Cat, Tiago and Emme, wondering why their cocktail cheer of ten minutes ago had turned serious.

'Well, it seems a bit insensitive, after what he did with Anastasia, and I know I'm a fool but –'

'Just don't say I didn't warn you,' Cat conceded, nudging into Emme's arm fondly.

Will strummed the first chords of 'Summer of 69' and Lydia looked up and smiled at Cat, who relaxed a little, despite her concern for her friend.

Tiago looked a little guilty for having brought it all up.

'Did I just kill the *tres mosqueteros* Christmas party vibe?' he asked, patting the girls each on the arm. 'I'll get another round in . . .'

Chapter Sixty-Seven

Walter and Lumi's stolen Friday afternoon in the Steinherr mansion had started with a game of backgammon by the fireplace, for old time's sake. Lumi had entered the home with trepidation: had it really been thirty years? So much had happened in both their lives. But as she walked the black and white tiled floor of the corridors, it felt like yesterday. The mansion smelled the same – of polished wood, aged leather and smoky logs in the hearth. The mansion looked the same. Apart from a rather disconcerting family portrait above the fireplace, but walking in politely in her Jaeger suit, Lumi felt at home again.

Viktor and Mika were still at loggerheads in Helsinki and wouldn't be back until Sunday; Anastasia was away in rehab; Dimitri was visiting his father in Athens; the children were still at school and would be returning with Nanny Iris tomorrow; and Vivian was busy at the Anna Maria, no doubt occupied by the hotel's busiest week so far. Christmas week at the newest, hippest hotel in town would inevitably be full-on.

Walter and Lumi played three rounds of backgammon before the maid delivered a carpet picnic by the fireplace and Walter instructed her to close the door and not to allow anyone to disturb them. An hour later, Lumi and Walter had transitioned to his marital bed. It felt reckless, or was it romantic, to be reconducting their affair in the family home in which the forbidden love had first ignited.

Walter stroked Lumi's radiant skin. The stretchmarks on her soft stomach sparkled silver.

'What do you want, my love? And I'll give it to you,' he asked.

'I want to leave Viktor,' Lumi said defiantly. She thought of the disdain with which he spoke to her. The disdain with which Benjamin his assistant ordered their lives.

Walter paused, and looked at Lumi with caution. Since his last appointment with Dr Blitzer, he was feeling more wary. He wanted to be with Lumi, but he didn't want to break her heart either. He shook his head gently.

'You don't want that, Walter? The children will grow to understand. Stella will be the hardest to explain it to but –'

'I do,' Walter said gravely. 'More than anything. Well, more than almost anything.'

He wanted to live longer.

'So what's wrong?'

Lumi sat up, alarmed, and pulled Walter's oyster-pink silk sheet around her. The bedroom clearly had the feminine decorative touch of Kiki, although no other trace of her remained.

'Don't end your marriage,' Walter confirmed.

'But I thought you wanted us to be together?'

'You will need Viktor.'

'Why are you saying that?'

Walter shook his head.

'I just want us to enjoy the time we have.'

A grey shadow dulled Lumi's luminescent features, realisation dawning on her.

'Oh god, Walter, how long do you have?'

She started to breathe heavily.

She knew it.

He looked grave.

'Months. A year at best. You will need the stability of Viktor to get you through.' And they looked into each other's eyes in calm horror because, yet again, this was to be a fleeting affair.

Chapter Sixty-Eight

It was the last day of term before the Christmas break, and Emme was on her way to collect Harry and Bella from school. The school day was ending a little later today, due to class Christmas parties, so Emme braced herself for the children to come out high on sugar and games. As Emme walked across the square past the Grand Hotel Sommar, its Havana Grey horse and cart waiting outside in the snow, her phone rang.

It was Tristan on FaceTime from a lush, sunny estate. Rolling green hills framed him in the background; his handsome, healed, face was sunkissed in shot.

'Hey,' Emme said, showing him where she was.

'Hey, I sorted my flight! I'll be back late Monday.'

Monday. Bliss.

There would be no school run on Monday, and Bill would be home for Christmas. Surely Lexy wouldn't need Emme for much, although she had certainly found excuses to keep her busy. A flash went through Emme's mind that perhaps she should keep it quiet that Tristan was returning, then she could get away with saying she was off Christmas shopping.

Can't wait.

'Shall I come to Zurich to meet you?' she asked excitedly.

The thought of riding in a helicopter back from Zurich to Kristalldorf next to Tristan gave Emme a thrill.

Tristan's broad, sexy smile filled the camera and she took it as a yes. She still couldn't really believe that Tristan Du Kok was into her, a temporary nanny from the UK, when he could have anyone in town. But his smile looked genuine. His electric touch was more than genuine, no matter how much caution Cat heeded.

Emme weaved through the school gates.

'I've got to go, the kids are coming out of school. I'll call you back later?' she said.

'Sure thing, speak in a bit,' Tristan said, as he kissed the camera and Emme hung up.

'Emme!' Harry shouted. 'I won the Christmas talent show for my taekwondo!'

'Well done, dude. That's great!'

'Emme! I got a chocolate reindeer!' Bella said, thrusting it in her face. 'For winning musical chairs!'

'Never in doubt!' Emme cheered.

Emme's contentment at how far she'd come turned to mild irritation when she remembered the chocolate reindeer she had bought the kids – and left up at Vitreum. It was fine, they didn't need any more right now.

'Stupid game!' Arjun said as he sidled up to Bella, a contemptuous and haughty smile on his princely face.

Cassie arrived.

'You didn't win?' she asked Arjun cheerily. 'Oh dear.'

The sarcasm in her voice was palpable.

'End of term, kids!' Emme beamed. 'Who's getting a visit from Santa next week?'

'Santa is a work of fiction,' Arjun harrumphed, as he

opened out his arms and waited for Cassie to put his coat on for him. She half threw the hood onto his head.

'And I am out of here!' Cassie said under her breath to Emme.

'Of course, when do you fly?'

'Tomorrow morning. Cannot wait!'

Emme relieved Harry and Bella of their bags and end-of-term artwork, politely appraising each piece as if it were actually good.

'When do *you* fly?' Cassie asked, thinking perhaps she had forgotten, but it hadn't come up in their conversations.

'Oh, I don't. I'm here all Christmas . . .'

Cassie looked almost horrified for her.

'It's fine!' Emme batted it away. With Tristan coming back, it really was.

Back at the apartment Emme was preparing an early dinner for Harry and Bella while they played in their bedrooms, shattered from the end-of-term parties. As she warmed a large *flammkuchen* in the oven, she sent Tristan a quick text from her phone on the island.

> Just cooking. Will call you in a bit. Cannot WAIT to be in your arms again. See you Monday! X

She put Spotify on. Al Green. 'Tired of Being Alone'. Songs they had made love to the night of the Kivvi Christingle. Emme was buzzing. Now she knew Tristan would be back on Monday, she considered Christmas and how it might look. As per Lexy's 'rules' she had Christmas Eve and Christmas Day off, and she was free to hang out with Tristan, lounging around Vitreum, cooking, sleeping and coming together.

She knew the Harringtons wanted her back for Boxing Day and the social whirl of their New Year. Lexy had mentioned Walter Steinherr's famous Kristall Ball on New Year's Eve and how wonderful it would be – especially so this year, after it didn't take place last December. Emme opened the fridge and took out a cucumber to cut into batons. Lexy was on the other side of the fridge door as she closed it.

Emme gasped, jumping so badly she had to smother the urge to attack her employer.

'Sorry, Lexy, I didn't hear you come in!'

Lexy gave a smile that looked more forced than ever.

'I wasn't expecting you home so soon,' Emme said, trying to smooth everything over.

Lexy motioned to the noise of the kitchen disco around them.

'Evidently not . . .'

Emme chopped the cucumber into batons as Lexy put her Aspinal of London folio case and Mulberry handbag down.

'The kids are just chilling in their rooms while I get dinner. They had great fun at their class parties . . . Both of them won a prize.'

Lexy didn't say much, she looked pissed off and affronted as she opened her mail.

Emme turned the music right down, then realised she may as well turn it off.

'That's better,' Lexy said icily. 'No devices during meal or snack time . . .'

Rule five, Emme thought. Although technically, they weren't eating yet, but Emme bit her tongue as she peered through the oven to check the *flammkuchen.*

'Ooh, while we're talking rules,' Emme said casually. 'I just wanted to ensure you're not expecting me to stay overnight on Christmas Eve and Christmas Day. As per rule three.'

Emme turned around to gauge Lexy's reaction.

Lexy wrinkled her nose.

'Hmmm, now that doesn't sound like you're asking permission to me . . .' she said.

'But I have those days off.'

Lexy put her post down on the island next to Emme's phone just as her screen flashed up.

A message from Tristan Du Kok.

Me neither. Can't wait to make you come again honey x

Emme clocked Lexy reading it and saw what looked very much like a searing rage rise up her face.

It seemed a bit of an extreme reaction.

'Is everything OK, Lexy?'

Lexy picked up Emme's phone and held it up accusingly, thrusting it towards Emme's nose as if she'd caught her out.

She wanted her phone back but Lexy was holding it like a hand grenade.

'After what that man did to Jenny?!' Her furrowed face was furious.

The timer buzzed and Emme switched the oven off and turned around to face her boss.

'What's that?' Emme scowled, tired now of Lexy's madness.

'Don't you wonder *why* she left town?'

'All the time,' Emme replied with a nervous laugh.

'Your *boyfriend* Tristan got *my* nanny pregnant! Left her

in the lurch. He even tried to rough her up when she told him she was keeping the baby.'

'What?'

'Did he get rough with you?' Lexy asked with an arched eyebrow. 'He's a very violent man.'

Emme thought about their tender lovemaking. His hands were commanding and skilled, his grip firm and manly, but he was never rough or violent. She was utterly confused.

No!

He said he'd never spoken to Jenny. Had Tristan lied to Emme as easily as she'd seen him lie to Vivian?

Emme shook her head. She wanted to cry but pride and anger stopped her. She turned around and looked at the *flammkuchen* bubbling in the oven, close to overcooked. She hastily removed the tart and took a deep breath.

Why was Lexy being so *nasty?* Emme turned back. Lexy was still standing there, hand on her hips as if Emme had done something wrong and she were her mother, waiting for an explanation. Except Marian would never look at her with such contempt.

Emme was doing everything she could not to cry.

Tristan? Jenny? Pregnant?

Emme stood tall. She was so exhausted by Lexy's psychodramas, her increasing demands, her *stupid fucking rules*. That she bit back without thinking.

'I assumed Jenny was having an affair with Bill, from the tension in this place.' She raised her chin.

'Bill?!'

Lexy curled up her nose. She was still clutching Emme's phone in her left hand, her knuckles white.

369

'Yes. Poor guy needs to let loose somehow. I assumed –
if he wasn't already getting his rocks off in Zurich in the
week, that maybe Jenny obliged him at weekends.'

Emme stood defiant.

'How dare you!' Lexy scolded, as she slapped Emme,
square on the cheek, the force of her right palm turning her
head. Emme gasped.

She held her face, looking utterly confused. The mother
of the house, her employer and caregiver, was the one being
violent.

'Fuck you . . .' Emme said, as she snatched her phone
out of Lexy's hand, looked around the kitchen, grabbed
her bag and coat, and left.

Chapter Sixty-Nine

With tears streaming down her face, Emme ran down the steps from Chalet Stern to the centre of town, breathless, shocked, panicking, as she clutched her cheek and wondered what the hell had just happened. She ran straight to the Steinherrhof hotel near the station, where Tiago was helping guests check in at the start of his night shift.

'Breakfast is served from seven am over there in the restaurant,' he said with a genial smile as he gave the guests their key cards and called for the bellhop to take the couple and their cases to their room. As he spoke he saw Emme come through the doors crying, eyes red and face flushed. She slumped into an armchair in the corner of reception.

'Are you OK?' Tiago asked, rushing over as soon as he was free.

Emme covered her face and sobbed.

'I have nowhere else to go!' She knew she could have gone to Cat but she wasn't ready for Cat to be right.

Tiago perched on the arm of the chair and put an arm around Emme.

'Hey hey, you're OK here. What's the matter? What's happened?'

He moved to the chair opposite and sat down, squeezing her knee as he rubbed it.

'She hit me!' Emme sobbed.

'Who? Who hit you?'

'My boss, Lexy, she slapped me!' Emme shook her head.

'Are you kidding?' Tiago looked around. 'Are you OK?'

Emme looked shell-shocked, and shook her head.

Tiago whistled to the restaurant manager, and asked that she watch the front desk for a second.

'Sure,' she nodded.

Emme sobbed. She wasn't OK. Tristan had got the former nanny pregnant and her boss had just slapped her.

'Not really.'

Tiago leaned his elbows on his thighs.

'Why did she hit you?' He could see the redness from Lexy's slap on her cheek.

'Because she's a psycho. She turned all weird on me because . . . because of . . .' Emme looked like she might be sick. 'Because of Tristan.'

Tiago frowned. He didn't approve of the guy, but he wouldn't slap anyone over it.

'I don't know what to do. I can't go back there. Not until Bill's home. I don't want to be on my own with her.'

Then she realised she'd probably lost her job after what she'd said.

Could she go to Vitreum and wait there until Monday?

No chance. She thought of Vivian Steinherr running out of the Kivvi party in tears. She had already known Tristan Du Kok wasn't a safe bet. She shook her head and cried. How could she be so stupid?

'Hey, I can see if we have a room here?'

Emme knew that rooms at the Steinherrhof cost at least 400 francs a night.

'I can't . . .'

'You can. If there's one available I'll put you on the manifest, you don't have to pay for it, and my manager, he won't know. But I gotta check we have a room first, I've only just come on shift . . .' Tiago walked over to the desk, thanking the restaurant manager for covering, who went back to the bustling restaurant.

He scrolled the screen with his syrupy gaze while he concentrated. Then he beckoned Emme over.

'Room 319, easy.'

'Tiago, I can't.'

'We don't lose money if the room's empty. It's fine. No hotel ever gets walk-ins in this town. It's available. It's a safe space. Don't be weird about it.'

Emme smiled. She'd heard Tiago say 'Don't be weird about it' before and liked his friendly bluntness.

He put a swipe card into a machine for room 319 and handed it over to Emme, along with three tissues he pulled expeditiously from the box on the desk.

'Thank you . . .' she said reluctantly.

'Take your time, no hurry. I can go get some of your things for you if you want, on my break . . .'

'No it's fine, really.'

'I could call Cat?'

'No – really – I'll work out what to do . . .' Except she had no clue. She felt a terrible wrench about walking out on the children, but there was no way she could go back.

Emme looked at her phone. A missed called from Tristan. He was expecting her to call him back. Lexy hadn't messaged. Why was she so furious with Emme when it was Tristan who had done that to Jenny?

*

Up in her cosy and plush room, Emme sat on the bed and thought about calling her mum. She thought about calling Tom. Their last conversation had been cut short, and for the first time in weeks she pined to speak to him, to seek his counsel, but she couldn't. She was so embarrassed. She thought about Tristan, and how he had lied to her about Jenny. As seamlessly as he had lied to Vivian about sleeping with Anastasia.

'Motherfucker,' she muttered to herself as she turned on the TV, not excited by anything she scrolled through.

Emme couldn't get Jenny Jones out of her head. What had she looked like? Lexy had left no trace of her, no photos or keepsakes for the children from a nanny they must have spent a lot of time with. When had it started with Tristan? How had he made *her* come? What was she feeling, back in England and pregnant? Emme felt sick just thinking about it.

Emme looked at her phone at a loss. Then she remembered the BUZZ doorbell footage and felt compelled to know more. Except Lexy said the app only saved video for thirty days, Jenny's history would be exactly that. History.

As Emme washed her face at the limestone sink, she examined her reflection in the mirror. She took a plump fresh flannel and soaked it under the hot water, before pressing it to her cheek. The warmth felt like a soothing salve. As she removed the flannel she could still see a red mark from where Lexy had slapped her. Maybe she had asked for it.

No, I hadn't.

As she tried to soothe the red mark away, Emme thought about Lexy's increasing volatility; how her tacit disdain had escalated into vocal admonishments. She examined her eyes and had an epiphany. Bella had accidentally bought the ninety-day BUZZ upgrade on the iPad. Lexy had berated her for it. She counted back. Emme had been in town for forty-two days, but ninety days would take her back to mid-September. Surely she would see what Tristan's lover looked like on some of the earlier BUZZ footage.

Chapter Seventy

Bill walked into the Harrington home to the kids eating their dinner. *Flammkuchen* and chopped veg with a bratwurst on the side for Harry.

'Hi kids,' he said benignly.

'Daddy!' Bella smiled.

'Hi Papa,' Harry said, more flatly.

Lexy was leaning against the kitchen worktop, arms folded, hovering over her children as if she were a prison warden, except her gaze was elsewhere.

'Everything OK?' Bill asked, as he put his attaché case on the sofa. 'Where's Emme?'

'She had to go out . . .' Harry said with an unnerved look.

Lexy turned away, towards the corridor and the bedrooms.

'Everything alright?' Bill asked again, puzzled.

'Yes,' Lexy replied frostily.

Bill loosened his tie.

'Do you know how long Emme's going to be? I thought you and I could go out for dinner,' Bill said, leaning in to kiss his wife on the cheek, but she flinched.

'Can we have pudding?' Bella asked.

Lexy looked at them, flustered for a second.

'Get an ice cream, you can have it in your rooms.'

'Yes!' they both cheered.

'But clear your plates first.'

Bill looked at the scene. Something was obviously wrong. Lexy could barely look at him. The atmosphere in the chalet was tenser than ever.

Harry and Bella negotiated over which flavour ice cream to have and happily went off to eat in their rooms, back with their tablets. Bill kicked his shoes off and put them in the cupboard.

'When's Emme back?' he asked again. 'I was thinking we could try 1865 tonight, Dirk Detzer said it's –'

'I don't want to go out for dinner,' Lexy cut him off.

'I thought after our disastrous anniversary meal last week, we should try again.'

Lexy turned to him sharply.

'What was wrong with our anniversary meal?'

Bill looked at his wife agog.

'Anyway, my hunches were right.'

'About Emme being sexy?' he joked.

'Bill!' Lexy scolded. 'I was right about her not being a good nanny.' She put her hands to her temples.

'What the hell's going on, Lex?'

Lexy couldn't tell Bill what Emme had really said, so she dug deep and shuddered.

'I think Emme has Münchausen by proxy. I think she's trying to poison the children.'

Chapter Seventy-One

Emme lay across the bed of room 319 looking at the BUZZ doorbell footage on her phone. She scrolled back to what she thought might have been Jenny's last days in Kristalldorf. She must have left in late October or early November because Emme started at the end of that first week. She whizzed back through the banal comings and goings, of Lexy with the kids. Bill nipping out to see a friend for a drink. Lexy toing and froing to work, and back to 1 November. There was nothing except Lexy leaving and re-entering the apartment with the kids, looking harried and hurried and stressed as she spun her plates without having a nanny.

Jenny must have left by then.

She continued to turn back time. Halloween. Time stamp: 8.58pm. A young woman appeared on the black and white footage, fresh faced and blonde with a long fishtail braid, bringing Harry and Bella home, excitedly clutching buckets full of sweets. But the woman looked troubled.

Jenny.

Jenny had a pretty, wholesome face, Emme could see that Tristan would find her attractive, and a pang of jealousy hit her like a silent punch. Did Jenny know a part of Tristan Emme didn't? If she was pregnant, she'd always be connected to him. Envy seared through Emme's body as she clutched the phone screen and searched back to the previous event. Jenny again, on her own this time, leaving the apartment at 7.18pm, except now her face looked angry rather than troubled. The BUZZ footage had no sound, but from the expression on her face, Jenny was not happy with someone inside. She looked like she might be shouting. Perhaps she was shouting at the children, except her eyeline was too high.

'Dammit!' Emme said, as she turned her volume up to maximum, just in case she could hear anything, but it was soundless. It always had been.

Emme continued to watch. Lexy came out of the apartment. But her face wore an expression Emme hadn't seen on her before. She wasn't helping Jenny in a crisis. Or even admonishing her the way she had just berated Emme. Lexy was *pleading* with Jenny. It was Jenny who looked angry. Her earnest face cracked into frowns and anger. She was shaking her head and reproachful. Jenny was the one who looked like she was telling Lexy off.

'What the fuck?'

Emme could understand why Jenny would be angry at her predicament, for being pregnant and ditched, and probably out of a job, but why was Lexy beseeching her?

She went to the previous event on the history list. Jenny arriving home on her own, rushing up the stairs and looking brighter, the time stamp saying it was only two minutes earlier: 7.16pm.

What had happened in those two minutes?

Emme went back further, and dropped her phone on the bed in shock.

No.

She picked her phone back up, her hand shaking. The previous event. Time stamp: 6.49pm. Lexy Harrington and Tristan Du Kok on the threshold of the family home. Kissing passionately, before he turned her around and pressed into her from behind as he pinned her against the door and threaded his fingers through hers. Lexy's sparkling ruby ring and wicked smile, fully facing the camera as she bit her lip.

Bastards.

It was there all along. No wonder Lexy was raging with jealousy. No wonder Lexy had seemed so especially jumpy when Emme first arrived in town. Video evidence was sitting on their devices like a time bomb and Bill was too stupid and too disinterested to notice. Was that why she relaxed a little at the end of November, after the thirty days had expired? Was that why she was so pissed off when Bella accidentally upgraded the BUZZ app to ninety days? Her tryst with Tristan wouldn't be so easy to cover up. That was why she turned psycho after she saw Tristan and Emme together at the Kivvi Christingle.

Was Tristan fucking both Jenny and Lexy? The guy got more and more depraved.

Emme went back one more event, 5.43pm, Jenny and the kids leaving the apartment, the children in their costumes. Jenny looking happy and nurturing as she closed the door and held Bella's hand.

Emme felt sick to the core. Her palms had gone in on themselves, she was gripping her phone so intensely. She looked across the room at her coat strewn on the chair and got up off the bed, her legs so heavy it was as though weights were tied to them. She had to find out how long Tristan and Jenny had been dating. She had to find out what happened on Halloween night, and thought of the one person who might have the answers.

As Emme threw on her boots she felt nauseous at the realisation that while Tom and Chrissy were having their first dance to 'Where the Wild Roses Grow', Tristan Du Kok was fucking Lexy in the Harrington home.

Chapter Seventy-Two

Bill walked down the corridor to look in on the kids and gently pulled their doors to. When he came back to the living room, Lexy was sitting on the sofa, her spine curled over, her shoulders hunched, her hands over her mouth, almost in disbelief.

He plucked a bottle of red from the wine cabinet and took two glasses out of the cupboard and poured them each a drink, then sat close to his wife, whose gaze was firmly facing forward, in the middle of the room.

'What the hell makes you think this?'

'I caught her red handed, pouring *immense* quantities of pink Himalayan salt into two glasses of lemonade as I came home. And it's not the first time . . .'

'What do you mean?'

'Remember Harry was sick last week, the night of our anniversary?'

Bill nodded.

'She'd fed him frozen bratwurst!'

Lexy was on a roll now.

'Are you sure?' quizzed Bill.

'I saw it in the bin!' She took a sharp breath. 'And Bella at the Kivvi Christingle. Emme was plying her with a solution as she went on her rounds. Bella was *sick* that night!'

Bill sounded unconvinced.

'But why would Emme want to do that?'

Lexy looked at him theatrically. Her eyes stung.

'Attention. It's why anyone does it.'

Bill pushed his wine away.

'Really, Bill. I saw her with my own eyes, tipping half a bloody container of salt into their drinks while she prepared dinner. I feel sick.' She put her fist to her mouth.

'Jesus, Lex, what is it with us and nannies?' Bill said, shaking his head. 'First Jenny steals from us, now Emme tries to poison the kids!'

Chapter Seventy-Three

Emme knocked on the door of Cassie's family's house. It was grand but gaudy, with a lion on either side of the chalet door. Arjun's family lived near the Steinherr mansion, on the left bank of the Glanzfluss, although their house looked a bit deflated next to the fairy-tale turrets of the mansion next door.

A maid answered.

'Hi, erm, is Cassie home?'

'One moment,' the meek woman said as she closed the door and went to check.

Within seconds Cassie came to the door, intrigued by who the visitor might be.

'Em! What's up?' she said, leaning on the doorframe. She was already wearing pyjamas and a robe, and had her hair wrapped in silk. 'I've just finished packing. What is it, last-minute Cadbury order?' she joked. Then she saw the desperation in Emme's eyes under the streetlights. 'Oh no! Is everything OK?'

'Please Cassie, I know you're obviously a wonderful, loyal friend, but I need to talk to you about what happened to Jenny . . . My boss – Lexy – I've had to get out.'

Cassie took a step back. A flash of hesitation flitted across her face while she tried to work out what to do. She looked down at herself, then nodded to the Anna Maria on the other side of the river.

'Give me a few minutes to get changed. I'll meet you over there . . .'

In the cosy bar a pianist was warming up for the Friday night clientele. No Christmas tunes here, he was playing jazz versions of rock standards. 'I Was Made For Lovin' You' by Kiss followed by 'Nothing Else Matters' by Metallica.

Emme was sitting by the fire, already nursing a G&T when Cassie arrived.

'I didn't know if you wanted a G&T or a cup of tea, you were in your jammies . . .'

'Oh hell, I'll join you,' she said.

Emme beckoned the waitress and asked for the same again.

'It's a double,' she said sheepishly to Cassie, who batted that little quandary away.

'So what's up?' Cassie asked, rubbing the top of Emme's shoulder. 'You look really spooked!'

Emme took a large sip and placed her glass down carefully on its mat.

'I need to know – did your friend Jenny get pregnant by Tristan Du Kok?'

If Cassie had her drink yet, she would have spat it out in shock.

'WHAT?! No!'

There was no uncertainty in her tone.

'But she and Tristan were having a fling?'

'Jenny?!'

'Please Cassie, I know she's your friend and her business isn't my business, but I need your help. Lexy. She *slapped* me.'

'She what?!' Cassie shook her head. 'Jesus Christ! That woman . . .'

Emme put her palm to her cheek and nodded.

'She was acting crazy, warning me off Tristan because he got Jenny pregnant and dumped her when she told him. But I've since realised Lexy was sleeping with him too.'

Emme shook her head in despair. This was all so grubby.

'Lies.' Cassie said firmly. 'Lies to cover her arse. She really slapped you?' she asked in outrage.

Emme put her hand to her cheek again.

'Then what's the truth? What happened on Halloween that made Jenny leave town? I really need to know about Tristan because –'

'Oh god,' Cassie groaned, shaking her head. 'You're not into TDK.'

Emme's eyes glassed over with tears as she nodded.

'Like nothing I've ever known,' she said, almost in a whisper. Embarrassed that she had arrived in Kristalldorf in unrequited love with her best friend, and now was hopelessly obsessed with the biggest player in town. A player who had made her feel exquisite for a few stolen moments.

Cassie let out a big sigh.

'Well I can a hundred per cent say Tristan did not get Jenny pregnant.'

'Was it Bill then?'

'No! Jenny isn't pregnant – not that I know of anyway . . .'

The waitress arrived with Cassie's drink and they stopped talking for a second, nodded and smiled their thank yous.

'Jenny has a boyfriend back home. Jon. She loves him.'

Cassie looked at Emme with caution.

'Look – I couldn't tell you about Lexy, it would have compromised you, but you obviously found out. How?!'

Emme didn't answer. She was just desperate to understand.

'What happened on Halloween?'

Emme thought back to her Halloween. The church. Chrissy's beautiful dress. The murder ballads.

'Jenny and I took Arjun, Harry and Bella out trick or treating – it's big here, of course,' she rolled her eyes. 'Spoilt brats . . . But Jenny forgot to bring buckets, and Arjun was being a turd about pooling sweets and sharing them, and there was just sooo much stuff . . .'

Emme was hanging on Cassie's every word.

'So while we were doing the rounds, Jenny popped back home to get Harry and Bella's Halloween buckets. I'd said I'd watch the kids.'

'And that's when she walked in on them . . .'

'Yes.'

'And had a row with Lexy over Tristan.'

'Yes – but no! Not like that.'

Cassie took another swig of her G&T.

'There was no Jenny and Tristan, whatever Lexy told you was a deflection, to take the focus off what she and Tristan were up to.'

Family friends.

'What, so Jenny and Tristan weren't shagging?'

'One hundred per cent not,' confirmed Cassie.

'So Lexy lied to me?'

'Of course she did! She's a nutjob.'

'Poor Jenny.'

'I know.' Cassie shook her head. 'She was so shocked – and uncomfortable. Lexy begged her to keep schtum and not leave, but I think she'd made Jenny's life so difficult before that – she wasn't the nicest boss . . .'

Emme nodded. That much she knew.

'Jenny knew it was game over for her job. A secret like that would weigh too heavily on her.'

'And Lexy was panicking about losing her nanny,' Emme said wryly.

'Plus Bill finding out, you'd hope . . .' quipped Cassie.

'So that's why she was pleading. That's why Jenny looked angry.'

'Looked angry?' Cassie asked.

'I saw some of it on the doorbell footage, but there was no sound.'

'Jenny just needed to get back to the kids, so when she came back with the buckets she was totally in bits. She knew this terrible thing about the kids' mother, and she knew it wasn't going to end well for her . . .'

Emme shook her head. *Fucking* Tristan. Fucking uptight Lexy Harrington. She wondered where in the apartment they were screwing when Jenny walked in.

'That night, after Jenny had put the kids to bed, Lexy hardened. She gave her an ultimatum. Keep it quiet or she'd fire her. Jenny had no option. She couldn't lie. She's so sweet. She had to walk. She handed in her notice there and then. She just wanted to get home to Jon.'

'What did Bill think?'

'I don't think Bill ever found out why she went so suddenly. Who knows what Lexy told him. Jenny just wanted to be out of that toxic place. I mean, Jenny said Lexy was a nightmare for months before that. I thought my family here were crazy . . .'

Emme shuddered.

'What a bitch.' Emme started to cry. 'What an utter bastard!'

Cassie rubbed her back. Vivian Steinherr walked past and stopped in alarm to see a customer not looking happy.

'Everything OK?' she asked Cassie with a sympathetic smile, trying to gauge Emme's face. Cassie nodded as if to say it would be OK, and Vivian moved along to meet and greet diners.

Emme felt even more ridiculous to have Vivian bear witness to her tears. It served her right. She remembered what Lexy had said to her in the laundry, the night of the Kivvi Christingle.

'Be wary of anyone who can break three hearts in one callous hit.'

She meant Vivian, Anastasia and herself, of course. He hadn't broken Emme's heart then. Not yet.

And Tristan. What a shit. His sunny FaceTime calls from Stellenbosch had all been such bullshit. She hung her head.

'I can't believe I was excited about spending Christmas with him.' She shuddered. 'I feel sick.'

'I'm so sorry babe, it's utterly shit. They're as awful as each other.'

Back in room 319 of the Steinherrhof, Emme paced in circles, trying to work out what to do: Bill would be home by now – should she go back and tell him why she had fled? Should she tell him about Lexy and Tristan? Should she hand in her notice? She couldn't work in that family with that atmosphere any more. Poor Jenny having to walk in on that. But poor Jenny wasn't hooked on the guy she'd walked in on, fucking her boss. She wanted to cry. She wanted to scream. *How dare they?*

Tristan phoned on FaceTime, a fourth missed call, and she ignored it, not knowing what to say or how to coherently tell him to fuck off.

What do I do?

With Bill home, the kids were not abandoned. She would take the weekend to work out what to do. Maybe Lexy would have to start looking after her own kids.

The phone rang again. Tristan on FaceTime, followed by a worried text.

Are you OK babe? Got a bad feeling x

Emme flipped her phone over, and cried herself to sleep.

Chapter Seventy-Four

On Saturday afternoon, Emme opened her hotel room door to see Cat standing there with a care package.

'You OK?'

'No,' she said, as she opened the door wider to let her friend in.

Cat placed the paper Migros bag on the desk in the room and took out some bits.

'I got you biscuits, chips, chocolate, and I brought you some clothes – some of mine . . .' she said, as she slunk into the chair next to the window.

'Thank you Cat, you're a hero.'

She nodded.

'I bumped into Bill in Migros and he asked if you were staying with me. Said he wanted to talk to you . . .'

'I bet he does. What did you say?'

'He seemed kinda angry.'

'Oh dear,' Emme said, a rash creeping up her neck.

'I said I didn't know where you were . . . which he knows is BS. But, you know, hoes before bros . . .' Cat tailed off and Emme appreciated the loyalty.

'Well, I just don't know what to do about that at the moment.'

Cat picked up a handful of grapes from the fruit bowl Tiago had sent up as he was ending his shift.

'Tristan's worried too. He called me, I don't know how he got my number but he asked if I'd spoken to you . . .'

'Great.'

Cat looked at her, puzzled by her sarcasm.

'What did you say?' Emme asked.

'I said Lexy had gone psycho on you, but I couldn't really talk . . . I was prepping breakfast, Gerard was in my ear.'

'Did you tell Tristan where I was?'

'No. Should I have? I wasn't sure.'

Emme didn't answer.

Cat twirled the empty grape stalk between two fingers. All Tiago had told her was that Lexy had slapped Emme over Tristan.

'I thought it was going great guns with you!'

Emme shook her head.

'You did warn me . . .'

Cat sat up.

'Wait, what's happened?'

Emme told Cat exactly what triggered Lexy to slap her. Because of Emme's comment about Bill and Jenny. Because Lexy was so wound up about Tristan and Emme and seething with rage because she had fucked Tristan not even two months ago. Perhaps more recently too.

'Motherfucker!' raged Cat.

'Well . . . quite,' Emme said, solemnly.

'I can't believe it!'

Cat was so livid, she looked like she might have been duped too. 'But . . . at the party . . .'

'What?' Emme asked.

Cat couldn't speak.

'So what are you going to do?' she eventually asked.

'He's back on Monday and I just can't bear to see him. He's such a liar, Cat! Disgusting. I mean, you warned me . . . I knew it myself! But *Lexy*?!'

'Yeah, he should have told you that perhaps there was a conflict of interest there. But, you know, after you told me and Tiago about you two, I was thinking about the party . . .'

'What?'

'When you guys went flying in a heap on the floor. He wasn't looking at Anastasia. Or Vivian. He wasn't looking at Lexy Harrington, that's for sure. He looked genuinely worried about you. I should have guessed about you two there and then. He was all for *you*.'

'Oh please, Cat! You of all people, after him and Anastasia . . .'

'I dunno. At least hear him out. Does he know you know about Lexy?'

'How can he? I doubt even Lexy knows I know.'

'Well he knows something is off. He's worried you're not answering his calls and he knows Lexy has gone nuts.'

'So what do I do?'

'Don't think about any of it yet. Let's hit the mountain. I have tomorrow off. The Kivvi men are flying back into the country tomorrow and having dinner in Geneva when they collect Stella. We'll get some air, the forecast looks great. I swear, the mountain always has the answer.'

Emme nodded. She had been skiing twice a week since

that magical day in the gondola; she was even starting to envisage loving skiing one day.

'For now, just stay here and keep ordering room service. Tiago's on shift tonight, right?'

Emme nodded.

'He'll look after you.'

And just like that, Emme felt bolstered.

Chapter Seventy-Five

Cat walked into the lobby of Seven Summits and froze when she saw who was waiting for her, on a sofa opposite the chalet lifts.

'Oh. I thought you were in –'

Tristan had his black holdall next to him. He looked like he had just flown in. He stood, and ran his fingers through his hair frantically.

'I got an earlier flight. I need to speak to Emme. Please Cat, where is she? She's stopped answering my calls. What's going on?'

Cat levelled him with a look.

'You're a grade-A creep, you know that, right?'

'What?'

Tristan looked totally bewildered, as if that were a past life.

Cat shook her head.

'Please, she's not answering my calls, and I can't go to her place of work.'

'No, funny that . . .' Cat said with a raised eyebrow. 'Look, I gotta cook. Nice talking to you,' she said sarcastically, as she pressed the button on the Chalet Edelweiss elevator.

Tristan picked up his bag in defeat and went to leave.

'Look, I didn't know about you and Anastasia,' he said apologetically. 'Not until Emme told me.'

Cat looked back at him.

'Would it have made any difference if you did?'

He didn't answer.

'I thought not.'

Cat was small, but she made Tristan feel minuscule.

'Really, I'm sorry.'

They stared at each other in a standoff as the lift arrived.

'Please, can you get a message to her?' Tristan begged.

The lift doors opened, and something in Tristan's desolate face made Cat think Emme might want to hear him out.

'She's staying at the Steinherrhof.'

Tristan looked puzzled. What *had* happened? How had she found out? But he was also relieved. If he could just see her, he could explain.

'Room 319. But you have to get past Tiago first.'

Chapter Seventy-Six

Emme sat cross-legged on her hotel bed and read a message from Tiago checking in on her.

I'll be on shift tonight, he said, although she had remembered. *See you soon.*

Thanks Tiago x Emme replied.

Emme looked at the calendar and pondered the mess she had got herself into in six short weeks. She wondered why the hell she had agreed to take a job that would pull her away from her family for Christmas. Two days off wasn't enough time to go home, and she had been so naïve to think she would have a lost Christmas of passion in Tristan's penthouse.

There was a knock on the door as she considered whether she really could fly back to London for forty-eight hours. She missed her mum, dad and Lucille terribly.

The knock rasped on the door again, this time more frantically.

'Shit,' Emme muttered.

She half hoped it would be Bill so she could show him the footage of Lexy and Tristan, but wondered what good that would serve. What about poor Harry and Bella? Emme climbed off the bed, checked her appearance in the vast mirror by the door and put her phone in her jeans pocket.

As she opened the door, all the feelings of lust, obsession and treachery came flooding back like a wrecking ball to the third floor of the Steinherrhof.

Chapter Seventy-Seven

Walter Steinherr walked into the lobby of the Anna Maria, ignoring his doctor's orders about avoiding crowds.

'Daddy!' Vivian said, her eyes lighting up as she crossed the foyer and took his hands. The Saturday before Christmas was the busiest time of year for any Alpine hotel, let alone the newest in town, and the Anna Maria was bustling with guests, diners, partygoers and holidaymakers, all sharing the collective self-satisfaction of being in one of the most Instagrammable places in the world right now. The beaches of St Bart's had New Year. The cherry blossom of Yoshino had spring. The jewels of the Greek Islands had summer. New England had the fall. December belonged to Kristalldorf, and this hotel was fully booked for weeks.

Her father didn't often visit the hotel he had gifted his daughters, he had wanted to let them flourish on their own.

'What are you doing here?'

'Oh I just popped in, I have Timo and the yumbo outside. I've just been to the lakes . . .' Walter omitted to mention he had spent a lovely day with Lumi, lunching lakeside under the gaze of snowy mountains.

'Would you like something to eat?' Vivian asked, excited by her father's visit. Vivian was a people pleaser, and there was no person she strived to please more than her father.

'You should come and eat in Avocet. The December menu is wonderful.'

She was aware that her father looked like he needed feeding up. The powerhouse of a man appeared to have shrunk in clothes that had stayed the same size.

'No, no, I just wanted to pop by, have a look at the place, see you in your natural habitat.'

His emotion was unnerving her. As if this would be his last visit. A smile of puzzlement curved her lips.

Vivian looked around.

'Daddy, are you OK? I know you're going to be fine without Kiki, I'm just a little worried about you, going back on your own.'

He waved away her worry with a liver-spotted hand.

'Why don't you stay and have some supper here? We can find you a table.'

'I'm fine! It's only over the river, I could probably swim home myself!'

'And freeze to death!'

She wouldn't have put it past him in his youth, although not in December.

Walter looked around in awe, at the bustle, at the décor, at the happy guests.

'I just wanted to stop by and let you know – I stand by my decision, Vivian. Anastasia will find her way back to us, but you are the right successor for all this.'

Vivian beamed.

'And you don't need to feel guilty about that.'

An athletic man with silver hair sauntered over, his grey-blue eyes in awe behind black rectangular glasses.

'Is this the genius who made all this happen?' the man

said, a delighted smile lighting up his face. He was definitely one of the tourists who appreciated how fortunate he was.

Vivian smiled.

'Hugh, welcome back!'

Hugh Van-Tam was a repeat guest – a widower in his fifties, who owned a chain of Pilates studios around the world and had the physique to show for it. Vivian kissed him on each cheek.

'Father this is Hugh, a regular now, who's here with his daughter. Hugh, you are correct, this is indeed the famous Walter Steinherr.'

Vivian looked adoringly at her father. His sentimentality of a few moments ago slid away as he smiled and pressed the flesh of the polite Englishman. Walter was the consummate hotelier, even in his old age.

'Would you care to join me and Holly for dinner tonight?' Hugh asked both father and daughter, but he was really looking at Vivian, his eyes glittering. 'Holly is *desperate* to get into hospitality and do a season out here, any nuggets of wisdom you can spare would be delightful . . .'

'Oh Hugh, I would love to but I'm so busy. Perhaps we can meet in the bar later, when things quieten down?' Vivian flashed her winning smile.

'Vivi, I will leave you to it,' Walter said, keen for one of his maid's hot whiskies, and to get his aching bones to bed. He had another date with Lumi tomorrow. The Lucerne Christmas fair. They had vowed to spend as much time together doing as many joyful things as possible. While they could.

Chapter Seventy-Eight

Anastasia Steinherr Diamandis stalked a poolside lit by candles and decorated with rose petals, her thin maxi dress billowing in the balmy breeze. Palms swayed and calming gamelan music chimed from hidden speakers among the verdant bushes as she paced the pool's edge, phone to her ear. It was only five days until Christmas, and she couldn't have been anywhere less seasonal and more tropical. It was so liberating, Anastasia had forgotten herself and accidentally answered her brother's phone call.

He'd been talking at pace for five minutes now, checking in on her, talking about Christmas and all his plans for it, avoiding any mention of the Kivvi Christingle and how she humiliated their family in front of everyone.

'We're spending it with Meg's mom and dad, upstate . . .' Lysander said. Anastasia hadn't asked and she wasn't really interested. 'Do you think you'll head back to KD?'

KD, Anastasia scoffed internally. Her brother was so bloody American.

'No, I think I'm going to need a little more time,' Anastasia said, following the figure of a woman as she cut her path towards a small cliff edge. Beneath it the ocean lapping the rocks was lit artfully, making azure dots shimmer out of the black night water.

Anastasia had stayed precisely one night in the austere Black Forest facility before remembering an article she had read in *Vogue* about a supermodel-turned-wellness-guru who had opened a string of state-of-the-art resorts in the Indian Ocean. It was more her thing. If she was going to be gone for a while, to really try to save her reputation, she may as well do it in style.

She had spent the past blissful fortnight doing gong therapy, juice cleansing, reading by the pool, and working on herself, her way.

'I'd better go Zand. I have chakra cleansing in ten.'

'At seven pm on a Saturday night?' Lysander said, his voice landing halfway between impressed and sceptical.

Actually it was midnight where she was, and the heady scents of frangipani trees in the gardens and the monoï oil in her slicked-back hair were intoxicating, filling her with an invigorating thrill. She looked to the woman, staring out to the ocean. Her serene beauty in profile made her look like an African queen.

'I'll check in with you soon,' Anastasia said. 'Promise.'

'OK sis. Maybe give Dad a call too, huh?'

Now he was ruining her chi.

'I have to go.'

She hung up, threw her phone on the lounger, and looked towards the diners in the twinkling restaurant beyond the long empty rectangle of the pool that separated Anastasia from the families. The detoxers. The couples. All of whom had chosen the idyllic tropical island for their wellness get-away too.

The woman on the edge of the sea, dressed in a cream silk slip dress that caressed her lithe body, glanced back.

She and Anastasia had been playing cat and mouse for days, and as Anastasia held her eye, she kicked off her flat gold sandals, pulled her maxi dress over her head and stood, naked and glistening in the moonlight, as she dived into the water and swam a tantalising length of the pool.

Chapter Seventy-Nine

'What are you doing here?'

Tristan stood broad in a checked shirt and sherpa-lined trucker jacket, his tanned face looked ashen.

'Emme please . . .' he reached out a hand.

'Get away from me!' she hissed, narrowing the door.

Tristan looked devastated.

He put his arm in the door so she couldn't slam it on him.

'Please.'

Emme didn't know he'd spent the week in South Africa thinking about her; telling his mother about her; and shunning every old flame because he had only one person on his mind.

'What's happened? Why are you staying here?'

Emme stayed silent. She was so furious and so hurt, she couldn't speak.

'We talked every day, look, I don't understand. But when you didn't call me back yesterday, you didn't answer my calls, I knew something was wrong. What's happened? What's changed?'

He had returned to Kristalldorf within twenty-four hours.

'You can't work it out?'

Tristan looked vague and panicked.

'You and Lexy Harrington. You and my fucking boss.'

He hung his head and looked at his feet, before letting out a huge sigh.

'Of all people! Why didn't you tell me?'

'Please, let me come in, I can explain . . .'

Emme opened the door and walked away from it, towards the window, her arms folded, her heart broken.

Tristan reached an arm out, desperate to touch her.

'Genuinely, it was nothing.'

'Nothing? You two go way back! How long have you two been at it?'

'Seriously, she's hit on me ever since she moved here . . .'

'You were here first?'

'Yes – her kids were really little and they were new in town. Of course she knew I was here – she knew what had happened to my father. Our mothers are friends. But I swear . . . I took them out for dinner and since then she has been relentless.'

'Gross,' Emme spat.

Tristan told Emme about the surprise on Lexy's face when she and Bill turned up to that one dinner. Tristan still owned Vitreum then, and Lexy's jaw almost dropped to the floor to see the boy Tristan Joubert, manly and ripped, in the restaurant of *his* spectacular hotel.

The last time they had seen each other Tristan had been fourteen, with fluff around his top lip and a skinny body – as a teen he hadn't dared look Lexy in the eye.

Tristan had welcomed Lexy and Bill with a hug and a handshake. He had always thought of Lexy as a much-older cousin, pin-up hot, but the pretty redhead was now a little tired from the ravages of parenthood.

'My, how you've grown!' she'd said with an avaricious smile, as she pressed her body into Tristan's, before pulling back, tilting her head to one side and saying, 'So sorry to hear about Charles.'

Tristan stroked his temples in despair as he told Emme how she'd plagued him ever since.

'She's been like it for years, hounding me at any opportunity, until I finally thought *fuck it.*'

'Nice,' Emme scowled.

'But I swear, it only happened once. A one-night thing after a wine event got crazy. I suppose my teenage self got the better of me . . .'

Emme shook her head.

'I explicitly asked you!' she said, tears stinging her cheeks.

'No you didn't.'

'I did!'

'You didn't!' Tristan said more firmly now, an obstinate twitch in his stubbled jaw. 'You asked me about a Jenny, I didn't sleep with Jenny.'

'Oh right but you conveniently omitted that you had fucked Lexy.'

Tristan shook his head.

'It was before I even knew you existed. I would never . . .'

'Why didn't you *tell* me then?'

'And compromise your job?'

'Oh fuck off!' Emme shouted. She'd had enough. 'You're toxic. Is there anyone in Kristalldorf you haven't slept with? Oh yeah, Cat, but you had to fuck up everything for her too . . . Jesus Christ what is *wrong* with you Tristan?'

As she said it, she looked at him and felt such a raging passion she wanted to be back in Vitreum, the two of them, naked on the bearskin. She felt like such a fool who couldn't control her own body and mind.

'I swear Emme.' He put his palm to his heart. 'I have not been able to think about anyone but you since I've been home. My mom said I look like a different person – she's dying to meet –'

Emme cut him off and raised her chin.

'I genuinely cannot believe anything you say, and now I've lost my job, and I'm holed up here, and –'

Tristan approached her and put out his hand.

'Don't!' she scolded, and he stopped.

'I was a fool to think you looked at me any differently.' Emme said.

'I do, honestly.'

'Get out of here, leave me alone.'

Chapter Eighty

When Emme came down to breakfast the next morning wearing the ski thermals Cat had squirreled for her, Tiago was nearing the end of his shift. He looked exhausted and overwhelmed, and she didn't want to add any more stress on his shoulders.

'Hey T, I'll be out of your hair later, I'm going to check out . . .' she said, as she squeezed him on the arm and walked to the breakfast buffet. Emme had decided. She didn't have to fly to London for a stolen forty-eight hours with her family. She was going home for good. She was going to tell Lexy and Bill she was leaving, although she assumed she had already been fired; she was going to show Bill the BUZZ footage of Lexy with Tristan. Then she was going to pack her clothes, hug Harry and Bella tightly, and take the last train down to Bloch this evening. She planned to spend the night in an airport hotel, and fly from Zurich to Gatwick the next morning. She'd booked the flight and not told her parents. It was going to be an early Christmas surprise for them.

His weary-warm smile wore a look of concern.

'Hey, you can stay as long as the room is available – although I might need to switch you around to a twin, I think I need that double back . . .'

'No really, I can't stay here forever. I need to go home.'

'Home home?' Tiago looked forlorn.

Emme nodded, as she put some muesli and yogurt in a bowl.

Camilla approached, looking harangued. The restaurant was half full with guests in their skiwear, eating plates of fruit, cheeses, meats and cereals. Staff were hurriedly waltzing in and out of the kitchen with refills.

'Dammit, Cecily has called in sick and Dieter's in a plaster cast . . . what can we do Tiago?'

He sighed at the ceiling.

'Damn Camilla, I gotta sleep some time!' He looked at Emme. 'Want a job?'

She laughed, then realised he was serious.

'Really?'

'We've been understaffed all season and people are letting me down left right and centre. Pietro is going to go apeshit.'

'I'm meeting Cat, we're going skiing,' Emme apologised. 'And then I need to sort out my shit.'

'Not now!' Tiago laughed, nudging Emme on the arm. 'But any time you do . . .'

Emme wasn't sure she could ever stay in Kristalldorf without her heart hurting too much, but it was nice of Tiago to offer.

Chapter Eighty-One

'You're going?' Cat exclaimed from their perch on the double chairlift. 'Noooo!' she bellowed theatrically into the pine forest nearby. A mountain hare scurried into its burrow, cotton tail bobbing as it darted away from Cat's voracious echo.

'Tonight,' Emme nodded. 'I'm sorry.'

'You better be!' Cat joked. 'What about *los tres mosqueteros*?'

'Well you must come visit me in London. I'll take you to Sheekey, Bouchon Racine and Scott's . . .'

Cat looked impressed. They were restaurants Emme could always get a table at, as long as she booked in Dominique's name.

'I can't change your mind?'

'Well, Tiago did just offer me a job. But no. I need to go home. Get as far away from Lexy and Tristan as I can. Plus, there are things I need to make right in London.'

She thought of Tom and what a bad friend she had been. She hadn't even called him back since the night Harry was sick. She had been so all-consumed by Tristan and the passion he had ignited in her — and how good that had felt — that she had neglected to fan the flames of friendship.

'But you just mastered parallel turns!' Cat lamented.

They'd done three blue runs already today, and although

the slopes and chairlifts were busier than Emme had ever seen, the sun was dazzling and the powder was perfect.

'It's a good way to go out . . .' Emme said, not quite believing that she would ever feel like she could ski. Cat kicked the snow off her board while they soared over the fenced-off wildlife area. She leaned over the chair, looking at three figures skiing beneath. Two adults and a teenager, from the look of it. The teen was wearing blue and red stripes.

'What?' Emme said, following their trail.

'They should not be skiing in that area . . .' Cat said, irritated. 'It's protected woodland.' She shook her head. 'Plus it's high avalanche risk today. *Malditas turistas.*'

Cat watched them sternly, the group was already near the bottom, so she figured they'd be OK, but bad ski etiquette pissed her off.

As they approached the top of a red run, Emme tried to soak in the view. The Silberschnee was stunning and the air was so fresh, such a far cry from London.

London.

She couldn't wait to surprise her family. To see Zara and Zack on Christmas morning. To put this ridiculous town behind her and get back to work. Maybe Dominique would even get rid of the temp and give Emme her job back in the New Year.

I hope so.

At the top of the chairlift both friends glided off expertly; Cat on her snowboard, Emme on her skis. Her entire wardrobe comprised Cat's spare clothes: a bright hotchpotch of vivid colours. Vibrant base layers. A multicoloured one piece. Mismatched socks and gloves and a well-worn Roxy helmet. Although she had managed to get her boots and skis from the Harrington locker by the ski train without bumping into Lexy or Bill.

They did two red runs together, and now they were doing a third. Cat faster and much more competent than Emme of course, but Emme felt that she might have nailed her technique. She had arrived in Kristalldorf paralysed and incapable; now she was flying. Flying away from Lexy Harrington. Flying away from her jealousy about Tom and Chrissy. Flying away from Tristan. Flying away from the sad, naïve girl she thought she might be. Remembering she was a strong woman. An exceptional assistant her exceptional boss relied upon. She had learned more about herself, her body, her passion and her boundaries, than she thought possible until now, as she flew down the slope, her sadness lifting into exhilarating joy.

Cat was ahead of her, twisting deftly, before she turned and looked back up the slope towards Emme. She shouted something and shook her head, as she crossed her arms overhead and veered left, into a woodland area. Emme didn't hear, but followed the trail Cat blazed with her board.

Through pine forests relieving their branches of snow, Emme struggled to keep her eye on Cat, whose pace had quickened as she boarded with an urgency. Ahead of her was another figure, one of the three who had been in the group before – the younger figure in the red and blue stripes – then Emme was struck with a terrible realisation: she had followed Cat into the protected wildlife area. None of them should be there.

Panic surged through Emme's body, her thoughts filling

with a primal fear, which she tried to reason with: terrible things didn't tend to actually happen.

Until they did.

She heard a thunderous bang, as a shelf of snow fell in one roaring thud, onto her shoulders, compressing her down with unyielding force.

Chapter Eighty-Two

At first, Emme felt as though she was in a washing machine. Tumbling in a cold cycle as her body was caught up in the crashing cacophony of snow, carrying her limbs like a Catherine wheel. Her first thoughts were confused.

What the hell is going on?

Then realisation.

This is actually happening.

I'm dying.

She thought about Cat. She tried to call for her, but no words came out. Emme's voice was muffled, as if someone had stuffed a heavy cloth in her mouth. She didn't know if her eyes were open or closed, there was a darkness enveloping her that was also piercingly bright; she felt a searing heat that was also freezing cold. Her body felt as if the weight of a thousand trucks had rammed her into a pillow of freezing cotton. The cartwheeling came to an abrupt halt with a feeling that she was being slammed into something sharp, alongside a million little pieces of debris. Then everything went dark. An eerie silence reigned, while Emme realised she was slipping away.

Emme opened her eyes, not sure whether seconds, minutes or hours had passed. It couldn't be hours. She remembered

Cat telling her how humans only lasted fifteen minutes under the snow, before they died of suffocation or hypothermia.

Perhaps I'm already dead, Emme thought, although she could hear muffled, muted screams in a distant realm. The sound of a helicopter. Sounds which suggested movement. Sounds which suggested life. She tried to look around her but was surrounded by white concrete, then she realised, she could be so many metres deep. This was really happening. All her optimism from just moments ago, the empowering soaring flying, had been crushed. This was the end.

She thought about her mother, father, sister, and niece and nephew as a chilling comfort washed over her. 'It's OK,' she told herself, as if she were reassuring Zara and Zack. Comforting them so they might sense she was at peace.

'It's OK.'

Her breathing became more laboured, the cold cloth expanding in her mouth. She tried to punch the snow around her but the weight of it pinned her arms, and she was frozen in her freefall, frozen in time.

'It's OK,' she told herself, as she felt herself slipping away.

Chapter Eighty-Three

Emme woke with a start and gasped for air. *Air.* She could breathe. Her panicked eyes opened and the first person she saw was her father, sitting at her bedside, a book on his lap. He looked up and gave a smile of harrowed relief.

She started breathing rapidly, in panic, until machinery beeped and whirred and she realised she was alive.

Her father looked across Emme's bedside, and she followed his gaze. Her mother was sitting on her left. She tried to move but her body ached, she felt pummelled.

'It's OK love, you're OK,' Marian said, clutching Emme's hand.

'We're here,' Geoff said.

Emme nodded.

'I . . . I . . .' she tried to speak.

'Do you remember what happened, love?' Marian asked.

Emme thought about the whiteout and the white noise, and then panicked.

'Cat – where's Cat?'

'It's OK, love,' her mother soothed her. 'She's down the hall. She broke her collarbone when she hit a tree. The boy broke both his legs.'

'You got off lightly!' said Geoff, with some relief. She

could tell from the sad sweep across his face that he didn't really think it. He was so immensely relieved.

Emme smiled. She was relieved too. She thought she'd died.

'How long have I been in here?'

'Three days darling. You've been drifting in and out for three days. The poor boy was in a coma but he woke up last night,' her mother said.

'How long have you been in Kristalldorf?' Emme asked.

Her parents looked at each other.

'Oh we haven't even got to Kristalldorf yet, we're in the hospital in Bloch. Do you remember Bloch?'

Of course.

Emme nodded.

A nurse came in to check Emme's vitals.

'Ahh she's awake! Hello sweetie,' she said in a German accent. 'Do you know what day it is?'

They went quiet as the nurse took Emme's blood pressure. As her parents waited on tenterhooks to see how much Emme might remember.

She shook her head.

Her parents looked at each other, more nervously this time.

'Well, it must be around . . .'

'It's Christmas Eve. Happy Saint Niklaus!' the nurse said cheerily, as she noted down Emme's blood pressure, pulse and temperature on her chart.

'The doctor will be in to see you soon, I'll tell her you're awake and she'll come on her rounds.'

'Thank you,' Emme said, her voice rasping her throat. She felt thirstier than she ever had.

How had she got out of there? How long had her parents been in Switzerland? Was Cat really OK?

She had so many questions.

'What happened? After the avalanche?' Emme mustered.

'You were stuck under the snow my darling,' Marian said. 'It was lucky you were wearing Cat's ski suit. It has one of those thingamajigs that send a signal.' She paused, as she pressed a tissue to her eyes. 'Search and rescue could find you more easily.'

'Not that easily,' Geoff said. It was like they were recounting a story that had been only half told to them. 'Search and rescue got to the boy and Cat first, they were nearer the helicopter landing point. Lucky to be alive because they'd hit trees.'

'You're lucky to be alive too,' Marian added.

'A local man had to get you out himself,' her dad said. 'With his shovel.'

'He had all the gear,' Marian said. 'He could see on his gizmo where you were below. He dug you out with his own hands.'

Emme gulped.

'The kindness of a stranger,' Geoff said, almost crying.

'Tristan,' Marian said.

'Tristan?'

'He's been here day and night, checking on all three of you. He knows the mountains very well apparently. Knew exactly what to do.'

'He could see search and rescue were having to make choices. Priorities . . .' Geoff said, shaking his head.

Emme's mother welled up.

'They weren't prioritising you.' She put her hand over

her mouth, dreading to think what would have happened if the kindly man hadn't been on the mountain with his avalanche pack on.

'*Guten Abend!*' the doctor interrupted, as she walked in with the nurse at her shoulder. She explained that Emme had suffered hypothermia, concussion and two broken ribs, which there was nothing that could be done about apart from taking ibuprofen and paracetamol to ease the pain. 'They heal on their own within three to six weeks and we usually recommend ice packs for broken ribs, but in your case, *nein*. No ice,' she said, with a wry smile.

'Why not?' Marian asked.

'Not when she's recovering from hypothermia and trauma.'

As the doctor looked at her clipboard she said she was satisfied with Emme's stats. 'You're making a good recovery, Miss Eversley,' the doctor added. Emme's parents glanced at each other with the pride of parents whose child had just won an award at school. 'Mr Du Kok is certainly the hero of the hour,' the doctor said with a smile.

And Emme was so shocked. So grateful. So tired, she fell back asleep.

When Emme woke again it was just her mother sitting by her bedside, crocheting a dress for Zara.

'That was a big sleep . . .' she said, as if Emme were a toddler.

'Where's Dad?'

'He went off to get some sandwiches. Your friend Tiago's showing him a better option than the hospital canteen, although I thought they were pretty good myself. They did a nice turkey and cranberry one yesterday . . .'

'Of course. Is it Christmas Day yet?'

'Not yet, love.' Marian tucked her crochet away. 'Cat was brought in but you were asleep . . .'

'Is she OK?'

'She's a bundle of energy, isn't she?'

Emme smiled.

'How long are you staying here for?'

There was a polite knock at the door before her mother could answer.

Tristan stood, one hand in his pocket. Denim shirt loose under his thick jacket. His face sunkissed and golden from the South African summer.

'Mind if I . . . ?' he looked at Emme hesitantly.

'Oh, do come in!' Marian said, all of a fluster.

His good looks were not lost on Emme's mother either.

'Emme, this is the gentleman who saved your life!' She stood up, almost as if she should curtsey.

'Tristan, hi . . .' Emme gave a small wave.

'Emme,' he said, almost in a gasp.

'Oh, you know each other?' Marian asked, delighted.

If only she knew how well.

Marian blushed as she made an unnecessary fuss about picking up her things.

'Maybe you want to talk, I'll leave you to it. Actually, love, I might go and call Dad, tell him to buy extra. You might want something other than hospital food – and would you like anything, love?' She looked to Tristan as she wittered.

'No, I'm fine thank you.'

'Will you be alright?' Marian hesitated.

'Of course Mum, find Dad, get some food.'

'I can stay with her,' Tristan said reassuringly. 'As long as you need.'

He looked at Emme cautiously. Aware that the last time they spoke she was furious with him.

Emme looked back at Tristan, feeling utterly confused.

I was dying, she remembered, realising she had no head space for anger right now. She was too spent.

'I'll come back with your dad and sandwiches as soon as I can. Visiting hours end at ten pm.'

Not for Tristan they didn't. He'd sat in the chair night and day in the waiting room, waiting for the right moment to see Emme.

Marian realised she was fussing. This man, this hero, who had saved her daughter's life, had that effect on her, so it was best she left them to it.

'Go Mum, it's fine.'

She kissed Emme's head, pressed Tristan on the shoulder, blushed, and walked out.

Chapter Eighty-Four

'Your parents are lovely.' Tristan said quietly, testing Emme's reaction to his appearance.

'My parents are grateful.'

There was a pause, and Tristan took a seat.

'*I'm* grateful,' Emme said. 'You saved my life.'

Tristan shook his head.

'How are your ribs?'

Emme put her palm to her left side, she could feel exactly which were broken. She gave her answer in her wince. But she didn't want to talk about physical fractures. It was the broken heart that was consuming her now she was conscious.

'I mean, I'm still so, so gutted . . .' she added, shaking her head and almost crying at his treachery. She so desperately wanted to unsee the awful video of Tristan and Lexy on the threshold. Knowing that within the week he would have slept with Vivian and Anastasia too. He'd ruined everything before they'd even started. But he had saved her life.

'I know, I am so sorry,' he said, face forlorn.

'But thank you. For the mountain.'

He let out a sigh as weary as a confession.

'I was so scared.'

Tristan took Emme's hand, scared she would flinch but

she didn't, so he raised it, kissed it, and held it to his cheek. His touch felt like the most natural thing in the world.

'I wasn't willing to lose someone else I . . . someone else I care about . . . to the mountain.'

Emme smiled gently.

'How did you know I was up there?'

'I didn't. I went skiing. I was so pissed off that the Lexy thing had undone everything – undone us – I did what I always do when I'm upset. I went to the mountains. Tried to clear my head. I was on the piste when I saw the avalanche.'

'You were?'

'I saw the snowboarder set it off . . .'

'You did?'

'I'd seen that there were people in the wildlife area. I didn't know it was you, but I just had a bad feeling . . . I would have gone to help whoever it was . . . but it was *you*.'

He looked genuinely terrified.

'It's OK, Tristan.'

He squeezed her hand and held it to his lips again. She looked at him and smiled. They were bigger than Lexy Harrington.

She realised, after all Tristan had been through that day with his father, after all he had done to get help and dig her out, there were more important things at play than a bruised heart.

'I am so sorry Emme,' he said, shaking his head.

'Don't be sorry, you save—'

'I'm talking about us.'

Emme steeled herself.

'I thought about you all the time I was in South Africa. I promise. Nothing has been the same since you, I swear.'

Emme felt so conflicted.

'What about all these women? I can't be with some-one who just sets everything ablaze wherever he goes. I can't be with someone who can't help himself. That's not me.'

'That's not me either!' he almost begged. 'Not any more.'

Emme was startled.

'Lexy, Anastasia, Vivian . . . what do they all have in common?'

Emme looked blank and shrugged. The effort of which hurt and she winced again. Tristan kissed her hand; his lips offering a salve. God, he was beautiful.

'They all came before you. Since . . . since we kissed in the alleyway, since that day in the gondola, I swear I haven't even looked at another woman.'

Emme blushed. She thought about the sensations of him, rippling inside her; the passion he unlocked in her. 'Not here, not in London, not in Geneva, not in Cape Town, not in Stellenbosch . . .'

Could Emme really believe a man she had seen lying?

'You breezed into my life six weeks ago and I have never felt so utterly sure about anything. I want to take you to the vineyards; meet my mother; show you the whales off Hermanus, show you the Alpenglow. I swear I have never felt like this about anyone.'

Emme shook her head.

'Why?'

Tristan looked genuinely confused.

'Why what?'

'Why me? You could have any woman in Kristalldorf. Why me?'

'All those fakes? All those entitled princesses? I don't think you and I are as different as you think we are . . .'

Emme pondered Tristan the outsider. Tristan grafting to find his way and fit in. Tristan with the luxury of choices, just like Emme had. Her flat in Balham was not quite the Vitreum, but she had *chosen* to move to Kristalldorf, and didn't they both feel like imposters in the end? Didn't they both want to be loved, wholeheartedly? To be their lover's priority.

'Look at you Emme! You are beautiful. You emanate kindness and warmth. You make me feel safe. I have never felt safe with any woman in Kristalldorf. When I realised it was you in the snow, I just . . . I just imagined losing you, all over again, and how I'd fucked it all up. And I vowed to do anything I could to make you happy. I promise. I will *serve* you.' He said it with such reverence, Emme was taken aback. She wove her fingers among his and beckoned him closer, until he was close enough to kiss. His kiss felt like medicine as she remembered all the passionate kisses he had furnished her face, her breasts, her stomach and her entire body with, since they had come together in the gondola.

Except this kiss had more depth. It felt more tender. It was gentle and loving and loyal.

'Anything?' Emme asked, as she pulled back.

'Anything,' he assured her.

'Then take me to Cat,' Emme said with a smile. 'I need to see Cat.'

Chapter Eighty-Five

Tristan wheeled Emme down the hall in a slick Swiss-engineered wheelchair to the room at the end of the corridor, where they could hear Cat chortling over the *tele-novelas* she was watching in bed.

'Knock knock,' Emme said, as she entered.

'*Me estás cargando!*' Cat said, delighted.

Tristan parked Emme next to the bed, and stood behind her, pushing his hair back out of his face. He smiled at Cat. Cat looked at him, pleased to see him.

'Can I hug you?' Emme asked.

'No. This side is fucked,' she said, nodding to her collarbone.

'In which case . . .' Emme gingerly stood up and kissed Cat on the forehead. Tristan held her up. She hadn't stood for three days.

'Let's just say I won't be chopping cilantro for a while.'

'I'm so sorry.'

Tristan helped Emme back down and smoothed her hospital dressing gown.

'Hey, it could have been a lot worse.'

Emme took Cat's hand.

'Lumi has been in – how nice is that?'

'Really nice.'

'I'll leave you two to it,' Tristan said. 'Do you want anything from the vending machine?'

They both shook their heads and Tristan ambled out.

Cat barely waited until he was out the door before she brought it up.

'You kids all good?' There was a twinkle in her eye. Perhaps she didn't think Emme was mad. 'I mean, he saved your fucking life, that has to be worth a second chance, huh?'

'We shall see . . .' Emme joked, cryptically. And then she turned to the burning question. 'What the hell happened on the mountain?'

Cat shook her head.

'That kid – he went down a second time. On his own.'

'Why did you go after him?'

'His parents were on the piste – I went after him to tell him how idiotic it was to ski off-piste, in a wildlife area, in those conditions – it was perfect avalanche conditions.'

Emme looked bewildered.

'I was trying to catch him. Give him a piece of my mind. Spook him. I was shouting at you *not* to follow me . . .'

'I didn't hear.'

'I know that now!' Cat laughed. 'And I was giving you the signal to stop, crossing my arms above my head . . .' The thought of attempting such a physical feat with a broken collarbone made Cat wince. 'But it's not so obvious without ski poles.'

'God, sorry, I didn't know.'

'A snowboarder set it off above you. A German tourist. Apparently he still doesn't even know! But, hey, none of us should have been there.'

'Shit.'

They looked at each other, scared, relieved, reunited.

'I heard the boy was in a coma!'

'Yeah, he and his parents learned their lesson alright.'

'God, Cat, what a fright.'

Emme squeezed her hand. Her friend. The first person she had met on this mad journey and the person she almost died with. She knew for certain that they would be friends for life.

Epilogue

'Are you OK? Are you sure you can do this?' Tristan asked, as they flew in Tristan's charter helicopter towards the Silberschnee. Emme nodded as she squeezed his hand, breathing calmly so as not to strain her lungs, her ribs. She wasn't ready to ski any time soon, but they had snow boots and crampons on and were ready, so they could walk the path around the Blocherpass. Emme nodded tentatively. She feared the sound of the rotors might trigger something; trigger her – but sitting next to Tristan, his hand clutching her thigh, gave her comfort and she knew she would be OK.

Emme had left the hospital in Bloch on Christmas morning, also by helicopter with Tristan by her side; with an excited Marian and Geoff gazing out of the window as they finally got to see Kristalldorf come into view. Emme and her parents had never travelled by helicopter before, and the ride was spectacular. They moved into the Vitreum penthouse and spent a quiet and languid day with Tristan, watching movies and having Christmas lunch sent up from the kitchen. Marian didn't stop talking about the changing weather through the exquisite panorama; Geoff kept accidentally triggering all manner of devices hidden among the sleek ergonomics of the penthouse.

Cat had to stay in hospital for a few days more, but Lydia, Will, Yannick and Tiago all brought Christmas to her: gifts, tinsel, and *The Grinch* on the hospital's pay per view, and they crowded around her bed and all laughed together watching it. Between her friends, Tristan Du Kok and Lumi Kivvi, there wasn't much else Cat could want for.

Emme didn't have the energy to deal with Lexy, but Tristan called Bill on Boxing Day morning and invited him up to the Vitreum restaurant for brunch. Bill was equal parts flattered and intrigued by the invitation – he hadn't dined with Tristan at Vitreum since he and Lexy were new in town and he had been shocked to hear Emme might be one of the three people injured in the Kristalldorf avalanche. Swiss privacy laws meant the press weren't allowed to name them, although rumours had swirled that Cat and Emme were among the injured and that Tristan Du Kok joined the search and rescue team with his own snow shovel. Plus Bill was keen to get to the bottom of Lexy's improbable Münchausen by proxy accusation.

Tristan gave Bill two simple instructions: bring Emme's belongings, and don't tell or bring Lexy. Bill was too curious to break Tristan's confidence.

Lexy had almost had a nosebleed when she saw Bill rolling Emme's huge suitcase out of Chalet Stern on Boxing Day morning and he wouldn't tell her why.

'Bill?' 'Bill!' 'BILL!' she had bellowed after him from the front balcony.

'Goodness, how are you Emme?' he later asked, as he ordered coffee, orange juice and eggs Benedict, and Emme and Tristan eased into the large round table.

*

When Emme showed Bill the BUZZ doorbell footage of Lexy and Tristan; and Jenny catching them out, Bill suddenly realised how Dimitri Diamandis had felt.

He looked at Emme, bewildered. Was she really with this cad?

Emme nodded, and the penny dropped. Not only had his wife cheated on him, it was also highly unlikely Jenny had stolen as much as a banana from them.

'And, erm, the Münchausen by proxy . . .' Bill said, clearing his throat.

'What?' Emme said, aghast, before explaining that Bella was sick from eating too much party food, Harry had a normal bug probably caught from school, and she had never even used the Himalayan pink salt, let alone tried to poison the children with it.

Emme told Bill about the slap and said that if they didn't pay her a decent notice period, she would be taking it to the police on the grounds of assault.

Bill, ashen-faced, wrote Emme a cheque, for double her rate through to April, and apologised profusely. Emme apologised too. She hadn't wanted to leave Harry and Bella in the lurch again, but she suspected there would be bigger upheaval ahead for them than the matter of a new nanny.

And none of it was Emme's fault.

'Sorry, man,' Tristan said as Bill left, Christmas cheer well and truly knocked out of him. He offered Bill his hand.

'You're a shit, Du Kok,' Bill Harrington sneered, refusing it.

Emme's parents flew back to the UK on Boxing Day, and Lucille, Ryan, Zara and Zack were all very understanding about why Christmas dinner was a day late, keen to hear happy news of Aunty Emme's recovery. Marian and Geoff understood that Emme might need a few weeks longer in Kristalldorf to recover before coming home. Having seen where their daughter's saviour lived, having understood that he was her special someone as much as he was her good Samaritan, gave them the security to leave her with him.

'I promise I'll be home soon,' she had said as she and Tristan saw them off on the heliport roof.

'I could get used to this,' Geoff puffed like a peacock, as they soared over the Alps towards Zurich.

Tristan and Emme spent four days locked away, making love with caution, eating, recuperating, talking. Over breakfasts and massages, films and confessionals, Tristan managed to show Emme how serious he was. How her physical recovery and mental wellbeing were more important to him than anything else. How there was nothing he wouldn't do to win back her trust and make her happy. How she was his priority. And Emme had to hand it to him, he had never in fact lied to her. How could she begrudge Tristan for being the person he was before they kissed? She had fallen for that person after all.

And now, here they were, the penultimate day of the year. Tristan had instructed the helicopter pilot to set them down on a ledge and return in half an hour, just a few hundred metres along the pass. He knew Emme was up to it.

Tristan's arms were slung around his girlfriend's waist, careful to protect her side. He dotted sweet kisses in her ear as they waited.

And then they saw it: as the sun hit the horizon, their entire world turned pink.

'There she is!' Tristan said, happily cocooned in his large grey puffa coat.

'Alpenglow!' Emme marvelled. She turned to him in awe and looked back. 'It's beautiful!'

They watched, mesmerised as the dark peaks of the Swiss Alps ignited a stunning, warm hue of rosy pink across their entire universe. She pressed her body back into Tristan's. She felt the strength of him pressing back. She felt entirely safe and nurtured for the first time in her life.

'I love you Emmeline Eversley,' Tristan whispered, before he kissed her.

She turned to face him.

'I love you too.'

They stood for twenty minutes, soaking up the peace, the tranquillity. Savouring every second and drinking in how lucky they were to be alive. How lucky they were to have found each other. A year was coming to an end, and she couldn't think of a better way to spend it than with him.

'Let's go home,' she said.

Tristan nodded.

As they traversed the slope carefully back onto the Blocherpass, Tristan led the way and held Emme's hand, checking the path was safe at every turn. The pink was fading now, and as the sun rose, a new light filled Emme's world with warmth. As they rounded a corner they could see the form of another walker heading towards them on the trail. A man with walking poles and straggly hair. In the distance they heard their pilot returning in the chopper. The sound of it, the cold, reminded Emme of the rescue.

Perhaps she had been aware of Tristan, holding her in the helicopter after he had plucked her out of the snow. Emme squeezed his hand, and then Tristan stopped abruptly as the walker's face emerged from the shadows of the rock and into the morning sunlight.

His sudden halt caught Emme by surprise.

'Tristan?' she asked, squeezing his hand again.

But Tristan was staring straight in front of him. Paralysed in surprise.

'Dad?'

Acknowledgements

Thank you, treasured reader, for joining me on this journey, from my home and yours to the mountains and valleys of the Swiss Alps. I am more grateful than you could know.

To my wonderful agent Rebecca Ritchie at AM Heath: thank you for getting *The Chalet Girl* out into the world and a deal at Penguin Michael Joseph no less. And a huge thank you to Florence Rees, for coolly and calmly watching the fort while Becky cooks up a new story of her own.

Penguin Michael Joseph was this author's dream publisher to land with, not only because of the incredible writer heroes of mine who are now stablemates, but mainly because my editor Hannah Smith is a genius. Thank you, Hannah, for your attention to detail and your brilliant brain. Thank you to Nick Lowndes and Katya Browne in production, to Fiona Brown for the seamless copy-edit process, and to Gabriella Nemeth for being pin-sharp. Thank you to Frankie Banks in PR and Courtney Barclay in marketing, to editorial assistant Kathryn Ramsay and to Lee Motley and Becci Livingstone in art. None of us expected to be scrutinising underwear on skis quite so attentively as part of the day job. Thanks to foreign rights champion Beth Wood and to publishing queens Maxine Hitchcock and Louise Moore. To know I have you both on my side feels like there is no mountain I can't climb.

Thank you to my author friends whose eyes lit up when I told them I was writing this, and their encouraging words along the way. To Elisa Frenz for her German help. And to a pocket-rocket Australian friend of mine, who lives in the Alps and hopefully doesn't regret inviting me to stay all those times. I adore you.

Finally, thank you to my husband, sons and cat for giving me the time, space, love and encouragement to write, although perhaps not the cat. She's hassling me to play ball right now. VPx

On a station platform, with nothing to read,
and a four-hour train journey stretching ahead of him...

That's where the story began for Penguin founder Allen Lane.
With only 'shabby reprints of shoddy novels' on offer,
he resolved to make better books for readers everywhere.

By the time his train pulled into London, the idea was formed.
He would bring the best writing, in stylish and affordable
formats, to everyone. His books would be sold in bookstores,
stationers and tobacconists, for no more than the price
of a ten-pack of cigarettes.

And on every book would be a Penguin, a bird with a certain
'dignified flippancy', and a friendly invitation to anyone who
wished to spend their time reading.

In 1935, the first ten Penguin paperbacks were published.
Just a year later, three million Penguins had made their
way onto our shelves.

Reading was changed forever.

—

A lot has changed since 1935, including Penguin, but in the
most important ways we're still the same. We still believe that
books and reading are for everyone. And we still believe that
whether you're seeking an afternoon's escape, a vigorous debate
or a soothing bedtime story, all possibilities open with a book.

Whoever you are, whatever you're looking for,
you can find it with Penguin.